Dead Wrong

Dead Wrong

• A Novel •

Alan Dennis
Burke

St. Martin's Press • New York

Design by Amelia R. Mayone

Library of Congress Cataloging-in-Publication Data

Burke, Alan Dennis.
   Dead wrong.
      p. cm.
   ISBN 0-312-05068-2
   I. Title.
   PS3552.U7213D4   1990   813'.54—dc20   90-37313

First Edition: November 1990
10 9 8 7 6 5 4 3 2 1

This book is dedicated to Dennis, Andrew, Aimee, Patrick, and Cathy.

We wish to extend thanks and heartfelt gratitude to: Mary Antonino, Christine M. Burke, Robert W. Burke, Ann Deveney, Attorney Thomas Dwyer, Honora Flanery, Dale Halloran, Peter W. Kitler, Elizabeth and Bernard Milton, and Susan L. Monach.

Dead Wrong

· 1 ·

I'm not exaggerating. When Tim Regan finally shows, smiling encouragement, I want to hug him. I stand as they unlock the door to let him in. He's smiling, sure, but I can tell he's embarrassed to see me here. I guess I look like hell— eyes red, hair askew. I'm in so much trouble I don't even care.

I wait until he puts his lawyer's briefcase on the table and then I lean over and say softly, "Tim, I never killed anyone. I swear to God. I couldn't do that. You're family. You know me."

He nods smartly. "We'll get this straightened out. Get you home."

And I'm thinking, wow, will it be that easy? I'll explain everything to Tim. He'll explain it to the police. And they'll let me go. God, I'm going to feel relieved walking out of here.

But, pretty soon, I'm looking at this kid. And that's the problem. He's just a kid, my second cousin, and sure, he seems to know his stuff when it comes to routine deeds and contracts, but . . . I mean, do I trust my life to a guy with that many freckles?

I have to tell him up front, "I'm broke."

"You can catch me later. After you've made your millions."

"Yeah." Made my millions. A bitter joke. Anyway, I'm grateful for Tim's generosity. Except, considering the stakes, generosity might not be enough. "Have you, uh, have you handled a case like this before . . . Tim?"

"Like this?"

"Yeah. Like, you know. A murder case. Have you defended someone accused of murder before?"

"Let's not get ahead of ourselves. You haven't been charged with anything yet."

"But if I am. Do you have, you know, experience?"

"Ronald Aiello?"

"What?"

"Ronald Aiello. Knocked or pushed a friend of his in front of a subway train. They were both drunk. Charged with manslaughter. Did you read about it? I represented Ronnie. I did a pretty good job on that one."

"You got him off."

"Uh, not quite off. No. I mean, he obviously did it. And I think I managed, or, you know, the sentence, uh . . . It could have been worse for him is what I'm trying to say. It could have been much worse."

"I see."

God help me.

Next, he wants to know what happened. "Everything you saw and heard." And I start off talking a mile a minute, not making a hell of a lot of sense. "Jesus," I say, "Jesus, what an awful thing."

"I know."

"There was a hole," I point to my forehead, "You could see, see—stuff coming out." I close my eyes. I'm going to be sick. "I don't understand why they've arrested me, Tim."

He doesn't reply at first. Does he really believe me? Maybe everyone, hearing the story, will assume I'm guilty. Oh, God.

"You were just in the wrong place at the wrong time," Tim says.

"Yeah." I nod vigorously. "Wrong place, wrong time. I mean, we just have to point it out to them."

"Sometimes that's all it takes."

I don't belong here in the police station lockup. I'd been brought in, handcuffed. With all these officers standing around. Guys I know personally. Like, I played pickup basketball with Matty O'Keefe for years. And Matt and the rest of them stood around, pretending not to know me.

Tim clears his voice. His short red hair is combed neatly, he wears a three-piece suit. Maybe it's supposed to make him look older, but he's like a kid dressed up.

He says, "Let's back up and start over. We want a complete statement. From beginning to end. The truth and all the truth. And think before you talk. Get it all organized in your head."

"Okay."

"And don't lie about anything, Kevin. If something makes you look bad, say it anyway. Remember, it's privileged. Between us. And if you can't trust me—what am I doing here?" His voice is kind, assured. Suddenly, I want to put my future in his hands.

I try to concentrate. Think back on everything. The Lundgren party is a good place to start.

Since my divorce there are so many "friends" I no longer see. Pat and Jack Lundgren are the exception—surprisingly, because Pat and Susan, my wife, remain close. My new career as an independent contractor actually meant that I was dealing regularly with the Lundgrens. They operate a very successful real estate agency in Norham. Naturally, we'd given them the exclusive rights to sell the homes of Indian Peak Estates.

The first step toward "making my millions" was Indian Peak, a thirty-acre site on the edge of the town forest where

I proposed to build twelve homes at a half-million apiece. Fifteen years a professional carpenter, I brought know-how and a small amount of money (every penny I had) to the project. Eventually, I envisioned developing upscale property all over the South Shore.

I met my partner, an attorney named Larry Dexter, through the Lundgrens, but in fairness, neither Jack nor Pat had recommended him. Larry was smooth—some might say oily—and well connected. There'd always been talk about him. People would kind of roll their eyes when his name was mentioned. He'd been the subject of a few malpractice suits, but, as he pointed out, what lawyer isn't these days?

Well, I really needed money to make Indian Peak Estates happen and I figured I could handle Dexter. And in the beginning it all went smoothly. Larry was able to obtain our permits, state and local. More importantly, he secured the mortgage, and he even promised to set aside a reserve of money in the event that the homes didn't move as we hoped. In fact, Larry expected the first to be sold even before it was completed.

"Nowadays," he insisted, "you can't lose money in real estate." Even the cautious Jack Lundgren admitted this was pretty close to true.

So, you see, going in it was a *can't-miss* deal.

I was the first person to arrive that night. I helped Jack prepare the playroom, erecting the Ping-Pong table. Later I distracted the twins, four-year-old Tony and Jessica, while their parents set up the bar.

Tony and Jessica had white blond hair and diamond-blue eyes and went to an exclusive, big-bucks preschool. They were dressed in designer clothes and fed a diet that eliminated sugars and processed foods. The two had come late in their parents' lives and I suppose it's not surprising they were spoiled a bit.

Well, let's be honest, it bothered me when Pat and Jack

lavished attention on the twins. Because I would have liked to spoil my kids, Michael and Molly, only that's pretty difficult when you only see them twice a week.

People began to arrive. I played Ping-Pong—beer in one hand, paddle in the other—with Jack and Shep Halloran. Later, upstairs, the place was packed. A lot of the guests were clients, realtors, people I didn't know. I found Larry Dexter sitting on the huge, white leather couch with Terri Pratt, who I remembered vaguely from my wife Susan's women's group.

Terri was a few years younger than Susan. She dressed modestly and had a pleasant round face, dark hair, a pale complexion, and a slim figure. I'm almost positive that Susan disapproved of Terri, which meant that she drank too much, or swore too much, or worse.

"Are you a tycoon too?" she asked as I came near.

"Excuse me?"

"Larry tells me he's a real estate tycoon and since you're his partner, you must be a tycoon too."

"Next year I'll be a tycoon. Just now I qualify for food stamps."

As this was the only vacant seat in the crowded living room, I sat beside her. It was a mistake because she began talking as if we were old friends and dammit, I wanted peace. Or was I afraid? To be honest, since the divorce I found myself actually avoiding women.

I talked past her, to Larry. "Where's Kikki tonight?"

"She either has a head cold or a brain tumor," he replied. "She stayed home where she could worry and not be distracted by the fun."

"How's Susan?" Terri asked me.

"Susan? Susan's fine." And I felt compelled to add, "We're divorced now, you know."

"You mean . . . legally divorced?"

"Yep." I looked at the floor, tipping my bottle up for a quick gulp. "All legal and everything."

"I'm sorry."

"Yeah, well, it happens."

"It's rough." She looked down at her ring finger, which was bare. "I've been there. . . . How many years were you married?"

"Fifteen."

"A long time."

"Long enough for one of us."

Larry, after waving to this odd-looking guy in a dark suit, turned and asked Terri, "Where's your date?"

"He's—" She looked about. "What have they got, some basketball game on in the den? I think he's in there."

Larry nodded to me, "Thith one's a male nurthe."

"Yeah," Terri retorted, "Just make some remark to him. I dare you."

"Why? What's he going to do? Hit me with a bedpan?"

I leaned over and told Larry, "That guy Rapolli from the DEQE called."

"I'm on top of it, partner."

"He says you won't answer his calls. Larry, you don't want to get these state guys pissed. They could shut us down."

Suddenly, Dexter leaned forward and called to the man in the dark suit. "Having a good time?"

"Great," the man raised his voice above the din.

"You see what I mean?" Larry looked to me. "Mr. Rapolli's having a great time."

"You mean—"

The representative from the state's environmental watchdog agency came wobbling towards us balancing a heaping portion of Pat Lundgren's cherry cheesecake. He leaned close to Larry and whispered, "Where is it?"

"I've got it in my car," my partner said quietly. "Let me know when you're leaving."

"I'm not going any time soon." He looked happily at the pie. "Does it have a frame?"

"Oh, sure. With all those squiggles and things." He made a loop in the air. "Wait'll you see it."

"It's small you say?"

"Well, sure. But size doesn't matter. It's age and quality that matter."

When Rapolli moved away, I grabbed Larry's elbow. "What the hell is he talking about? What's in the car he's so interested in?"

"Not here," Larry said. "I'll tell you later."

"So what have you been doing with yourself?" Terri interjected. "Going out on dates yet?"

"Uhh." I was still staring at Larry. "What? No. I've been working."

"You can't be that way. You've got to get out. Get back in the swing."

Terri acted very familiar. It wasn't so bad having a pretty woman play up to me. And gradually, the queasy feeling I had over Dexter and the state inspector subsided.

At some point, Terri's date, a tall, thin fellow with a sparse mustache, came hovering over us. "Nice place," he said, admiring the Lundgrens' modern home with its bare beams and sharp angles.

"Good game?" Terri asked.

"They lost."

He stood uncomfortably, none of us offering to push over and give him a seat. "Did you tell them?" he asked suddenly.

Terri made a face.

"Tell us what?" Larry asked.

"Terri was big hero today. Saved a patient who was choking to death on—what was it?—popcorn I think."

"What'd you do?" Larry asked. "That Hemlock maneuver?"

"I just did my job," she insisted.

"Guy must've weighed two hundred fifty pounds. I didn't want to get near him. Terri, she practically tackles the old bastard. Gets her arms around his gut. Saved his life. No shit."

"I just did my job," she repeated, then she began talking to me. I don't remember what she said. The point was she ignored the guy. He finally asked, "Want to get going?"

"No. I'm staying awhile." She actually put a hand on my leg. Her date drifted away. And the story about the Heimlich maneuver comes back now because of the irony. On the day I met Terri Pratt she saved a man's life.

When Larry went off to the bar with Rapolli, Terri remained at my side. She kept at me about why I wasn't "going out" and after a few beers I found myself admitting, "I suppose I'm still in love with Susan."

"Of course you are."

"Sometimes I think I should just go over there. Tell her, 'Let's stop this foolishness. We belong together . . .' but . . ." I studied the bottle wedged between my legs. "If it was that simple, we wouldn't have split up in the first place."

"It's hard to accept when it's over."

"I have this sense of failure. I guess everybody says that, feels that."

"It's the world, Kevin. The way the world is today. Years ago people had a dozen kids and stuck together no matter what. Because that was the only way. Today, we have choices and freedom. And everybody thinks freedom is just good, good, good. But there's bad about freedom too. It can mean your husband's free to run off and leave you raising three kids alone."

She asked dozens of questions—though she already knew far more about me than I knew about her.

"Didn't you go to college, Kevin? Somebody told me you went to college before you decided to build houses."

"That's right."

"What did you study?"

"Oh, lots of things. Business, engineering. Even philosophy for a semester. But, you know, I always liked to work with my hands. I didn't like the idea of, my whole life, having a sit-down job. So, I got into carpentry."

"That's where the muscles come from." She reached out, touched my biceps, and then smiled. Because I was blushing, couldn't help it.

I drove Terri home. Her date, his nose out of joint, had left hours before. It was barely one in the morning. "Who's watching your kids?"

"My mother," she said.

"I'm trying to remember what you told me. Three, three kids?"

"Robin, thirteen, Louraine, six, and Kelly, five. Three girls."

"The world can't have too many girls."

"They're great kids. You should meet them."

Yeah. I might like that.

We went to a Chinese restaurant. "So you were a life-saver today," I commented over egg rolls and pork strips. "I'm impressed."

"Any nurse would have done it."

"But you did it. That's the point. You made a difference. Or that man might be dead now."

"He'll die soon anyway. He's nearly eighty."

"It doesn't matter. It's life. Every day is precious."

I liked her face, very sweet. And when she turned away, I studied her body, trying to make out how it looked under her loose clothing.

After nearly a year without a woman, the joke was on me. I'd always fantasized on freedom from Susan, picking from a menu of interesting ladies. In fact, I avoided women, the idea of sex had become an invitation to pain.

Until tonight, as Terri listened attentively to everything I said and laughed at all my jokes. And the possibility that I might have her had me bubbling. I explained all my dreams for Indian Peak; how I would provide for my kids when the money started pouring in. "These days, you need a ton of money to put kids through college."

We stayed more than an hour, eating and drinking, then she looked at her watch and announced it was past time to be home.

Starting my pickup, I took a deep breath before asking,

"What . . . what time do you have to be back? . . . I mean, if your mother's there I guess, you probably don't have to be back till late."

"It is late."

"Well, then. Till later."

"Well, I—" For the first time she seemed uncertain.

"How's about we do something? Go somewhere."

"There's no place open, Kevin. Even the Chinese restaurant is closing."

"We could just sit somewhere."

She didn't answer.

"Really, Terri, I like talking to you."

"I like talking to you too, but it's—"

"Maybe this sounds all wrong. And maybe I had too much to drink and maybe everything will look different in the morning. But. I hate the idea of saying good-bye to you."

Looking away, she said softly, "This is going too fast. I need to think." After a pause, she said, "Sometimes, after a breakup, divorce, a person gets so lonely for someone. Anyone. And, well, the thing is I'm not just anyone."

"You're not."

"To be sure I'm not. We should take, take it slow. Slow." She reached for her bag. "Let me give you my number."

"Great."

Driving home, Terri got very quiet. And it had been so easy to talk before, words just poured out. I worried that I'd spoiled it all somehow.

Her home was a little Cape in the poorer section of Norham. A light was on. "My mother. She's probably fallen asleep in her chair, waiting up." She turned to me, "It's like when I was a kid."

"Well—"

"Listen, Kevin. I don't know. Maybe it's not such a good idea if you call me. I mean, it's not you. In fact, I wanted you to like me tonight. I tried hard so you would. Only now I'm wondering if I'm being fair. To you, I mean."

"I don't understand. Being fair. How—"

"The problem is I'm . . . I'm involved with somebody else just now."

"The guy at the party?"

"No. It's, it's somebody you don't know. I've been going with him a long time. Years."

I stared ahead at the darkened road. Christ.

"Don't be upset," she said.

"You're not married to him, are you? Because if you're not, there's no reason we can't go out."

One hand on the door, she looked down at the floor. "Honest to God, Kevin, you don't want to get mixed up with me."

"I'm going to call you."

Finally, she leaned over and gave me a little kiss on the cheek while picking her bag off the floor. Just to see what would happen, I gently held her. When she didn't resist I kissed her flush on the mouth. She moaned. God, she moaned. And my tongue was in her mouth, my hands all over her, and best of all, she was fighting past the wheel to get at me.

"Come home with me, Terri."

She looked up and showed white teeth, like a hungry animal. "Drive fast."

On the way she pulled something in a cellophane wrapper from her purse. "I probably shouldn't show you this."

"What?"

"I don't want you to get the wrong idea about me."

I kept fighting not to look at her, but to watch the road.

"A girl at work just gave me these today. As a joke. I never dreamed—"

I stopped for a red light. "What are they?"

She giggled. "Edible panties. Cherry flavored." Pressing her lips to my ear, she whispered, "I could try them on. Are you hungry? Would you like something to nibble on?"

I roared through the red light.

Back then it all seemed wickedly exciting. Only later would I wonder about a woman who went about with edible panties in her purse.

I still got kind of surprised, waking up in a cottage in Hanbroke, instead of the big house in Norham. It's a pleasant spot though and I could see tree tops and red-orange morning through the skylight. And Terri Pratt, naked, astride me, eyes almost closed, pure white teeth closed on her lower lip as those marvelous hips rocked up and down, up and down.

Wake up, you're having sex.

"Did you know," she sighed, "you get erections in your sleep?"

"I do now."

"Well, didn't your wife ever tell you?"

"Never mentioned it."

"It never came up with her." She giggled softly. "Want me to stop? I'll stop if you're sore."

"Don't."

"You'll tough it out." She smiled and kissed me, her face so incongruously sweet and innocent.

I was a little sore, to tell the truth. Out of practice. In fact, not since the early years of my marriage had I had anything near this much practice. And it was a little frightening the way she kept coming back, smiling eagerly, wanting more.

I thought, my God, I'll never be able to please her.

"Do you want to come?" she asked, still rocking. "I'll stop, unless you want to come."

"I—I think all my come is gone."

She smiled, then rolled off and snuggled against me. Her hand went to my cock, absently toying with it. Most of the night, even when we slept, she'd been hanging onto it like she was afraid somebody would steal the thing. I myself didn't give it that much attention.

I didn't know what to make of Terri. My wife, Susan,

was not like this, not hardly. And Susan was really the only woman I'd ever had.

"This soldier has had it." She offered a playful tug.

"Well, give me a few minutes and—"

"No, no, Kevin. I don't want to wear it out." She grinned. "You've been great. Really. You can go and go and go." She kissed me. "Where have you been all my life?" (I'm not bragging, just telling what she said.)

"You *inspire* me," I told her.

She glowed. It turned out she loved compliments.

So we lay in each other's arms, relaxed, warm. She ran her hand over my chest. "You have a beautiful body."

"I think yours is pretty great."

"Mine's not as good as Susan's." She looked down at herself. "Is it?"

"Well," I shrugged. "Susan, her breasts sag a little."

"Because they're big. Of course they're going to sag as she gets older."

"Yours don't." I leaned over and pressed my face against them.

She rolled onto her back. "Yeah. I always used to envy girls with big ones. Only now, their tits are down around their navels. And mine are still firm and nice." Her brow furrowed, "Because everybody's got to wear clothes all the time nobody knows how nice mine really are."

"Life is unfair," I laughed.

Terri phoned her mother. I prepared breakfast, trying not to eavesdrop. But, after all, this was a one-room cottage. I could hear things like, "Oh, the party was real nice . . . I met a great guy . . . No, he's not like that, ma. He's very nice. . . . He has a little girl Louraine's age. . . . No, he's divorced. . . . Of course, I'm sure. . . . Well, I didn't see the papers if that's what you mean. . . ."

Over breakfast, she said, "Did you have a good time? Don't answer. Just—I had a great time. From the minute you sat next to me. I had a great, great time." She wore a white blouse, white panties with red hearts, and a terrific grin.

"You were great, Terri."

"I'm a good piece of ass?"

"You—you're a human amusement park, you are."

She seemed quite pleased. I noticed she had almost unconsciously reached down to play with herself. Amazing. I'd never before encountered a woman who spoke so directly about sex, in language more graphic than I would dare use; who took her pleasures without apology or embarrassment or shame. Apparently.

Almost lovingly, I gazed at her from over my Rice Crispies.

Ravenously hungry, we ate again at a little diner in Assinippi. Between bites, Terri talked of her ex-husband. "You met Eddie a few times."

"I don't remember."

"Yeah. At the Lundgrens' party a few years ago? He was clowning and knocked the barbecue grill into the pool."

"I wasn't there. But I heard something about it."

"He couldn't drink, Eddie. That was one of his problems. We didn't go to parties at the Lundgrens' after that."

She gazed thoughtfully at her pancakes. "He was nice in some ways. But not reliable. You know? Whenever things were going good, he'd do something stupid to mess them up. After he started with the phone company, the money was good. But he lost ten thousand dollars in Atlantic City. I could have killed him. Instead, I started taking money from, you know, from the household budget. Putting it away in an account he didn't know about. He was always complaining how come we never had money. But we bought the house. I bought it. Or we'd still be on Dot Ave."

"Where is he now?" I asked.

"After we moved to Norham, I told him, 'This is my house.' I let him think I'd gotten the money from my mother. Which was probably a mistake. But I didn't want him thinking he could borrow on it or sell it out from under us." She shook her head. "I guess it offended his dignity. The idea he was living in *my* house. About four years ago, he left. Told the kids he was going to California. It wasn't a surprise. We weren't on good terms by then."

"And you got a divorce." I said.

"Not right away. But I did."

"And now you're seeing someone."

"What?"

"Last night. You told me you were seeing—"

"I'm not seeing him anymore."

"You're not?"

"I—I was. I was seeing someone. A guy. For a long time. But that's over now. Done."

"You weren't sure about me last night," I said, smiling. Because I'd figured something out about her.

"What? . . . how do you mean?"

"You weren't sure. That's why you kind of exaggerated that story about having a boyfriend. Because, I don't know, something, something about me you didn't . . . weren't sure of. What changed your mind all of a sudden?"

"If I wasn't sure, last night would have convinced me."

A free woman. Terrific. And I was impressed because she'd told me how she'd slickered the house from her husband. She wouldn't want that story repeated. I thought, she must trust me. And I never made the simple deduction, if she played tricks on Eddie she would also play them on me.

Look, for more than sixteen years I'd dealt with Susan, straightforward, honest Susan. I had no experience with women like Terri.

"How often does this happen to you, Terri?"

"What?"

"Us. The way, the way we were. Last night. Does it happen a lot?"

"Not like this."

I said, "It's . . . I felt like I was swept right into bed. Like I didn't have a choice. God, Terri, I wanted you so bad."

"I wanted you just as much."

"I still want you. Right now. And if I stood up everybody here would know it."

She smiled, amused and gratified.

"The thing that galls me, and scares me: I could have lived my whole life with Susan. My whole one and only life and never known this feeling."

Unhappily, Terri worked at the nursing home on Sundays, starting at four o'clock. I had to have her home long before that. We took a roundabout route, driving along the ocean, where we admired the many beautiful homes.

"Me and Eddie used to come out this way," she said, "and we'd talk about winning the lottery and buying one of these houses."

"You'd have to win big."

I pulled onto a shoulder that looked down on a sweep of ocean, rock, and sand. The sky was very blue and the sea bluer still. I put my arm around her.

"How, how do you get along with Susan?" she asked.

"You mean what? Now? How do we get along now? Uh. I don't know. We're friendly, I guess. She acts friendly."

Terri nodded.

"To tell the truth, sometimes I think she doesn't know if she loves me or hates me. Like she's stuck in the middle, hasn't made up her mind."

Terri stared out at the ocean for a long time before asking, hesitantly, "And how do *you* feel about *her*?"

"It's over, Terri. The papers are signed. All that. It's over."

"But how do you feel about her?"

"I don't, I don't know. It's complicated. I haven't sorted it out yet."

"You still love her."

"I couldn't live with her."

"But you still love her."

"She's the mother of my children. I spent half, almost

half my life with her. So." A shrug and a pained expression summed it up.

"What if she asked you to come back—"

"She's not going to do that."

"But if she did?" She turned toward me, smiling. "I'm just curious."

"Listen, Terri. I don't want to go back to her. I hope she's happy. And I'd be sorry if anything bad happened to her. But Susan is the past. I could no more go back to her than I could go back to being twenty years old."

Terri leaned against me, looking out at a freighter, just a dot on the horizon. She said, "Divorce sucks."

Something sad came on the radio as we watched that ship come slowly toward us. I said, "You wonder what it does to our kids."

"Did you leave her?" Terri asked.

"Not exactly. I said I'll leave if you want. And she said go. Maybe she was surprised I actually did it. Maybe she expected I'd come running back. But. I. didn't."

Terri looked very thoughtful. "You must have been happy with her at some point. In the beginning maybe."

"Well, sure. In the beginning. But that was almost twenty years ago. There's been a lot of hurt feelings since. Each one disappointed at the other."

"Disappointed about what though? I mean, I look at Susan. She's beautiful. And she's real competent the way she runs the children's library. Your kids. Everytime I see them. They're perfectly dressed, perfectly behaved. And Susan's sweet to everyone. Nice disposition. In fact she always made me a little uncomfortable because she's so perfect."

"Not quite perfect."

"Well. Why? What's wrong with her?"

"I don't want to blame it all on her." I shook my head. "But, let's put it this way. Susan lacks passion."

"Passion?"

"Yeah."

She looked out to sea a moment. "You mean she doesn't like to fuck?"

"She . . . yeah. She doesn't like to . . ."

"And that's why you got divorced?"

"Well, it was more than that, of course. We had lots of problems. But I don't think taking out the trash would have been such a sore point if we hadn't had that one big problem in back of it all."

I wasn't comfortable discussing my divorce. I really didn't have answers for a lot of the questions—kind of like the driver in a car wreck. After, he's not quite sure what happened.

"You're going to be late if I don't get you home." I pulled out onto the road and soon, the ocean behind us, we were swallowed up by tree-lined streets, the houses set on huge lots, including mansions hidden behind hedges or meadows or hillocks.

Terri asked, "Was she always that way?"

"What?"

"She never liked fucking? Why did you marry her? Why did you stay married to her?"

I grimaced. "When you're eighteen and your girlfriend doesn't want to have sex you figure she's supposed to say that. When you get married and she seems a little cool . . . well, she's about the only woman you ever had. You figure they must all be like that. Besides, when she was young I could kind of coax her into things. It wasn't until the kids came. Either she got less interested or I wasn't trying hard enough anymore. I don't know."

I turned, gesturing, trying to make her understand. "While I was married, I respected my wife. I treated her good and I'd never touch another woman. And I had offers."

"I can believe it." She pointed. "Better watch the road."

Both hands on the wheel, I stared straight ahead. "I used to ache when I'd see a pretty woman like you. Like, at a party or somewhere. And all you'd do is smile. And I'd want you so bad. I'd be afraid I couldn't control myself. And maybe I shouldn't have been that way. Because I had a great-looking wife who I loved and seeing her naked I wanted to explode all over her. But she just wanted to get dressed—which made me frustrated as hell. And, besides that, it hurt. I know it shouldn't have, it was her problem. She explained many times. She'd be that way with anyone. But I just got sick of getting pushed away again and again. Of being . . . tolerated."

"She doesn't do it at all?" Terri asked.

"It's her attitude. Like she's making a big sacrifice. I mean, when I heard myself once promising to paint the garage if she'd go down on me. Even I could figure out, this is not the way it's supposed to be. Don't laugh."

"I'm sorry."

"If she had one—one ounce of what you've got, Terri."

"Did you try foreplay? Some women need time."

"You mean, like long body rubs with oils and stuff?"

"Yeah."

"She fell asleep."

"Oh, God."

"I tried different things, but nothing seemed to work."

As we drew close to Terri's house I didn't talk for a while, thinking of how miserably it had all ended. "I got to be past thirty-five. I got to thinking my life was half, more than half over. And I'd been waiting all that time for something. And it wasn't coming. Susan would never loosen up, become like, like . . . like you. So, I felt cheated. And without meaning to, I started to resent her. Which made her confused and hurt. Because she expected I'd always love her the same. That sex wasn't supposed to matter when she loved me. I didn't want to cause her pain. But I couldn't spend the rest of my life pretending that this mismatch was a marriage." I turned to Terri. "Maybe I should have married someone like you."

She looked down. "I wonder how that would have worked out."

No sooner had I said good-by to Terri than I was calling her on the phone, "Just to see that you got to work okay." That night, as I plotted tomorrow's activity on the job site, I could not get her out of my mind. I'll tell you how bad I was—like a kid—I wouldn't change the sheets because they had her smell.

I lay back, imagining the future. And it was Terri. Hand in hand, right into the retirement village. And it would always be as it was last night. So easy to talk, so easy to float into bed. Bed, where Terri would understand everything I wanted and Terri would want it just as much. Not that it was all sex. No. I liked her. I liked her just to talk to. Really.

Suddenly, I sat bolt upright. Okay. Okay, who am I kidding?

I surveyed my domain, a single room, secondhand furniture, kitchen in the corner, closet-sized bathroom. What woman could resist? The pond looked nice, but it was too shallow for boating or swimming and occasionally dried up completely.

If I wanted a future with any woman, I needed money. So. More than ever, my happiness hinged on the success of Indian Peak Estates.

Of course, I was getting ahead of myself and knew it. I had a lot to learn about Terri Pratt. Nor could I completely banish from my mind an old prejudice; that there must be something wrong with a woman who enjoys sex so thoroughly, who is wildly immodest—an exhibitionist in fact—who uses the language of the bedroom, every filthy world, like a native.

Well, she didn't learn all that watching Dr. Ruth.

· 2 ·

Almost by default, Big John Finnerty acted as foreman on the Indian Peak project. More and more I found myself on the phone to suppliers, to the architect or the various inspectors; or chasing down subcontractors who never arrived on time, who left with the job half-finished or not done to standard. In my absence, John took charge, recruiting and supervising the carpenters, inevitably his sons or cousins from Galway.

Independent, they often communicated in Gaelic, which irritated the hell out of my partner. "Kevin," Dexter rasped, "tell those micks to speak English. I don't want them talking about me behind my back when I'm standing right in front of them."

Indian Peak was a name Dexter pulled out of his hat. The site was to peaks what Greenland is to green. In fact, it was slightly depressed. The road had been monumentally expensive, involving tree cutters, earth movers, blacktoppers, utility workers, landscapers. Red tape in gaining permits had delayed construction until November and we'd since lost additional weeks because of weather. Even now, amidst a warming trend, we'd had rain.

Despite the bad luck, Dexter was already considering sites for our next project. "We're going to have a reputation," he enthused. "With the work you do, Kevin, we're going to be the preferred builder of luxury homes on the South Shore. Just watch."

I could only hope. With both my cottage and my wife's home mortgaged to the hilt, I didn't want to think what might happen if Indian Peak wasn't completed and occupied on schedule. In the meantime, I drew a monthly stipend from the Indian Peak Corporation.

My heart beat a little faster as the massive colonial came into view, a solitary structure at the end of the road. Our first-born, so to speak, it was virtually complete, on one and a half acres with an attached garage, Greek revival columns soaring two full stories, and a spacious backyard deck. I thought proudly, I must bring Terri to see my good work.

I began snapping out orders the minute I hit the ground. "John, make sure somebody seals up the knots on those dining room doors. They're going to be painted and we don't want them to bleed. Whoever laid the plywood in the kitchen didn't countersink the nails. Have Pete do that today before the linoleum goes down. And make sure the treads for the back stairs are glued down as well as nailed. I hate squeaky stairs. What's the matter with you? You look like your dog died or something."

"My dog's fine. But your basement's a bit wet."

Standing on the last, dry step I muttered, "It's one thing we get water. But not this much. It only rained a little."

Moments later, the worst possible time, Jack Lundgren arrived with clients, a young couple. We didn't hear them until they were on the cellar stairs. "What have we here?" came a woman's voice.

At the top of the stairs, Jack's smile faded. Bending for a better view, the woman muttered to her husband, "You could hold a regatta down here."

The couple left. Jack stayed, staring glumly. "You've got to do something about this, Kevin."

"I will, Jack."

"I've got Dexter on my ass ten times a day about selling this house, and then when I bring someone . . ." He gestured to the dirty black water with bits of wood and cigarette packages floating on the top. "Too bad. Those two seemed really interested."

With a small pump, we began draining. As John pulled the hose through a basement window I asked, "What else can go wrong?"

Almost in answer, Larry Dexter's wife arrived in her new Mercedes. She'd brought the two youngest of her five children, tiny Erica, who had to be carried, and three-year-old Mathew.

"Christ." John took off his cap, ran a hand through his gray hair. "I'll be making myself scarce."

Kathleen Dexter was a short, blue-eyed brunette with a bit of a weight problem. She came striding up to me. "I heard."

"Heard what, Kikki?"

"The basement. Jack Lundgren told me. What I want to know, is it actionable? I called Larry and he said it must be the fault of the cement people. If they don't make it right they'll find themselves in court so fast."

"Well, I don't know." I stepped back. "Basements leak. It's not necessarily the cement. A basement is not a boat. Sometimes water comes in through doors or windows. Kikki," I pointed, "Mathew is on the street."

"Mathew!" She screamed so loud I winced. But the boy continued, unconcerned, walking across the road. In a padded winter coat he was almost as wide across as he was tall. "Well," she turned toward me.

"Well? Well what?"

"Are we going to go inside and look at the damage or not?"

"Yeah. Yeah, sure. Don't you think you should get Mathew—"

Before I could finish she had turned, shouting again, "Mathew! Mathew, come with mommy." Then, she adjusted the baby in her arms and plunged inside. I could see the boy was not listening. I ran and fetched him myself.

"Is the oil burner okay?" Kikki stood on the basement stairs.

"Fine," John explained, hat in hand, bootless in two inches of water. "That's the reason it's raised off the floor. In case of water—"

"What's damaged?"

John shrugged, "Nothing, as far as I can tell—"

"These stairs should be painted."

"Yes, m'am."

"We don't want the buyers to see water marks."

"No m'am."

"How did this happen?"

John looked around, "Rain, m'am."

A worker's laugh was just barely audible.

"Why don't you get some buckets?" Kikki demanded.

"Buckets?"

"To get the water out."

"The pump does that, m'am."

"Good God, why wait for the pump? With buckets it'll be gone that much sooner. What's wrong with you people? Do I have to tell you your business?" She turned to me. "Get them busy, Kevin. Get it done in case Jack brings more clients."

Upstairs, in the gleaming new kitchen, I played goalie, blocking Mathew from the stairs, which he returned to again and again. Little sister sat in the center of the room watching, as if taking lessons.

Kikki tried the sink. "Damn, the one place you should have water."

"It hasn't been turned on yet."

Nonplussed, she went to the electric range, to the dishwasher, to the garbage disposal, making certain that each operated.

"I've done all that, Kikki. Everything works."

But there was no stopping her. She switched off the oven lights and turned to me. "You went to the Lundgren party?"

"Yes," I sidestepped to catch Mathew.

"I couldn't go."

"We missed you. Glad to see you're feeling better."

"Who said I am?"

"Oh, I—"

"So I hear you made a new friend," she said.

"What?"

"Terri Pratt." She came close, smiling unpleasantly. "Of all people."

"What?" I nearly had to leap in order to stop the boy, who had executed a nifty end run, tearing up the stairs. "What? She's very nice."

"So I've heard." She gave a lewd chuckle. Then, in one motion, she scooped up the girl and reached to grab Mathew by the hand. "I've got to get going. Have that cellar cleaned before noon." Half dragging little Mathew, she left as abruptly as she'd come.

From the foyer, watching the sky blue Mercedes pull away, I guessed the meaning of her smirking attitude toward Terri Pratt. Kikki was still friendly with Susan. So she wanted order restored, she wanted me back with my wife and family. Naturally she disliked anyone who threatened the restoration.

"Why don't you tell Dexter to keep his woman away from here?"

I turned to Big John Finnerty.

"She makes me nervous," he continued. "She makes my boys nervous. It takes up too much time answering her damn fool questions."

"Watch it, John. You're tracking water." I looked up the street to see the last of her. The land was bare trees and mud to the main street—not another house visible. Grass. Grass will cure the water problem.

I was determined that nothing would wreck my positive mood.

"I don't know why you put up with her." John continued. "Bossing you around when she's got no right to do it. You don't work for her."

"Kikki? I make allowances for Kikki. She's had a lot of problems."

"I couldn't put up with either of them."

"Yeah, well without Larry we wouldn't be in business. We're alongside the town forest. You need state permits to build here. Larry got them. Besides that, if we don't sell this first house right away, we're going to need more money. And Larry's got the money."

We moved back to the cellar. Only a thin film of water remained on the floor. John sat and removed his shoes and socks.

"Get brooms," I told a worker, "sweep what's left toward the pump."

Wringing out his socks, John declared "I don't envy you."

"Why's that?"

"How many hours do you put into this?"

"How many hours am I awake?"

"Thank Jesus I'm not boss. After five I don't even think of this place. You have to think of it all the time. And be nice to her. And her husband. And bankers and clients and inspectors. I couldn't digest my food if I had to be nice to all those assholes."

I laughed.

"Whatever you're getting out of this, Kevin. I hope it's worth it."

I hoped so too.

"I'm exhausted," Terri explained that night over the phone. "I'm off work at midnight and I'm going home to collapse. I have to get three kids out to school in the morning."

"I understand." I swallowed my disappointment.

"But I'd love to see you, Kevin. I've been—all day—wanting to see you and be with you."

"Better get your rest. That's the important thing."

Finding time for Terri was not easy. I had to be on the job site almost constantly. Thursday morning I could clear a few hours—but her kids had dental appointments. The problem Friday night was landing a baby-sitter. "It's my mom's bingo night," she lamented.

All Saturday I would have my kids. "And I'd love you to meet them, Terri. But I think I should prepare them. They're not used to me dating."

"That's wise."

"What about Sunday?" I asked.

"Sunday! I'm free Sunday. Except I have to be at work by four."

"Sunday it is." After a moment I said, "That gives us a whole three hours. A week from now."

She groaned sadly.

"If things were different, I'd be with you every minute. You couldn't get rid of me." In fact, finding time together would be a chronic problem

At twelve-twenty Terri had just arrived home from work. I rapped softly on the door, nervous because she might think I was pushy, a pest. Even worse, her mother might answer.

She came to the door in her bathrobe. I thrust forward a bunch of roses. "I, I just couldn't go a whole day without at least looking at you."

"God." She smiled, pushing back her hair. "God, Kevin. These are beautiful. I can't believe you did this." She felt them against her face. "I wish I had something for you."

"Just let me look at you."

"I'm a mess." She looked down at the bathrobe. "This ratty old thing."

"Oh, Terri." I slid my hands inside of it to the flannel nightgown.

"God, God . . ." She giggled as I went down on my knees, my face between her legs. "Kevin . . . Kevin, someone might see us."

She led me through the living room. Quietly, so as not to wake her mother or children, we made love on the queen-sized bed.

It wasn't as good as before. We had to hurry. But there was a moment where she wrapped me in her arms and for the first time in nearly a year, I felt close to someone. "We need each other, Terri. That's what I think."

But she was looking grimly to the ceiling.

I mean, I started to worry. "What's the matter?"

"I'm scared."

"Scared? Scared of what?" I glanced around the room.

"I'm scared that I'll fall in love. But you won't love me back."

I responded carefully. "I can't make any promises. But I had the time of my life the other night. And ever since all I can think of is you and how I want to be with you."

She said, "For a long time I've been really down. Thinking. Thinking suppose I never find anyone. I should prepare. Because it's possible I'll live the rest of my life, you know, single. Sitting, watching television with my mother. And then, some day, with the girls gone off, alone, watching alone."

"No."

"Look, I'm not getting any younger and I've got three kids and I've got to be realistic. And not hope for too much."

"You're not alone now," I said—but I don't know if she believed me.

Susan was unusually sullen when I came for the kids on Saturday. In her bathrobe, no makeup, my wife still looked young—not so different from the pretty cheerleader I romanced in high school. I felt an urge to kiss her and say, "I still love you." But of course that would only have complicated matters. Instead, I complained, "I thought you'd have them ready."

"They were up late."

"Susan, you know I come early."

"They stayed up late to watch some Disney thing on TV. If I woke them now they'd be cranky and you'd blame me for that."

"I'm not blaming you. It's just I don't have much time."

"Well whose fault is that?" she asked.

"Whose fault is that? I don't know. I have to work. It takes time to keep you living in the style you've become accustomed to."

"Yeah, kids' night at Burger King is hard to give up."

"Let's drop it," I muttered.

It's not fair introducing Susan like this. The sarcasm was out of character. I figured she'd been tipped off about me and Terri, probably by Kikki Dexter. Of course, she had no right to complain. I was free. And did she think I'd joined the seminary?

While I sat at the kitchen table, she remained at the sink, grimacing unpleasantly, occasionally sipping coffee. I thought, maybe from now on I should wait in the car and blow the horn. Don't come in. Don't have anything to do with her.

Still, in Susan's place I might be even angrier. And I couldn't help feeling a little guilty about the situation. So, I managed to check my temper.

"How are things with you?" I asked.

"Oh, marvelous. Things are marvelous with me."

"How, how have the kids been? . . . Susan?"

"Molly's teacher called again."

"About her reading. You mean reading? We'll go over that tonight."

"Good." She sipped, stared out the window. "Good."

See, I was trying but getting nothing back.

The kids charged in—"Dad's here!"—landing in my lap for hugs and smiles.

I laughed. "How's my best girl and my best boy?"

Susan turned her back.

At the cottage, Michael and Molly lay side by side on the convertible bed, blankets to their chins, firelight from the wood stove catching their eyes and smooth, soft, flawless skin. We'd had a full day running from the mall to the movie theater to the toy store.

"Can we watch television?" Molly's face was framed by blonde curls.

"It's way past bedtime. Anyway, there's nothing on for kids this hour."

"Put on a tape."

"Yeah," Michael echoed, "the Muppets."

"No TV. I want to talk to you guys. About something important." I sat on the edge of the bed and took a deep breath. "Remember what we said about things changing? How people are always leaving one place for another. Trying new things. Getting, you know, making new friends?"

"We know all about it," Molly said.

"You know all about what?"

"You and some lady."

"What do you know about me and some lady?"

"That's she's your girlfriend."

No doubt they'd heard or overheard their mother discussing this with someone. No doubt they'd gotten a rather slanted view.

"I don't think you know *all* about it. Let me explain what's happened so you'll understand. Okay." I cleared my throat. "Daddy's met a very nice lady. And I want you to meet her too."

"No," Molly declared.

"Don't be like that, sweet."

"I don't have to meet her if I don't want to."

"I know you'd like her. She's fun. She has some real nice girls of her own. One of them just your age."

"Louraine Pratt. She's a geek. Nobody likes her."

"I'm sure if you gave her a chance—"

"You only like her because she's got young cookies."

"What?"

"Well, I heard mom say you like young cookies."

I smiled. No point pushing. Let her get used to the idea.

"Would you like to meet my friend sometime?" I asked Michael.

"Okay." I figured it was all over his head, but then he asked, "Do you like her, Dad?"

"Yes. I like her."

"More than us?"

"Hey, listen." I bent low and spoke softly. "You two are the most important people in the world to me. There's no one I like, there's no one I've ever liked more than you two. My best girl and my best boy."

"Not even mommy?"

"Well, I liked her in a different way."

"But now you don't like her."

"Of course I like her."

"What's horny?" Michael asked.

"Some of this stuff is just for grownups, pal."

"When will you come home to live?"

"Michael, you ask me that every time I see you. The answer is the same. I'm sorry. But this is my home." He looked very sad. I stroked his hair. "But I'm here, pal. Whenever you need me. I'm right here."

"Can we watch television till we go to sleep?" Molly asked.

"I . . . I'll put a tape on. Muppets? Okay?"

Terri thrived on attention. In our few hours Sunday she never stopped performing. Whoever said that nudity was asexual hadn't ever met this lady. She'd dance naked on the bed, directly over my face. Or she'd take a wide stance and bend at the waist to pick something off the floor. Sometimes she'd stand at the picture window, gazing on the pond, playing with herself.

"Hey, somebody might see you."

"I thought all those cottages were vacant." She backed away.

"Sometimes people come down on weekends. Even in winter."

Somehow, within minutes she was right back at the window.

For sure, Terri was Susan's polar opposite. And that contributed to my fascination, not to mention a nagging sense of dread. We were making love when an ad came on the radio: *Remember this message from your Better Business Bureau, if it sounds too good to be true, it probably is.*

I actually stopped in the middle of things. Were they talking to me?

Terri had a nice taut body. Her breasts were small but pleasingly shaped; hips firm, bottom small, smooth. And, to be honest, as much as she enjoyed displaying herself I enjoyed watching.

I declared, "I don't know when I can spare the time. But we're going to Bermuda some weekend. Soon. Three days sitting on pink sand and we'll really get to know each other."

"Yeah." She was suddenly pensive, sitting on the bed, looking down at the floor. "We'll really get to know each other."

"What's the matter? Don't you want to go?"

"Of course, I do."

"Well, why—"

For the first time, she pulled at the sheets, wrapping them around herself. "If we really get to know each other—"

"What? If we get to know each other, what?"

"I'm not . . . I'm not so wonderful as you think I am."

"I'm not so wonderful as you think *I* am."

"I have faults, Kevin. Things about me you haven't seen. A past."

"I have a past too. I mean, my wife threw me out. She must have had reasons. Maybe after a while you'll want to throw me out too. But I'm willing to chance it that you won't."

"You know what I think?" she looked up, the sheets falling away.

"What?"

"I think your wife should have her head examined."

My God, it was great to hear her say that.

In the following days, I was lucky to see Terri more than once a week. But we spoke by phone daily, sometimes for hours, about kids and jobs, our hopes for the future. And sometimes . . . I mean, the things she'd say, about *wanting* me, wanting my body, wanting a specific part of my body. It wasn't poetry, but if Susan had spoken this language I might still be married.

It was time to meet the kids.

We decided on a day trip to the Cape. I drove Terri's old Chevy. We two adults sat in front, little Michael between us, the four girls wedged in back. "This'll be fun," I declared optimistically.

The three Pratt girls seemed eager. Michael was quiet. But Molly grumbled, "I have no room." It was just the beginning. Throughout the trip, nothing and no one could please her. She made no effort to socialize with the Pratts, addressing me in a somber monotone and Terri not at all.

As we traveled, I seemed to hit it off especially well with Robin, a younger version of her mother. Louraine and Kelly laughed heartily at all my jokes. Unfortunately, the more I talked to these three, the more hostile Molly grew.

"Are you hungry, Molly dear?" Terri asked.

When no response came, I barked, "Answer the question!"

"No!"

Terri tried again, "You wouldn't want a hamburg—"

"I said no!"

"Don't raise your voice!" I shouted.

"I just said no. You told me to answer!"

"Don't you dare raise your voice to Terri. Or to me. Understood?"

"I want to go home."

Off season, the Cape was unhurried and beautiful. Eager to keep the kids happy, I stopped at ice cream parlors, arcades, and toy shops.

The Pratt girls fawned over Michael. "Isn't he cute." And he responded, chattering about his new school.

We also visited a flea market in a mall parking lot. The Pratts pawed over the dress racks, their mother smiling and attentive.

"You get along good with your kids," I said.

"My kids are my best friends." She gazed at them. "They're great kids."

"They are. My kids. Well, Molly. I wish you could see her when she wasn't acting like a little brat. She's not really like that."

"She hates me," Terri said.

"No. No way. She's just a little upset—"

"Take my word for it. She hates me. She'd hate any woman you brought home. I understand. It's divorce. My girls went through it. I went through it myself a long time ago."

"But your girls have treated me great," I protested.

"They've had four years to adjust. My kids. And just now they're a lot like their mother. They love having a man around. The right sort of man. And feeling for a little while like a regular family."

I wanted Terri to see Indian Peak Estates, to prove I wasn't just another divorced father living in a crummy room. I had prospects.

Nonetheless, it was more than a month before we found time to get out there together. As we pulled up to the house with its grand columns, she seemed awed. "You really built this?"

"I had help."

She toured the rooms wide-eyed, gasping, "God, Kevin. It's beautiful."

"We use quality stuff," I explained eagerly. "Dexter's always bitching about money. But if you want a reputation you can't use inferior material. It'll show. See." I knocked on the door frame. "Hardwood mouldings, special order. Oak flooring. In the master bedroom, the bath has gold fixtures, a Jacuzzi *and* a shower."

"Gold fixtures."

"Well, gold plated."

"How much?"

"For the house?" I smiled. "Half a million."

"Oh, my God."

"I couldn't afford it myself. But if it sells, and everybody seems to think it will, we'll build another. Then another. We'll develop this whole street. Maybe by the time we get to the next project I can build a house for me." I reached out, held her. "Would you like that? Would you like to come visit me in my new house?"

She gave a vigorous nod and smiled.

For a long moment, I couldn't take my eyes off her. Then, I heard Big John's crew outside, furiously wacking away, setting up forms for the foundation of the second house. "Come on, I'll show you the master bedroom."

On the stairs we passed unconnected electrical fixtures, the wires, snakelike, reaching out at us. It spoiled the look and I apologized, "We're not quite finished in here."

In the master bedroom she went first to the elegant bow window that offered a view on the town forest, an impenetrable tangle of black branches. "God," she said, "wait until spring. It'll be so green."

"In winter you can put a few logs in the fireplace over

there. You can climb into bed with someone you love and"—
I pantomimed with my fingers—"watch the first snowfall
drifting down."

"Someone's going to be so happy here," she stared out
the window.

I moved past her, gesturing out the window. "Where
we're standing. No human being ever stood up here. Until I
put the floor in. So. You're seeing the world from a completely
new perspective."

"I never thought of it that way."

I used my fingernail to clear a speck of paint from the
window.

"You really love your work," Terri said.

"You know, some people who knew me all my life never
understood that."

"Susan?"

"Well, I was thinking of my father. . . . His family came
from a little French village in Nova Scotia. Fishermen. My
mom used to tell us how he'd get furious when the other kids
teased him. *'Rory get your dory, there's a herring in the
bay. . . .'* He worked so hard to better himself. For years, he
had a full-time job and went to college nights to be a lawyer.
And God, was he ever disappointed in me. Becoming a carpenter, working with my hands. Just not good enough. Not
for his son."

"I wish—I wish he could see this house."

"I don't know if it would make any difference, really."

"He'd be proud of you, Kevin. He'd be very proud. Just
like I am."

"God, I need you. I've always needed someone like you."
I kissed her.

I grew excited and reached beneath her winter coat, bur-
rowing into her pants—one hand down the back through the
smooth, giving flesh of her behind, and one down her front,
over coarse, thick hair—until my fingers met. Her legs bowed
slightly and she made a low, involuntary sound.

I don't mean to harp on this, but Susan would have pulled
away. *Not here, Kevin. You're ruining my slacks.*

"What a woman you are."

She smiled like crazy.

John Finnerty appeared at the threshold. We broke apart abruptly, awkwardly, Terri turning to the bow window, pretending to admire the view. I thrust my hands into my pockets.

"Yes, John?"

"Sorry to bother you, Kev. Dexter is here wanting to see you."

"Be right down. Thanks."

John gave Terri a rather stern glance and departed.

"He saw." She was flushed, straightening her coat.

"We're not breaking any laws."

"He doesn't like me."

"Everybody likes you. Why wouldn't they?"

She forced a smile. "You're prejudiced."

"Come on downstairs. I got to talk to Larry Dexter.

"I'll . . . I'll stay here and look around. I want to see the gold bathroom."

I could hear Larry as I came down the stairs. Uncharacteristically, he was out on the street, shouting, leaning into Kikki's Mercedes. When he moved I caught a glimpse of the driver. Strangely, it was not Kikki, but some wild-looking guy in a fatigue jacket.

And this character started hollering back. "If you don't like it get somebody else to deliver your shit."

"You're supposed to have your own car."

"It's in the shop. You want I should get my bicycle?"

Larry passed him a rectangular, brown package, saying, "Deliver this and get back to the office. No detours."

"What's that all about?" I nudged John.

"Whatever that man's involved in," John replied, "I don't want to know."

Dexter was still talking to this guy—I couldn't hear what he was saying—when, without warning, the car roared forward. Larry leaped to the shoulder or the thing might have run over his toes. It squealed away in a fog of exhaust.

"Son of a bitch! Goddamn!" Larry came storming up the driveway toward his own gleaming, burgundy red BMW. Seeing me, he put out a hand, palm up. "See what I'm stuck with for temporary help? Goddamn psychotics. It's the fucking welfare and unemployment causes that."

"Yeah," I observed, "the decent people are all home collecting."

"You can laugh, Bourque. He's not driving your car." Then, recovering his cynical smile, he looked up at the bedroom window. "Not working today, I understand."

"What?"

"Am I interrupting anything?"

"I'm showing the place to a friend. That's all."

He chuckled. "I don't think it's in her price range."

"You wanted me, Larry?"

He reached into his pocket and produced a circular, "I got this in the mail. From the Wood Shed. It seems the price they're offering the public isn't much higher than the contractor's price at Shea's."

"The difference is that Shea's delivers a better grade—"

"Wood is wood."

"Larry—"

"What does it matter with studs? You can't even see them."

"It matters because you don't want your floors to sag or your walls to warp so the plaster cracks and the windows won't open. I mean, are we in this for a quick buck or what?"

"We're not going to have any bucks at all by the time you're through."

"We've got financing to build two houses. So let's not cry poor mouth."

Larry folded the circular, put it away. He was trim, well dressed, and not as tall as he looked thanks to elevator heels. "Just be aware. The market is a little soft. And it might take longer to sell than we originally thought."

"Yeah, well, you've got that rainy day fund. That'll keep us going if the first house doesn't sell right away."

"That's for emergencies only," he turned away briefly. Larry had insisted from the beginning that he could lay his hands on lots of additional cash if the project required it. Back then I didn't care because I never expected, still didn't expect that we'd need it. For months the housing market had been booming.

"You *do* still have this rainy day money?" I asked now. It made me nervous the way he suddenly didn't want to talk about it.

"I said I can get the money. Okay? Just, that doesn't mean you should go on spending like there's no tomorrow. We're not going to make a nickel if you don't get the costs down."

He was exaggerating, of course. I used quality materials, sure, but we'd always intended that. Besides, I'd saved thousands doing a lot of the labor myself, working nights and weekends.

I asked, "What gives between you and that Rapolli from the DEQE."

"I invited him to Lundgrens' party. That's all."

"Why should you do that?"

"To stay on his good side. You said it yourself. We don't want those state guys pissed at us. They could shut us down. Rapolli, he's from Weymouth. And he was just tickled to see how we live across the tracks in Norham."

"He was asking about something. Something in your car."

"Yeah."

"What was it?" I demanded.

"A painting. An old painting I picked up when I went to Europe that time. Just a piece of tourist junk really. I got a bunch of them and sometimes I give them away. It impresses people."

"A bribe?"

"A bribe?" Larry laughed. "These things cost five bucks tops. You can't bribe a state official for five bucks. Five hundred bucks maybe."

"I guess you'd know," I said darkly. "For the record: it

might cost more, but I do business above the table. Get me? I want no part of bribery—"

"It wasn't bribery I keep telling you." Then he smiled and backed into his car. "Who's been putting these sordid ideas in your head, partner?" Finally, he glanced up at the bedroom and gave a leer that I did not like at all.

It wasn't only the Dexters giving me funny looks over Terri. I met Pat Lundgren at the market, shepherding the twins. "So what's this about you and Terri Pratt?"

"Has it been in the papers or something?"

"You know, I feel kind of responsible. It started at my party."

Was she apologizing for that? "I feel kind of responsible." Like she was joking, but, then again, like she wasn't.

· 3 ·

We'd left three inches of snow at home, but Bermuda wasn't too great either, damp and chilly. On the plane, Terri and I had our first fight. She'd been late, you see. I complained and she went into a pout.

We walked a deserted beach, hands jammed in our jacket pockets, noses red with the chill. Terri was still not talking and I knew there was more on her mind than our little tiff. Obviously, she'd found something wrong with me. The romance too good to be true was coming apart too soon.

"You really know nothing about me," she said.

"Theresa Tucci Pratt." Smiling hopefully, I held her. "Brown hair, brown eyes, and very large nipples. I know all the important things."

She didn't even smile, but pulled away. I got more worried because she'd hinted around like maybe her past was a little *too* interesting. Possibly I was better off not knowing about it.

"I love you, Kevin, but something tells me I can't hold you."

"Come on—"

"It's my pattern. People leave me. Back to my own father."

"Anyone would be crazy to leave you."

"Yeah, well maybe you'll be crazy too." She looked up. "I want to tell you some things."

"You don't have to tell me anything."

"I don't want to spend every day worrying. That you'll find out. And then hate me for *not* telling you. I'd rather you heard the worst from me."

The worst? God, what had she done?

"I want you to know that I've had a lot of guys. Uhhh. Even when I was married, I had guys."

I kind of winced. "I guess your husband wasn't giving you—"

"It was his idea."

"It was?"

"My husband's. Eddie."

I was hoping I'd misunderstood.

"He'd find couples. He'd sleep with the wife. I'd have the husband."

"Uh . . . God. Are you telling me he made you do it?"

"Not, not exactly." So, she began telling me about this. Her lips, red and moist, were in a sexy pout, while her voice came in and out like headache pain. And the more she talked, gushing with information, the more she tried to justify herself and the more she got caught up in the story.

". . . It was like drugs. You can't imagine the high. . . . I'd just lie there and get all that attention. . . . It seemed intense, exciting. I even thought I liked it. And I thought I liked the people. Cared for them. . . ."

Mostly, I wanted to get the hell away from her, but—and this even I can't understand—some part of me was dying to take her right back up to the room because obviously this woman was hot.

She said, "Back then you could live that way and you weren't taking your life in your hands. My husband encouraged it. So I never realized how wrong it was. Back then . . . you remember how things were. Everybody just doing what they felt."

"I, I read about it."

She stopped and looked closely at me. "You don't like this. Oh, Christ." After a silence, she asked, "Should we go home now? I'll pay for my ticket."

"When . . . when did all this happen, Terri?"

"Mostly at the beginning of our marriage. . . . I was young. And stupid."

"And since then?"

"I've had a few, uh, relationships since my divorce, which, which I will tell you about. But nothing, you know, kinky."

"Kinky? How . . . how many guys were there?"

"I didn't keep a count. I could try to add them up. If you want."

"Oh, Jesus. . . . Are you seeing anyone now?"

"You. You're all I want. If you still want me."

You know, it was like suddenly watching the world through a mirror and you can't quite figure left from right. Appropriately, it began drizzling.

She said, "If you hate me now. Tell me."

"What sort of things did you do? I can't—"

"You know what we did."

"Kinky things. What does that mean? When you had sex with these guys. Were there others in the room? I mean, watching?"

After a long time, she said, "Yeah. Sometimes."

I shook my head. "And would you have sex with, with more than one guy at a time?"

She took a breath, "You really want all the details?"

"Women? You'd do things with women?"

"I like men. Someone told me it's because of my father. But. All I know is I like men. See, for a long time I had this, I guess you'd call it low self-esteem. And then I found I had this power. I'd meet these guys. Some of them doctors and lawyers and important people who spend all day telling everybody what to do. And I'd have them completely." Her eyes lit up. "I'd have their very balls in my hand or their cocks between my teeth. And they'd beg for me to do things. Little me. I felt so womanly and strong."

A glance my way—I must have looked like a guy who'd just been clubbed on the head—and she knew she'd said too much. "Afterwards I'd feel so empty, Kevin. I had to stop. I told Eddie, no more."

Which I suppose makes it all better. I didn't know what to say. I mean, I always figured she was free, even wild, and I loved that. But this, this was something beyond, something dirty and ugly.

On the other hand, if I wanted purity, I had had that in Susan.

Maybe you can't get both in the same woman, virtue and wild passion. I mean, maybe that's the point. Wasn't Terri's background of a piece with her whole approach to sex? In fact, I'd sometimes feared worse.

I began to picture friends, laughing at me. "Who knows about this? Anybody we know? Anybody I know?"

"It's not something I tell anybody. I never exactly even confessed it."

I turned away, shaking my head.

"I didn't have to tell you, Kevin. But I want to be honest with you. Tell you everything . . . I knew it was a risk." She walked to the water. "I guess we're all finished. Is that right?"

"I . . . I've got to think. Okay? I've got to think about this." Abruptly, I began shuffling down the beach, leaving Terri standing at the edge of the ocean in the rain.

I tried to make sense of what I'd heard. Well. You can't blame someone for having a past. She was under the influence of an immoral man. And now, she has the decency to come clean, admit everything. I wondered if I'd had a good influence on her.

It's no wonder she was so good in bed. My own sexual history pales by comparison. (It's embarrassing to admit how pale it is.) Some won't believe this, but beside my wife I'd had relations on two occasions with one other woman (Susan and I had briefly broken our engagement, at the time.)

It's unsettling to think that every time you go to bed you're being measured against a small army.

I walked a long time in the drizzle, trying to think up an excuse not to just leave her flat. The fact is, I didn't want it to end. Terri had given me my first happy moments in more than a year.

I returned to the room to find her staring out the window. We scarcely talked at dinner. Retiring early, we took separate beds, lying awake, silent.

"Kevin?"

"What?"

She rolled over. "Listen. If you want to stay together. After what I told you. I know you don't. But in case you do. There's one thing."

"What's that?"

"I told you this. About my past. Okay. But you can't ever throw it up at me. I didn't tell you this so you could call me names. Or tell your friends."

"You think I want my friends to know about this?"

She sighed. "It really bothers you."

Now I rolled over. "How do I know you're not going to do it again?"

"I'm not," she snickered at the idea. "I'm not, never. I'm older and wiser. I know there's nothing better than having one good man to love and to love me back. I swear that's all I want. You."

"But maybe you've had better than me. And maybe someday you'll want that again."

"Every night," she wore a kind of half smile, "to help me sleep, I bring myself off. And since the party, I can't come unless I imagine I'm with you. No one else." And then, after a moment, "Do I have to sleep alone?"

"I . . . Just, I'm kind of tired now."

Well, Terri was not one to take a slight lying down. At once, she was banging into furniture, turning on lights, opening drawers.

"What are you doing?"

"Taking a shower!" She stripped at the foot of my bed and disappeared into the bathroom, running the water. Thereafter, she pranced by four or five times, always managing some loud noise lest I fail to notice her.

She sure wasn't like Susan. And I was glad of that. Besides, I wasn't marrying her or anything. And she swore up and down she'd be faithful.

"About the guys you've, you know, slept with."

"What?" She looked over.

"Uh. Anybody I know?"

"Well, I don't know everybody you know."

"I just, understand, I just don't want to be running into these people."

"The people from those days, I wouldn't remember them if I fell over them. And they wouldn't remember me. It was long ago. It's a closed, closed chapter." A small smile came at the corner of her lips when she knew she'd won. She came across my bed on all fours, the smile growing. And I didn't care where she'd been or what she'd done. I had to have her.

"You liked it? Those things in the past."

"It was a long time ago."

She slid her naked body beneath the sheets, against me. And I still don't fully understand what I did next. I said, "Tell me that you liked it."

"I . . . I liked it."

"Tell me again. Just say the words."

"You mean . . . I liked it. Okay?"

"Keep saying it."

"I liked it. I liked it. I loved it. I love to fuck. I can't help myself. I love to be fucked. I need to—"

"But—Wait. But only with me."

Stopped in mid-moan, she looked up. "Right. Only with you."

* * *

Just as we'd had rain on our vacation, it had been gloriously warm and sunny at home, bringing unhappy results.

With the colonial largely completed, the second house was progressing swiftly. The foundation set, Big John had already built the deck and stud walls of the ground floor. Yet both basements were badly flooded.

"What the hell is this?" I high-stepped through sloppy mud. "Did you have a monsoon or something?"

"Snow melted," John shrugged, "and the water wouldn't drain."

"Look." I plunged my fingers into the ground and retrieved a handful of grey mud. "It shouldn't be like this." I squeezed, the stuff running between my fingers. "Something's wrong, and I think it's the perk test."

Larry Dexter, who had insisted on arranging the test himself, didn't answer for a moment. "If I remember right the perk test was fine. I can show you the results."

"Yeah, I'll bet you can. In the meantime, I've been up to my ankles in mud since we started. You can't tell me this site perked properly. You played some angle here and I want to know what!"

"The land's buildable," Larry went on. "That's all that counts. The land's buildable and we've already built a whole house on it."

"We didn't pass the perk test. Did we? Instead you made some deal with the guy Rapolli. Am I right?"

Larry shrugged.

"You had no right to do that."

"If I hadn't, we'd be out of business now."

"We could have got our money back!"

"I don't want my money back. I want to build houses. Don't you?"

"Houses? We should've built boats!"

"We can handle the water."

"You lied to me. You said you didn't pay any bribe, you said you gave him a worthless painting. You lied to me."

"Oh, but you're wrong. I *did* give him a worthless painting. I just didn't tell him it was worthless."

"You mean you told him it was some kind of original fucking work of art? I don't believe this. Suppose he has it checked out?"

"He's not going to do that." Dexter was maddeningly composed. "It's a religous painting. He gave it to his mother. He's not even going to be looking at it. And even if he did have it appraised, he already gave us the permit. He's not going to sue us for misrepresenting his bribe."

"And what if the police or somebody finds out about this? Bribery is against the law. We could go to jail. God!"

"I gave a friend a cheap painting from a flea market. That's a bribe? I don't think any jury would call that a bribe." Larry smiled at his own cleverness. "Thanks to what I did you can go on building. And we can make a fortune." He leaned close and nodded, "And don't think this sort of thing isn't done all the time."

"Is it?"

"Yeah. It is."

"And what about finding someone to buy a house in the middle of a fucking swamp. Is that done all the time?"

"We'll have buyers—"

"I don't get involved with this kind of underhanded shit. I just don't."

"If you can't bring yourself to go along," Larry gave a sneering smile, "give the attorney general a call."

I didn't reply.

"Go ahead," he goaded. "I'll give you the number."

My hands became fists. The fact was, if the true condition of the drainage became known to state officials we might be forced to shut down, even to dismantle the project board by board. I would lose everything. I'd been given a choice: acquiesce in Dexter's crooked deal or be ruined.

No doubt he could see on my face how angry I was.

Certainly, I got a warning look from John Finnerty, who appeared now, as if sensing trouble. But I held my temper and walked away.

"Every cent," I told Pat and Jack Lundgren. "Every cent I've got in the world is tied up in Indian Peak."

Sitting in their living room, I didn't mention the perk test. The less people who knew the better. Besides, water was only one of my problems.

"Where are the buyers, Jack? A few months ago there was a place up the road. They were *charging* just to look."

"I'm getting hurt too, Kevin. Unsold houses all over town. Prices drop and still they don't move. We're letting agents go. And it happened overnight. The bubble just burst."

"I've got to unload that house, Jack."

"I'm trying."

I took a calming breath. "Don't misunderstand, I appreciate everything you guys have done."

Pat said, "I bring out anyone even remotely in that price range. But not many people have half a million to spend on a house."

The Lundgrens lacked the aura of successful realtors. Jack was short, balding, and overweight. As a salesman, he was not particularly compelling, yet he worked hard, knew the town.

Pat has lovely black hair, though I suppose she's not considered attractive, with a receding chin. A conscientious mother, she'd given up most of her real estate work to care for the twins.

Anyway, both these people had been kind to me and I was always grateful for their help and advice. I put the check on the table.

"What?" Jack asked.

"Bounced."

He examined it.

"Shea Brothers Lumber sent it back while I was in Bermuda. They said they could wait a few days until I got the money straightened out. But of course, they're not going to deliver any more lumber in the meantime."

"Well, what happened?" Pat asked. "Don't you have the money?"

"All the money we had—most of it from the building loan, the funds of the Indian Peak Corporation—were in this account. So. Apparently the answer is no. We don't have any money."

"Don't you always know how much money you've got?" Jack asked.

"I'm building twelve houses. I don't have time to be auditing bank accounts."

"Well, how much do you have in there now?" He put the check down.

"They said I had no money in there. Zip. *Nada*."

Pat asked, "How much did you expect was in there?"

"We started with enough to prepare the site. Put up two homes. And pay my expenses until August." I shook my head. "I just made a lot of purchases. And I know we were running over budget. But, no way we should have completely run out of money. We only just started the second house."

"Oh, Kevin," Jack said, "you've got to keep a close eye on the money if you're going to be in business."

"I figured that's what my partner was for. That was his job."

"Have you talked to Larry?" Pat asked.

"I'm afraid of what he's going to tell me."

Jack suggested, "Maybe he put the money in another account."

Oh God, let it be true.

Pat said, "You don't think Larry is, I don't know. I don't want to say it."

"Larry can play fast and loose sometimes," Jack added, "but I don't think he'd . . ." He didn't want to say it either.

"You don't think he'd steal the money?" I asked. "Well, you're probably right. For one thing, if we run out he's obligated to come up with more cash to keep us going. Besides that, he's in as deep as I am. He put his house up as collateral on the building loan. And his cars. And his vacation place. So. If he skims money, he cuts his own throat. But." I paused. "He's just stupid enough to borrow from the account. Thinking he'll put it back. Thinking he's got a sure thing on some investment. And he'll put it all back. Except the asshole loses it."

"You've got to ask him straight out," Jack said. "What's the story?"

"Yeah. I should. Ask him straight out. But if he gives me a straight answer it'll be a first."

Over the phone, Larry Dexter was unperturbed. "This is a bank screw-up. Something about my signature on the wrong form."

"I called the bank, Larry. They didn't mention any screw-up. They said something about insufficient funds."

"Horseshit."

"Yeah. Well, what can I tell you?"

"Just write another check, Kev. I'll straighten out the bank."

"I don't enjoy apologizing to people for rubber checks."

"It'll all be cleared up tomorrow."

"If that account's wiped out then I've got nothing to live on. I'm in the poorhouse and my whole family with me."

"The money is there, Kevin. I'll drop off some cash for you just for the time being, until we get this mess cleared up."

That night, I told Terri little of my business worries, yet it must have been evident that my mind was elsewhere. She was a bit nervous as we headed out for an evening of dinner and shopping. "This proves we don't have to go to bed to have a good time," she insisted. "Not that I mind when we do."

As I drove she kept looking sideways at me, studying my face and expression. "Is it all better now?" she asked.

"Is what all better?"

"Am I forgiven for . . . those things I told you in Bermuda."

"I asked you to tell me. So there's nothing to forgive. It's the past. It's done. The past can't hurt us."

I wanted it to be true, but as I spoke I think we both realized it wasn't. Nevertheless, Terri smiled and laid her hand on my shoulder. "You won't be sorry, Kevin. I'm going to be so good for you. You'll never regret it. I swear."

I nodded.

"The other day I was going to cook pot roast," she said.

"What?"

"I was going to cook pot roast. I cook a good pot roast. So I went to the market for vegetables. And I saw this nice-looking guy buying frozen dinners. And I got to thinking there must be a million single women who cook great. And there must be a million guys, lonely guys like him, who'd love for someone to cook for them. A nice supper. Only these people, it seems they never get together. So, finally I thought about us. And how lucky I am because I can cook a nice supper for you. And it made me so happy." She drew a line down from the corner of her eye. "Big tears came down." And now tears came again. "God, I don't want to lose you and be alone again."

And I decided that it was weak and immature to hold the past against her. An attractive, exciting woman was vowing to do almost anything for me. What more did I want?

"We underestimated costs," Larry Dexter finally admitted. "We've got cash flow problems." The temperature near zero, winter had come boomeranging back, along with half a dozen bounced checks. We sat in the Lundgrens' kitchen, reviewing the books.

Pat stood in the background, offering drinks, advice. Jack looked almost as concerned as we did. He had urged this summit and even agreed to host it. But, incredibly, Larry used the occasion to lash out at him.

"I gave you an exclusive listing, Jack."

"Well, I know, but—"

"I gave it to you expecting results. Quick results. Some results."

"We've had a major market turndown and—"

"Spare me."

"It's true," Pat added, "don't you read the papers?"

"Jack's put in a lot of hours on this," I insisted.

Larry snickered. "All I know is houses in our price range have been going, sold, before the first spade was turned. Now, we got a beautiful house in a beautiful location. And you guys can't fucking sell it."

"Watch your language," Pat glanced upstairs, where the children slept.

"I had two people who were very interested," Jack reminded him, "until they got a look at the basement. You pay half a million for a house you don't want water in your basement."

This quieted Dexter. The water was all his fault.

Larry had produced figures showing where the money had gone. "What would you say," I said as I picked over the mountain of receipts, "if we got an accountant to review all this?"

"Sure. We got nothing better to do with our millions. Hire some guy to tell us what we already know."

Larry's snappish attitude was an ominous sign. In the past, no matter how grim matters had seemed, he had remained optimistic and cool.

I continued. "If we got cash flow problems like you say, we can't borrow more money. And what we need to avoid total collapse, we need the reserve we talked about."

Larry sat back, dragged on a cigarette. His expensive suit jacket hung off the back of the chair. He wore a Rolex and two gold rings. "What reserve?"

"What reserve? What reserve? Is that your answer?" Suddenly, I stood. "I mean, what is this? You told me you had money! I never would have gotten into this except—"

"I don't see why I'm expected to come up with more money when it's your extravagance and poor business sense—"

"No way I spent all the money! I know what I spent, goddammit."

"I know what you spent too." Larry waved some receipts.

"Oh, yeah?" I bent down to within inches of him, "Well, we're going to find out about that. Okay? Someone, someone impartial is going to go over these books. But, in the meantime, it doesn't make one bit of difference if I spent all the money or if you lost it at the fucking track—"

"That's a damned lie!"

"It doesn't make any difference because we agreed. Going in. We agreed if we had difficulty selling the properties. Or unforseen expenses. Or any shit like that. We agreed you'd put up the money to keep us going. Did you agree to that?"

"Don't—get out of my face."

"Did you agree to that? Go ahead and deny it if it's not true."

When he didn't, I stood straight and turned to Jack and Pat. "He can't deny it because it's down in black and white on our letter of corporation."

"All right." With professional deftness, Larry now changed his line one hundred and eighty degrees. "That money. Sure I've got that money. I said I had a reserve I could tap. Isn't that what I told you?"

"Many times."

"Well, I wouldn't bullshit you. I don't bullshit my partner."

"How comforting," I said.

"Now don't get temperamental on me. You're a nice guy, Kevin, but some day that temper of yours is going to put you in the shit."

"Tell me about the reserve, Larry."

"I've got a reserve of money I can tap. And I can lend it to the corporation. Okay. But I never said it was my money."

"Jesus Christ almighty."

"Now, don't get your bowels in an uproar. It's there. I'd rather not go to it. Frankly. But it's there."

"What is this? Shylock money?"

"It's not for you to worry about," Larry insisted.

"Pardon me if I worry anyway. Because I'd just as soon not be paying interest at thirty percent and have some guy named Vito come break my arm."

"Nobody's going to break your arm. It's going to be a reasonable rate of interest. Like we agreed."

"Where does this money come from?" I asked.

"That's not your concern. Except. Except for this. I want you to know that dipping into this reserve is a step I'd rather not take. Except as a last resort. Because of the consequences."

"Consequences?"

"Which don't concern you. It's nothing for you to be worried about."

"Then why tell me?" I demanded. "Why tell me there are going to be consequences if the goddamn consequences don't concern me?"

"Just so you'll understand. That's all. So you'll understand why I'm reluctant to do it, to tap into this reserve."

Obviously embarrassed at this line of malarky, a grim-faced Jack Lundgren leaned away from the table and sighed.

I looked at Jack. "Do you know what he's talking about?"

The agent could only smile weakly and shrug.

I turned back to Dexter. "Have you got another crooked deal here? Drugs or loan-sharking or something."

"What are you talking about? I couldn't be involved in something illegal. I'm a member of the bar."

After Larry left, I lingered despite the late hour, thanking the Lundgrens for all their help. "He should never have talked to you like that."

"Well," Jack shrugged, "he's under a lot of pressure, he's—"

"He's an asshole. Don't defend him."

Pat waved at the smoke. "If it wasn't so cold, I'd open a window."

"He's going to leave me in the goddamn lurch. I *know* it! All that rigamorole about the money. He hasn't got any fucking money."

"He said he had it." Jack tried to be positive.

"Why did I ever trust that guy? I wanted this to work so bad. All I could think of was money. Money for my kids, my family. So Susan could quit that library job and just be a mother. See, I wanted to make it all up to them, everything. I wanted it so bad that I closed my eyes to Dexter, to what he is."

"He's got a lot of influence through his father-in-law, Mr. Foley," Pat noted. "A lot of people have done business with Larry for that reason alone."

"And a lot of people have regretted it. I mean, I knew. I knew he'd been sued. I knew all that. But he just sweet-talked me. And I shut my eyes. I just threw my better judgment into that fucking swamp Indian Peak."

I went next to Terri's. We'd had trouble lately and now, my business near collapse, now was the time to discover if she could truly be counted on.

Her car was not in the driveway. At quarter to one it should have been. I waited—she had to be along any minute. The heater blowing, I stabbed compulsively at the buttons on the radio, chasing dark tunes. Half an hour ticked by. First time I ever really needed her, dammit, and where was she?

Quite possibly she'd had car trouble and gotten a ride home. Sure. Right now she was inside, sound asleep.

Or was she in trouble? Stalled at the side of the road. Walking home in the dark and cold. Or . . . Jesus, I began imagining worse things.

I drove directly to the nursing home, fifteen minutes away. Looking carefully, I did not see her car stuck anywhere along the route, nor did it pass me. At the home, I could not find it in the lot.

I drove back to her house, my concern growing. The car was still missing.

It must be in the shop. And Terri is sound asleep in her own bed. It's the only logical explanation. I worked to calm myself. See, I've always been an alarmist with those I love—like Susan and the kids. Conjuring up endless horrors whenever one of them is more than ten minutes late. I get a little carried away when I'm anxious and upset.

Past two o'clock I reached my cottage and prepared for bed. Terri must be okay. If something bad had happened her house would be blazing with light, the whole family awake. So, relax.

I could call in the morning just to make sure.

I slept little that night. When I relaxed about Terri, I agonized over Indian Peak, a worry that could not be eased by a phone call. If the project was collapsing I needed to protect myself. Get a lawyer. And an accountant to audit the books. But, my God, how to pay for these people?

Dexter was a lawyer himself and he had access to money and high-powered friends. Ominously, he was already blaming the trouble on me.

I'd been foolish leaving the money in his hands. Suppose he accuses me of theft, kickbacks, anything. How would I defend myself?

I called Terri moments after waking up. "So, I guess you had car trouble last night."

"What? No, I didn't have car trouble."

"You—well . . . what time did you get home?"

"Same time as always. Just after midnight."

God, God. "Where did you park?"

"The driveway. Where I always park. Why—" Now came a thoughtful pause. "Well, maybe it was later. That's right. My relief was late. So, I got home late."

"How late?" For a long time she was silent. "Terri? How late?"

"What difference does it make?"

"I'm curious. Okay? When did you get home?"

"I don't punch a clock."

"Make a guess," I urged.

"I . . . You know, I don't think I like the tone of this conversation."

"I sat in front of your house waiting. I was there till past one in the morning. Way past one. Now. Where were you?"

"Where was I?"

"That's the question."

"I told you I was at work."

"Suppose I went there. After midnight. And you were already gone from work."

Again, silence.

"Where were you, Terri?"

"You . . . what . . . I mean, are you trying to imply something?"

"I'm asking a simple question."

"I don't . . . I don't have to answer—"

"Fine."

"If you didn't take that tone like you're my father or something."

"I'm not your father, Terri. I'm not your husband. Or your conscience. Or anything else. So. Fine."

"Why, why are you making a big issue over nothing?"

"I want to know where you were last night until one, past one o'clock in the morning. For all I know, you never went home at all. Is that right?"

"I should think you'd respect my privacy. And not be spying on me."

"I wasn't spying. I went there to see you. Because I had big problems. I needed help. Do you hear what I'm saying, Terri? I needed you."

"What, what's the problem? Tell me."

"Never mind that now."

"Well," she said, "it couldn't have been much of a problem."

"Not compared to the problem we've got right here.
Right now."

"What?"

I repeated, "Where were you last night?"

"Why . . . why do I have to say where I was?"

"You don't."

"I don't see why you can't just respect my wishes. If I
don't want to—"

"It's a little more involved than respecting wishes, Terri.
Because I'm in love with you. I'm in love with you and I want
to know, I have a right to know what you were doing last
night . . . Terri?"

"I'm sorry . . . I . . . Please . . . can't you just trust me?"
She began to cry. At that point, I felt ill, dizzy. I had my
answer. What remained was the ugly formality of hearing it
aloud.

"You were with someone last night."

She sniffled.

"Were you with someone last night?"

"Yes."

"A man."

"Yes, but—"

"Two o'clock in the morning practically, you were out
with him."

"I was with that guy I used to see, okay. But we
didn't—"

"You were out getting layed. To put it bluntly."

"No." She was crying louder now. "It was wrong to see
him without asking you. Okay. And it was wrong to lie about
it. But all we did was talk—"

"You must think I'm stupid, Terri."

After a pause she complained, "I think you've just made
up your mind not to believe me and nothing I say is going
to change it."

"You got that right."

"Don't hang up. Please listen, Kevin. I'm sorry."

"Sorry comes so easy after you've had your fun."

"I want to explain," she was crying. "Don't hang up! *Please!*"

I was putting the phone down when, impulsively, I brought it back to blurt out, "I hope you enjoyed yourself. Terri? Hope it was worth it."

I was due at Indian Peak, but I pulled into Mister Donut's parking lot and sat, watching traffic. People had tried to warn me about Terri—even Terri had tried to warn me. I'd been too big a fool to listen.

Obviously, she was a nympho or something. And a liar. I felt dirty. For all I knew she'd been fucking any number of guys. Oh, God. Had she given me the venereal disease of the month? Was I to be sterile? Impotent? Dead?

I wasn't as angry at her as I might have been. Mostly, I felt sad—and stupid for ever believing a word she told me.

Admittedly, I was spoiling for a fight when I arrived at the job site.

The new construction was cagelike, including stud walls, with no attic. On his knees, John Finnerty nailed down two-by-fours for interior walls, the BANG! of the pneumatic hammer echoing for miles.

Big John looked ill at ease for he was surrounded by Dexters, Kikki, Larry, and the five kids. None of his crew was to be seen. At first, the implications failed to register. I had that woman on my mind. What she'd done to me. What I'd have liked to do to her. Terri. And, oddly enough, Susan.

Oh, to hear my wife's soothing voice. Suddenly, her faults seemed trivial. Better to have a woman who loved and cared for you, who would not break your heart.

Almost louder than the hammer, four kids raised hell on

the second floor. It gave me an excuse to shout as I came across the yard, "Jesus, Larry! Get those kids down before they fall down."

"That's what I told him," Big John stood.

"Get them out of our way. I've got work to do." I lifted my circular saw. I was eager to lose myself in physical labor.

Dexter turned to his wife. "Get them down, dear."

Kikki passed the baby to Larry and hurried up the plywood stairs. She hollered, chased them about. Meanwhile, Larry left the baby to sit on the bare floor in the middle of the "room." Not moving, little Erica looked up at us in nervous alarm. With parents like these, I couldn't exactly blame her.

At some point, while playing out the cord for my saw, I asked about the crew. Larry explained, "I've had to let them go. Until I get that financing. Which should be tomorrow." He turned to John. "Two or three days at most."

"If this is for a few days, fine," John replied. "But we can't be laying about longer than that. I have a chance to sign on to a job up in Leominister."

"I'm raising the money," Larry began smooth-talking both of us. "No question of that."

I sat slowly on the staircase, which climbed toward the crisp, blue sky. Well, that ties it, I thought. Larry didn't have the money. Obviously, there never was a reserve of cash. Indian Peak was done. Things can't get any worse.

The kids charged down the stairs, shouting, knocking into me. Kikki followed. "Go outside."

"But we are outside," protested Robert, the oldest at thirteen.

"Out, out of the building. Don't argue. Go."

Outside, they ran in circles, screaming in the cold.

"That yard's full of nails and boards," John pointed out.

Kikki stood where the front door would be, above a plywood ramp subbing for stairs. "Play across the street," she told Robert. "Take them across the street." Mathew, the toddler, was already on his way.

I still sat, the big saw in my lap, while Larry continued selling the future. Coming from a man plunging into bankruptcy, it sounded bizarre.

"You're too easily discouraged, Kevin. You gotta have faith. I give you my word, in a few months the money's going to be pouring in. And you can marry some girl and buy a house as big as this." He turned to John. "I've got big plans for my winnings. Going to invest. Fine arts. Paintings, stuff like that. Never loses value. How about that?"

Kikki lifted the baby. "Larry has an eye for art."

"Better collect my tools." Big John went off, grumbling.

I stood. "Couldn't you have asked me before you sent everybody home?"

"Kevin, we can't pay them."

"It's going to rain and this whole structure is open to the elements."

"Whatever gets wet will dry I'm sure."

"Plywood flooring warps! For Christ sakes!"

"Calm down," Larry said. "This is only a suspension. Temporary. Like I told you, the money's in the pipeline—"

"Bullshit!" Blood rushed to my face. "Pipeline. That's just shyster talk for '*I don't have the money*'!"

"Listen, Kevin—"

"I'm up to my ass in mud and debt because I listened to you."

"You can't talk to my husband—"

"I've got the money." Larry waved her to silence. "I keep telling you."

"Where is it, Larry? I want to see it and touch it. Because without it I lose my cottage and my house. And my kids are on the street!"

"I wouldn't answer anyone who spoke to me in that tone," Kikki said.

"Well, he better answer. Because I'm too fucking old to go back banging nails by the hour." I moved close and lowered my voice. "You said I could count on you. You said you'd be there. Now, where I come from, when somebody says he's going to be there, he goddamn well better be."

"I told you—"

"Get that money."

"I've got it."

"Sell your cars or your rings or your fucking house. But get it!"

I guess the baby, in its mother's arms, began to cry.

"You'll be sorry if you don't."

"What? What's that suppose to mean, Kevin?"

"It means what it says."

"Are you threatening me?"

"Take it how you like."

"Are you threatening—"

"You're not getting away with this, Larry. *All* you people who think you can shit on me and nothing happens to you? You're going to find out different."

And suddenly, Big John was between us, saying something in a soothing tone. Larry Dexter was backing away, his face pale. The baby screeched. The four older kids were lined up just outside, looking in.

Frankly, I was a little out of control, louder than I intended to be. But it's not like I was going to hit somebody or something. I have a temper. And I was angry. But I'm not violent. Not at all.

I threw myself into building the attic floor, as if it really mattered anymore, as if I cared. Kicking on the compressor, I lugged the air-driven hammer up the ladder, trailing its long transparent tube. I generally avoided this tool. The safety was broken, and it was liable to blast out nails at the slightest touch. Mostly, I'd used John's hammer, but John had taken that with him.

I worked doggedly, hauling massive two-by-ten boards up two stories. I took satisfaction slamming nails home with a terrific BANG! I've always enjoyed hard physical labor, losing myself, losing my problems in it.

Once, a board balanced on my shoulder, I made a misstep, plunging between the joists, catching myself painfully at the elbows, breaking my fall to the second floor. Wrapping a cloth around my bloodied forearm, I returned to work, scarcely giving this near disaster a thought.

Since becoming a "developer" I did a lot less heavy lifting. My mistake, thinking I should wear cleaner clothes and give orders. Still trying to please my old man?

It was dark and windy when the Lundgrens pulled up.

"Come down," Jack waved. Apparently they'd heard that I was bad off, maybe from Dexter—maybe even from Terri.

"Got to finish," I called, pumping nails into a beam.

"It's too dark, Kevin," Pat called. "Come down before you get hurt."

So I climbed down, turned off the compressor, and tossed the tools into a corner.

"It's not hopeless," Pat insisted. "There are things you can do."

"Sell the lots," Jack urged. "You should talk to Larry. Get him to sell some of the lots." As we stood on the road, he spoke of the advantages. I pretended to listen.

"I can't talk now," I finally said, and I could have left it at that. Should have. But I swung round and let loose. "What makes you think I can talk to *that* asshole. Fucking thief with a briefcase! Well, he's going to find out he made a mistake. Him and someone else I could mention. They're going to find you can't fuck with me and walk away laughing."

At the time, I was thinking of maybe a lawsuit against Dexter. Unfortunately, I didn't say this to the Lundgrens.

At home, bone tired, I still couldn't sleep. I finished off a bottle of Irish whiskey. It seems to me there was about an eighth remaining, maybe more. I zapped a steak, but couldn't eat it.

I tried to see the bright side of my situation, but there was none. Forget any career as a big-shot contractor. Forget huge profits. I would be happy, thrilled, just to avoid total ruin.

We had to sell two homes at top dollar to keep even. But we had already run clean out of cash with just one house built—a house no one wanted to buy.

Susan had shown faith, allowing me to remortgage our home to gain capital. And now I was on the verge of actually losing it. How would I tell her? How would I explain it to the kids?

I had failed. As a businessman. As a builder. As a husband and father. And the failure was total. I stared into the blackness for hours.

· 4 ·

Nearly midnight, I was lying on the bed in my bathrobe when I heard knocking. Stumbling to the door, I found Terri slumped in the freezing drizzle. She looked as miserable as the weather.

"Can I come in?"

"What?"

"Please. Can I come in? I won't stay long, Kevin, I've got to be at work in fifteen minutes. . . . Please, it's raining."

I pushed the door open wider. "Suit yourself."

She came in, eyes down. "Can we talk?"

I collapsed on the couch, my hurting head in my hands. "About what?"

"What I did."

"What you did? Ha. I really don't want the play by play."

"Please, it isn't what you think."

"Believe it or not I've got bigger problems to deal with."

"I don't blame you for being angry, but—"

"You're wasting your time, Terri."

"Just—you don't have to say anything. Just hear me out. Do that. And then I'll leave. I'll just leave."

I didn't look up. She started talking and I wasn't listening, had no intention of listening. Screw her, barging in, babbling about her petty problems when I faced total ruin. I didn't care about Terri anymore.

Except, I would catch a word here and there. And sometimes an answer would occur to me. Like, I once imagined marrying you and I loved you and you went behind my back to someone else. And in all my life, no one ever hurt me like you did.

So. I discovered that I did care and very much.

". . . It was wrong to do what I did," she continued, "but understand when I did it, I never thought it could hurt you."

"What!?"

She paused, tensing because now she had my attention.

"You know I have these . . . deficiencies, kind of. Which I'm going to change. The thing is, I never expected you'd even know. And with the way I used to think, I thought, 'If you didn't know, how could it hurt you?' "

"Fucking unbelievable."

She crouched to my knees, closed her eyes. "I know that was wrong thinking. I know I justify my behavior sometimes and it's not right. But the point I'm making, even though I've got these flaws, even though I'm not a good woman like you're used to, Kevin, I love you. And what I did. Going out with my old boyfriend. You won't think it was so bad when I tell you why."

"I can guess why."

"No."

"Gimme a break. You're going to tell me you went out with the guy but he never touched you? Is that what you're going to tell me?"

"I saw him to, to make clear that I wasn't going to see him again."

"And that took till two in the morning, I suppose."

She looked down, didn't have an answer.

"It didn't involve one for the road? For old times sake?"

And after a moment, she admitted. "Okay, maybe it went further then just talking. But we didn't fuck. I swear we didn't.

I'm, I'm trying to tell the truth. I could have lied, made up a lie about where I was. But I told you the truth."

"After I caught you in a lie."

"I know—"

"If you wanted to just talk you could have called him on the phone. But you wanted more than that. Right? I'm not . . . I guess, it's just I'm not enough for you. Good enough or something—"

"Don't ever think that. No, no. You are all I want. Only . . . sometimes I'm weak. And foolish. I do things without thinking."

"And what was it you did last night, Terri? Without thinking. What did you do with him? Exactly what?"

"He wanted to fuck. But I wouldn't let him."

"I didn't ask what you didn't do. I asked what you *did* do."

It took a long time for her to answer. She looked down and then spoke so softly she was barely audible. "I sucked him off. That's all."

"That's all?"

"I . . ." She looked at me and swallowed. "He wasn't going to let me go until I did it. He acted like I owed it to him."

"For Christ sakes!" I'd intended to wound her with coolness. This sordid mess is trivia compared to my business troubles. And yet, I couldn't even pretend not to care. "You could get some disease doing what you did. Ever think of that? You could get a disease and pass it to me."

"But I didn't . . . oh, what's the use." She turned away, her lips vibrating. "I know you hate me now." She held back the tears. "I've always lived a certain way and it didn't seem to matter. It never mattered to other guys. And even when I started seeing you. I didn't expect to fall in love. I didn't even realize how much I loved you until this morning. When I thought I'd lost you. I'd done a stupid thing and you were gone and maybe forever."

"There's no maybe about it."

"No."

I sat back on the couch. Why did she have to behave like a whore and spoil everything between us? God, I loved her and I wanted it to work.

"Your arm!" she exclaimed. "How did that happen?"

"Now you're all concerned because I might be hurt. Sure."

"You should put something on that."

"When I needed you, really needed you. You were with someone else."

She looked away sharply, as if she'd been slapped. "Tell me the problem you came to see me about? Maybe I can help. I want to help."

"I don't need your help."

"Let me prove myself. If you need money. I don't have much, but whatever i've got is yours. Let me help, Kevin. Please."

"All my problems are going to be taken care of. Okay? I've got my own resources for solving these things. I don't need you."

But even as I said it I was thinking that I sure needed help. Terri owned her own home and I was desperate enough to take that into account.

But then I remembered precisely what she'd be making amends for. "How could you do that?" My voice was layered with contempt.

"I got into a situation. I couldn't get out. It was stupid, stupid, stupid." On her knees, she bent like someone with a stomach ache, "Sorry."

"Sorry." My voice broke with pain. "Sorry doesn't stop the hurt. Like, like somebody just cut me up the back. The last person I expected. A person I trusted and loved. She cuts, cuts me up the back. Worse than my worst enemy."

She buried her face on the couch, crying, looking very alone.

I suppose I felt sorry for Terri. I mean, that's probably why I let her in the first place. I wondered if the infidelity had been less a reflection on me, more the symptom of some sick, self-destructive compulsion.

I stared a long time. She looked vulnerable, sexy. And suddenly, incredibly, it actually seemed that I wanted her. I gave a shake and barked, "Just go home. Go home and forget me like I'm going to forget you."

Eventually, she got up. It was very quiet. At the door, she asked, "Can I see you again. Just, we can talk?"

"We have nothing to talk about."

"Don't say no. Just leave me with some hope. That I'll see you again. And talk. Maybe find some way to make amends. Please, don't say no, Kevin. Despite what I did, I love you. And I could change for you. I could."

I suppose I should have told her no. For some reason, I didn't answer at all.

Early next morning, I arrived at Indian Peak Estates in a muddle.

It was still drizzling. With no roof, the wooden frame of the house was glistening wet. For a long time, I sat in the cab just staring at the place.

I stepped carefully through the mud to the new construction. Inside, I was overcome by despair. I could not stay in this monument to failure longer than a minute.

I trudged to the back of my beautiful colonial, thinking vaguely to check the basement for water. Icy rain stung my face. I covered up with my arm.

Had I made a mistake with Terri last night? She went off imagining we would speak again. Wouldn't it have been far better to cut clean? It still made me angry to think of her betrayal.

Unlocking the back door of the colonial, I found more bad news. "Goddamn, this is not my week." The house had been trashed. I went from room to room, outrage to outrage.

Beer bottles and cans were everywhere. Someone had used a felt pen to write "Lisa" again and again on the walls. Windows were broken. Dirty footprints appeared every-where, even on the ceiling. My stunning oak floors were gouged. Obscenities had been scratched on the Jacuzzi.

"Holy Christ." John Finnerty whistled, coming through the front door. He found me in the kitchen, sitting on the floor. "Goddamn sons of bitches." He looked about. "Hope your policy's up to date."

"It'll take forever to collect and I don't have the cash to make repairs in the meantime. So, how do I sell this mess? Goddamn!" I kicked a beer can across the room. After a moment, I looked up. "What are you doing here?"

"Forgot my drill."

"Must be over in the second unit."

We went out the back door together and as we trudged through the mud, John commented, "I've got a job, Kevin. I've got to drive up there presently. But I wouldn't mind helping you out over the weekend and you pay me when you get the money. At least, we'll get that house weather tight."

"That's decent of you, John. I can use the help."

"Where's Dexter?" he looked back toward the colonial.

"At this hour? Sleeping soundly no doubt."

"In his car?" John asked.

"What?" I had to hustle after him, bounding onto the first floor of the unfinished house, slipping between the studs of the skeletal outer wall. "Here it is." John moved for the drill, which lay on the plywood floor near the top of the cellar stairs. Then, he gasped, "Holy Mother of God!"

The stairway resembled a dark pit, a hole in the floor, not quite surrounded by a cage of studs. John stared into it.

"What?" I came up beside him and looked below at Larry Dexter. It seemed he had fallen backwards down the stairs. I remember the thick black heels of his elevator shoes. "God." I moved at once to aid the man, pushing past John. But I got no further than the second step before halting. The scene came forward in sharp detail.

Dexter was sprawled on the bottom steps. All around him were bright, gold-colored nails protruding from the stairs at odd angles, as if a child had attempted to pound them in. His face was frozen with eyes opened, like a stopped clock. Larry had encountered something horrible and had struggled frantically to escape it. Panic was in the wide eyes, the crooked line of the mouth.

He was dead, surely.

I felt unsteady, afraid.

In the center of Larry's forehead was a dark blemish. I studied it a long time before realizing it was a hole. "God."

I noticed the nail gun, with its coils of clear plastic tubing, resting on the first floor within reach of the open stairwell. John watched me carefully. Watched *me*. I thought it odd at the time.

Slowly, reluctantly, I went down the stairs.

"Better leave him be," John advised.

"We should make sure he's dead."

"He's dead."

"Somebody's got to make sure."

I stepped carefully to avoid the nails protruding from the stairs. From the sixth step up, I ducked under the banister, dropping to the floor. Only then did I cautiously approach Larry.

His head and shoulders rested on a plank of plywood at the foot of the stairs. The rest of him was draped awkwardly on the steps, his thick, gray coat disheveled, pulled taut beneath his shoulders. The right hand was up near his face, palm out, kind of like a traffic cop ordering "Stop!" There were punctures on it, some bloodless. A few of the gold-colored nails protruded hideously from his hand and wrist.

The left arm flopped behind his head. I took a deep, calming breath and lifted his wrist to search for a pulse. Though still warm, he no longer felt human. His Rolex ticked on faithfully. Repelled, I dropped the arm.

Turning away, I had to lower my head, let my stomach settle.

"He's dead," I croaked.

"Better leave him be." John had come down a few steps.

"Yeah. He's got to be dead."

* * *

Three Norham cruisers arrived, one behind the other. Then a pair of state police vehicles came, followed by an ambulance. Flashing lights played off the trees, blue and red, vivid in the gray overcast.

Next came vehicles from the district attorney's office, the medical examiner, and the newspapers and TV stations. Before long, the quiet cul-de-sac was thick with cars and people. The muddy grounds were stomped into soup.

Dazed, I answered questions. I replied in succession to local police, a state police officer, a state police detective, and someone in the district attorney's office. Each asked more questions than the last.

How did I find the body? "John Finnerty found it." Had I looked down the basement stairwell prior to John's arrival? "No. I was only in the house a few minutes." Did I know anyone who might have wanted to hurt Larry Dexter? "I . . . I don't know anyone who could do *that*."

Had I seen or heard anything suspicious?

"Well, somebody tore up my house. Next door. Beer cans everywhere. Vandalism. I assume whoever did that, Larry must have caught them."

In the street answering questions, I studied Dexter's BMW in the garage of the colonial home. John Finnerty had seen it, but somehow I'd walked past the garage twice and not noticed it.

The car meant a lot to Larry. His initials were stenciled on the door. Alongside the plush, reclining seats were a phone, a radar detector, a state-of-the-art stereo. And later a stranger would come drive it away.

You'll know he's really dead when someone else drives his car.

I felt very temporary, as if whoever killed Larry might come for me.

"Would you mind visiting the station for more questions?" a state police detective asked.

"Anything I can do to help."

By the time Kikki Dexter arrived, the unfinished house was crammed with people, including a still and a video photographer. A wall of uniforms and suits gathered around the basement stairwell.

As Kikki charged from her Mercedes, I nudged Matt O'Keefe, the Norham officer. "She shouldn't see that."

Matt passed this along to a sergeant, who conferred with a state police detective. Others joined the huddle. Meanwhile, Kikki advanced across the mud field leading to the death scene. No one stopped her. But maybe no one could have.

In the building, she disappeared amongst the men. Not for several moments did I hear a long, hoarse wail. The street grew silent.

Every eye was on Kikki as she emerged, at first supported by two officers. Then, seeing me, she came eagerly across the mud. I went forward to offer my sympathy and help. Whereupon she threw herself at me, her face a ferocious snarl, fists flying.

I was knocked back, into a parked car. She pressed her advantage, arms and elbows flailing. It was all I could do to cover my face. "Stop . . . Kikki . . . what—?" Police pulled her off.

"You bastard, you killed—killed my husband." As they held her, she spit. "You made orphans of my children!"

Her rage spent, she allowed herself to be carried away. Friends, relatives, and officials closed around her.

Looking about, all I saw was police.

"Jesus." I dabbed above my eye. Came away with blood. "Jesus." Hoarse with shock, I looked to Matt O'Keefe. "What a thing to do. Jesus."

"See if we can't get a Band-Aid or something for Mr. Bourque."

"Unbelievable." I was stunned and embarrassed. "What got into her? Didn't somebody explain I only *found* the body? I didn't kill him."

Matt said nothing.

It began to sink in. See, no one apologized for the assault.

Or offered sympathy. And I realized finally that these officers had been at my side since their arrival—not asking questions anymore, just watching.

Was I some kind of prisoner? How absurd. I attempted to walk to my pickup. Matt put up a hand. "Appreciate it if you stayed here, sir."

I gave him a long look.

The police officer shifted uncomfortably. "As a favor, Kevin. Please."

Murder? I mean, I knew Matty O'Keefe. I knew many Norham officers. They must realize it's ridiculous to accuse me of such a thing. For Christ sakes. Let her calm down and even Kikki will see that.

When they insisted I ride to the Norham police station in a cruiser instead of my own pickup ("We'll take care of your truck, Mr. Bourque"), I resisted the significance. This is just some kind of procedure.

I sat in back, separated from the driver by steel mesh. I asked hesitantly, "Are they going to read me my rights and all that?"

"I can do that now, Mr. Bourque."

"Yeah, just. Before you do. I just want to say, Uh, I want to call my lawyer. Okay? Before I answer anything else."

· 5 ·

"Well, what do you think, I mean, isn't it crazy to arrest me?"

Tim Regan drops his pen, has to search under the table. "Just a minute." I roll my eyes and wait for the kid and the pen to reappear. "Okay," he says. "Now. First thing up, bail. We'll try and scare up a judge tomorrow."

"Tomorrow. I go to court tomorrow?"

"*If* we can find a judge. On the rare chance we can't—Monday."

"Monday?" I grimace. "I have to spend the weekend here?"

"It could be a lot worse. You're here instead of county jail."

"Yeah, but—"

"Your wife's going to bring you a nice suit of clothes for court."

Susan. Oh, God, I don't want to see her. Not like this. My eyes sting.

"You agreed to answer questions?"

"Yeah, with you, with my attorney present."

"Well, forget it."

"But why, I've got nothing to hide."

"It's just not a good idea." He's pawing through his briefcase.

"Timmy, once I lay out the facts. And they see they got the wrong guy—"

"You know what they'll do? They'll take your statement and use it against you. That's what they'll do."

"How can they use it against me if I just tell the truth?"

"Because you could make a mistake. A perfectly innocent mistake. You could say, 'I wore white socks the day of the murder.' And then, on the witness stand months later, they ask, 'What color socks were you wearing?' And without thinking, you say 'Black.' At which point the prosecutor jumps down your throat. 'Here it is in plain English, Mr. Bourque. Your signed statement that you wore white socks. And what else are you lying about?' "

Slowly, I look down at my socks, which are blue.

"Now, bail. As I said. We're asking nominal bail. But in case they don't go for that. Be thinking where you can lay hands on some cash."

"I don't have any money."

"Well, you own your own home," Tim points out.

"Mortgaged and remortgaged."

"What about Indian Peak? You can borrow on that."

"Not without my partner's permission. Kikki Dexter."

"Oh."

"You see the problem."

He rubs his chin. "There's always the bail bondsmen. Anyway, don't worry about it. With your background bail shouldn't be a problem."

"Listen, Tim. I want to know what you think of my story."

He puts down his pen, his expression softening. "I wasn't surprised."

I'm holding my breath

"I was sure this mess was a police screw-up."

"You don't—"

"They always get their man—or whoever happens to be handy."

"Right. That's exactly right." I almost smile. Someone took the time to listen and now he sees the truth. "I was just there. What happened to Larry was horrible. But I was just there and they grabbed me."

"I've seen it before."

"Then why don't I explain it to the district attorney? Just the way I explained it to you. He'll send me home. Drop the charges."

Tim looks pained.

"This is ridiculous. The whole idea that I killed Dexter. Nobody could believe it. When I sit down with these guys. When I tell my side. They're going to realize they got the wrong guy. And they're going to let me go."

If Tim agrees, he gives no hint of it. "Don't talk to anyone without asking me," he cautions. His eyes are fixed, his voice firm, serious. My apprehension increases.

I'm on television, the camera staring down from just outside of the bars. It's cold. They've given me a thin blanket and I lie on a thin mattress, taking care not to roll against the wall which is iron and cold as ice.

Strange, they've taken my belt and shoelaces. I'm not to hang myself. They want me to die of pnemonia.

Sometimes, I see patrolman Joe Devine. Long ago we played softball together. He asks, "How you doin'?" I stare at the floor and shake my head. I feel ashamed and humiliated. I'm relieved when he goes off duty.

During the night the cells accommodate a whining, screaming, thumping crush of drunks, druggies, and crazies. From somewhere comes a drunken voice, crying, "I am the recollection . . . the resurrection . . . what is it?"

"Just the usual Friday night crowd," an officer remarks.

I think most were collected from the strip of bars and restaurants across the expressway—a part of Norham that is not really Norham.

"I gotta see a doctor," someone shouts, pitiably. "Help me. I gotta see a doctor!"

"Someone needs a doctor," I alert a passing officer whose offhand reply jolts me. "All you assholes need doctors," he says.

My God, he thinks I'm one of them.

Later, I complain, "I can't sleep in all this noise."

"You're lucky. You're in isolation. Or you'd be sleeping sitting up. We got four to a cell already. And the night is young."

"I can't take much more of this."

"If you think this is bad, wait till you get to county jail."

"I won't . . . I won't be going there."

The officer is moving away, "It's not up to you, ace."

"I'm going home Monday," I call. "On bail . . . If I'm not released first." And it's true. I haven't done anything and they can't keep me. So, I won't worry about county jail. I don't have to and I won't.

Not for a moment does the noise abate. Lights dim, but burn through the night. A fight breaks out and policemen rush in to referee. Later, someone vomits loudly. Another prisoner suffers from diarrhea. The stink never leaves. Toilets flush all night.

If county jail is worse than this what must it be like? Oh, please, I don't want to go there.

But suppose they send me anyway. Christ. And then to Cedar Junction. Innocent people have been tried and convicted before. I see it in their faces, from Kikki Dexter to Matty O'Keefe. They believe I did it.

I don't sleep, thinking . . . thinking I wouldn't be here if I'd been more careful, less greedy, a better husband, father, person. Oh God. I am exhausted and so low I almost wish I was finished with it all. Maybe I should do away with myself. But they must be reading my mind because there's always a cop walking past, looking in on me.

Joe Devine is home. Watching TV with his kids. God. What I wouldn't give to be sitting at home with *my* kids. Bail tomorrow. Suppose you don't get bail. Suppose you never get out of here. Never. The ceiling is wire mesh. No place for a rope if I had a rope.

I can't lay down. I stand and turn and turn and turn. Someone's watching—the damn camera. I stare back, but the thing doesn't blink.

Bail tomorrow. I feel myself gagging on the air.

In the next cell someone sings, sort of, an idiot lyric, "Going to have it all. Then scrape me off the wall," which he repeats endlessly.

"Shut up!" I finally shout. Someone slams the partition violently, the iron shakes. I'm terrified. No doubt if he could reach me he would kill me.

Saturday and I wait for Tim Regan. My fellow prisoners leave, one by one. It disturbs me that some of these creatures are let loose. But what does it say about my situation that I remain here?

Regan arrives in the late afternoon. "I've been chasing judges all day. I think I'm getting my chain yanked if you want the truth. My calls aren't returned. People promise things. Then, when I call back they're not in."

I nod.

"I don't understand. It's a simple, ordinary murder. Why's everyone running for cover? Is it the nail gun angle? That *is* pretty freaky, but . . ."

"Larry's in-laws have a lot of influence," I suggest.

"You mean her father? Dollar Bill Foley? But he hasn't been active in fifteen years. I don't think he has any influence."

When Tim leaves, I'm taken back to my cell, more depressed than ever.

It's quiet now and I try to read the paperbacks he brought, but the words might as well be Greek. I think of nothing except my situation. And that I have no chance to improve it sitting here.

* * *

Susan stares for a long time.

"Don't say it. I look horrible. Right?"

"I . . ."

"This has been pretty bad, Susan. Christ." I cover my face a moment. "If I could just sleep." She keeps staring and half of me wants to crawl away while half of me wants to embrace her. Maybe she wants that too, but so much hurt and anger stands in the way. Besides, she is clearly confused, finding me here.

"You look wonderful," I manage to say. "Good, good of you to come."

"Of course I'm going to come when you're in trouble."

Like an angel come to visit hell, her skin is clean, smooth, and glowing. I look down. "I'm sorry putting you through this."

"Never mind me."

"The kids? Are they—"

"The police say I can bring them in tomorrow—"

"No! No, I don't want them coming here!"

"I just—"

"No! No!" I must be loud because Susan looks away nervously. I ask, "What do they know? Have you told them? Did they find out?"

"I've tried to explain."

I imagine. *Do we all know what jail is, children?*

"They don't really understand. And I don't know what to say exactly. So many times over the last year, I wished you were there to talk to them. Because, I don't . . . I don't have the words to explain."

"Just, just tell them it's all a terrible mistake. That I'm staying here . . . I'm staying here until, until I can make everyone understand. That it's a mistake. And then I'll come home. Okay?"

She nods.

"Tell them it's a misunderstanding."

She nods some more. "But . . . don't you think we should like prepare them? Tell them the truth. So that later on—"

"Susan."

"What?"

"That is the truth."

"Oh."

"I didn't kill Larry. How could you think I did?"

"I, well . . ."

"You thought I killed him?"

"Well. I didn't know you were denying it."

"I'm not just denying it. I didn't do it."

"Oh. Okay."

"All the years we lived together and you think I'm a murderer?"

"No . . . No, I thought if you killed him, if you did, he probably did something to deserve it. I don't know. I never trusted him."

"Don't cry."

"I'm sorry. I should have known you wouldn't do such a thing."

"Don't cry, Susan. You just make it harder."

"I'll stop. Okay. I'm not crying."

But she is. And I have to jab a fingernail into my palm to keep from crying myself.

"I brought clothes," she says.

"Thank you."

"I got them at the cottage. It was an awful mess. I picked up a little."

"Thank you."

"They said they'd give you the clothes on Monday when you need them."

"Good. Fine."

"You have to wait until Monday?" she asks.

"I guess. For the bail thing."

"So you'll be in this awful place all weekend."

"Let that be a lesson to you."

"What?" she asks.

"Never get arrested on a Friday."

Still sniffling, she laughs for the first time. I could always make her laugh. "I want to help. I'll do anything. Just tell me what to do."

"Well, I might need money for bail."

"I wish I had some."

"So do I, Susan."

"I'll find some money somewhere . . . I'll pray for you." After a moment, she points. "You're not wearing your ring anymore."

A faint white band marks where the wedding ring had been. "I took it off a while ago, Susan." I see she still wears hers.

"Kevin, how did it come to this?"

"This is just a misunderstanding. I told you."

"I mean us. What happened to us?"

"I don't know, Susan. Maybe I could think about it. Later on when this business here is settled. Then I'll be able to think about it. Get it all sorted out. What went wrong."

We sit not speaking. For all the bitter scenes in the final days of our marriage, never before has our failure and loss seemed so permanent.

Terri tries to see me on both Saturday and Sunday, but they are restricting visitors to legal counsel and family.

"Afraid you hate me," her note says. "Don't let past mistakes keep us apart. I only want a chance to explain. Please hear me out. I believe in you and I want to lend support in this time of trouble."

Her "indiscretion" seems very small beer under the circumstances. "Need all my friends," I write in reply. "See you Monday."

They wake us early Monday. The sink in my cell seems designed for humiliation. It sits atop the commode, which I must straddle in order to wash. I'm allowed my electric razor. With a fresh shirt and tie, for a moment I feel human.

Matt O'Keefe looks away as another officer cuffs my wrists to a chain around my waist. Finally, I am shackled to a line of five grim, worn men. Mostly younger, they regard me with curiosity.

Matt calls our names, pronouncing mine as if he'd never heard it before. Then we are hustled out to a police wagon, which is unheated. Bumping along to the courthouse in Brockton, I can't quite zipper my coat because of the chains. I wrap my arms around myself and shiver.

Someone is whispering, "Is it true Lee got sent away?"

The guard at the door looks over and the whispering stops.

Sometime later I hear another voice, "Him and Sean got picked up in Manomet. Lee got five years. Concord. But the joke was Sean."

"What?"

"Same charges. Different lawyer. Probation."

"Christ."

"Motherfucking lawyer. Bastards get paid either way."

"Cut the chatter."

I've seen Brockton a hundred times, but from the inside of a police wagon it looks like a foreign country. The courthouse comes into view as someone says, louder than before, "Never trust no sorry-assed lawyer. He ain't going to be doing the time."

Unloading in a basement garage, I move too soon and someone yanks the chain, nearly pulling me off my feet. I wheel. But before I can hit back an officer has roughly spun me around again. "Keep moving!"

The other prisoners seem surprised to find we are surrounded by court officers, some with sidearms, one with an automatic rifle. Apparently, this is not routine. The heavy guard is for me. In a line of scummy degenerates, I'm the one everybody's afraid of.

Herded to a shabby room with barred windows and iron doors, I keep my head down, thinking. Lawyers. Can't trust them. Of course, Tim Regan is not just a lawyer. He's my cousin—but only a second cousin. Add to that, his father was a big shot in the state police, which maybe counts against him.

In any case, I don't know him very well and goddamn he's young. If it's a mistake to trust him, I could have thirty years to sit and regret it.

These millionaires are always killing their wives and getting away with it. They hire experienced lawyers, get good advice.

Besides, I have the feeling Timmy doesn't respect me. I mean, he hasn't said anything. But sometimes I hear this tone, like he's talking down to me. I look at my calloused hands.

An officer opens a door to a huge room with enormously high ceilings, a courtroom. I swallow hard. I hear the echo of loud voices and I can see a few dozen people. My lawyer walks in and out of view.

Separated from the others, my wrists are still chained to my waist. I try to ignore the chains but when I move they rattle. I try not to move.

"This way." I'm ordered into court, to a sort of dock. I hear mutterings, "There he is." I'm flanked by armed officers.

I see familiar faces. I'm breathing very hard, sweating. There's Susan and a row of reporters with note pads and way in the back, Terri.

I close my eyes. This humiliation will be over soon. And you'll be free.

Anyway, here's my chance to explain that they've arrested an innocent man. After which, they can find out who really killed Larry Dexter.

"Smile," an officer tells me.

"What?"

"Smile. You're on television."

The camera, across the courtroom, points directly at me. Sure, let the whole world see. I can imagine my third grade teacher tuning in.

I should probably hide my face. All the criminals do. Only I'm not a criminal. I haven't done anything wrong.

"Ready?" Tim Regan leans over the railing.

"What?"

"We're all set on bail. Susan borrowed ten thousand. What a dynamo she is. She must have called everybody in her family and everybody in ours."

"God bless her."

"We won't need the whole ten grand. We only have to post ten percent."

"When do I get to talk?"

"Let me do the talking. You'll be on your way home in a few minutes."

I'm encouraged at the sight of the judge—a small plaque identifies her as Hon. Andrea Sussman. I expect a woman to be sympathetic, understanding. Except she seems reluctant to look at me, but watches the lawyers intently.

The assistant district attorney, Robert Toomey, is tall and stocky. He matter-of-factly declares, "The county asks bail of one million dollars."

Tim Regan looks up sharply from his papers.

"Who'd he kill?" whispers a court officer.

"The county will show that prior to the murder the accused and the victim quarreled. That Bourque threatened to harm the victim. That he did, in fact, strike the victim. After which, he, Bourque, had to be physically restrained. Additionally, he threatened the victim with the very weapon, a pneumatic hammer, that killed Lawrence Dexter a few hours later. All this, your honor, happened in the presence of two witnesses who will so testify."

If it wasn't so serious I'd laugh. My God, I never struck Dexter. I never threatened him and I certainly never threatened him with a nail gun.

"The county will show that the accused made good on his threats the following morning. That he pushed the victim down a flight of stairs. And then, as Mr. Dexter lay helpless, he *turned on the air compressor,* a premeditated act. He waited at least a full minute for the compressor to build up pressure. And finally—" Toomey pauses, his voice thick with emotion.

"Your honor, this is a horrific crime. The medical evidence shows that Mr. Dexter was fired on with three-inch nails . . ." He holds one up, thick, with a shining coat of gold-colored glue, ". . . coming at him with tremendous force. As he lay helpless, fighting desperately, vainly, for life, the assailant emptied the weapon of nails. In all, Lawrence Dexter, husband and father, was shot eight times. And the final shot, through the face, exited partially at the back of the skull, penetrating a piece of plywood and the cement. In fact, this particular shot literally *nailed his head to the floor!*"

Spectators groan. I wince. No matter what you thought of Larry, it's pretty awful. And they think I did it. This guy Toomey, he seems positively convinced of it. God, my shirt is damp with sweat. Aren't they even going to give me a chance to explain?

"Kevin Joseph Bourque is a man with a notorious, *hair trigger* temper. He was known to have blamed the victim, his partner, for recent business reverses. In addition, there were personal differences between the two.

"The accused has been placed at the scene *at the time of the murder.* Other physical evidence will link him to the killing. Including a partial thumbprint on the murder weapon. Further, he was one of the few who knew the peculiarities of this nail gun."

Up to now, even when depressed, I was confident my innocence would finally become self-evident and I would be freed. But if you look at all this a certain way, the way Toomey is telling it, the way he's lying, maybe I don't get out . . . ever. For sure, the more he talks the worse it gets for me.

I tap my foot, breathe with my mouth open.

When we get our at-bats, Tim's voice is high and whiny, lacking authority. And he can't rebut the prosecution, doesn't know what to say. He's telling what a swell guy I am, a good risk for bail. And, Christ, they're all looking at me, remembering poor Dexter with a nail through his brain.

I watch the judge. Our eyes meet and her face is pinched and sour. The court officers scowl. I sense that the prosecutor's open contempt for me is more than courtroom theatrics. And suddenly, I know that these people are playing for keeps, that they mean to bury me as quickly as they can.

Oh, Jesus. County jail. I imagine the faces of hard, violent young men, people I've spent my life avoiding, waiting for me.

"I'll make bail no problem?"

"Well—"

"I'll be on my goddamn way home." I slam my fist on the table. A grim-faced court officer peeks into the interview room, but Tim waves him off.

My head is on the table and I'm trying not to cry. Jesus. I want out of here. I do not want to go to the county jail. "I HAVEN'T DONE ANYTHING!"

"Hey." Tim pats my shoulder. "At least she didn't hit us with the full million. We only have to come up with, what? Five hundred thousand."

"Don't you understand? I don't have fifty cents!"

"We'll appeal. Or go to a bail bondsman. We have options, Kevin."

"Do any of them get me out of here right now, today?"

Tim gnaws his lip and looks uncomfortable.

"Oh, Christ."

"Whatever you do, don't quit, Kevin. Keep up your courage. I'll have you home in a day or two."

"That's what you fucking told me two days ago! Jesus." My hands shake. I try to check my temper. I'm not violent. I'm certainly not "notorious" like that asshole prosecutor said. On the other hand, I'm only human and as anger and frustration mount, I will lash out. In the county jail that might even get me a knife in the gut. I see it as a distinct possibility.

"I want to talk to the district attorney's guy."

"Now . . ."

"That Toomey there. If I talk to him, if I explain how it is, I'll get it through his thick head that he's wasting time with the wrong man."

Tim tries to change the subject. "I got a load of information this morning. Tells us the sort of case they've got on you."

"You mean there's more?"

"First. Because, apparently, none of Dexter's valuables were taken we can eliminate robbery as a motive. Now. Here's what the medical examiner says. Thinks. What happened." He spreads out his notes. "Dexter went backwards down the stairs. Pushed. Probably pushed. And the fall immobilized him. Maybe he pulled his back out or something. But he couldn't get up. So the killer turned on the compressor. Then he—or she—fired from the top of the stairs and kept on firing as he descended. They figure this from the pattern. Some nails just barely stuck into the stairs. Some went in deep. Some got Dexter in the arms and hands—which shows he was conscious, trying to defend himself. One went right, completely into his skull. That's the one that killed him and the one . . . well, you heard in court."

My mouth is completely dry.

"Someone did a job on the man."

"They can't think it was me, Timmy."

"I'm afraid, when they ask bail of half a million dollars it's a good clue that they think it was you."

"Some of that stuff they said in there was just lies, made up."

"Made up?"

"I never hit Dexter. I mean. I had an argument with him. I told you that. But I didn't lay a finger on him. And I certainly never threatened him with the nail gun. Where do they get that shit? How can they say something that's just an outright lie?"

"Toomey wouldn't, wouldn't make it up out of whole cloth. He said he had witnesses." He consults his notes. "John Finnerty and Kathleen Dexter."

"Kikki? It's not like she's unbiased."

"And I'll make sure everyone understands that. Oh, I can deal with her testimony. It's something like this," he taps his notes, "that's damaging."

"What?" I lean forward.

"Time of death. Six-thirty. A neighbor heard the gun going off and noticed the time."

"Wh-what? Why is that damaging?"

"Because the police know you were at the scene at six-thirty."

"How could they know that?" I demand.

"They know because you told them."

"I told them?"

"When they talked to you at Indian Peak. You said you were at the scene a full half-hour before John Finnerty arrived. And Finnerty claims he got there at exactly seven. He says the news came on the radio just as he turned down the road." Tim looks up. "I warned you about talking to police."

"Well, I didn't know I was a suspect then. I was just trying to help."

"We'll try to get it thrown out. Because, frankly, the earlier they place you at the scene, the worse it looks." He puts down his papers. "Did you see anyone when you arrived? Or another car? Anything out of the ordinary?"

I try to think. I'm shaking my head. No.

"You must have got there just minutes too late."

"Could they have the time wrong?"

"Who?"

"Anyone," I say. "Finnerty. Maybe his radio station gives the news at quarter past. Maybe this person who heard the gun at six-thirty. It's a little pat. Six-thirty. Like he rounded it off. And maybe it was earlier."

"Possibly." Tim gives an optimistic smile then returns to his papers. "The police are real interested in blood. Blood on the compressor switch."

"It's probably mine."

He looks up.

"I was working the night before. I fell between the attic joists. You can go up and see the blood." I show the scabs. "I mean I'm a carpenter. I bleed for a living."

"Well. It's probably not important. Like the thumbprint

they got off the nail gun. It's your gun. Why shouldn't it be there?"

"Were there other prints on the gun?"

"No," Tim says. "Unfortunately no. But. It's almost impossible to get prints off a machine like that. They were lucky to get the partial. And as far as the blood goes, we don't have to concede it's yours in any case."

"But, they can find out."

"Not unless you tell them."

"No. They can test it. They can tell it's my blood."

Tim smiles. "They can find out if it matches your blood type. Right. But lots of people have the same blood type."

"I don't think that's right. My understanding is that they got this DNA. It's like a code of your DNA from the blood. No two people have the same code or readout, whatever. So they match it up. See if it comes from you."

Tim is sitting there with his mouth slightly open.

"You never heard of this? DNA? It's been on the news. Everywhere."

"I heard something, something about it. Let me just . . ." he starts scribbling notes.

Up to now I've been impressed by his questions. But, God, I've heard of DNA and I'm just a carpenter. What sort of cases has he been trying?

"I think I'd like to talk to the prosecutor."

"Kevin, we've been over that."

"If I can explain I can convince him I'm not involved here."

He clutches his pen, groans.

"Tim, I followed your advice up till now and look where I am."

"The high bail is because you were right about Dexter's family. Very possibly they've got influence with the court. And that's not my fault."

"I was right about that. Maybe I'm right wanting to talk to Toomey."

"No, no—"

"Don't forget I know a little about the law. My father was a lawyer."

"Your father was a tax lawyer."

"It's not like I'm going to let them put words in my mouth. You'll be there. You can object. Interrupt."

Tim doesn't like this, plainly. I half hope he quits. "You think you can answer Toomey's questions?" he asks.

"I'd just tell the truth. What happened."

"All right. Because I've got information. And I think I know what some of his questions would be. You want to try them on?" Tim begins exploring the bottom of his briefcase.

"I'm not afraid to answer his questions. Or yours."

"Okay." Tim stares at me. His expression says that he's been holding back—but now he means to let me have it. I grow nervous. "First Toomey will ask for an alibi. For the time of the murder. Six-thirty in the morning."

"I guess I was on my way to the site. In my car."

"Anyone see you? Did you drive past anyone who might have?"

"I wasn't exactly looking to wave hello to anybody."

"Did anyone see you leave your house?"

"All the cottages around me are empty this time of year."

"Okay," Tim nods. "No alibi. That's not a crime. So. Let's talk about the argument between you and Dexter on the eve of the murder."

"Yeah."

"You said Toomey was making things up about that."

"Yeah."

"When he said you struck Larry Dexter. When he said you threatened Dexter. When he said, in particular when he said you threatened him with the nail gun. You say he made that up."

"Somebody made it up. Maybe Kikki."

"Suppose I told you that I've seen a transcript of Mrs. Dexter's statement. And she says unequivocally that she saw you strike her husband. And she heard you threaten bodily harm with the nail gun."

"I told you, Timmy. She's lying."

"Is John Finnerty lying too?"

"Is John—what?"

"Finnerty essentially supports Mrs. Dexter on each point."

"I don't . . ." Christ. I'm knocked dizzy. I feel my collar constricting.

"Why would he say that, Kevin?"

"He wouldn't. I don't believe he said it."

"I've seen his transcript. He doesn't say you *struck* Dexter. He says you pushed him. He didn't mention the nail gun until he was asked directly. Then, he corroborated Mrs. Dexter. They agree you held the gun in your hand. You raised it and made a threatening remark. Something to the effect that Dexter would be sorry if he didn't come across with more money."

"I didn't do that."

"You didn't—"

"I didn't touch that gun. I didn't threaten Larry. Nothing like that happened. Nothing."

"You say you didn't threaten him. But you've already admitted to me that you said, during the argument, you said that Dexter *was going to be sorry,* those words approximately."

"Well, I might have said . . . something like that. But it wasn't a threat. Not like you make it out. I just meant, I meant I was getting accountants to go over everything. And I wasn't going to take all the losses myself. Okay?"

"But you didn't strike him?"

"No."

"Or push him? As angry as you were. You didn't push him? Or even bump him accidently? John Finnerty is lying about that?"

"I . . ." I'm thinking, remembering the scene and how Dexter was moving backward, away from me.

"Is it possible you bumped him in the excitement? And being so upset. You forgot. Or didn't even realize you'd done it. Is that possible, Kevin?"

"Uhhhh . . ."

"Is it possible?"

"I, I suppose it's possible, but—"

"Would John Finnerty have any reason to lie about this?"

"I can't think of any."

"Does he have some special relationship with Kathleen Dexter—"

"No."

"—that would cause him to support a false version of events?"

"No."

Again, I picture Larry reeling in undignified surprise. Did I bump him? I can no longer be sure. What else have I forgotten?

"But you say definitely that you did not threaten Dexter with the gun."

"Definitely. That, I'm positive of that."

"Do you remember what you told me during our first interview?"

"What? I never mentioned any nail gun."

"You said you arrived at the site carrying something. Remember?"

"I was carrying . . . what? You mean the saw. The circular saw."

Tim nods.

"Well, so what?"

"You mention carrying it into the house. Having it in your lap when you sat on the staircase, listening to Dexter talk."

"What do you mean? You're saying . . . I, I had it in my hand. I remember that. But so what? What does it prove?"

Tim asks, "Do you think Kathleen Dexter knows the difference between a circular saw and a pneumatic hammer?"

"They don't look alike."

"Is it possible. Because you were so angry and so loud neither one of them paid much attention to what you had in your hand. They remember you had *something*. A power tool. And when Mrs. Dexter decides it must have been the nail gun, John Finnerty just agrees because he's not really sure."

"I might have had the saw in my hand, okay, but I never threatened him with it, for godsakes. It's a tool, not a weapon."

"You were pretty worked up."

"Jesus, Timmy, I remember what happened."

"Could you have acted in a threatening manner without, not meaning to."

"This . . . wait a minute . . . you're getting me all screwed up here."

"Terri Pratt."

"What?" I look back at Tim.

"Do you remember telling her on the night before the murder, telling, rejecting her help. Telling her, *All my problems are being taken care of, by my own resources.* I'm paraphrasing."

I've got to switch gears. Terri. "I . . . yeah, I guess I told her that."

"And she—she's a big help. She repeated that to the police."

Squinting, I don't get the point.

"When you said that. Don't you see, Kevin? It looks as if you were planning to solve all your problems by killing Dexter."

"No. I just meant it in a general way. Like. I was just telling her I could solve my problems without her help. I mean . . . Besides, how would killing Dexter solve my problems?"

"The insurance."

"Insurance?"

"Larry Dexter had several life insurance policies, including one for over two million dollars which lists Indian Peak Development Corporation as beneficiary." He stares. "Two million. That'll take care of all your problems. And then some."

"I never heard of any two million dollar insurance . . ." And I get back this skeptical look. "I swear I never heard a word of this before."

Jesus, I'd imagined sitting with the prosecutor and speaking from my heart, convincing him that I couldn't kill anyone. Instead, *my* lawyer throws me one curve after another. I'm beginning to doubt my memory. I haven't got smooth answers for these questions. I grow hot and uncomfortable.

"Why do you suppose Larry took out life insurance and never told you?"

"I'm sure, I'm damned sure he wasn't thinking of me. He was thinking of his family. He probably figured, if he dies, it'll keep the project going, provide for them down the road. That's my guess." I lean forward. "How about Kikki? I'm not accusing her. But if there's insurance who benefits most? Not me."

"Kathleen Dexter was preparing breakfast for her five children and her brother—that's William Foley Junior—at the time of death. It's a pretty convincing alibi."

"Hey, I'm not accusing her, just . . ."

Tim consults some notes. "There are questions. Some inconsistencies I noticed. In your version of events." He smiles. "I've heard Toomey's raised some of these very points with his people."

"What? What inconsistencies?"

"On the morning of the murder. When John Finnerty arrived."

"Yeah?"

"You were in the colonial house there."

"That's right."

"Well, the question is, what were you doing there?"

"What was I . . . ?"

"What were you doing there, Kevin? There was no work to be done in there. So, what reason did you have to go in there?"

"Well, I explained. I was depressed, discouraged. I didn't feel like working. So. I went over to the colonial. I explained that."

"If you didn't feel like working why not just get in your truck and leave?"

I look about. "What, what difference does it make?"

"It makes a difference," Tim says. "You went into that house. Now. Why? You must have had a reason."

"I had a reason."

"What?"

"I had a reason." But I'm getting so nervous, so hot, I can't think straight. Tim is friendly and low-key, but he springs his questions like traps. "I don't . . . I don't see the point of this."

"There is a point, Kevin. Okay? The assistant DA is going to say you went in that house to break things. To throw beer cans around. To write on the walls. He's going to say you were planting evidence, to make it look like there was this wild band of drug addicts or psychopaths at the scene of the murder. He's going to say you were trying to mislead the investigation."

"No, I didn't, I didn't do that."

"He's already got handwriting experts trying to prove you wrote 'Lisa' on the walls and 'Fuck the Cops' in the Jacuzzi."

"I wouldn't wreck my own house." I'm grasping the bottom of my chair so hard my fingers ache. "The reason I went into that house, like I said, the reason was because I was really down. And I wanted to walk around inside of my house. Timmy, my whole life was falling apart. And this was the one decent thing still standing. Something I was proud of. And it made me feel better to walk around inside of it. Understand?"

"Will the prosecutor understand?"

"Anyone, anyone who's ever built anything will understand. And—wait a minute—if he thinks I planted all that trash. Does that mean he's not going to look for those people who wrecked the house?"

Tim shrugs.

"Christ, those are the prime suspects. Find out who wrecked the house and you find out who killed Larry. I can't believe he won't at least look for them." I undo my top button. "It's, it's hot."

"You never saw Dexter's car in the garage? When you drove up, it was visible from the street."

"I didn't look."

"Later on, you walked into the colonial house and you walked right past the car. You went around the back of the garage, sure. But there's a window. You could have looked in the window and seen it. It's odd you never saw it."

"Are you saying you don't believe me?" I demand.

"I'm saying it's odd. But Mr. Toomey. He might say something else."

"Who gives a fuck what he says."

"Well, I thought you did. Isn't that why you want to see him?"

I glare back. Damn lawyer tricks.

Tim begins, "Toomey's going to make a lot of the weapon. The fact that the killer had to know how to activate the compressor."

"It's a simple switch. Click."

"And he had to know how the gun worked."

"A monkey could figure out how it worked."

"Your hammer had a malfunction, isn't that right?"

"Well, yeah. Most of these hammers, you've got to put the thing on the wood and push down. That releases the safety. Then you fire. But on my hammer the safety was broken. It fired in any position. Like a real gun. It's dangerous. I never leave it lying around. Except, it just happens that night. I was so wrung out. I just threw it in a corner."

"How many people knew the gun was dangerous?"

"Anybody who picked it up would find out fast."

"But," Tim repeats, "how many actually knew?"

I shrug. "Whoever worked on the site. John Finnerty. All his people."

"What do you think Larry Dexter was doing at Indian Peak Estates at six-thirty in the morning?"

"I don't know. Usually I never saw him before noon."

"Dexter's wife says he got a phone call. Very brief call that woke them both. And Dexter went out without saying where he was going, or who had made the call. Now, apparently he made a date to meet someone at the Indian Peak development. And the thing is, that's not the most convenient place for a meeting. It's isolated. Hard to find if you haven't been there before. So, who would he be meeting there? Unless it was you."

"You're saying it was me? You think that?"

"That's what the prosecutor's going to suggest."

"He wasn't meeting me. Okay? It could have been anyone. It could have been a customer, a buyer. Or. Or, he might have been dealing with loan sharks. Ever think of that? He borrowed from gangsters and he couldn't pay them back and they killed him."

"Loan sharks don't kill people, Kevin. You can't collect from the dead."

"If I was going to kill Larry, would I do it on the job site? Right where all this suspicion would point at me? Would I use my own hammer? Huh? Come on. That doesn't even make sense."

"It might if you acted impetuously. In a rage."

He's talking like he actually believes this.

"You've acknowledged that you have a temper, Kevin. And Toomey might make the case that you snapped and threw Dexter down the stairs. And then, because he was badly hurt, you felt you had to kill him. And solve all your problems. So you grabbed whatever was handy. And you did kill him."

"Oh yeah, good plan. Except I'm arrested for murder."

My face is hot and moist. My shirt sticks to my body.

"You weren't thinking of that. You were thinking of what Dexter had done to you."

"Was I?"

"How he'd involved you in bribery on the perk test. How he'd promised money and then didn't deliver. How he'd conned you into this project. Got you to do all the work. Put up all your money. And you were going to lose everything but he'd still be living in a big house on the North River."

"I didn't kill him. I wouldn't."

"And then, when you found out he was sleeping with your girlfriend—"

"That's a lie!"

"That he'd been sleeping with her all along. That she was his mistress. That they'd been together for years. That they'd been—"

"It's a lie, a fucking lie!" I can't listen anymore. I rise and swipe at his papers, which fly everywhere. A bit startled, Tim leans back.

"It's a lie." I stand stiff, my face burning. But I know it's true.

I remember the note Terri sent me in the Norham jail. "I only want a chance to explain." She'd guessed that I'd been told about her and Dexter.

At the Lundgren's party, she'd been at Larry's side. She focused all her attention on me. Was I so charming? Or was she simply trying to make her lover jealous? Then, she made that sordid confession. Was she afraid Dexter would tell me if she didn't? Was she working up to tell me about him?

"Are you all right?" Tim asks.

I sit down woozily. I can't begin to sort out the implications. Was Terri involved in Dexter's murder? Was I the designated patsy?

"And you want to spar with Toomey?" Tim shakes his head. "If he'd been in here your little eruption would have been on tape. It would have been shown at your trial. And you wouldn't be heading to county jail for a few days. You'd be off to Cedar Junction forever. . . . Still want me to call him?"

At this point, it's a rhetorical question. I stare straight ahead for a long time before looking up, asking, "Do you think I'm guilty, Tim?"

"No, I don't. But, I'll tell you frankly. We have our work cut out for us."

·6·

My knees nearly buckle as they chain me for the trip to county jail.

"Don't worry." Tim speaks from behind steel bars. "I'm going to work on the bail. I'll be doing nothing else until I get you out."

The officer jerks the handcuffs and I feel I may collapse. I concentrate on what Tim is saying. "It's a very old jail. Too many prisoners. People sleep on the floor. Radios everywhere. Very noisy."

"Right," I keep my eyes down.

"Mind your business. That's best. A lot of those guys are dangerous. Either the court doesn't trust them on the street or they've fucked up so many times their families won't go bail anymore."

"Okay." They're really doing it. Putting you in jail. A real jail.

"Keep a low profile, cousin. Don't lose your temper."

"No."

"I'm going to get you out. Very soon. Maybe today or tomorrow."

I'm taken to the door. I'll be sleeping in the county jail tonight. I'm not going to cry or faint or anything. I grit my teeth.

I am afraid. But there is something else now. Anger. Someone committed this crime. Someone is free, untroubled, while I'm sent to hell. Why do I keep seeing Terri?

I wait while an officer adjusts his ring of keys. "Just a minute," Tim says. "Could you hold a minute?"

The officer, key poised at the lock, looks annoyed as Tim confers with another man in blue. "What is it?" the officer finally asks.

"Bail," Tim calls triumphantly. "They put up your bail!"

Thank God! I feel like laughing. And I owe Susan the biggest kiss.

"I'm going to scoot you out the back," Tim says as a court officer checks off and returns everything taken at the time of my arrest. "We want to duck any reporters. Remember, talk to no one from here on."

"Right." I've learned my lesson on that score. "Where's Susan?" I look to the lobby.

"Yeah. Well. I've got to tell you something about that."

I'm looking past him still.

"It wasn't Susan put up the money."

She comes into view, smiling nervously, giving a quick, hopeful wave.

"Mrs. Terri Pratt. She put up the money."

I'm staring at her, my face a scowl. "I don't believe it."

"Well. It's here in black and white." He notices I'm looking off, turns, sees Terri, whose smile has dissolved into a look very doubtful, nervous. "Is that the lady? She must love your ass, partner. She put up her house."

I can't make a lick of sense out of this. If she's involved in some scheme to frame me for murder, why bail me out of jail?

She realizes that her welcome will not be warm. As we

approach, she actually pulls back a little. "Hi. Uh, I just wanted to make sure you're okay."

"Are we grateful to you. This poor guy was on his way to county jail."

"I couldn't bear that. When he didn't have bail I knew I had to do something." She looks me in the eyes. "I know you're innocent, Kevin."

I'm glaring back and I don't say anything.

She clears her throat. "Do, uh, do you need a ride home?"

"Tim's driving me."

"Well . . ." She looks from one to the other. "I guess . . . well, I'm glad you're out. I'm so glad you're out and now you'll fix all this. So. I just wanted to see how you are. And . . . I guess I'll go."

As she takes a few steps away, Tim whispers, "You didn't thank her." But I can't bring myself to do it.

On the drive home, Tim advises, "I don't know your plans. But if you were thinking of going to Larry Dexter's funeral, that would be a mistake."

"I wasn't."

"Mrs. Dexter's brother called to say he'd punch you out if you showed." He smiles ironically. "Just thought I'd let you know."

"Thanks."

"And one more thing. Stay away from Terri Pratt."

I come home to find my cottage immaculate, floors vacuumed, furniture shining with polish. This is Susan's work. I call her and the children at once. "I'm really grateful, it gave me a lift coming home to a clean house."

"Who put up the bail? I've been calling all day trying to raise money."

"That's nice. But anyway, a friend put up the money."

She seems to know, without being told, who the friend is.

*   *   *

Even in the cool quiet of my cottage, the euphoria of freedom wears off quickly. I am still charged with murder and the state intends to put me in prison for the rest of my life. I pace in silence. I stare into the dark. Mostly I think through the events surrounding the murder.

Try to figure Terri. First she deceives me, then she risks her house to get me out of jail. If she means well, why volunteer to the police what I'd told her about all my problems being taken care of? She must have known how damning that would sound just hours before Dexter's murder.

Had Terri romanced me in order to set me up? But why kill Dexter? Was it madness? Some involved scheme of revenge? Another man?

I toss the proposition over and over in my head. I don't watch television. I don't listen to the radio. I don't eat. I just think about Terri's actions and all their ramifications. I go to bed thinking about them.

Yet, it's a relief to lie here in peace—suddenly this lousy little room seems like a palace. And when I use the toilet I close the door behind me. I'm in terrible trouble, I must literally fight for my life, but just now I allow myself to forget and sleep.

I am awakened by the phone shortly after two in the morning. I think it's been ringing a long time when I answer, half awake, "Hello?"

The caller does not speak.

"Who is it? Hey. Who's there?" When no one answers I hang up. A crank. You expect that sort of thing when you've been on television.

The phone rings again.

"Who are you?" I demand.

Again, no answer. But the line is alive, someone listens. And I have an almost supernatural sense that this is no crank. The longer I hear that eerie nothingness, the closer intuition comes to conviction. The voiceless caller is someone involved in Larry Dexter's murder.

"Tell me what you want," I say.

Just speak. Say a word.

When he doesn't answer a chill runs up my arms. I breathe faster. "Answer me. Come on, you gutless son of a bitch."

But the caller does not respond and does not hang up the phone.

I slam it down. In the dark, fear takes hold. I am vulnerable, alone in my cottage, not another occupied home within shouting distance.

Don't they call sometimes to make sure you're home? Just before they come after you?

I stand at the window, trying to see through the trees. Whoever called Larry to Indian Peak Estates, whoever called him to his death, had just called me. What happened to Larry might yet happen to me.

The floor is cold on bare feet. I strain to hear. What was that? A rustle in the trees? But there is no wind. I wish I had a gun, a real gun.

Ring!

I'm sweating. It rings and rings and rings. I disconnect the thing and sit in bed, eyes wide, watching the faint light of the moon outside.

By day such calls seem less sinister. Must have been a crank. I can't worry about that nonsense. I'm focused on finding a way out of this box. I replay the last few days again and again. I study them from everyone's point of view. When at last I happen on a flaw in the county's case I rush, jubilant, to the phone.

"The thing is, Tim, I couldn't have used that hammer on Dexter. Precisely *because* I know how it works."

"I don't get it," Tim says.

"I know how it works. Don't you see? The killer didn't. He fired half a dozen nails into the stairs. Shots all over the place. Because he didn't know what he was doing."

"Good," Tim says. "Of course, the prosecutor will say

you shot erratically because you were in an emotional state. But it's a very good point to throw at them."

"Yeah." I'm encouraged for the first time since the bail hearing. "What, what else should I be doing, Tim? Just . . . what?"

"Look, it'll be months before trial and in the meanwhile you've got to get back to a near-normal existence. Go build houses."

"But aren't there steps we should be taking? If I didn't kill Larry, who did? I mean, we've got to find out."

"It doesn't work that way, Kevin. We don't care who killed Mr. Dexter. It's not our business."

"It's not?"

"The county has to prove that you're guilty beyond a reasonable doubt. Which is a very high standard of proof. My only job is to prevent them from doing that."

My pickup is still in custody, so I pull on work clothes and hitch a ride to Norham and the Indian Peak site. I make small talk with the driver, but mostly I stare out the window, thinking through everything. Terri. Why should she kill Dexter? I must check on her alibi.

What was the purpose of her midnight visit? Did she intend to keep me up late, ensuring I would also sleep late? Asleep at six-thirty, I would not have an alibi. Up and about, I might be on the phone, getting gas, or having breakfast in the diner at the precise time of the murder. As it turned out, I got up early and it didn't do me a bit of good.

At Indian Peak, the colonial house has been cleaned and repaired—but by who? Perhaps it was a kind gesture from John Finnerty. Possibly Kikki had directed repairs.

I walk the frozen ground, hands in my coat pockets, approaching the murder scene slowly. I'm distracted as a car approaches, slowly. The passengers, a young man and two young women, gawk. Curiosity seekers, they apparently abandon ideas of getting out when they spot me.

Once they've gone, I climb into the uncompleted house, moving cautiously, almost reluctantly to the top of the cellar stairs. I see no sign of the killing, except that the bottom steps have been removed.

I would work, but my tools have vanished, probably stolen.

"Oh, Jesus." A few weeks ago I was a real estate developer. Now, I'm a guy with no car, no tools, no job, and a life sentence hanging over his head. Maybe something good is around the corner. If things can deteriorate this fast, why can't they improve just as fast?

I'm trudging up the road as a car approaches. I don't look up, thinking it's another sightseer. Only it stops.

"Kevin."

I look up to Pat and Jack Lundgren. Cleaners and tools clutter the back of their car. Grim faced, Jack rolls down his window and I retreat a little.

Well. Do they think I'm dangerous, a murderer? Will they denounce me? I can't bear that from my friends.

And Pat, God bless her, senses my anxiety. She climbs out of the car and calls across the roof, "Kevin. Come with us. Come on."

I smile, can't help it. And Pat Lundgren is positively beautiful to me.

"Jack and I repaired the damage in the colonial," Pat says. "So we could show it for you. It's a hard sell now. With, with what's happened here."

"The police took some of your tools," Jack explains. "The gun. Some other things. But I got the rest. Or they would have been left to rust."

"Thanks, Jack. Thanks to you both." We walk through the unfinished house where Larry Dexter died.

"Are you okay for money?" Pat asks.

"I've got a few hundred in my checking account. That's all."

"Any assets?"

"You're walking on them."

"Have you considered selling some of the lots?" Jack suggests.

"I need Kikki's permission. And the way she feels, she won't do anything to help me."

"Well." Jack gazes up the plywood stairway to the sky. "Maybe I'll talk to her. She stands to lose a piece of change herself if this place goes under."

"My cottage. See if you can sell that."

"Cottage prices aren't what they were."

"I just need money, Jack."

"If you sell your cottage," Pat asks, "where will you live?"

"The state has made some suggestions."

"That's not funny." She seems genuinely angry that I'd joke about this. "No one believes you did this, Kevin. No one who knows you."

"You ought to talk to Susan."

"Don't you dare. Susan is behind you one hundred percent."

I walk to the cellar stairs. "What was Larry doing here at six in the morning?"

"Waiting to talk to you?" Pat suggests.

If true, then Dexter's mysterious morning phone call and his appearance here were unconnected.

Pat continues, "I think those kids, the ones who trashed the house, I think they were taking crack or something, something that leads to violence. And it wouldn't surprise me if one of them is out there. He murdered Larry. And now he can't even remember doing it. That's how those drugs work."

"Did they find drugs in the house?" I ask.

"Did they look?" Jack responds.

Pat says, "By the time they started looking a million people had been in that house. Police made more mess than the vandals."

"Drugs." In fact, Dexter's bizarre murder might relate to some druggie weaving in and out of reality. "It takes a certain type to kill, to kill that way," I note, "to go up to Larry—I mean, sure he's an asshole. But, he's also a guy with five kids. And they looked him in the eyes, pulled the trigger, and drove a three-inch nail into his brain." I nod. "Do we know anyone insane enough to do that?"

They go pale. I'm chilled myself, as if Larry's ghost is amongst us, as if his screams for mercy still echo among the walls and the trees beyond. And beneath our apprehension is the simple fact that the killer remains at large, even his motives unknown. So, can any of us feel safe?

"Kevin," Pat asks, "how did you get yourself into this mess?"

Maybe I'm hypersensitive, but I hear something other than irony in her voice. Despite her kindness, I wonder if Pat suspects that I *did* kill Larry.

Only now I see a gentle smile and she clings to my arm with two hands. "Don't be discouraged. We're with you. All your friends are with you."

With the tools Pat and Jack have salvaged, I begin working to complete the attic and roof, covering the walls with plywood. It's a backbreaking task, but it suits me. I can think. About my case.

Like an old man obsessed with his illness, I think only of the case.

Tim Regan has invited me to supper—a nice gesture because he knows I'm broke. I wait in my cottage, thinking that he might just save my life. He'll be motivated—this case could make his reputation. When the bell rings, I stand eagerly, but sit back down at once. Luckily, I have the lights off.

It's Terri Pratt. I guess she's working the overnight shift this month. Maybe she's loony enough to think she can spend time with me.

She rings a long time, leans close, cups a hand over her eyes trying to see through the window. "Kevin. Please talk to me. Please. I saw you in there. Come on." But I don't speak or move from the shadows and after fifteen minutes the racket stops.

"You asked me about an alibi." Tim Regan picks through his salad. "Terri Pratt. You wanted to know if she has an alibi for the murder."

"Does she?" I'm holding my breath.

"She was working. Punched in at twelve-forty midnight and punched out at eight. In fact, at the precise time of the murder, six-thirty, she was reading to a patient."

"Well, that's not much of an alibi. She could have had an accomplice. I'm not saying I think she did it, understand. I'm just pointing out that you could pin this on lots of people if you wanted to try. Right?"

Tim smiles tolerantly.

"I think it's pretty thin. The stuff they've got against me."

"Kevin?"

"I can explain everything I said. Everything I did."

"Kevin?"

"What? Like *my* thumbprint on *my* nail gun. Ask Toomey if his prints are on his briefcase."

Tim puts down his fork, pushes away his dish.

"What?" I ask.

"Kevin, don't underestimate the prosecution's case. Granted it's mostly circumstantial. But sometimes thumbprints and insurance policies give better evidence than eyewitnesses. I had a witness to a rear end collision. He was great in my office, relaxed, full of details, he even told jokes. But on the stand he froze, he couldn't remember his name."

Something in his quiet, measured tone frightens me. And I don't like the way he gives an auto accident as his example. Didn't he *ever* handle criminal trials?

"Now listen carefully, Kev. I've been consulting with

some people I respect. People with years of experience on just this sort of case. And they agree, Toomey's got the makings of a pretty persuasive prosecution."

"But I thought . . . you said he had to prove guilt beyond reasonable doubt."

"That's true. That's the legal test. But there's another side of it. A side we've got to be thinking about. And, that's really the reason, one of the reasons I asked you here."

"What? What reason?"

"Well." He exhales. "The jury starts from the proposition that Dexter has been murdered. And they want someone punished for it. Now, they've got your prints on the weapon. They've got two witnesses who claim you were on the verge of violence with the man. They've got life insurance. They've got you and Mrs. Pratt. And you're placed at the scene behaving in a way that might look strange to some. They've got all this and Toomey's just started."

This isn't what I expected, what I wanted to hear. I place my hands under the table because they're shaking. "I've . . . I've explained all that stuff."

"And maybe the jury will believe your explanations. But then there are some things they're going to find difficult to believe. For instance. Why didn't you know about Dexter's relationship with Terri Pratt? Lots of people knew. How did *you* miss it? Why didn't you know about the life insurance policy? How did you manage to walk past that garage and not see Dexter's car big as life? Now. It's all circumstantial and we know it's just a horrible series of coincidences. But it might be hard to convince a jury it's nothing more than coincidence."

I stare at the salad, my stomach churning vigorously.

"I want to try something out on you, Kevin. Keep in mind, this is just something to consider."

"What?"

"I was with the assistant DA earlier. Speaking informally. Feeling him out on certain things."

"What things? What are you talking about, Tim?"

He takes a breath. "It might be possible to get this settled quickly. Get it behind us. It might be possible to strike a bargain with Mr. Toomey. Settle the case. Changing our plea. From not guilty of murder in the first degree to," he clears his throat, "to guilty of murder in the second degree."

My shock is total. I can't get my breath. My heart races. "Change . . . change our plea?" I feel dizzy. Is this a heart attack? It's hard to hear what he's saying for the pounding in my ears.

"Are you all right, Kevin?"

I manage a nod.

"Are you sure?" He gives me a close look before continuing, "I know this is hard to accept, because you haven't committed any crime. But it would be a light sentence. And you wouldn't go to Cedar Junction with the dregs of the earth. I mean, as it is, we're facing life. And even here, a life sentence can send you to prison a long time. When you get out, if you get out, you'll be an old man. Kevin, I don't know if you want to take that gamble. The second degree sentence, I think you can be out in thirteen years. Maybe less. You've still got time after thirteen years."

"Thir- thirteen years . . ." I guess I'm not going to explain my way out of this. The authorities don't believe me, my own attorney doesn't believe me. And suddenly shame and prison are probabilities. I want to run away.

"You don't have to decide tonight."

But by an act of will, I collect myself to face Tim's proposal. "You want me to change my plea?"

Tim grimaces, shrugs. "I'm only asking you to consider—"

"I won't, won't even consider it. Not for a minute. Not for a second."

"Okay."

"I haven't done anything. I'm not going to lie and say I did."

Tim manages a kind of smile, "I thought you'd say that. You have my respect, Kevin."

God help me, my own lawyer thinks I'm guilty. He

wouldn't have proposed such a thing otherwise. I remember the furtive voices in the police wagon. Don't trust the lawyers. If I want to be saved, I must save myself.

After a day with my kids, I settle in the kitchen with Susan. Since the final divorce decree I no longer feel at home here, despite the welcome and sympathy. "She put up her house," Susan says.

I nod.

"Nice of her." My wife speaks softly. "Very kind."

"I suppose."

"Of course, I would have put up this house."

"I realize that. You've always been there when I needed you, Susan."

"A lot of women in my position, they'd say to hell with him. I don't owe him a thing."

"You've got a generous heart. I know I don't deserve it."

"The kids, did they ask you about it today?"

"We talked about it over pizza," I say. "I told them that I'd soon have everything explained and the police would be apologizing to me."

She looks hard at the table. Susan has this thing about being honest with the kids. Tell them there ain't no Santa Claus and we'll see dad again when you graduate from college. What my wife cannot see is that reality head-on is sometimes more than anyone can bear.

"I spoke with Linda about moving in," she says.

"Linda and her kids? Where are they all going to fit?"

"It's the only way to keep the house. You're not contributing anymore. I'm not saying it's your fault. But you're not and who knows when you'll be able to."

"I'm selling the cottage."

"That's not a long-term solution. This problem could be with us for the long term. And I have to put food on the table. If I take Linda in, with my job at the library and hers at the bank, maybe, just maybe we can squeeze by."

"I didn't . . ." I avoid her eyes.

"Don't think I like it. Back to sharing a room with my sister."

"I'm sorry, Susan. Honest to God. I didn't want this."

"Well . . ." her voice fades.

I can hear the kids yelling in the backyard. They're in high spirits. I've spent all day hiding the truth from them but I find suddenly I can no longer shield Susan. "It looks bad." I blurt it out. "Very bad."

Susan is visibly upset. "How bad?"

"I think they've made up their minds that I did this thing. They're determined to railroad me into prison. And maybe I can't stop them."

She clutches one hand with the other, her eyes well up. "No . . . isn't there anything you can do?"

"I'm fighting. I won't make it easy for them. Right now. Well. They have this legal thing called discovery. The right to know everything the state knows about my case. It's a whole pile of records and interviews."

"Yeah?"

"Well, I'll take that stuff. And by going over it carefully, maybe something will jump out at me. A reference, a name that shouldn't be there."

"The name of the killer?" Susan asks.

"It's a long shot." I shrug. "The other thing I'm doing. I'm going to talk to people. I'm going to ask questions."

"Are you supposed to be doing all this?"

"Who's going to do it if I don't?"

"What does Tim Regan say?"

"I don't need his permission."

"But don't you think it might be dangerous, Kevin?"

"It's more dangerous to do nothing."

Susan nods uneasily. "Who are you going to be talking to?"

"I want to find out who was in the other house that night. Made all that mess. It must have been kids."

"Kids. That's not much to go on."

"If they broke into that house, chances are they've broken into others. And chances are they've been caught at it and the police know who they are. So, if I can get the names, I'll talk to them."

"What if they won't talk to you?"

"If someone won't talk. Well, that tells me something, doesn't it?" I'm nodding. "Kikki Dexter won't talk to me or my lawyer."

"She won't talk because she thinks you killed her husband."

"Maybe. On the other hand, there's something about Kikki's story that just, I don't know, it jars."

"I don't get you," Susan replies.

"Well, it's like, Kikki says that on the morning of the murder Larry got a call. Then he went out, never telling her who called, what they called about, or where he was going. Now. If somebody calls at six in the morning, don't you think she'd ask, 'Who was it?' And if he rushes out at that hour. Wouldn't she ask, 'Where are you going?' Wouldn't anybody ask that?"

"Maybe she did and he didn't answer. Or maybe he was always rushing off at that hour so she didn't care. Why? You're not saying Kikki had anything to do with Larry's murder?"

"You know," I reveal, "he wasn't faithful to her."

"Everybody knew that."

"Everybody knew? What?"

"He made moves on any woman who crossed his path. Kikki had to know it." She tilts her nose upward. "He made a pass at me once."

"He what?"

"Of course, there were lots of sly remarks over the years. But once I ran into him at the mall and he flat out asked me to go off with him."

"That son of a bitch."

"And, my God, was he persistent."

I used to think I knew the world. "What . . . what did you do?"

"I laughed at him."

"How come I never heard of this before?"

"Do you think I told you about every guy who made a pass at me?"

"You didn't—uh, and you think Kikki knew about this?"

"She must have known how he was." She shakes her head, puzzled. "I always thought he married her because of her father, his connections and his money. But Kikki has this face to the world like hers is the perfect marriage and Larry the perfect husband. Well, maybe she just shut her eyes and convinced herself it was true. After all, they survived Billy. It's not uncommon. When a child dies. The marriage breaks apart."

Neither Larry nor Kikki had any knack for teaching their youngsters discipline or even plain caution. The kids were forever rushing into traffic or swinging from the highest tree. So, it was ironic that ten-year-old Billy Dexter had died from the bite of a mosquito infecting him with equine encephalitis. No amount of caution would have prevented the tragedy.

At the wake Kikki came at me, wobbling under tranquilizers. Not quite focused, she found my hand and squeezed hard. "Watch your children, Kevin. Hold them. Hold them." I figured she'd suffered about as much as anyone could so I was thereafter mostly tolerant of her overbearing manner.

"They stayed together," Susan concludes, "and even had two more kids. I often think there must be something redeeming about Larry. He must love children to have so many. Maybe, in his way, he even loves Kikki."

"And maybe he just conned her. Year after year. Until she couldn't pretend anymore. So, she started hating him. And maybe she hated him bad enough to kill him."

Susan thought, then bent forward slightly and spoke in a low voice. "Women will kill their lovers. But they never kill their husbands. No matter how bad they hurt them."

As I am leaving, I call Susan close. "Did you happen to tell the police about Larry making a pass at you?"

"I refuse to talk to the police."

"Good girl. Uh. But just to be safe. Don't repeat that. To anyone."

She looks a little uncertain.

"It could be used against me," I add. "If I knew he was after you. Don't you see? It gives me another motive, supposedly, for killing him."

In the backyard I call the kids.

"Will you come back tomorrow, Dad?"

"Not tomorrow."

"He'll come back on the weekend. Huh, Dad."

"That's right."

"Then will you live with us again?"

I sigh, "We've been over that before."

Molly explains, "Because him and mom are divorced he can't come back and live with us. It's against the law."

"Why?"

"Cause him and mom hate each other."

"*We do not hate each other.* What a thing to say. Where do you hear that stuff?"

I have thrown myself into the backbreaking work of completing the second house at Indian Peak, constructing the attic, roof, and plywood walls. Unfortunately, unless I find money for roofing materials and siding, the job comes to a standstill soon.

With Dexter's insurance settlement tied up, I'm desperate to sell the colonial. The big house with its grand columns sits alone at the dead end of the road, bordered by mud and gray, leafless trees. Of course, it's attracted some ghoulish attention, but, as one of Jack's agents explained, "It's a beautiful whore. Everybody wants in, but no one wants to marry her."

Kikki Dexter adds to the confusion. Both our signatures are required to sell anything. I have approached her, tactfully, through the Lundgrens. So far the only reply has been a rumor—passed by Susan—that Kikki is outraged by my efforts to complete the house where her husband died.

Does she expect me to level the place out of respect or something? Soon to collect a whopping death benefit, she might be content to let the whole thing collapse. I cannot afford such gestures.

I'm on the ladder as John Finnerty arrives. Shyly, he walks completely around the house before approaching. "I thought I might not be welcome."

"Sure you're welcome." It's better to be friendly and perhaps turn him toward my version of events. I climb down slowly.

"What I told the police. I thought you wouldn't be too pleased to see me."

"You only told the truth. Right, John?"

"Yeah." He looks away. "They had me all confused, Kevin. They told me that, that you'd . . . that you'd—"

"That I'd killed Dexter."

"That you'd admitted it."

"Well. I didn't. I didn't kill Dexter."

"No. And afterwards I discussed it with my wife. And we decided you couldn't have done it. You're not the sort. Jesus. Dexter had more enemies than the British Army. I don't know why they should settle on you." He looks away for a moment. "I'm sorry what I told them cops."

"All I ask is that you tell the truth. You saw me threaten Dexter with the nail gun. Okay, I don't remember that. But. If that's what you saw—"

"I never did," he insists.

"No?"

"You had the nail gun in your hand and you were shouting at Dexter. All right. But I never said you threatened him. With the gun."

"It was the saw," I explain.

"The what?"

"The circular saw. I had it in my hand. But I didn't threaten him."

"I never said you did. Never said it. And I won't . . . the saw you say?"

Whether out of guilt or friendship, John pitches in for several hours. More than his help, I appreciate his company. I've spent too many hours alone, brooding.

Once, during a break, John stands over the basement stairway, staring down into the shadows where Larry Dexter died. When he realizes I'm watching he walks away, embarrassed.

"Never liked the man," John admits.

We're sitting on the front steps in the dark, each with a beer.

"Shouldn't speak ill of the dead. God forgive me. But that bastard . . ." He takes a sip of beer. "He wanted us to work cheaper. Did you know?"

"Well." I put the bottle to my lips. "He mentioned it."

"He said I should be glad to have the smaller amount because he was keeping the immigration away. I told him to fuck himself." He grimaces angrily. "One of my boys, Pete—"

"Your cousin?"

"My cousin. From Galway. There was a question on his work permit. Pete is strictly legal. You saw his papers, you should know. But there was a few weeks when his work permit was up for renewal. You could cause problems. No doubt about it."

"Larry shouldn't have done that."

"You go about threatening people. The way he threatened me. Is it a surprise when someone kills you?"

I put my beer down. "You, uh, John, you're not saying Pete—"

"No, no, no. You don't kill over an immigration problem which can be sorted out right enough." He smiles. "But generally speaking. If you do business by threats, isn't that going to rebound on you one day?"

It's an interesting point. Larry was never shy about blackmail, or "leveraging," as he put it.

Nonetheless, I'm suddenly reviewing all I know about John Finnerty. The tough Irishman had the opportunity to kill Dexter—he knew how to operate the defective nail gun, he could have called Dexter in the morning and brought him to the site. Finally, he undoubtedly hated the man.

His statement to the police failed to get the details right even as it incriminated me. Possibly, the genial man beside me, sharing a beer, is working to put me away for his crime.

At once, I am sad and terribly alone. I can't trust anyone. I have no friends.

"Did they ask you—"

"What?" he responds.

"Did anyone ask you about your whereabouts? At the time of the murder."

"I was at home with my wife."

I nod. "That's good. They won't be bothering you then."

"I did not like the man. But I wouldn'ta killed him."

"I didn't think—"

"Put your mind at rest." He grasps my shoulder. "Would I have told you about Pete if I'd done it? Do you think I'd come find the body? No way. I'd stay as far from here as I could get."

We leave it at that. Though I resolve to have Tim Regan ask around about John's alibi—and his cousins'.

A big-eyed little boy who can scarcely reach the knob swings the door open wide. "Can I, can I see your dad?" I ask.

At once, his mother appears, her pretty face tense as she protectively yanks her son away and closes the door almost shut. "I'll get Matt," she says, running off as if she intends to call the SWAT team.

Turning, I take in one of Norham's older developments, the homes small, yards close together. Terri lives a few streets over. Susan's house, my house, which is a little larger than these, is less than a mile off.

"Can I help you, Mr. Bourque?" Matt O'Keefe swings the door wide.

"What's this, uh, what's this Mr. Bourque stuff? Huh?" I'm smiling, hopefully. "It's Kevin. Remember?"

"Listen." He looks past me. "We probably shouldn't be talking."

"There's no harm talking, Matt. I was even hoping for some help. You know?"

"Help?"

"Some, some information."

"Uh, if it's about the case you ought to go through the department."

I reach out. "Matty, if this happened to you, I swear I wouldn't be so quick to believe you were a murderer."

"I never said I believed it." He's looking past me still.

"At least hear me out. Can't you? Matt?"

He thinks for a time. "Okay. Go around back. But I doubt there's anything I can do. And one more thing. Be careful what you say. If you incriminate yourself, I'm going to report that. It's my job."

On the back porch I ask if the police have looked into the trashing of the colonial house on the day of Dexter's murder.

"This is a state police investigation." Sitting, on the top step, O'Keefe wears his patrolman's jacket and tan pants. "You think they tell us peons anything?"

"Are they at least looking for the kids who broke in?"

"Trouble is, who were they? You say kids. It could have been anyone."

"I'll bet there are kids in town. They've done that sort of thing before and whenever there's a break you suspect them right off."

He looks up.

"You know some kids like that?"

"I might."

"Well? Were they questioned? Did their names go to the state police?"

"If you want the truth, Kevin. You won't like this. But the whole focus of the investigation, as near as I can tell, is you. Gathering evidence to convict you. No one cares who may or may not have broken into that house."

This is no surprise, but when he says it I feel the life draining from me. For a moment, I perceive the forces arrayed against me as a tangible thing, a wall so high I can't see the top.

I sigh. "Now you can see why I need help."

"I can believe you need help."

"Give *me* those names, Matty. The state police won't talk to those kids. I will."

He stands and comes down the stairs, walks away.

"I'll talk to them, Matt. Even if they weren't involved. They might have seen something. Or someone."

For a long time, he gazes up at the stars. "Nobody's to know I did this."

"I swear."

He looks back at me. "I doubt any kids'll talk to you. But. Seems like somebody ought to make the effort."

"All I ask is a chance."

"I'll see what I can find out, Kevin. I'll be in touch."

"You won't regret this." I'm all smiles. I shake his hand. "I'll never forget. Never. I owe you. I owe you."

Sometimes, I get more weird calls. The phone company puts me on a four-month waiting list for a tap. "Right. I'll just tell them to call back then." But I don't take it lightly. My partner is murdered and the silence on the phone is like a call from the dead.

Ring . . . ring . . . ring.

"Hello." I try to sound indifferent when I pick up.

This time, a voice. "Kevin?" It's Terri. "Kevin?"

Now, I'm silent.

"Please, answer . . . Kevin? Why won't you talk to me?"

"Yeah?"

"Why treat me this way? I love you. I put up your bail because I love you and I want to help."

"Have you been calling here?" I ask.

"I called a bunch of times this week and no one answered. And I came to your place twice. But I guess you weren't home."

After a wait, I say, "What do you want?" Despite Tim Regan's warning, it just makes sense to talk to her. Odds are that Terri is mixed up in Dexter's murder and if we talk— even if her purpose is to disarm me—she might slip and give herself away somehow. Even if she's innocent of murder, she was involved with Larry. Lovers confide. Terri might know something helpful to my defense.

Anyway, she no longer has a hold on me and I'm not afraid to meet her for breakfast at a cafe in nearby Assinippi.

At a both in back, she wears a stylish jacket, fancy black jeans, and a tight sweater. One look, damn me, and I feel a jolt.

No problem. Just a sign that I'm recovering from the shock of my situation. I can handle it.

"I was afraid you weren't coming," she says.

"I had to hitch. Police still have my pickup."

"I would have gotten you."

"You wanted to talk."

"I want to do more than talk. I want to help. I want to do anything you think will help. Anything."

I look away.

"Just . . . just tell me what you need, Kevin."

"There's nothing. There's nothing I need from you."

She stares at her coffee. Her lips quiver, then she twists them. "You're mad. You found out about me and Larry and you're mad." She gives a helpless shrug. "What can I say? I'm sorry. I know I should have told you."

"It was Dexter you spent the night with that time."

"Yes."

I must be sneering. Jesus, I'd like to pop her one, the lying bitch.

"Would the gentleman care to order?" the waitress smiles.

"Nothing for me . . . coffee. Maybe coffee." As she leaves, I continue to stare at Terri.

"You seem so bitter," she says.

"Excuse me. But I don't see anything to be cheerful about."

"It's not—"

"I can't play your little games, Terri. I've got too much at stake. When I deal with you. When I'm near you. I can't trust anything I see. Or anything I hear. Of course, you're fun. I'll admit that. You've had lots of practice and you're a good lay. But, frankly, you're a luxury I can't afford. Under the circumstances."

"You're trying to hurt me."

"I'm going to prison for the rest of my life, so—"

"No, you're not."

"—sorry but I don't care one way or the other about your feelings. Let's just cut the crap and you tell me what you know about Larry's murder."

"I don't know anything."

"Come on."

"I give you my word," she says.

"Your word? I'll sleep sound tonight with that."

She closes her eyes tight. "You can be cruel."

"I can be honest. That's the difference between us."

Neither one of us looks up as the waitress serves my coffee. When she leaves, Terri says, "Please, believe me I had nothing to do with what happened to Larry, or what happened to you."

"Sure."

"What can I do to make you believe me?"

"Try telling the truth."

"I am. What can I say to make you believe it?"

"Nothing. There's nothing you can say. That's the reason

people value the truth, see? Because once you toss it away you can't just have it back because now it's convenient to be believed."

"You're not being fair," she protests. "I lied about one thing. For a good reason."

"You came to my house. To make up to me for cheating with another man. You told the truth about that. But in the next breath, ha, you lied, you lied about who he was."

"I know, I know. It was stupid."

"Sometimes you lie. Sometimes you tell the truth. And I'm supposed to sit around trying to figure which is which while they put me away for the rest of my life. Well, you know what I say to that? Fuck you, Mrs. Pratt. Okay. Fuck you."

She looks down, very sad. "I just want a chance—"

"A chance? You expect me to take you back like nothing's happened? Be serious."

"I thought I could make up for it. Now that you're in trouble. And it's so serious. I could help."

"It is serious. You're right there, Terri. Fucking serious trouble. But what makes you think I can use *your* help?" I reach over and grab her wrist, squeezing until she looks uncomfortable and a little frightened. "The kind of trouble I'm in. I really don't know who I can trust. Understand? I don't know who to trust." I let go of her, sit back. "Except. I know *I can't trust you.*"

She glances down again, looking sad. But maybe playing for sympathy. She's a dishonest woman who's been caught again and again. She's given this performance before.

The only question left. Is she also involved in murder?

"You've been awfully cooperative to the police," I say.

"I tried to help you—"

"By digging my grave?"

"No!"

"You tell them I'm going around saying how, how *all my troubles are going to be taken care of.* A few hours before Dexter's murder. That's real helpful. Even my own goddamn lawyer's wondering about that one."

"But you said it, Kevin."

"You didn't have to tell them I said it. You knew how it would sound."

She looks distressed. "I . . . I thought it would help you."

"Help me? Jesus!"

"They asked about financial problems. And I thought they were getting to the idea that you killed Larry over money. And I told them it couldn't be. You told me yourself you'd made arrangements so all your problems were being taken care of. Solved. Done."

Well, it's the truth or a damned clever explanation. Anyway, I can't say anything to rebut it.

She asks softly, "Why *did* you say that? I mean, if you still had money problems, why did you tell me you didn't?"

"To get rid of you."

Her eyes well up and she says softly, "I am a liar. I lie . . . But. I don't know if it will make a difference. But let me try to explain. And you won't forgive me. But maybe you can understand a little."

Let her talk. I'll listen carefully.

"In Bermuda, when I told you about my past . . . I intended to tell you about Larry then. But you kept asking if these men lived in town. Do you remember?"

"Get to the point."

"You said you didn't want to be meeting them. Or to know them even."

"So?"

"Don't you see? That's why I didn't tell you about Larry. I started to. But what you said scared me off. He's your partner—"

"Was."

She looks down. "Was. He was your partner. And if you knew, knew I'd had a long affair with him. I was afraid." Tears began to gather again. "I was afraid you wouldn't want me anymore."

She shakes her head. "I knew you'd find out about Larry eventually. But I couldn't tell you then. If you knew that morning that it was Larry I'd spent the night with, when you were already mad, you would have hated me for sure. And I couldn't bear that. So, I thought. I'll tell you . . . everything. But later. Because by then you'll love me so much it won't matter."

"Stop it," I snap. She's flushed, dabbing her eyes with napkins. *"Don't make a scene."* With my notoriety, I don't much like being out in public and I like it even less with her calling attention, putting on a big performance.

"When I met you at the party I was still seeing Larry. You were passionate and tender, but you never mentioned marriage or the future so I wasn't always sure where I stood. Except, I knew I had Larry."

"What do you mean, you had Larry? He was married."

"But we'd been going out for years. He was married. But I had him when I had him."

"That's pathetic."

She looks down.

"I suppose he was promising to leave his wife."

"She didn't matter to him. Kathleen. She's crazy. They should ask her some questions, if you want my opinion. She's violent, you know. He told me. She hits, throws things. He would have left her and married me except for the kids. We used to talk about that back when I thought I loved him. We were in love once. So you can't think I'd want to murder him. You can't."

"Can't I?"

Tears came rolling down. "It's not fair. You're taking all these things against me that are just . . . suspicions. And you build them up to prove I did something awful. And that's exactly what the police are doing to you!"

She's hit a nerve there.

"If I was part of some scheme," she continues, "to kill Larry. It's just ridiculous that I could hurt anybody. I don't even hit my kids, for God sakes. But if I was part of this, this plot. Why would I bail you out of jail? Why?"

"To put me off. You knew I would have raised bail eventually and—"

"If I was the monster you say, I would have left you in

jail as long as possible. Where you wouldn't be a threat. Instead, I put up my house. My kids' house! And everybody says I'm crazy because if you run away I'll lose it. But when I saw you in court, chained, confused, and scared, I couldn't bear it. I love you and I want you free where you can prove that you're innocent."

For the first time, I've got nothing mean or doubting to say. And as she can see that I'm softening, her voice grows hopeful.

"I went to Larry that night to tell him we were through. I was going to see you, only you. Oh, God." Her voice is close to breaking again. "I've been alone a long time. And there's nobody decent out there. Just jerks. Then I met you. I knew I'd never find anyone so nice, so kind and sweet. And I thought, don't blow it, Terri. Hold on tight. I can't blame you if you hate me, Kevin. But, I swear to God I had nothing to do with Larry's death. And I wouldn't ever do anything deliberately to hurt you. I wouldn't. I wouldn't."

In the parking lot, in Terri's car, I want to know about Larry Dexter. I don't necessarily trust her, but again, it can't hurt listening.

"Larry handled my divorce. You don't know how lonely and rejected I felt then. And he was very considerate, kind . . ."

She plunges her hands between her legs. Well, it's cold. "He was in a bad way too. They'd had trouble. The boy dying. They almost split. She was under a doctor's care. He carried the load himself. Three kids. I guess we got together to feel sorry for each other."

She sighs, almost smiles. "When he took me out it was always to nice places. Even New York once. Always places we wouldn't be recognized. I mean, it was no fun sneaking around. But it was fun to go to nice places. We'd take his BMW with the stereo and head for some motel with an ocean view. We'd always get a room because I don't do it in cars."

"Did Larry have other girlfriends?"

"He barely had time for me. Like, in the beginning, he wanted to see me every night. But that wore off. And at the end it was like we were married. We'd spend most of the time talking kids and things. But it was always hard for him to get away. What with work. And she watched him like a hawk."

"Did Kikki know about you two?"

"I think she would have divorced him if she knew. Or killed him—" She stops, realizing what she's said.

"You say she could be violent?"

Terri stares at the traffic. "Whenever we met he had a story about her. The all-time hysterical female. She tried to maybe kill him twice that I know of. Once with scissors and once with a knife. It was over something . . . over nothing probably. I can't even remember what touched her off."

"When did this happen?"

"With the scissors? Last year. He told me one story. When they first got married she got mad and threw his stereo out a second-floor window. Big, expensive stereo smashed all over the driveway. People think she got the way she is because her little boy died. But she was always that way."

"Did Larry ever talk about money problems?"

"No. Never. But Larry was one of these people. He lived good. He'd take you to some fancy place and tell you to order anything on the menu. But then he'd be careful which credit card he used."

Damn, I'd also noticed Larry shuffling through his stack of credit cards, but I'd been too blinded by greed to face what it meant.

Terri continues, "I don't think his law practice was so successful. I know he got work from his father-in-law's friends. But that didn't make him rich. And Larry wanted to be rich."

"Did he ever mention where he was getting the money for Indian Peak? Did he ever mention any partners besides me? Anything along those lines?"

"No."

Christ. I exhale loudly. I'm not learning much.

"He did say this," Terri offers. "He told me he had lots of friends. People who owed him. And if he needed help he expected to get it."

Terri's car has a bench seat. I could lean over and touch her. That would feel good, my head on her breasts as she stroked my hair. I would have a lover and an ally in this bitter time.

But this woman is a known quantity, she lies and steals. She promises love, but chances are good that she's connected to Larry Dexter's murder. Chances are she's digging my grave as we sit here.

I say, "He was married."

"What?"

"Larry. When you met him he was married with five kids."

"Three." She's looking straight ahead, not getting it. "When I started seeing him he only had the three. Plus the one that died. Poor little boy."

"A decent woman doesn't mess with somebody else's husband."

"I guess I'm not so decent. Is that the point?" She looks down. "Maybe I'm not. But I didn't put a gun to his head. He came after me. Took advantage of how lonely and un-happy I was. Lawyers aren't supposed to do that. So, at the time I thought, oh well. If he's not with me he'll be with someone else. I thought he loved me. And maybe he did for a while. But at the end, when he was asking me to sleep with other men—"

"What?"

"At the Lundgrens' party. That's how come I was flirting with you right in front of him. He spent the whole night trying to get me to sleep with this shrimpy guy in a brown suit."

"Rapolli? The guy from the state?" And then, "I guess the cherry panties were meant for him. Jesus."

"I just, I wouldn't go through with it. I couldn't. And I was hurt that Larry asked me."

Driving me home, she speaks very little and I'm leaning on the door, as far from her as possible. She's perfumed, hair nicely done. And this is no accident. She's trying to win me back. But I'm not stupid.

Her face is still young, the kind of face they use in paintings, Madonna and child. This added to my wonder when she performed her bedroom tricks. But I can't get distracted by all that now.

Stopping in my wooded driveway, she says, "You don't have your truck. I can drive you. Lend you my car."

"I'm getting the truck back tomorrow."

"I'm due three weeks vacation. Whenever you need me, I'll take it."

"I'll think about it." And I open the door to a gust of freezing wind. It's beginning to snow.

"Oh, God," she reaches out. "Let me hold you. Don't go."

I turn toward her and that's all it takes. She is on me.

"Please don't push me away. Give me another chance. You won't regret it. You won't."

I can't believe how good it feels to be held after all this horror. But when I shake loose and step outside I'm surprised because more than anything else I feel sorry for her. She looks lovely and wounded—and suppose everything she's telling me now is true.

"I don't think this is a good idea, Terri," and because she is near to crying, I add, "just now."

"We'll talk again," she pleads.

"I'll . . . I'll be in touch."

"I can help. I want to help. Let me."

"I'll call you."

Tim Regan is reluctant to have me wading through the materials sent from the district attorney's office, six cardboard boxes full.

"I know you're motivated, Kevin. But I think a professional should do this. An accountant. From what I've seen of contractors, and maybe this doesn't apply to you, but a lot of them can barely add up their bills."

He's closer to the truth than I care to admit. But I insist I will be extremely careful. I've even borrowed a calculator with a print-out as an aid.

Kikki had allowed the DA free access, not only to Indian Peak data (we were entitled to that) but to Dexter's personal financial records. In a stroke of luck, someone at the prosecutor's office had carelessly given all of this over to Tim. The files stretch back to college where Larry drew from a dozen sources of student aid, including one reserved for Native Americans.

I arrange it all chronologically across the cottage floor, tax returns, loan agreements, credit card statements, even pleas for donations from the Catholic school where Larry sent his kids.

I also find a third grader's Father's Day poem and a snapshot of Billy Dexter. What sort of person murders the father of five? Someone demented? Or a person consumed by hate. No doubt, Larry could inspire that.

I'd imagined that something here would leap out at me. But it's not going to be so easy. The whole mess has to be perused document by document with emphasis on the period of our partnership.

I sigh. Can't be done. I lie in bed, staring at the ceiling, papers scattered everywhere. They always said I couldn't do math to save my life.

Soon, I rouse. I have nothing better to do. A burst of work takes me far into the night. Though I finally collapse, bleary eyed, into bed, I awake early and get right back to it.

It doesn't take long to confirm Terri's observation. Dexter's earnings consistently lagged behind his spending. He frequently paid huge interest fees to credit card companies. Several notices mention legal action if bills aren't honored.

More than once he paid a late filing fee to the Internal Revenue Service.

Not until the evening of the second day, my eyes sore, with paper covering just about every inch of floor, bed, table, and chairs, do I find an intriguing reference to something called European Import Consultants.

The financial statement gives no hint that anyone was involved besides Dexter. The company's earnings were erratic, with a whopping profit of over sixty thousand dollars four years ago, nearly twenty thousand three years ago, and only six thousand last year.

European Import Consultants? Evidently, Dexter was offering his expertise on imports—but what expertise? What was imported? The statement gave no inkling. I rummage through the papers with new interest. But I find no further reference to this mysterious company. Have some papers been filed elsewhere or even withheld?

Dexter had made almost eighty-six thousand dollars in total. And not a clue how. Well, it's pretty odd . . . odd enough to be connected somehow to the murder. Even Tim Regan has to admit as much when I call—though he's quick to point out that it went back a few years.

"Let me know if you find out anything else about it," he advises.

Next, I bury myself in the finances of the Indian Peak Development Corporation. It takes two days to organize the endless invoices. Apparently, Dexter *was* borrowing from the account—probably to pay personal expenses. Withdrawals are noted, but absent are corresponding payments to lumber companies or subcontractors.

Now we're getting somewhere!

But further checking reveals a series of mysterious deposits. Apparently, the unauthorized loans had been returned as quietly as they'd been taken.

So. Larry Dexter hadn't exactly cheated me. It's a pity.

· 7 ·

Pat and Jack Lundgren surely believe in me—otherwise they'd never let me near the twins ("The Christ child and his sister," Susan calls them). In their extraordinarily normal living room, Jessica is rapt as I read a story, while little Tony bounces on and off my lap.

My tension eases until I notice that at least one parent is in the room at all times, watching closely. But then, maybe I'm oversensitive.

At bedtime, I get hugs from the kids. Just now such uncomplicated affection is particularly moving to me. Once the little ones have gone to bed with their mother, my eyes tear. I look down so that Jack won't see.

"Great kids," I say, aching for my own.

Jack begins softly, "So, tell us about this scheme of yours. This plan to find Larry's killer."

"Sounds dangerous," Pat hunches her shoulders, gives a shudder.

"The real worry is the odds against me. This murderer

could have been a million different people. Larry was into so much shit. It could have been some deal. Like drugs. And maybe he was going to sell drugs to save the business, like Delorean. And if it was something like that, how would I know? How would anyone?"

"So discouraging," Pat says.

"If it was a thing out of the blue. If he was killed by the crazies who trashed the house. Like Pat thinks. And now they're in California or somewhere. And they did it for no reason. No motive. Well, no one's ever going to find that out. See what I'm saying?"

Jack nods.

"The police, they decide right off it must be this guy. Me. Meaning me. So they look to confirm their prejudice. And why go after people a thousand miles away when you've got a perfectly good suspect right here."

Jack says, "It's a tough spot."

"Well, you see why I've got to get involved in this myself."

"If there's anything we can do to help," Pat adds. "Anything."

The words are right, but these two are uneasy—especially Pat. I'm not imagining this, I've been around them a lot lately and I sense it.

"Did you find anything in Dexter's records?" Jack questions.

"Well. I'm not sure. There was one strange reference. It might mean something to you guys. Larry ran an outfit. For all I could tell, a one-man operation. European Import Consultants. Does, does that ring a bell at all?"

They share puzzled looks.

"He made a lot of money off it the last few years."

They look back blankly.

"Anything you can think of that might be connected? European Import Consultants. Anything?"

"His . . ." Pat hesitates.

"What?"

"Well, I don't know if it's connected. But I've heard him

talk about his father. His father was German. Came over after World War II. Anyway, that's a European connection, I guess."

Nodding, I suddenly remember hearing something about this before.

"Larry didn't like to talk about his father," Jack adds. "Something, something in his past. Political stuff."

"What?"

"Something . . . I don't know. He was, I think, a Nazi. No wait. A communist. I think he was a communist because he got into trouble back in the fifties. At least, I remember Kikki telling me something about that."

Dexter's father a communist? It didn't add up—not with Larry the swashbuckling capitalist. And how did this relate to his murder?

"European Import Consultants," I repeat. "What was Larry importing?"

"He went to Europe on business a few years ago," Jack says. "But I never asked him what the business was." Jack points to the wall. "He brought that back with him."

It's a dark, weathered painting on wood depicting Jesus as a young man. I walk toward it. I guess it's a match to the flea market fake that Larry palmed off to Rapolli as an antique. "It's not real, is it? I mean, it looks old, but . . ."

Jack laughs. "He only charged us a few hundred dollars."

"It's treated to look antique," Pat explains. "Tenth century or something. This guy overseas specializes in them. Larry got it for Kikki. She didn't like it. So we bought it . . . I took medieval history in college."

"It's not the kind of thing you kill for," Jack offers.

To my disappointment. Sitting, I ask about Larry's last days.

"He was desperate to sell that house," Pat says. "Of course, he'd never admit it. But when he called every day. Sometimes twice a day. Well."

"Did he ever talk about money? The money he supposedly had in reserve. The money to keep Indian Peak Estates going. Where it would come from?"

Jack replies, "He never said a word about it to me."

"Me neither," Pat adds.

"Larry went to the site. Apparently to meet someone. Can you think who it might have been? Maybe some buyer wanted a second look."

"If it was a buyer," Jack shrugs, "I knew nothing about it. It's possible someone contacted Larry directly. If you think it'll help, I can give you a list of names. Everyone *we* ever brought out there."

"Do either of you know anything about John Finnerty?"

Jack looks up. "Your foreman?"

"He lives here in town," I add, "and I thought maybe . . ."

"I've met his wife," Pat says. "She's sweet. But shy."

"Why are you asking about him?"

"I'm asking about everybody."

"Jack and I were both in the office at the time of the killing," Pat shrugs. "We're each other's alibi."

"Pat!" Jack complains.

"Well. Kevin said he's asking everybody. I'm just volunteering the information to avoid any embarrassing questions."

"Thanks," I say. In fact, I've already seen their statement to the police. "Getting back to Finnerty."

"I've seen him around town," Pat says. "I know who he is. But I don't really know him."

"There's one story . . ." Jack is looking up at the ceiling, trying to remember something. "Finnerty, Finnerty . . . it seems to me he got in some trouble once. A few years ago. There was some gossip that he'd come to blows with the hockey coach up the high school."

Pat leans forward. "Michelle Sollivar was on the school committee at the time. She told me the whole thing was over Finnerty's boy Doug. He was on the team. But the coach wouldn't play him. When the father complained—"

"I think they actually came to blows," Jack completes the thought.

"It was all smoothed over afterwards. They got rid of

that coach. He had run-ins with a lot of people. Finnerty was barred from school grounds."

Jack notes importantly, "Finnerty has a temper."

I've seen evidence of John's temper. Once, when he thought he was being stiffed on a job up in Westwood, he nearly drove his pickup into a company trailer. Sure, he's got a temper. Yet I can't see him using that nail gun.

In the minute or so it took for the pump to gain pressure, the hottest rage would have cooled enough for him to face the horror of murder. Temper might have played a part in this killing, but whoever fired a spike through Larry's skull surely had a sustaining reason.

We're interrupted by faint cries from above. Pat nudges Jack, who dutifully bounds up the stairs to the twins.

What follows is one of those moments of almost painful silence. Pat smiles, then stares grimly ahead. I have the discomforting impression that she's afraid to be alone with me.

I say, "I keep asking, why has all this happened? And why to me?"

"You shouldn't have left your wife," Pat says.

"What?"

"You shouldn't have left Susan." I realize she's not fearful at all, but angry.

"Susan kicked me out, to be accurate."

"Honestly, Kevin, whose fault was that?"

"Why does it have to be anyone's fault?" I'm shaking my head, trying to understand what all this has to do with Dexter's murder.

"You didn't get everything your way and you sulked and bitched until she couldn't stand it anymore. That's what happened. That's what really happened so don't let's kid each other. Okay?"

"Pat." I'm trying not to get angry back at her.

"If you'd stayed where you belong with your wife and your family you wouldn't be in all this trouble now."

"How do you get that?"

"Leaving your wife is how you got involved with that,

that Terri Pratt. And if you hadn't gotten mixed up with her this would never have happened."

"What, what's the implication here, Pat?" I'm on the edge of my chair, on the edge of rage. "You think I did it. Right? You think I killed him."

"I do not. But if you weren't seeing Terri Pratt the police would have no reason now to accuse you."

"That's not the way the police see it."

"God help me," she says, "I should have told you about her and Larry."

"You mean you knew? You knew and didn't tell me?"

"Everybody knew. We all thought you'd find out too. If she had any decency she would have told you herself."

"Jesus Christ, you let me walk right into this—"

"None of it would have happened if you just stayed where you belonged! Married. That's what I'm telling you. Bad things happen when marriages break apart. It destroys, destroys the natural order of life. People think it's going to be better with someone else, but they just end up multiplying the misery. I've seen it once, I've seen it a million times."

"I don't think—excuse me, Pat. But where my family is concerned. I don't think you're in a position to judge."

"The problem with you, Kevin, is you had it too easy all your life."

Now I'm too astonished to even answer.

"You were the big jock who married the prettiest girl. Susan loved you, she'd do anything for you. But still you weren't satisfied."

"That's Susan talking," I say.

"No it isn't. It isn't Susan talking. I've got eyes." She looks right at me. "I used to envy you. Once I thought you had the perfect life. It isn't that way for everyone, you know. It wasn't for us. I was past thirty when I got married and up to then I hardly ever had a date even. Did you know that? I'd given up on ever being loved. It was the hand of God that I met Jack."

"Pat—"

"You had two beautiful kids. As soon as you wanted

them. Ever stop and think what a blessing that was? Happy, healthy kids. With, with Billy Dexter in his grave and me, with four miscarriages." Her eyes well up, her voice cracks.

"I appreciate my kids, Pat. And you have the twins now, so—"

"Do you know what that cost me?"

"I know, you spent months in the hospital."

"That was the easy part. I'm talking about running to specialists who think up tests to humiliate you and your husband. But I did it. And Jack went too because he loved me. Would you have done as much for Susan? Do you know what she's suffered since you left? Do you know that sometimes, when I'm over there, she excuses herself and goes into another room to cry."

"Enough!" She's trying to hurt me—out of some long-closeted jealousy I think. "I'm not listening anymore." I move to get up.

"I should have told you how I felt. When you separated. Instead of now. When it's too late to do anything about it."

I clear my throat. "I . . . I always thought we were friends—"

"If I didn't care about you, I wouldn't say a word. I'm just sorry, sorry that now I'm speaking out and it's too late."

When Jack comes down he looks from one to the other. "What was all the hollering?"

"Nothing," Pat says.

"Well, I heard you—"

"It's nothing."

But the visit is over. Slowly, the truth in what she said is sinking in. If I'd stayed married, given the extra effort, if I hadn't been pressed by the need to provide for two households, well, it's unlikely I would have gambled with Larry Dexter—or his mistress.

As I leave, Pat asks, "How much money do you have?"

"What?"

"Here." She pushes an envelope into my hand. "Pay me back when we sell that house."

Jack looks a little uneasy, but doesn't protest.

"I don't want your money, Pat."

"I wish we could do more."

I'm proud. But I'm also broke.

In my pickup, I count out ten one hundred dollar bills.

At home with those piles of documents, I take special care to examine Larry Dexter's credit card statements when he traveled abroad, the year he made over sixty thousand dollars with European Import Consultants.

Restaurant and hotel bills tell me that he stayed several nights in Vienna. I note the dates in chronological order. I find that while in Austria he incurred expenses on July 9, 10, and 14. Well, what happened to July 11, 12, and 13? Did he use cash those days? If so, why?

"I've got a theory," I excitedly tell Tim Regan over the phone. "Now. Don't laugh. But all this, particularly the three days where he didn't spend a dime on his credit cards. What does it suggest?"

"Oh," the lawyer muses, "the bank screwed up. It happens."

"He was in Vienna. Okay?"

"All right."

"And he used the cards for his room, for food, everything."

"Yeah."

"So. I figure. The three days he apparently used cash. It was because he'd gone someplace they didn't take credit cards. The East. Czechoslovakia. East Germany. Behind, well, back then it was still behind the Iron Curtain."

There is a pause. "So what?"

"So what? I told you what the Lundgrens said. And,

okay, it sounds wild. But they seem pretty sure about it. Larry's father was a communist."

"And you think—"

"I think it's possible that Larry was a communist himself. Or at least he dealt with communists."

"Dealt how?"

"I don't know. Maybe he was a spy. Some kind of spy."

There's a very long pause. "A spy?"

"Or he was selling secrets or something."

"What secrets did he have to sell?"

"I don't know. That's something we'd have to look into before—"

"Kevin, just because someone goes to Europe. Even to Eastern Europe. That doesn't make him a spy."

"Well . . . I'm not saying he was a spy. I'm just raising the possibility."

"Okay, so you've raised it. Now what?"

"I mean, Tim. The major thing here is sixty thousand dollars earned in a single year and where did it come from?"

He doesn't have an answer. And while he promises to pursue the matter with his sources in the state police, I don't know if I trust him to follow through. That plea bargain business sure shook my confidence in Tim.

"One more thing," he says. "Your friend Finnerty. The carpenter. His alibi is solid."

"And his cousin—"

"His cousin has resident alien status. There was a paperwork screw-up on him a few months ago, that's all. He's legal."

"Well, that's good then. John's probably in the clear. Probably."

It's not that I'm afraid to see her, but I quiz Terri Pratt on European Import Consultants by telephone. My tone is businesslike.

"I've never heard the name," she says. "I'm sorry."

"It's a company Dexter started. It was pretty successful about four years ago. Do you remember anything about it?"

"Sorry." She sounds genuinely disappointed.

"What do you know about Larry's trip to Europe a few years back?"

"It was business, wasn't it?"

"Yeah, but *what* business?"

"You know, if we got together, in person, I could remember better—"

"He went to Europe. He must have said what he was doing over there."

"He didn't. Honest. Lawyers aren't supposed to tell, you know?"

"What do you know about Larry's father?" I ask.

"Like what? What about his father?"

"Did he get along with him? Did he talk about him much?"

She sighs thoughtfully. "His father was from Poland or Switzerland or somewhere."

"Germany?"

"Somewhere like that. I remember Larry saying his father tried a lot of businesses but none of them really caught on. Larry's mother was always worried they'd be out on the street because the bills were never paid. And Larry didn't have nice clothes or a bike like other kids."

"Did he tell you his father was a communist?"

She kind of gasps. "No. Was he?"

"Did Larry ever talk about communism?"

"Larry never talked politics. Except who can get you jobs."

I let out a long, low groan of frustration.

"Want me to come over?" she asks.

"Listen. One other thing I want to ask about. Do you remember you once told me that John Finnerty didn't like you? Do you remember that?"

"I remember you had your hands down my pants and he walked in on us. I remember that."

"Yeah. Well, why doesn't Finnerty like you?"

"I don't know. I mean, I don't really know the man. It's just how he acted the few times I was around him."

"Do you know whether he was involved with Larry? I mean, *before* Indian Peak. Any involvement between those two?"

"I've never seen them together if that's what you mean. Why? Do you think he might have had something to do with Larry's murder?"

"I've got to run now, Terri."

"Please, can we talk a little longer?"

"I—Look, we'll talk later. I'll be in touch."

"I just want to say—"

"Bye."

To reach the place you have to walk uphill, through a stand of trees. The house is all crazy angles and built over an outcrop of granite. A few feet at one end actually cantilevers over the driveway.

I lean out of my pickup, toward Matt O'Keefe in his cruiser. "That's his address," Matt says. "Paul Koutrobis. Got a long record for house breaks."

"He's one of them?"

"We're pretty sure he was one of the kids who trashed the Indian Peak house. But the state police interviewed all of them. And they all tell the same story basically. The kids left about two A.M. None of them saw anything."

"You believe that?"

Matt shrugs. "You get ten kids in separately and they all tell the same story. I'd say you have to believe it."

I can't afford to believe it. Suppose one kid went back?

"Something else I heard." Matt looks reluctant to talk. "About Kikki Dexter. It's a rumor some of the detectives were talking about. They didn't think it was important, really. But I thought you should know about it." He leans closer. "Now you didn't hear this from me."

"Of course."

"It happened in Wollaston some time back. Quincy police got called into some Chinese restaurant to break up a disturbance. A shouting match or scuffle that involved Larry Dexter, Kathleen Dexter, and a second man."

"A second man? Who?"

"I don't know."

"What was the fight about? When did this happen?"

"I'm telling you, Kevin, this is a rumor. It didn't come with details."

"So you don't know for sure if it even happened?"

He pauses. "Well. I think, from what I've heard, it happened. But because someone had influence there was no report and there's no record."

"Are the state police looking into this? They're not, are they?"

Matt shrugs. "They say there's nothing to it. And maybe there isn't."

Nevertheless, I will pass the information along to Tim Regan.

This guy in a wool pullover answers the door, looking tired, like he's just home from work. "Sorry to bother you. Mr. Koutrobis?"

"Conley. Fred Conley."

"Oh." I'm confused, wondering if Matt pointed me to the wrong address. "I'm looking for Paul Koutrobis, Junior."

"Jesus Christ. You're not with the police, are you?"

"I just—"

"You better talk to his mother." He closes the door. I hear harsh voices, but can't make out the words until a woman cries bitterly, ". . . and his name's *not* the little bastard."

Opening the door, she's surprisingly young, giving me a quick, cold glance. "You're not with the police."

"No. I told your husband—"

"Paul's been clean for months now. He's really trying."

"Mrs. Conley, I'm not a police officer. I'm involved

in . . . a litigation. And I want to talk to Paul as a potential witness. That's all."

"A witness? Like to a traffic accident?"

"That's right. That's it exactly."

"Well . . . I'm—" Her manner changes. "I'm sorry for what I said. See, uh, Paul used to run with a tough crowd. Uh, how can I help you?"

"I need to talk to Paul."

She glances behind. "I'm afraid Paul's not home at the moment."

"I can come back."

She grows still more uncomfortable.

"I can come back at nine? Ten? Eleven?"

"Ah . . ." Apparently, she just doesn't know where the kid is.

"Maybe he's at a friend's house," I suggest.

"He was going with a girl. Bonnie Levin."

I take down the name. Before I leave she reaches out, "Uh, if you do find him, could you ask him to call home?"

The Levins live in a simple garrison with a small front yard and conservation land out the back. Mrs. Levin explains, "We haven't seen Paul in months. Bonnie doesn't see Paul anymore. Isn't that right?"

Bonnie sits at the supper table with her younger brother. She's attractive in a tight sweater, gold bracelet and earrings. Brown hair touched with blonde sweeps to her shoulders. I have to look a moment before realizing she's only fourteen or fifteen, not much older than Molly.

"Bonnie?" the mother asks. "Isn't that right?"

"Isn't what right, Mom?"

"That you don't see Paul anymore."

"I don't see Paul anymore. That's right."

"He's not in any trouble," I say. "I only want to talk to him because of this litigation. There could be some financial reward."

"Money?" Bonnie comes upright.

"We haven't seen him," the mother says, "and we're not likely to."

Walking slowly down the driveway, I spot her in the bushes. How she got here so fast I can't say.

"Hey mister," Bonnie asks, "how much money is Paul gonna get?"

We take a long walk, skirting the Levin's yard to the conservation land in back. It's quite dark as we pass into the forest. "Where we going?" I have trouble keeping up. I'm barely able to see the street lights through a tangle of branches. God knows what might come leaping out of the dark.

We stop at what I slowly perceive is a wooden ladder climbing to—of all things—a tree house, a weathered plywood box balanced on two sturdy limbs. Yellow light seeps from a trap door at the bottom.

Bonnie turns. "Don't tell my mom about this. Okay?" She climbs.

Paul Koutrobis is camped out with a space heater, portable TV, Coleman lantern, and a supply of beer. The tree house smells and there's barely room to lie down, but it's warm, insulated with old blankets hung from the walls and ceiling. Paul is wrapped in a sleeping bag. He greets Bonnie with a belch, "Sugar ass," lunging for her crotch.

"Paul!"

I emerge from the trap door, standing on the ladder, watching him retreat into the corner. He says, "What'd you bring him here for? Jesus." It's as if he knows who I am.

"I'd like to ask you a few questions, Paul."

"Hey, I don't have to fucking talk to you."

"I thought you'd rather talk than face charges of breaking and entering."

"No way. Cops promised if I cooperated they'd be no charges."

I climb a few more rungs until I'm sitting inside, legs dangling. The lantern makes a hiss, casting sinister shadows on the walls. Empty beer cans and pizza remains are piled in the corner.

"First. Who's Lisa?"

"I don't know what the fuck you're talking about."

"Lisa?" Bonnie turns to Paul. "Who's Lisa?"

"Shut up."

"Well, I have a right to know—"

"I said shut up." And he actually pushes her.

God I don't like that, pushing a little girl. But I hold my temper, saying, "Tell me about the Dexter murder."

"I don't know nothing about no murder."

"Murder!" Bonnie pulls away, astonished, frightened.

See, I don't like this kid, I don't like his setup or the way he treats this little girl. How do kids end up this way?

"You broke into my house at Indian Peak. On the day Larry Dexter was murdered. You were there. You wrote 'Lisa' on the walls. And I don't believe this shit about leaving at two A.M. Where'd you have to go at two A.M.?"

"None of your business."

"Did Dexter find you in the house? Is that what happened?"

"You better get out of here, man."

God damn! He's not going to talk. Suddenly he's in my hands. "I want answers!" My teeth clenched, I've got his coat front clutched like a ball and his eyes are saucers and he doesn't dare move.

"I didn't do nothing, don't hit me, don't hit me." His tone is much changed. "We partied, then everybody left. I came here to sleep. That's true. I'm telling the truth."

"He is!" Bonnie pleads. "Leave him alone!"

I release him, take a deep, calming breath. God, got to keep control or I'll wind up back in jail. "What did you see that night, Paul?"

"What?" He's straightening his coat, rubbing his throat.

"Did you see or hear anything out of the ordinary?"

Slowly, he shakes his head.

"Anyone who shouldn't have been there?"

Suddenly his eyes brighten. "A van or pickup or something. I guess it was a pickup truck. We had to hide. It parked in front of the other house for a while. Somebody making out. But they must have had a fight because they didn't stay long."

"Did you actually see them? Did you see what they were doing?"

"Well, no. It was dark and—"

"Can you describe the truck?"

He's shaking his head. "Just, just one of those pickup trucks."

"Did you tell this to the police?"

"No. I didn't, didn't remember it until just now when you asked me."

At a red light I scribble down my impressions of Paul Koutrobis.

The kid *was* there. He's got a police record for drug dealing and he surely uses the stuff himself. And that's a possible wild card, because who knows that these drugs can't transform a whiny teenager into a killer.

But Koutrobis couldn't kill anyone. I'm amazed how he let me push him around. More intriguing is his story of the pickup truck. Of course, it might be completely unconnected to the murder. And, no doubt, if the police find out they'll simply add it to the case against me, assuming it was my pickup and that I was out there scheming to kill Dexter in the morning.

Nonetheless, I can't forget someone else who drives a pickup truck—Big John Finnerty.

· 8 ·

By the time I reach the cottage road, I'm wondering more and more about John Finnerty. Why had he told me about Pete's problems with Dexter? Was it a clumsy attempt to deflect me from any inquiries along those lines? My speculation is interrupted when, pulling into my driveway, I see a note protruding from my mailbox.

It is crudely printed in pencil on a torn brown paper bag. "Information essential to your defense. Time: one hour past midnight. Place: beach parking lot across Long Bridge. Walk across the bridge so I will be sure you are alone. Involve the police or anyone else and you will never hear from me again." It is not signed.

I'm elated. Surely, someone out there knows I am innocent and is willing to help prove it!

"Sounds like a joke," Tim Regan says over the phone. "It sounds like the Hardy Boys. Someone's having fun with you."

"Maybe." I remember the crank calls. "But I don't mind going."

"Now, wait. Wait. Because regardless of how it sounds,

going out there in the middle of the night could be danger-ous."

"I'll just have a look, Tim."

"No."

"I don't even have to get out of my truck. I'll see if there's anybody I recognize. I could take down tags. Like that."

"This is not a game, Kevin. There's somebody out there who doesn't mind killing people."

"Whoever killed Larry is going to leave well enough alone. He wants me alive and on trial. You know, I'll bet I'm the least likely guy to get murdered in this whole business."

Tim says, "I think I'll drop dead from shock if you ever took my advice."

"The way I see it, I've got no choice. If I don't go, I see myself. And I'm in prison. I'm wondering what I would have heard on that bridge. And I'm in prison and I've got my whole life to lie there thinking about it."

I leave after midnight. Only a block from my cottage I pass Terri's car traveling in the opposite direction. I hear her horn, but pretend not to notice.

Long Bridge spans a gut of ocean to connect the mainland with a sandy, uninhabited island. I hadn't expected it to be so forbidding. A lone street light on the island illuminates the beginnings of the deserted parking lot and the cold dunes behind it. I'm sure as hell not walking this sucker.

On the other hand, I feel reasonably secure pulling onto the bridge in my warm, powerful pickup. When I reach the opposite side I stop, roll down my window, and listen. Icy cold. I hear only the wind off the water.

The parking lot is long and narrow. Across the inlet are the lights of huge ocean-front homes. But the water itself is black, not even reflecting the lights. I drive for several minutes looking in vain for a car or person. The place is deserted. God, I've been a fool!

I turn the truck quickly. No doubt someone delivered the note as a ploy to get me out of the cottage. At this moment they're stealing my VCR and television, or ransacking the place for information. They want to know how close I am to Larry Dexter's killer. (The truth should give them comfort.)

I approach the bridge, moving pretty fast. Damn, this business is discouraging. I've been working hard to prove my innocence, working for days with—let's stop kidding ourselves here—nothing concrete to show for it.

You know, it's almost as if someone knew everything about me. He knew the perfect time to kill Larry, when suspicion would inevitably fall on me. Now, who knew me so well?

Jam on the brakes! I slide to a halt on frozen sand. "Jesus," I say aloud.

I haven't seen a soul on this island. Yet someone has stretched a chain across the parking lot entrance. "Jesus, Mary, and Joseph." I lock my doors. Someone wants me trapped in here. In the middle of nowhere.

"Shit." Is someone coming out of the dark, coming for me the way they came for Larry?

Okay. Keep cool. Let's calmly assess the situation. It's a thick steel chain stretched between two cement posts. Can I get around it? Piled to the right is a bank of boulders, to the left, sand dunes. Room enough for pedestrians only to pass.

All right. Maybe the chain is just wrapped around the post and easily taken down. Rising to see over the hood of my vehicle, I can't really tell.

I leave the truck reluctantly. Make this quick. I find one end of the chain is bolted into the thick cement pole; the other is held fast to an eyebolt by a very large steel lock.

I don't see anyone and I can't hear anyone. But the wind is blowing and I'm surrounded by sand dunes, fences, and brush. Whoever locked this gate could be mere feet away, unseen, waiting his chance.

"Now you've done it, asshole." I keep making wrong moves, trusting the wrong people. Timmy was right again.

Fetching a tire iron, I work to pry the lock free. By headlights, I grunt and pound. The wind blows so hard I can't hear the metal clanking on metal. The tire iron is almost too cold to touch.

I keep turning, as if I expect to see someone standing there with a nail gun. I wish I could hear better. If I'd asked Terri to come she could watch my back. But with friends like Terri . . .

Face it, whenever she's out of sight I don't trust her. She knew my situation, habits. More than anyone she was in a position to frame me. Is she capable of murder? Well, she dances round all the rules, why not that one?

Suppose Dexter promised to divorce Kikki and marry Terri. Suppose he strung Terri along for years with empty promises. I can guess how she'd feel. It makes you mad to be played for a fool, mad enough to kill.

Now I've got the iron jammed into the eyebolt. I try to pry it from the cement. I put all my weight and muscle and anger into it but the bolt holds fast while the tire iron actually begins to bend.

Look out. What was that? I swing round, gasping. I swear I heard something. But I see only sand and my own breath swirling skyward like a cloud. Got to get out of here.

I consider crashing through. I'll start at the back of the lot, get up steam, and snap the chain like a string.

But it's pretty damn thick. And low. It might just flatten my tires, burst my radiator, even flip me over. If I broke through clean, I would have to whip right to avoid the rocks. I could end up in worse shape.

Where I was sweating a moment ago, suddenly I'm just damp and shivering. My hands feel the undulations of cold pain. My nose is running. I climb back into the pickup, but carefully, checking all around.

I'm afraid. Okay, good. It won't kill you to be afraid.

Warming up, I curse my stupidity. Always listen to your lawyer. Who has trapped me here and why? Hey, I'm the guy least likely to be murdered!

I can stay all night. I've got enough gas to keep the heat going. By morning the cops will let me out. No problem. I put the pickup in drive and allow it to nudge the chain. Slowly, I depress the gas pedal.

The tires begin to spin. The chain grows taut, apparently across the front bumper. The speedometer reads twenty miles per hour. A huge brown cloud dances with the wind behind me. Sand and stones pepper the undercarriage like hail. More gas! Thirty-five, forty . . . The front bumper creaks as it slowly bends. The whole truck shakes. The smell of burning rubber fills the cab. The rear wheels begin sliding left.

I step off the gas, back up. The chain swings, undamaged.

Well, this is ridiculous. I mean, I've been out here playing around for twenty minutes or more. No one's going to attack me. There's bound to be some innocent explanation for this—though just now I can't imagine what it might be. Anyway, a ten-minute walk across the bridge will get me safely into one of those houses over there.

There's nothing to stop the wind out here on the bridge. I wish I'd dressed warmer. As a precaution, I tuck the tire iron beneath my arm. It's cold as an icicle.

My hands, deep in my pockets, are jammed into fists and still ache. I can't feel my toes. Oh, to be warm, snug in bed under piles of blankets.

The bridge is remarkable, made entirely of wood, including a narrow sidewalk. Very quickly I am one quarter of the way across. Water laps at the pilings beneath my feet.

Pick up the pace. Get the old heart pumping to defeat the cold. Behind me, the single street lamp illuminates my truck, which waits faithfully for the silvery chain to be removed.

God, I can't get my mind off this cold. I'll be in one of those houses soon. Come sit beside the fire. What fool locked the gate with you still inside? I hold out my hands to a crackling hot flame.

Halfway. Keep moving. If something was going to happen it would have happened by now.

Except that now I see headlights.

"Christ."

I just stop. I'm not thinking of the cold anymore.

I can't tell how fast the car is moving. It's on the bridge, coming from the mainland, coming toward me.

It could be the police or lovers come to park, or a driver making a wrong turn. It could be anyone. Slowly, I resume walking. I don't take my eyes off the car.

His high beams come on. My hand rests on the tire iron. Where do I go if he tries to run me down? And the car—what a relief—slows, coming to a stop mere feet away. I stay on the sidewalk as the door opens and the driver pokes his head up.

He's about medium height. I can't really see him with high-beams in my eyes. But if he meant to do harm the ideal weapon was his car. Right?

"Trouble?" he asks.

"Yeah, I'm afraid somebody shut the gate with me inside."

"Gate?"

"A chain," I point. "Someone locked me in with a chain."

"What?" He leaves his car, looking at the truck off in the distance.

"Someone took a chain and locked me in." I point again just as I'm hammered, sent staggering, the world gone red. The tire iron thunks on the deck. I reach for the railing. Miss it.

I'm falling. Can't help it. Shot. Or struck on the head. Oh, God.

But I don't fall. Instead, I find myself rising, incredibly. I'm in his arms. Something has hit me from behind and this stranger saves me. He grunts. I feel the top of the rail, the wind, and nothing. I float on air.

But not for long.

The second shock is striking the water, hitting so hard I think for a moment it must be iced over. I'm going under. My face gets colder as I drop down and down. I wonder why I don't float anymore.

I must, must take a breath! I fight my way to the surface. "Ahhhh . . ." Gasping for air, I get a gulp of salt water instead. Coughing, choking, I must not panic. The freezing ocean penetrates my clothes. For a moment I feel nothing, then awful pain. Can't . . . can't breathe.

My work shoes are dead weights. Kick them off! I thrash about, raising my head above the choppy waves. A breath. Thank God. I'm breathing.

It is not the end of my problems, just the beginning. In the middle of the gut. In deep water. I am fighting cold and the waves. Half a mile from shore. It seemed so far to walk. Now I must swim.

"Help," I shout at the man on the bridge. Surely, he will not stand by and watch me die. But I can't see him or his car. "Help!" Nor does he answer my desperate screams.

"You son of a bitch!" I want to kill him. I would throw him in here. Watch him struggle and not raise a finger to help. I vow to get revenge on the bastard. Track him down and kill him. If I live.

"God, God, God." Keep your head up.

Get moving. Only minutes remain before the freezing Atlantic sucks the warmth of life from my body.

"Help," I shout into the wind, hoping someone ashore will hear. "Help."

I swim. Water slaps at my face. My muscles contract painfully. My head aches. I'm sick to my stomach as if I'd been kicked square in the balls.

Ignore it and swim. Swim with your arms. My coat is getting in the way. But keep it on. For warmth. It will retain heat.

I can't go more than a few strokes without stopping. Moaning all the time. Blood retreats to protect the heart and brain from the cold . . . but I need arms and legs to survive.

My hair is coated with ice. My teeth chatter uncontrollably. My lips are so numb I'm not sure when my mouth is closed, and I'm constantly swallowing salt water.

I push off on one of the pylons beneath the bridge. I use

my hands, but feel nothing. It's as if I have no fingers or toes. My limbs are stumps.

I kick hard, passing another pylon. I repeat the names of my children, "Molly. Michael. Molly," like a prayer. It's cold. But people swim in the winter for sport. If they can survive, so can you.

Only it's so far away and already—ominously—the pain begins to fade. "Help, God. Oh. Someone." And I panic, deciding that I haven't traveled any distance at all.

Current. The current is playing a cruel trick. It defeats all your efforts, Kevin. Swim and swim. Fight like hell. But you don't move an inch because *you're swimming against the current*. Somewhere, someone is having a good laugh. Look at him thrashing like a crazy man, getting nowhere.

I'm dying. Sad and frightening. I could cry. Because I don't deserve this. It isn't right. Isn't fair.

What'll my kids think?

Guilt-ridden, the suspect in the Dexter murder has committed suicide, throwing himself into the freezing ocean off Long Bridge.

After I promised them that everything was going to be all right. God . . . let them forgive me for not being stronger. I sink completely under the water, dropping for the last time.

And I feel something. Just barely . . . what, what's that? *There!* Almost convulsively, I plunge my legs down. I can stand! Incredible. I'm still nowhere near the end of the bridge, but in the dark I see that much of what I'd taken for ocean is in fact mud. The shoreline is actually quite close.

Swimming, leaping, pushing off rocks, I am rejuvenated. Quickly in waist-high water, I slosh forward. "Help, help, help, help." Once I stumble face first in sea water, but I get up. The waves are at my knees.

I feel somewhat warmer, which is to say the numbness fades and everything hurts worse. I cough, spitting, clearing my nose and throat. I crave warmth. I'm not saved yet.

A thin crust of ice covers the goo at the water's edge. Each step brings a tinkle like breaking glass. I stagger, sway, almost fall, but I have not fallen. I'm lurching forward. "Help, help, help."

Anger returns. Staying alive was an incredible achievement. Someone should be here to take note and help me off to blankets and hot water bottles. Look out your windows, goddammit! What's wrong with you people? Don't you care about anyone but yourselves?

"Owwwwww!" I screech and no one hears. The nearest house is still many yards away and I can barely walk. My skin is a suit of pain aggravated every time I move.

I emerge, gasping, from a stand of reeds quite close to the bridge, but my foot, which I cannot exactly feel, gets tangled. I pitch forward, splat into the mud. And I don't want to get up.

I hurt. Nothing easy about freezing to death. And then there's that point where you'd rather quit. Get up and blood circulates faster. It brings pain wherever it goes.

I raise up on my hands, but my arms wobble and I fall back down. Can't. Just can't do it. I rest the side of my face on the icy mud. The wind sings, cutting through the bridge with a mournful wail. How sad. Then, footsteps. And I know.

He watched the whole time, to make certain I went under. He will come now and press my face into the mud.

I must be more alive than I realize, because I'm afraid. I try to crawl backwards, into the reeds, but I don't get far. And he comes right at me, saying, "What . . . what in the name of God?"

I crane my neck, groaning.

"Kevin? Is that you?"

I blink up at Tim Regan.

"They say there's a bad current and no one knows why you weren't carried out to sea." Susan speaks softly.

"Somebody up there likes me—now and then." I sit up in my hospital bed. "If Tim hadn't come looking for me I'd still be there, frozen stiff in the mud."

"He told me he saw your truck, but he couldn't find you. He was about to leave when he just happened to see something. He didn't know what. But he went out to have a look. And thank God he did. Thank God."

She says it as if my survival really matters to her. "And you don't know who pushed you?"

"No." I could pick out his voice in a crowded room. But his face remains a specter, vague, hovering over the rail, haloed by high beams, watching at his leisure as I struggle and drown.

"Did the police have any ideas?" Susan asks.

"The police." I give a bitter laugh. "They think I jumped."

"Jumped? And do they think you hit yourself on the back of the head? My God, what's wrong with those people?"

"If I was going to jump," I wince, trying to wiggle my toes, "I would have jumped closer to shore. And closer to July."

She smiles. "It's good you still got your sense of humor."

"Yeah." I try to smile back, but it's really not funny. Everything has changed. I'm not waiting for a trial somewhere in the future. Someone tried to kill me. The guy is still out there.

"The kids wanted to come," Susan says.

"Tell them I was thinking of them. Uh, tell them that's what kept me alive. Thinking of them . . . of my family." I can't look her in the eye as I say this because I don't want to cry.

We talk about the kids. Susan leans close, her eyes warm, voice filled with concern. I feel a little thrill. But it ends abruptly when we look to find Terri Pratt at the door, a heart-shaped box of candy clutched to her chest.

Terri's very tentative smile dissolves when she sees the dark look on my face. See, I'm wondering at the coincidence of passing her on the road to Long Bridge. Did she rush to phone an accomplice: "He's on his way"?

"Ahh . . . ah, I'll come back later. I . . . I just stopped to see how you were doing and . . . and drop," she places the candy on a chair, "drop this off."

"Thank you."

"Also," she continues, "there was something I wanted to tell you. Something I remembered about, uh, Larry, that might be helpful."

"What's that?" I come up so fast that Susan reaches to restrain me.

"Well, I can tell you another time. It's nothing major . . . ah, well . . . you look good. Considering . . ." It's a moment before she leaves.

For a long time Susan stares at the empty doorway. "I better go."

"Don't."

She stands and gives that tight little smile of hers. "Take care of those toes. Wouldn't want to lose them."

"You don't have to go, Susan."

"I don't want to keep you from your friend."

"She's not coming back. Don't be like that, Susan."

"Like what?" Still smiling. "Really, I have to go."

She leans over, pats my head (for a second I think she's going to kiss me). "Thank God you're safe, Kevin." Her eyes fill for a moment. "Thank God."

Evening. The hospital corridors are quiet. For the second time, they have asked all visitors to leave. Pat Lundgren is uneasy, sitting in a corner behind a large curtain. "Don't go yet," I urge.

"They're going to kick me out."

"The nurse already came by. She didn't see you." I get up. "Excuse my wardrobe." Holding the back of the johnny together, I hop painfully to the door. The nurses are preoccupied at their station.

"You shouldn't be on your feet," Pat says.

"You're telling me." I stagger to bed. "Jesus." It's a moment before I can speak; my feet and fingers throb. "Listen, Pat. Remember when you hollered at me the other night? You said it was for my own good. Because you cared. Remember? Well, you said you cared. And I'm calling you on it."

"What . . . what do you mean?"

Standing, I reach for the closet. "I want you to get me out of here."

"I . . . I don't follow."

Clothes in hand, I slump onto the bed. "I want you to drive me home."

"But the doctor—"

"Someone is trying to kill me, Pat. What's to stop him from coming up here tonight and putting a pillow over my head while I sleep?"

"But you could lose your toes—"

"I could lose more than my toes staying here." I unroll my trousers. "I'm going to put my clothes on. Please watch the door?"

I escape down the back stairs. In my stocking feet—I can't put on my shoes—I must stop every few steps. It feels as though my feet and hands are expanding, purplish skin stretched to the breaking point.

Pat brings the station wagon to the side door. I hop to it. As we drive away I am trying not to groan. "My place."

"If you're not safe in the hospital," Pat asks, "what makes you think you'll be safe at your place?"

"I never said I'd be safe. Safer."

"Come to our house." She looks over. "At least for tonight. You can sleep without worrying."

She grips the steering wheel so hard that her knuckles whiten.

"Who could have done it?" asks Jack Lundgren.

"I wish I knew." I drain a second glass of milk at their kitchen table.

"Horrible," Pat mutters, "horrible."

"Not altogether. Because what they tried to do to me, that told me something. That told me that the killer is afraid. Because I've brushed close to the truth, see? I've asked something or heard something they didn't want me to hear."

"What?" Pat asks.

"I don't know." I start to stand, but pain brings me quickly back down. "It also proves that Larry's murder wasn't some random thing. It wasn't some drifter or crazy who's gone off somewhere. Larry was murdered by someone I know. Or someone I could get at if I keep working, keep looking."

"But it couldn't have been someone you know," Jack suggests. "You say you didn't recognize the guy."

"I didn't recognize him. No. But then again, I didn't get a real good look at him either. And there's also the possibility that the guy was sent."

"Sent. You mean like a hit man?"

I ask, "Do I know anyone who could get a man to kill for him? Or her?"

"Pretty remarkable person," Pat observes. "Points a finger. And someone is killed."

In fact, I can think of several people who could be capable, for example, Kathleen Foley Dexter. While murder might be a little out of her father's line, he's a man with vast contacts and clout.

John Finnerty has an endless supply of rough and ready cousins to call on.

At last, I must consider Terri. Because she is remarkable in her way and no doubt a man might kill for her. "You guys remember Terri's husband?"

"Eddie?" Pat asks.

"Do you know where he is? Terri told me he was in California."

"He's up the North Shore," Jack says. "Still with the phone company."

I remember distinctly Terri saying her husband had gone to California after their separation. A pretty sad picture she drew then, mother of three left alone.

Another lie added to her collection.

"I don't remember," I continue, "Eddie Pratt. He was . . . how big was he?"

"About average size," Pat explains.

"Physically fit?"

Jack says, "A lineman. That's a very physical job. Besides, he works out."

"He's big enough he could lift me? And toss me over a railing?"

No one denies the possibility.

I'm uneasy, sleeping downstairs in the basement guest room. But I'm mad too. There's something humiliating about being unceremoniously knocked on the head and dumped into the sea. I'm tired of taking all the punches. Sometime soon I'm going to start giving them out, so help me.

Don't tell Tim Regan, but William P. Foley, Sr., has agreed to see me. I was pretty surprised myself, working out the whole thing on the phone through his very doubtful housekeeper.

Dollar Bill Foley made a reputation moving behind the scenes in a national campaign long ago. They say he's still consulted by the senior U.S. senator. Larry Dexter surely sought his father-in-law's advice on matters great and small. And I remain convinced that Foley's hand is behind much that has happened to me—the high bail, for example.

First, I walk past his house twice. This can't be it. The Foley place is tucked between two decaying three-deckers and badly wants painting.

The grey-haired housekeeper swallows hard when she sees me. I'm as inoffensive as can be, but whichever side of the room I am on, she slides off to the other. This is what bad media will do for you.

I'm escorted down the hall, which smells of cigar smoke.

The furnishings are nice, but clearly, the old guy hasn't bought anything new in two decades. (I guess he's been a widower that long.)

I find him behind a desk, in polka dot pajama pants and a T-shirt. This get-up might reflect eccentricity, or it might be calculated to show me my station. Foley is bald and fat, his sparkling blue eyes incongruously young.

To one side of the desk is a large, green oxygen tank, the mask hung atop it. The walls are covered with portraits, mostly of Kikki and a younger boy—no doubt the brother who is Kikki's alibi. Peeking over Foley's head, looking me right in the eye, is a bust of John F. Kennedy.

"I'm grateful you agreed to see me, Mr. Foley." I'm also confused to see him alone save the housekeeper. Isn't he afraid that I might be dangerous? I listen for bodyguards lurking nearby, but hear nothing. "Uh . . . could I maybe sit down?"

"You think you're going to be here that long?" His voice is clear, full of vinegar. Apparently, Bill Foley fears little—and he wants me to know it.

I must hunt up a chair in the adjacent living room. Actually, it's the bench for a baby grand piano. I drag it over. "I was surprised you agreed to see me at all. And grateful. I'm sure you must think—"

"I was curious. I said Ha, tell the son of a bitch to come over. I have to see a man with balls that big."

"I don't know if this does any good, Mr. Foley. But I didn't kill Larry."

"Do tell."

"No really, I'm—"

"Mr. Bourque. I'm a lawyer fifty years. All that time I dealt with politicians. I've heard the best liars in the world."

"I'm not lying."

"Whatever you're doing. Get to the point and get out."

"I'd like to ask some questions. Because, I mean, possibly Larry told you things that could prove my innocence. He wouldn't get involved in a deal like Indian Peak without, somewhere along the line, going to you for advice."

"Advice?"

"At least he might have told you something, something about how he was raising money. That's mainly what I want to know. About the money."

"He never came to me for advice."

"I see."

"As to how he was raising money, I can answer that."

I lean forward.

"He was trying to borrow from me. But I gave him money in the past and I wouldn't give him more. I told him so."

I'm stopped. If Foley was Larry's secret source of capital, it wrecks my theory of a link between the money and his murder. Surely this old man didn't roll his own son-in-law downstairs and nail his head to the floor. Or did he? Is it too fantastic to speculate that he arranged such a thing?

Don't underestimate him, I remind myself. This is a man whose voice was heard when judges were appointed and attorneys general selected. And you don't amass that kind of power by reciting the rosary.

I ask, "When did this happen, sir?"

"When did what happen? When did I turn him down? I turned him down more than once because he wouldn't quit. Very persistent fellow, Mr. Dexter. Should have been a peddler." He stares as if he wants my comment.

"He had . . . a lot of energy and enthusiasm. Larry."

"Tell you frankly, Kathleen Foley was courted by the sons of the most important men in this state. In the country. And they were impressed. I'd hear from their fathers. And if she'd just given one of them half a chance . . . But she wanted *him*."

"Mr. Foley, when did you give Larry the final turndown on the loan?"

"Around Halloween. I suggested if he needed money, he should rob the Brinks. I was blunt, so even Mr. Dexter had to accept my answer as final."

Fall. But Larry was still promising his "secret reserve" only days before his death. The questions remain, did he even then have some hope of wheedling the money away from the old man, or did he have another scheme in mind? Or was it all just so much hot air?

"Larry ran this outfit, European Import Consultants. Ever hear of it?"

"No."

"Do you know why he went to Europe four years ago?"

"No."

I'd feel better if he gave these answers some thought. "This company. It made eighty, more than that, over eighty thousand dollars. Importing. Or helping somebody to import something, I don't know what."

"Art?"

I sit right up. "What . . . why art?"

"That's what his old man did after the war." Foley reaches for the key prop of his era, a big cigar. He takes a quick look-out for the housekeeper and lights it. I lean away from the stink. "I bought that from him." He points the cigar at a small religious painting on the wall behind me. On wood, in the style and size of the Lundgrens' Jesus, this one portrays the Blessed Virgin.

I stand, peering closely at the thing. "Is that antique? You think he made eighty thousand importing paintings?"

He laughs. "I paid a hundred bucks for it. I doubt it's worth twenty. They make 'em at some goddamn factory. So it's as phony as he was. But, it's going to make you think. Because when Dexter's old man did business with the Bolsheviks, he dealt in real antique art. Got it cheap all over Eastern Europe. I researched the man, so I know. Of course, he was a red himself, the father. You won't understand what that meant back then. Nowadays you can't get tenure at a state college unless you're a goddamn Marxist."

I nod. Keep him talking.

"Dexter's father. Whatever his name was because it wasn't Dexter. Bastard was a red. A bush league Armand Hammer. Importing from behind the Iron Curtain through some sort of cover. And he got caught. It's all forgotten now. But the point is, this was a sorry excuse for a man. In my opinion. No loyalty to the country that took him in. No loyalty to his family. Abandoned his family. Divorced his wife. And if the father will do that—I warned Kathleen—if the father will do that, the son will do it too."

He points the cigar at me, "That doesn't mean anything to you either. Divorce, communism. We're all so sophisticated about such things today."

"I didn't—"

"It's the fashion to live like an alley cat. I don't say we were saints in my day. But a man stayed with his family. Was a disgrace if he didn't. Men today. They've got three wives and two children by each. Can't pay the bills so the state does it for them. It's a different world. Years ago, they used to scare us. They used to say, 'If the reds take over, the government will steal your kids and raise them.' Today. People run around with signs, *Please, government, take my kids.* Ha. They're all begging their way into slavery."

He looks away now. "I have a son. I can't tell you the things he did. Deliberately. To embarrass and humiliate his mother and me. Police at the house all the time. But we didn't abandon him. Because he was mentally ill. You understand? Took me a long time. But I came to see that this, this did not reflect on me. It was no disgrace or failure. No more than if he'd gotten polio. A misfortune and a tragedy, but not a disgrace. You see?"

He looks over at a picture of the boy, about ten, smiling, without a care. "His mother and me. We were up that hospital every week. Kikki too. Sometimes twice a week. I still see him, send a few bucks when I can. See, it's not always easy but you stand by your family. And then one day, when you find yourself in trouble, maybe they'll stand by you."

Clearing my throat, I ask, "Were Larry and Kikki breaking up?"

"He wasn't much use. But he stayed with her. I'll give him that. And Kathleen. With all she's been through. Losing . . ." He pauses and for an instant his eyes go dead. "Losing the little boy . . . She'd no more leave her husband than join the Moonies."

He holds out the cigar, staring at the end of it. "Years

ago, I had him followed. And it didn't take long before we had something. But Kathleen . . . I could have gotten her an annulment. I'd even spoken to the cardinal. But she . . . she tore the pictures up without looking at them. See, we taught her loyalty. To respect her vows. And she stood by what we'd taught." A difficult breath, and he flicks ashes into a huge glass ashtray. "That's one reason I didn't give him money. I could guess where it went. Whoever killed him, it could just as well have been a jealous husband."

"You don't think I did it?"

"I don't think about you, Mr. Bourque."

"Then why have you been trying to keep me in jail?"

"Who says I have?"

"And you don't know about someone pushing me off Long Bridge?"

He laughs. "Throwing people off bridges. That was never my style."

"Your style is pulling strings."

"If I knew for certain that you'd hurt my girl, Mr. Bourque, I tell you true, I wouldn't pull strings. And I wouldn't throw you off bridges so you could swim to shore. And you wouldn't leave this house alive."

Limping for my car, I find a police officer watching from his cruiser. His partner hurries past to confirm that all is well at the Foley place.

Speeding away, what sticks in my head, oddly enough, is Foley's painting of the Virgin Mother. I remember the bribe to Mr. Rapolli of the state environmental office. And I remember Larry Dexter one afternoon at Indian Peak, thrusting a package on a wild-looking temporary employee, who then roared away. In fact, the parcel was exactly the size of the paintings that Bill Foley and the Lundgrens bought from Larry.

I've set up a motion detector at the foot of my bed. The switch is on my night table. It's a sort of box with a grill, and according to the instructions anyone moving in front of it will set off a loud wail.

I don't think I could sleep without the thing. Last night, I woke several times, expecting to find someone hovering over me in the dark. For defense I've left a huge iron wrench at the bedside.

· 9 ·

In the morning, I phone a travel agent to ask about Trans-Atlantic, the now-defunct airline that flew Larry Dexter to Europe four years ago. The payment had been quite large.

"Their record keeping was a disaster while they were in business," the agent says, "so don't expect any passenger list. I've got a rate book—I'll have to dig it out—that can give you the price for a first-class ticket back then."

A day passes before she comes back with the surprising information. Even first class, round trip, costs about half of what Dexter paid.

So, isn't it reasonable to conclude that he did not travel to Europe alone? And I begin to imagine who he might have gone with, what they might have done, and how it all led to murder.

Terri pulls into my driveway one evening, just as I am pulling out. She rolls down her window. "Where have you been? I've been calling. I've been so worried. How's your recovery going?"

"I'm going over to baby-sit my kids."

"Oh, over Susan's house. I see." She cranes her neck, looking up. "Are we ever going to get together to talk, Kevin?"

"Sure, I guess."

"When?"

I look up the street, then back. "I've been wanting to ask you, Terri. Where were you going when I saw you that night?"

"What? When you saw me what night?"

"The night I got attacked. I passed you on the road and you blew your horn. I'm just asking where you were going?"

She's shaking her head. "Me? You saw me? I don't think so. I had to work that night. I was working. You didn't see me."

And maybe I didn't. I suddenly remember that I saw the car and not the driver. Well, there are plenty of cars on the road just like hers.

"Where's your husband, Terri? He's not in California. Is he?"

"Why should he be in California?"

"Because that's where you told me he was."

She scrunches up her face in puzzlement. Christ, maybe she should have been an actress. "He's living in Revere."

"Then he's in two places at once?"

"No. I told you—"

"What?"

"I wish you wouldn't look like one wrong word and you're going to pounce on me."

I glance away. "I'm just waiting for the explanation."

"It's simple. When we split, yeah, Eddie went to California like I said. He took a pile of our money and had a good time for himself. But he came back. I mean he has a job and he came back to it. He still sees the girls."

"I got the idea he was out of your life." My voice isn't firm. Her explanation is simple and reasonable—and I feel oddly relieved about that.

She opens her door like she's going to come out and

stand alongside my pickup. "Don't do that," I say forcefully. "I've got to go. I'm late already."

So, she stays in her car, looking a bit confused. "Okay. Then, you maybe got the idea that Eddie was out of my life completely because I just never mentioned him. And the thing of that is, I don't talk about him when I'm with you." She looks down. "I suppose it sounds silly, but when I'm with you it's like there never was anyone else."

"What does he look like? Your ex-husband."

"He's . . . I don't know. He's ordinary. Fair. Fair skin, light brown hair, brown eyes. Why is this all of a sudden so important?"

"I'd like to see his picture."

"Okay. I can get one. That's no problem."

I look down the road. Despite myself, I want to stay and talk.

"Eddie and me, we have nothing to do with each other. Except for the kids. He's got a girlfriend he lives with."

"Okay, okay." Do I believe that? She's so good at explanations. "You were going to tell me something. Something about Larry Dexter."

"Oh, yeah," she says. "Unless, maybe you already know this."

"What?"

"A few years ago Larry was worried sick about the U.S. attorney. He didn't say, but I think he was afraid he'd be indicted."

"Indicted for what?"

"Something to do with immigration. Helping get people in the country who maybe they weren't supposed to be here."

Suddenly, I'm picturing John Finnerty, his Galway relations swarming all over the Indian Peak site. Hiring Finnerty had been my idea, but now I'm not sure if Larry hadn't brought up his name first: "How's about we get that mick friend of yours lives down on Old Oaken Bucket Road?"

Terri continues, "I know Larry did some work helping people bring their families in the country. Up in his office, once I saw an Iranian and that's what he was there for. I wondered how he knew to come to Larry way out in the suburbs. Another time he arranged for this guy to bring over a mail order bride from—I think it was Manila. I even met her."

Is it rather too convenient that this little tale points to Finnerty? I'd mentioned his name to Terri the last time we'd talked. While I try not to seem too excited, I'll certainly be asking Tim Regan to check on it.

"Well, if you think of anything else about this, let me know. Whatever you can remember I want to know."

"Don't go yet, Kevin."

"Terri, I'm late."

"I just want to say. It's . . . I don't think you're safe here." She nods at the cottage. "It's so isolated. And what they tried once they could try again."

An obvious point—but she's one of the few people besides me to raise it.

"Stay at my place. No one will know where you are. I've got a finished room downstairs. Or, you know, you can move in with me, in my room, if, if you want. The girls say you might as well move in. I talk about you so much."

"Oh, they can't wait to take in an accused murderer?"

"They don't think of you that way."

"Don't they read the papers?"

"They know you're innocent. We all do."

I grunt uncertainly.

"You'd be good for them, Kevin. Having a man around. It's important for young girls to have a father—I mean, you wouldn't be, I mean, you can leave when you want. When you think it's safe. I won't make any commotion."

I'm looking ahead, avoiding her eyes, her generous lips. Maybe I should take her at face value, maybe she's just in love with me. Maybe. "I've got to get going, Terri. I told you, I'm late."

"Well, will you think about it?"

"Yeah." I drop the transmission into drive. The pickup strains against the brake. "I'll think about it. And you get me that picture of Eddie."

* * *

The Pilgrim Trust is an ordinary suburban bank, but I dread coming here. I'm sure Mr. Simpson, the loan officer, thinks—along with most of the population—that I killed Larry Dexter.

The truth is, I don't like to go out at all anymore, except at night. In the dark, I feel secure in my truck, high above the traffic. (I made my mistake at Long Bridge in getting out of the truck.)

The place is swept by spotlights and everyone, customers and tellers, seems to look as I walk the blue carpet. It's as muffled as a library and I hear whispers. No doubt someone saying, "That's the guy with the nail gun."

Simpson ushers me to his office, a smoked-glass cubicle behind the tellers' windows. I shift in the chair, waiting for the moment when his eyes narrow, or he can't meet my gaze—because I'm a dangerous fellow. A killer.

Intead, I find that Simpson is consumed by money. He's asked me here because he's out on a limb over this loan. "The Pilgrim Trust does not want to foreclose, Mr. Bourque. As I told Mr. Dexter. It's in our interest that your project is a success, that you resume your schedule of payments."

"Yeah." He talks about Larry as if he's gone off on vacation.

As we go on, some kind of movement continually appears in the pebbled glass behind him. Distorted, almost surreal, I don't make sense of it at first. But I have the feeling of being spied on. Of course. It's the tellers, young women, passing on some errand and unable to resist a peek, probably through the quarter-inch, clear border where the glass meets the frame.

Come see the local murderer. God, I'm humiliated. I turn quite red.

Simpson shakes his head. "I spoke to Mr. Dexter of the possibility of some sort of financial bail-out."

"Uh . . . What?"

He glares. Nothing's more important than the loan.

"It's not bank policy, Mr. Bourque, and I shouldn't even

suggest this. But I know someone who is seeking a project exactly like the Indian Peak Corporation. Someone with the cash to keep you going. Shall I continue?"

"Well . . ." It's a strain to keep my mind on business. "Yeah."

"Understand, I don't guarantee anything. But if I had your permission, I could approach this potential investor on your behalf."

"I, I would appreciate it. Yes. Sounds good to me."

Damn. I hear giggling. Two or three people are out there. I'm not a goddamn circus, you know. "How long is this going to take?"

"How long is what going to take?"

"This. Being here."

"You've only just arrived, Mr. Bourque."

Goddamn, I bet they're calling their friends over for a peek.

You know, I'm the same guy who came in last month with Michael and everybody came around, "Isn't he cute, looks like his dad."

"I made this offer to Mr. Dexter. Did he tell you?"

"No. What? What offer?"

"To introduce him to a potential partner. Did he discuss it with you?"

I shake my head. "All he told me. He . . . he just told me not to worry. That he was taking care of the money."

"That's what he told me. He said he wasn't interested in partners. That he had the money. And the debts would be satisfied. Plus late penalty. Within days. Well, obviously, either he was wrong, or he failed to make the arrangements before, before . . ."

For the first time, Simpson squirms, looks down.

But he's told me something important. Larry was so certain of getting money—from somewhere—that he rejected an outside investor. It confirms that I've been on the right track from the beginning. Find the source of this money and discover the killer.

"Did Larry say where his money was coming from?"

"No."

"I mean, he didn't say anything? Anything? So, you could maybe make a guess where the money was coming from?"

"No. I have no idea where the money was coming from."

"What did he say?" I ask. "What were his exact words on this?"

"I'm sure it was pretty much as I've told you."

"He was murdered."

The bank official avoids my eyes. "So I understand."

"And I think his murder, and the money, they were connected."

Simpson gives me a brisk nod and then clears his throat. For a long time neither of us speaks.

"I . . . I wasn't the one who killed him."

"Uh . . . no."

The man swallows, his tie knot bobbing. He's not looking at the papers on his desk any longer. I don't think he believes me.

"I mean it. I didn't . . . k-kill him."

"Well. I expected as much, uh—"

Goddamn, there's another one. A face at the glass. I leap from my chair. "What is this? A goddamn sideshow?"

Simpson's open hands go up to his face, defensively.

I see a blur of dark hair, eyes, nose, mouth, frozen behind the glass.

"Why don't you just come in here and have a good look?!" I demand. I turn, wrenching open the door. "Here, I'll make it easy for you." I storm around the box-shaped office where I find a woman, a girl really, bent over . . . the coffee machine. She is literally shaking in fright.

I must be out of my head. You can't see through the pebbled glass. Business has stopped at the Pilgrim Trust. Everyone is staring at me for sure now. I turn, clasping my own hands. "Excuse me," I mumble.

I see the aged bank guard moving this way, reaching for his pistol. Jeez, I must have been loud.

"Excuse me," I tell Simpson, "I've made a mistake. I'm sorry."

I'm meek, soft-spoken. People begin to return to their work. "I'm under a lot of pressure just now."

"I . . ." Simpson is flushed, sweating, yet he tries to pretend that all is well. He blurts out, "I'll set something up with that investor."

"Yeah, sure, uh . . . I, I'd better go."

Tim Regan is very well dressed, a young bachelor with a gleaming red sports car. His cramped office reflects a somewhat different style. The desk top is hidden beneath piles of documents. I wonder darkly if anything vital to my case is buried there. I'm not surprised to learn the place was once a janitor's closet.

I'm careful to keep cool. I lost control back at the bank and misjudged the situation because of it. My very life depends on sound judgment. Where else have I gone off the track? Who or what else have I misjudged?

"I wish I could tell you different," Tim is saying. "The story checks out to a point. Yes, Kathleen Dexter and her husband got into a loud argument in a Chinese restaurant in Wollaston. About a year ago. The police were called. But, there was no question of a love triangle or anything of the sort. It was strictly an in-the-family squabble that got out of hand."

"They're covering up for someone."

"Come on, Kevin. Whole police departments haven't decided to frame you for murder. I mean, there are honest people in law enforcement. And besides, really, does Kathleen Dexter look like the kind of woman who meets strange men in Chinese restaurants?"

Picturing Kikki with her perpetual entourage of kiddies, I suppose he's got a point. Even so, I'm still not satisfied with the explanation.

"Now," Tim continues, "on Larry Dexter's background. I've got some information—I won't go into detail about how I got this—but some of it comes from state police sources and some of it from FBI files."

Tim pulls notes from his pocket. "Dexter's father was an Austrian, came to this country a few years prior to World War II."

"Prior?"

"Before the war. His name was Rudolph Dressler. He changed it to Dexter because it sounded more American. By all accounts, he wasn't a spy. There were rumors that he was a communist. But, then, during the war he was accused of being a Nazi. So take your pick. In fact, there's no record of any strongly held political convictions whatsoever. The communist charge grew out of some trouble in the fifties. He was importing art and there was some unhappiness because it came from Eastern Europe."

"Art?" There it is again. "What kind of art?"

Tim looks at his notes. "Paintings, carvings, tapestries. Like that. Some antiques. Mostly religious objects. Communists didn't have much use for religion, but they sure needed money. Western currency. Dollars, pounds, francs. Their paper wasn't worth shit."

"So they sold art to Dexter's father. And he paid dollars."

"Apparently. The point is, Dressler wasn't a communist spy. His heart belonged not to the revolution, but to the Rotary. Unfortunately for him, when customs started poking into the operation his retailers ran for cover. The rumors started and Rudy decided to find some other line of work."

"There's no stigma today," I say.

"What?"

"Doing business with the East. There's no big stigma. Even back four years ago before all this *glasnost* stuff. It wasn't against the law or anything."

"Not unless you dealt in strategic items."

"Is it possible that Larry revived some of his father's old contacts?"

"Revived his father's old contacts? Possibly. Was he importing himself? Not likely. For one thing, he didn't have a license."

"You need a license?" I ask.

"Sure."

"What if you're smuggling?"

Tim shrugs. "You got me there. Smugglers don't need licenses."

"But smuggling what? What do they sell over there?"

"I looked into that too." Tim smiles. "A friend of the family. Used to be with the State Department. Teaches at the junior college over here. Yers ago he was posted to Rumania. Bucharest. Vice-consul. Name of Gary Healy. I asked him what they might have to sell. And they don't have much. Raw materials. Furs. People."

"They sell people?"

"The East Germans, anyway. Before they tore down the wall. I mean, they didn't have a slave block or anything. It was done in a civilized way. The West Germans granted trade credits and the East Germans let a certain number of folks go to their relatives over the wall."

"Well, obviously, Larry wasn't buying people. Or raw materials. I can't connect him to furs. What about art? His father's line?"

"Again, it's possible," Tim concedes. "But, lately, even the communists appreciated that those objects, religious art, that it's part of their heritage. Irreplaceable stuff. So, it's been tougher to get."

"Which would make it worth more. Would also make it more likely that Larry'd have to smuggle it in on this end because he wouldn't have all the right papers."

I'm remembering the icons, one hanging in the Lundgrens' den, the other in old man Foley's office. Suppose they're not fakes, after all. Do Pat and Jack become suspects now? Isn't there anyone I can trust completely?

I grumble, "I wish somebody could talk to Kikki about European Import Consultants. Let her explain the sixty thousand Larry earned four years ago."

"Somebody has talked to her." A sly smile crosses Tim's face. "I went to some friends in the state police with that whole Import thing and they ran right over to talk to her.

Unfortunately, she claimed she didn't know a lot about it. She said she never had much to do with her husband's business."

"Oh, come on. At Indian Peak she drove my people crazy with her interference."

"Kathleen's story is as follows. That Larry founded a company helping people do business in Europe. Supposedly, a few years ago, there was interest in this. The banks made a lot of investments in the Eastern Bloc."

"Who paid eighty thousand dollars to consult with Larry Dexter?"

Tim replies, "Kikki says he had a client."

"A client? A single client?"

"And she says this client was the reason Dexter went to Europe. The client paid a great deal for his expertise. But after that, European Import Consultants ceased to be real active."

"Did she make the trip to Europe with him?"

Tim looks back at his notes. "She says no."

"Who was the client?"

"She doesn't know."

"That's her answer? She doesn't know. What about twenty thousand he made a few years later? And the six thousand last year. Who paid that?"

"Again. She claims she doesn't know."

"Well that's pure bullshit." I'm shaking my head. "Don't the police find this suspicious? He's earned all this money. And no record who paid it."

"*I* find it damned suspicious. And if I was the assistant district attorney I wouldn't want to go to trial until I knew the source of this money. It's the kind of thing can blow up in their faces."

"Yeah." I want to cheer.

"Of course, it would be better if we found some provable link between the money and the murder. But even as is. Eighty thousand. That's going to put any jury in doubt. And doubt is the mother's milk of the defense."

"If we could only find out for certain where the money came from. . . ."

Tim says, "The assistant DA has now seen this same information. For his own protection, he'll find out where the money came from. Just, just wait a bit on this, Kevin. See if I'm not right."

I'm not sure about the waiting part.

"Anyway," Tim concludes, "if this European trip pans out. If it is connected to the murder. It lets your friend Finnerty off the hook. I don't think there's a whole lot of Irish immigration from Vienna."

"I suppose not." Had Terri, in casting suspicion on Big John, purposely pointed me in the wrong direction?

Producing my own notes, I explain how I've matched Larry's credit card statement with the cost of a round-trip ticket to Brussels.

"He paid twice the rate. Obviously, he didn't go to Europe alone."

"Unless the money went to freight," Tim suggests.

"Freight?"

"His company was involved in imports. Freight is a possibility."

I stare ahead. Freight. It hadn't even occurred to me. From the moment I'd calculated the numbers, I'd imagined Dexter boarding the plane with Terri Pratt right behind him.

It's late—an inconvenient hour—but Susan smiles broadly at seeing me. It never took much to make her happy and I wonder that I didn't do a better job of it. "Kids still up?"

"No."

I'm so obviously disappointed that she offers to wake them.

"Better not, Susan. They've got to be up in the morning."

She grins at Michael's drawing taped to the refrigerator. "Recognize me? He's going to put on my hair when he gets time."

We laugh and I'm startled at how good it is to be close again, even for a moment. Still, something stands between us. I shouldn't feel guilty over Terri. I've had little to do with her since the murder. But I do feel guilty.

In the den, I open the hope chest and pull out the photo albums. I work backwards, seeking the most recent likeness.

"What are you looking for?" Susan asks. "Maybe I can help?"

"I'll get it."

She sits across the room. I study snapshots; here I am before the separation, tense, unhappy—thinking I have real problems. Then, it's summer on the back porch, Susan on my arm, looking fantastic in jeans. This was when we were seeing the marriage counselor. Hope fills her eyes.

God, I hate to think how she was disappointed.

"What are you after?" Susan asks.

"Uh, I got it." I remove a good, clear snap of Larry and Kikki Dexter.

The manager of the Chinese restaurant wears a name tag, "Andy." Yet his English is barely comprehensible. "Please," I wave the photo, "this man," I point to Larry, "and a second man got into a fight over this woman." I point to Kikki. "And you had to call the police. Don't tell me you don't remember."

"Don't remember fight."

"Come on, how often do you have the police in here?"

He looks annoyed. The Cathay Palace is the kind of place where your shoes stick to the floor. It's hard to imagine the status-happy Dexters here.

"Look, this won't get you in any trouble. Just tell what you remember." I wave a twenty, hoping he doesn't want it. My finances are at rock bottom.

He takes it. So, I hold out the photo. "Was this man involved in the fight? This guy?" I touch Larry.

He squints, then he reaches over and puts his finger on Kikki's pinched grin. "She here many times."

I'm holding my breath. "Alone?"

"Always with man."

"You mean this guy? Her husband?" Again, I point to Larry.

"No," the manager answers flatly.

"Okay." I want to jump up and down. "She came here a lot with a man, not her husband. A second man. And this guy, was he involved in the fight?"

The manager waits a moment, "Not remember fight. I toll you."

"You must remember something about it."

"Yelling. Much yelling. Call police."

"I guess there's no chance you remember what the yelling was about."

He squints impatiently.

"Okay, okay, do this. Describe the second man. Anything about him."

"Come many times. Sit with lady." He points at Kikki.

"Sits with her. How does he sit with her? I mean, do they sit close together? Like, like lovers. In love. Kissing. Touching. Love. You know?"

I get back the blankest look I've ever seen. Well, it doesn't matter. I've stumbled on Kikki Dexter's lover. (Who would have believed it?) And why are the police covering up about this?

"Let me ask you something, Andy." I hold out the photo one last time and indicate Larry Dexter. "Are you sure you don't know this guy? Name's Larry Dexter. A lawyer. You ever have cause to use his services? He's helped a lot of people bring relatives into the country."

An embarrassed smile comes on Andy's face. "I don't understand."

"This man?" I ask. "Has he helped you on immigration matters?"

"No. No. I don't understand." Shaking his head, he is still smiling.

"I wish Tim could have come," I tell Gary Healy.

He stares back with the bitter air of a Quincy Junior College professor who fully expected to be an undersecretary of state by now.

"I'm interested in what goods were sold from Eastern Europe, say, four years ago."

"You mean back in the bad old days?" He sips at the expensive drink I've paid for. "What did they sell? Not enough. Ran up billions in debts to Western banks for precisely that reason."

"Well, what I'm wondering. If a guy had gone over there and he came back with a pile of money in a few weeks. What, how did he make it?"

"Have you considered espionage?" Healy smiles, as if this is a joke.

"Tim kind of dismissed that."

"Was your Mr. Dexter representing any high-tech companies?"

"I don't know who his clients were. . . . Maybe I should find out."

Healy smiles. "That might help."

He picked the restaurant and I can't believe the prices. I'm paying and this guy orders lobster. Not only that, but he eats so fast I worry that he's going to order seconds.

"If he's not a spy," I say, "what else could it be? Any ideas?"

"Well." He motions for another drink. "He could have been negotiating for someone. It used to be like Rubik's cube over there. Get all your reds lined up before you can do business."

"Could he make sixty thousand for two weeks of negotiating?"

"Depends on the deal. Buying diamonds and furs in the USSR, well why not?" He shrugs. "I could be more helpful if I knew which country he was in."

"I don't know. To tell the truth, I know he went to Vienna, but I can't exactly prove that he ever went behind the Iron Curtain. It's a pretty good guess that he did, but—"

"You say he was of German-speaking parents?"

"That's right."

"Well," Healy adds, "if he went East, it could have been for personal reasons, to visit relatives. All those countries have pockets of German speakers. He could have visited relatives East while his business was West."

"But—" I don't even want to think about that possibility. "Okay, I forgot to tell you. His father did business in Eastern Europe years ago, trading in art. Mostly religious art. Old paintings, carvings, tapestries. Antiques."

Healy's eyebrows bounce. "A lot of what's worth having in the East is antique. Samovars. Jewelry. Especially religious art. Turn your churches into rec halls and you're going to have a lot of that stuff floating around. Of course, some places it's illegal to export. But there's ways around that."

"Ways around it?"

"When money talks," he nods knowingly, "there's no language barrier."

I watch quietly as Healy attacks dessert. For some time, I've felt that Larry's business in Europe held the key to his murder. Again and again the evidence is that his business was art.

I laugh. "For a while—this is going to sound crazy—but for a while I thought all this had something to do with Irish immigration. You know, bringing in illegals. But I guess you don't go to Vienna to import Irishmen."

"Why not?" Healy cuts into his pie with a fork.

"What?"

"Irish are everywhere. Another triumph for socialism, Ireland. No work at home. So they scatter all over the world. They're in West Germany, thousands of them, as guest workers. I suppose they could be in Austria too."

I'm not laughing now.

I might not take Gary Healy's remark about the Irish in Austria very seriously, except, suddenly, John Finnerty won't talk to me. He hangs up the minute he hears my voice. When I visit his house, on a wooded road, his son insists, "Dad's not home," though his pickup sits plain as day in the driveway.

"How can he do this?" I demand of Tim Regan. "He

could have information vital to my case. He can't just refuse to talk."

"He can. You can. Anyone can. I've heard Finnerty isn't very forthcoming with the police either. And there's nothing they can do about it because no one has to give information that might incriminate them."

"Well, isn't that suspicious? He's admitting there *is* something that could incriminate him."

"Look, Kevin, it's possible he just doesn't want to get involved. Murder can be a load of trouble even if you're completely innocent."

"You're telling me?"

"With a big investigation. They lift the rug and sweep out the dirt for everyone to see. And Finnerty. He might be afraid if he answers questions it will lead to some of his illegal cousins. Even if they have nothing to do with Dexter's murder they don't want their names in the papers for the INS to read."

"And maybe that's why they killed Dexter in the first place, to keep him from turning them in to the INS."

"I haven't seen any evidence of that."

"No one's looked for it! The cops won't even question Finnerty. For God sakes, Tim, let's *make* him talk to us."

"Whoa, Kevin. I'm trying to tell you, you can't compel testimony. In this country no one can be forced to talk."

I feel the heat rising up my neck. "You mean's he's maybe got information to prove my innocence, and we can't even ask about it?"

"We can ask. He just doesn't have to answer."

"I'm supposed to accept this? I'm supposed to shrug my shoulders and go off to prison because he refuses to talk? Well to hell with that."

"Listen, Kevin. Listen to me. Stay away from John Finnerty. If you want to talk to people—I don't like the idea, but do it your way—talk to anyone who'll talk to you. Only, if you make a big enough pest of yourself, you'll be eating off the county PDQ. Okay. Do you understand?"

"I understand."

"I'm not kidding around about this, Kevin."

"I said I understand."

I've trudged to the top of a Dorchester three-decker and I'm winded. It's cold in the corridor. The stairs squawk like birds. I slide my hand along the massive mahogany banister. Once grand, it's cracked and battered now with about twelve coats of aging varnish. I don't dare lean on it.

A young woman answers the door wearing her parka in the house.

"I'm looking for Pete Sullivan," I explain.

"Pete's not here."

"I really have to see him. It's—I'm his boss, you see."

She gives a long look. "Can you wait a few minutes?"

I wait in the dim, yellow light at the top of the landing. I assume she is making a phone call. The television mumbles in the background as I rehearse questions for Pete Sullivan, one of my Indian Peak carpenters and John Finnerty's cousin.

Sullivan's work papers had been in order, according to Tim Regan. As a result, I'd dismissed the possibility that he'd been involved with Dexter. In fact, the very opposite might be true.

I guess most Irish illegals enter the country on tourist visas and simply fail to leave. They don't need slick lawyers like Dexter for that. However, to get forged papers or to obtain residency, strings must be pulled and corners cut.

Suppose Dexter had helped bring in Finnerty's cousins— possibly from Vienna. And suppose Dexter was leaning on John, demanding more money, threatening to call the INS if it wasn't forthcoming. Well, it's not difficult to imagine a confrontation between Big John and Larry coming to violence.

Understand, I don't expect Pete Sullivan to admit to any of this. Yet maybe, when I ask, he'll show something in his eyes or say something and I'll know I've hit a raw nerve.

The ground floor door opens with a buzz and I look over the railing to see two guys in overcoats come into the foyer and head up the stairs. Right away, I've got a bad feeling. I've been kept waiting a long time—too long really. I begin to move urgently downstairs, closer to the ground.

I'll have to confront them on the narrow stairway. They're making a lot of noise, taking the steps two at a time. Head down, between the second and first floor I slide against the banister to let them pass.

"Are you looking for Pete Sullivan?" one asks.

"Yeah." I turn and at once they push up against me and I feel something sharp on my ribs. It pokes painfully through layers of clothing. "Hey, wait—"

Backed into the banister, I fight to keep my footing. A draft from the bottom floor cools the back of my neck. I could be flipped over in a moment. God. "I don't want trouble."

"You've got an odd way of avoiding it."

"My wallet's in my inside pocket."

"Do you think you can ease your troubles by spreading them to us?"

The knife bores in. I notice an accent, apparently Irish. I glimpse red faces, bad teeth, and a beard. I try to lean away but the banister gives an ominous crack. Below is a checkerboard marble floor. "This . . . this hurts."

"You're hurting people," one says with anger. "Children, families. They're frightened. You frighten them."

"It can't be tolerated," says the other.

"You're tearing my coat." It's not a knife, it's a screwdriver, but it feels plenty sharp. "I'm just trying to find the truth."

"Let's go somewhere and talk about the truth," one of them says and my heart races. I don't want to go anywhere with these guys. I try to sidle to the second floor landing, but one blocks me. I'm urged down.

"Don't make a sound," I'm warned. "Don't say another word."

The screwdriver hurts so bad I try to knock it away.

They pin my arms to my side. We scuffle. Off balance, I can't fight. "Okay. I'll go!" The banister sways dangerously. "Give me room, please!"

At first I don't realize why—but they back off. An elderly woman has appeared at the top of the landing with a small dog on a leash.

My assailants lower their heads as she passes. I force an opening between the two. A powerful hand wraps around my elbow. "Excuse me, ma'am," I say cheerfully so the woman has to stop and turn. So they have to let go. "Let me take that leash for you. Until you get down the stairs."

She is uncertain, but I manage—somehow—my friend-liest smile.

"Well, okay," she passes the leash. "Vixen's usually more manageable. You need your walk, girl. Don't you." And then, "Nice of you to offer."

"Well." I glance up to the second floor and the two men staring down darkly. "I was on my way out anyhow."

My ribs are black and blue. Not only have I been physically attacked but there's not a damn thing I can do about it. I can't identify the assailants, nor connect them to John Finnerty. Even if I could, the police simply don't care what happens to me.

I lie in bed trying to sort through all I've learned. For example, do I now eliminate smuggled paintings as a motive in the murder? Or was Dexter's real scam illegal immigration? Remember, in the past he had apparently gotten into hot water with the U.S. attorney over the same thing. Of course, I got that story from Terri and Tim says there's no record of it—which doesn't mean it didn't happen.

These guys in Dorchester behaved like killers—was it one of them who threw me off the bridge? I reach beneath the bed to make certain my oversized wrench is there.

On the other hand, my escape was easy, as if the intention had been merely to frighten me. I rub the bruise and wonder how I can find the truth.

For some reason, I picture Dexter handing his mysterious package to that temporary employee in Kikki's Mercedes. What was in it? Where was it delivered? Wouldn't it be useful to have that driver's name?

Dexter goes to Europe and earns a fortune doing God knows what. Meanwhile these odd little paintings that seem to be antiques but supposedly aren't appear on people's walls. Dexter's family has a history of importing antique art. The man had to be smuggling. And isn't it also plausible that the paintings *are* valuable; that they're worth killing for?

I should talk to Terri. If she's innocent in Dexter's murder—and I'm leaning toward that belief (obviously she has no connection to those thugs in the three-decker)—she'll be helpful. A little honest help. And who knows, maybe I can begin to trust her again.

Suddenly, I hit on a better idea. The only way to find the truth is to open Larry Dexter's *professional* records, his legal files. Find out if John Finnerty or anyone in his family was ever a client. Get the names of temporary workers.

Instead, the assistant DA is telling the judge, "Bourque is a failure. His business is in ruins. He's divorced and shacked up with a woman of low morals. Finally," his face comes within inches of my own, "he savagely murders his partner."

The judge glares down. I must tell my side, but Tim Regan signals to stay silent. I'll get my chance, he says. Except, at some point, they take me off. And I ask, when?

The trial is over. When do I get my chance?

As I lie on my prison bunk a frightening apparition takes form in the shadows, smiling, taunting. In terror I shout. And then scream, "The killer!" a howl so loud it pains my ears. I try to stop, but can't. The noise grows, obliterating every sound. Have I gone insane?

"Jesus!" I dive to the floor, fumbling for the wrench and silencing the screaming motion detector. Where did he go? I shake. A moment before a man stood over my bed, staring down at me.

*   *   *

"We've been around the house twice and there's no sign of forced entry." Two police officers, one with a flashlight, are on the front stairs.

"Someone was here."

"Can you give a description?"

"I—I only saw him a second. He must have been . . . at the window."

"Those motion detectors," one officer says, "a leaf can set them off. Paper falling to the floor."

"Brings you right out of your dreams."

"It was no dream," I insist.

One of the policemen points his flashlight to the pond.

Again, they don't believe me and don't care.

Thereafter, I listen to every tick and creak. I spot a paper half off the bookcase, flapping, blown by forced hot air. It might have set off the alarm. The face over my bed might have been a dream. But in the dark I can't make myself believe it.

· *10* ·

As a freezing night rain clatters on the picture window, Terri removes her coat, trying not to shower all over the floor. Her hair is wet, curling, and her cheeks bright red. "I can't stay long. But I'm so glad you called."

I keep to the shadows. I'm nervous, like for a first date or something.

"I, I know you've been avoiding me, Kevin. You still don't trust me. . . . I guess it's understandable. . . . My own fault really . . . Please say something."

"I need to ask a few questions."

"Can I sit down?"

"Sure."

"I just got off work and my feet are killing me." She sits.

"One of the things I need to know, Terri." Get right to business. "I need to know more about Larry's trip to Europe."

"I've told you as much as I know." She puts her coat on the back of her chair. "Kevin, that trip was years ago. It couldn't be connected to all this." She's tucked nicely into a new uniform.

"Did you know, when Dexter went to Europe somebody went with him?"

She studies the tablecloth.

"Did you know that, Terri?"

"No. I thought he went alone."

"You've never been to Europe?"

"No."

"I have the dates of his trip. Exact dates. And if you could prove where you were on those dates then no one could say you went with him."

"How do I prove where I was four years ago?"

"Work records. Payroll. If you were working. What?"

"Just, no. I wasn't working. I had very young children. I was home with them. So how could I go off to Europe? What would I do with my kids?"

"Your mother—"

"My mother couldn't manage three small girls. I mean, really, you have kids. How easy is it to drop them for a week?"

"It can be done."

"Well, it wasn't. Not by me. I didn't go to Europe."

I move closer, settling in a stuffed chair. "Larry ever talk about art?"

"About what?"

"Art. Paintings and things. He brought back some paintings from Europe. Did you know that? And he sold them to different people."

She's shaking her head slowly, looking puzzled.

I continue, "It turns out his father imported art from Eastern Europe. And Larry once talked about getting into that business."

She shakes her head again.

God, her skin is very smooth, young, and I feel a definite lift, knowing that in my bed across the room she'll do anything—positively anything—I ask. But I remind myself that she's a cheat and a liar, I take a risk just being with her. "Did you bring that picture of your husband?"

"I . . . I'll bring it next time. You should have reminded

me . . . Please don't look that way, Kevin. I'll have it next time. I'm not trying to hide anything. God. I'm not involved in Larry's murder. How can I convince you?" She rises from the table as if to approach me.

"Stay there." I point.

And she's startled, even frightened.

"Just stay there," I say more quietly.

Sitting, she looks sad, and I feel sorry for her. The thing is, she always has an answer. And the evidence so far hasn't implicated her. More and more, I want to believe she's innocent, in love with me, concerned for me. And how I need the sort of comfort she can give. God, Terri, if only you were honest.

"I wish I could be mad at you," she says. "But it's my own fault you don't trust me."

"Just now I don't trust anyone."

"You shouldn't!" She comes to life. "You shouldn't. Because I didn't kill Larry. So, somebody else did. Maybe it's someone you think of as your friend. I've always thought, whoever did it, the way it all worked out you look so guilty. Was that an accident? Or did they plan it? Because maybe they wanted to get at you and ruin you. They wanted to do worse than kill you."

Yeah! I sit up straight. You see it too—the possibility that this whole nightmare was aimed at me from the start. So, I'm not just paranoid.

"It could have been done by someone you've hurt. Someone, maybe eaten up with bitterness. That kind of thing. Someone who knows you well enough, they could wait until all the pieces were in place and then—"

"It isn't Susan," I say flatly.

"I'm just thinking out loud," she insists. "You know Susan better than I do. But. I mean, isn't it possible that she couldn't accept losing you? Isn't it possible she had a crazy idea that this would punish you *and* drive you back to her? You'd be in prison, sure. But, no one else would have you."

I manage a laugh while, God help me, a chill runs down my back. I mean, it doesn't sound like Susan. And yet, we've been so long apart. God knows what goes on inside a person's head, the resentments, anger. It's also true that Larry would have come running for Susan.

But Jesus, it's something I simply can't believe. I change the subject, asking, "What do you know about Kikki Dexter having an affair?"

"I don't know anything about that. I don't believe it. Not Kikki."

"It's true."

She shrugs doubtfully.

"Did Larry help John Finnerty get his family in the country?"

"I told you before. Larry got foreigners in the country. But I don't know anything about Finnerty."

"He could have mentioned Finnerty's name and you've forgotten—"

"What does Finnerty say?" she asks suddenly.

"Well, uh, as a matter of fact, nothing. He won't talk to me. He won't even see me."

"Well," her eyes light up.

"No. He might have his own reasons for not talking."

"For not talking to *you*? I thought he was your friend."

"I thought so too. . . ." I look off muttering, remembering Tim Regan and his goddamned Fifth Amendment. "Anyway, there's no way to make him talk."

"Why not?"

"Why not?" Is she reading my mind?

"Yeah. I mean, why can't you, you know, like corner him somewhere and he'd have to talk to you or at least he'd have to listen."

"Corner him?"

"I, I could even help you. I could call him, tell him *I* have information for him. And then, when he comes, we'll make him sit down and you put it to him that he's supposed to be your friend. And you only want some answers."

Is this good advice given in good faith? "If he complained to the police I could wind up back in jail for bothering a witness."

"Sounds to me like he's more scared of the police than you are."

I'm thinking this over when she offers, "There's something I should have told you before, but, for some reason, it didn't come up, I didn't remember it. About Larry and Pat Lundgren."

"Larry and who?"

She takes a breath. "Remember, Larry had appeal. And Pat, she's no prize in the looks department. I'm sure she was flattered by the attention. I'm sure she was easy pickings for a guy like Larry—"

"Are you saying they were lovers or something?"

"All I'm saying, at one time, they saw a lot of each other. I'd go to his office and I'd have to drive round the block because her car was there. We had fights about it. He said it was business. Yeah. Like I believed that." She looks up. "Ever notice those twins don't look like Jack? And this was right around the time she had them."

"That's bullshit."

"It's . . . you know, I'm not the first to say it. And everybody knows she wanted to get knocked up in the worst way and Jack couldn't do it."

"You've got no right to talk about Pat like that."

She looks down for a moment. "Let's face it, it was pretty strange to have Pat and Jack doing this real estate business with Larry."

"Why is that strange? I did business with Larry too."

"You didn't hate his guts."

It's true that the Lundgrens never had much use for Larry Dexter. It's possible that they did hate him. But certainly their work on Indian Peak was on *my* behalf, not Dexter's.

"You know, he would have gone out to meet *them* that morning," she says. "They would have called. Said, we've got a buyer, potential buyer here. And he would have been there like a shot."

"That doesn't work. They couldn't know if Larry would tell Kikki where he was going. Who had called. So. That doesn't work."

I'm relieved she has no answer. Instead, she looks out on the pond. "I'm telling you everything in my head that might help. To me. Pat Lundgren. I wouldn't cross the lady. She's sweet to people, sure. The perfect hostess, perfect mom. But for me she's the type—if you got in the way—she could knock you flat and never look back."

"Yeah, well you got your story a little confused, Terri. First Pat has an affair with Larry, children with him. Then she hates him. Which is it?"

"I'm saying Pat Lundgren was in love with Larry Dexter. And then it turned to hate. You can figure out how that works, Kevin."

I pause. "Except Pat never had a problem getting pregnant. Her trouble was staying pregnant. It seemed like every year Susan had to hold her hand over another miscarriage. Larry's services weren't needed."

"I just meant—"

"Is this how you get my trust? Backbiting? Taking Susan or Pat and twisting the good they do, twisting it round like they're against me?"

"No, I—"

"The only woman who I know for sure had an affair with Larry is you."

"Tell me." Now she leaps from her seat and crouches beside me. "What can I do, Kevin? How can I make you trust me again?"

"I don't know."

So, this encourages her because it's not a flat rejection. She keeps after me. Can she run errands? Lend money? Anything?

She comes closer. "I've got a new outfit. What do you think? Oh Kevin, I miss it so much, the way you used to care what I wore. How I looked. Now I get dressed and I know there's no one to care."

So, I glance at the outfit, a white blouse and blue skirt hugging her trim body. "That old one-piece," she complains, "I felt like a mechanic."

She wants to help. And what a boost to have an ally in

this. I need tenderness. God, I suddenly admit to myself how lonely I am, how good it would feel to hold her and be held. After cold horror comes warmth and love.

"Would you . . . would you take off your top?" I'm sorry as soon as I ask, but I don't tell her to stop.

She unbuttons, then strips off the spotless white blouse in one motion. She unhooks the bra and it drops. Her breasts aren't large, but pronounced, with dark nipples. There is something carnal about them, something that belies the innocent face. This is what she's really about, these hot red nipples she hides away.

"You are *something*," I say.

She stands, smiling, occasionally looking down at herself.

"You said you'd do anything for me."

She nods, seeming to point those nipples right at me.

"Suppose I went back to my wife. Would you be my mistress?"

"You're . . . no, you're not going back to her." Terri's face goes dark.

"When I go back to her. This is the question, Terri. When I go back to my wife can I still call on you when I want to get laid? Like Dexter did."

"Yes." Then she smiles. "You're not going back to her. Are you?"

"Get me a drink."

I don't understand the drift of this conversation. It's as if the pressure and my ambivalence about Terri has brought out a sick streak of meanness which I can no more control than I control my desire to have her.

With one hand, she steadies a wine bottle in her naked bosom, pulling the plastic cork with the other. "Ooo. Cold." She takes the bottle away and touches her chest. Then, she pours two glasses and approaches me on the stuffed chair. But when I reach for mine, she leans back and spills part of it over her nipple. It must be something she's seen in a movie.

Rivulets of red wine curl downward, around her navel, staining the waist of her skirt. And I lick my way up. This is what I want.

"I love you, Kevin." She reaches to put the glasses on a nearby table, but she sighs and I hear the glass falling to the rug.

I'm on her nipple, licking, sucking until I can't taste the wine anymore.

"I . . . oh . . . I love you," she moans, stroking my head. "Love me back, Kevin."

I rise to give her a kiss. "You'll do anything for me?"

Swaying, eyes almost closed, she's like someone under the influence.

"Will you tell them you did it, Terri? Tell them you killed Larry."

"They won't believe me."

"Will you tell them? To save me."

"Yes."

"Is it true?"

"No." She leans back, deadly serious. "God take my kids if I lie. No."

I have to be impressed by such an oath. I kiss her on the lips so hard she squeals. And I whisper, "If you *are* lying again, Terri. I'll kill you."

Only two cars sit in the parking lot at Wampatuck State Park and one is empty. Nonetheless, John Finnerty circles twice before picking out Terri Pratt's Chevy and pulling up beside it. After a few minutes, with her gesturing eagerly, he climbs in.

"I don't like this," he says. "What do you want with me, girl?"

I pop up in the back seat.

"Jesus." He is more angry than surprised.

"I want to talk, John."

"Well, this is a hell of a way to go about it."

"It's the only way you gave me." I'm nervous, hoping he won't run and gambling that Terri's right about his aversion to police. "John, I need help."

He glances at the door.

"I thought we were friends," I say softly. "I'm in trouble. The least you can do is talk so I'll know where I stand."

He waits, then rubs his chin thoughtfully. "Well, I might talk to you. But you can be goddamn sure I won't talk to *her*."

"I'll take a walk," Terri says. Leaning into the front seat, I pat her shoulder in thanks. So far, her scheme is working.

After she leaves, John says, "I worry about you, Kevin. When I see the company you keep."

Let that pass. "John, I happen to know you went to Indian Park on the night—early morning actually—of Larry Dexter's murder." I pretend to know this as fact. "You were in your truck. Now, I haven't told the cops about this, and maybe I never will. But first I have to know why you were there."

"I was looking for my drill. I told you I left my drill. I was out late and I stopped to get it."

"But the drill was still there in the morning."

"Sure, I couldn't find it in the dark. I had no flashlight."

"Why didn't you tell the police about this?"

"I, I didn't think it was important."

It's not exactly a compelling answer. I drape my arms into the front. "Some guys roughed me up the other night, John. Some guys, they talked like guys just off the boat from Cork. Okay? Know anything about that?"

"Some people value their privacy."

"You know your cousins or relatives or friends, did they ever live in Europe? On the continent? Maybe West Germany? Austria?"

"Pete spent a year in the U.K. But then he got a visa to come here."

"Who got it for him?"

"He got it himself at the U.S. embassy. In London, probably."

"He didn't have anybody help him through all the red tape? Maybe a politically connected lawyer on this side of the ocean?"

"No."

"Where is Pete?"

John leans back. "I'm not sure. He's looking for work. Maybe Florida."

"His papers aren't right, are they?"

"I told you there was a small problem, but—"

"Listen, John. If you lie to me I'm going right to the police."

He gives a longing glance to the door.

"Pete's papers aren't real. Are they?"

"Pete's papers are fine. I told you. Mike and Derek. Those boys only have the Donnelly visas they came in on. Both of them could be sent back tomorrow, which would be a sin. They have families."

I'm watching Terri, a long way off, following a path through the woods. "Did Larry know this?"

"No. No fucking way."

"He could have guessed," I suggest. "Or he could have helped those guys get in the country in the first place. And he could have been asking for money to keep quiet."

John shakes his head. "It wouldn't be worth the risk. All they can do is send you back. If you have a family here they have a hard time doing that. Immigration trouble is not enough trouble to kill for."

"Is it enough trouble to throw somebody off a second floor landing?"

"No such thing happened."

"Well, it almost did!" I answer fiercely.

"Those boys want to be left alone. They don't want the authorities coming round asking questions. So, sometimes—" he begins to contradict himself—"one will try to help the other and get overprotective. A lot of my people have no insurance, no unemployment, no government program to help them. When one gets sick we've got to all chip in. We've got to know it could be any one of us standing there needing help." He makes a chopping motion for emphasis. "We look out for each other."

"Tell me, John. Tell me the ways your people look out for each other."

His face brightens. "If you think we paid for Mr. Dexter's help—well, it makes no sense. Lawyers cost money. My people come here because they have *no* money."

"They earned plenty when they worked for me."

He turns to look me square in the eye. "I don't want your troubles splashing all over my family. That's true enough. That's why I wouldn't talk to you. But if I'd killed Mr. Dexter do you think I'd stand by and let you take my blame? You've known me almost ten years. And is that how you think of me? Is that your low opinion of me?"

I look down, chastened and, well, disappointed. Because it isn't.

I have to chase all over town before finding my lawyer in the district court. Then I have to stand around for over an hour waiting while he tries some foolish drunk-driving case.

I've got this bad feeling, like maybe I'd made a mistake trusting Terri, letting her near. Except, I can't see what harm she's done. In fact, she arranged the meeting with Finnerty— even if it led nowhere.

She looked hurt when I sent her home with a mere "Thank you."

Tim plants himself on a corridor bench. Dozens of people pass as he explains, "It's just like I said. The assistant DA doesn't want to go to court until he can explain where Dexter's eighty thousand dollars came from. And, from what I've heard, he's explaining it just the way you are."

"Just the way I am?" I sit down beside him.

"The art work. Smuggled art. They found more paintings in a closet in Dexter's house. Documents too. Export licenses granted to European Import Consultants from one of these East Bloc governments. And records showing Larry eventually sold three paintings for nearly one hundred thousand dollars. Supposedly, they're from the goddamn Middle Ages. Religious paintings. Jesus, Mary, and the whole Holy Family."

"Who, who . . . ?" I'm not just astonished, but panicked, trying to fathom the implications.

"It seems that Dexter smuggled the paintings into the country and broke a shitload of laws doing it. But. He made a big profit. Apparently the paintings are worth what people paid. These things are fucking old."

"Do his records say who bought them?"

"Your friends the Lundgrens bought them all. One hundred thousand worth. Eighty of that was profit for Dexter."

I watch the hustle of three-piece suits rushing past us. At first, I can't even respond. "I . . . I saw one painting at the Lundgrens'. But Jack and Pat told me they got it from Dexter for a few hundred dollars."

"The Lundgrens have flatly refused to talk to the police about this. But the assistant DA thinks that's because they want some kind of criminal immunity. They didn't pay the sales tax, which is substantial. And they might be liable for the customs duty, fines, and who knows what else."

"They won't talk . . . because of the sales tax?"

"Your friends probably think it's more serious than it is. The bottom line for the prosecutor is this. Nothing here points to murder. The eighty thousand is accounted for. It was just a business transaction."

"No, no, no, don't you see?" I'm red in the face, excited. "This is part of Dexter's scam. It's . . . it's a cover for something."

"A cover for what?"

"I don't know. Maybe Dexter sold the real paintings to someone else. We have to look at his papers. We've got to get the names of all his clients."

"His clients?"

"Look at Dexter's legal files, Tim, and you're going to find the killer."

"Unfortunately, Kevin, no one has the right to see a lawyer's files."

"Here we go again."

"Sorry, those files are privileged. The court is not going to allow it."

"My fucking life is on the line, for Christ sakes!"

"Be reasonable, Kevin. Would you want police rummaging through our correspondence, all the notes I've made on your case?"

"I've got nothing to hide."

"That's not the point. Give third parties the run of an attorney's papers, it could destroy an individual's trust in his lawyer. See what I'm saying?"

"No."

"If we could tell the court what we're looking for it might be different. But you're talking about a fishing expedition—"

"I know what I'm looking for."

"Tell me so we'll both know."

"I'm looking for the man who paid Dexter eighty thousand dollars."

"The prosecutor's going to say it was Jack Lundgren."

"That's crap! The Lundgrens wouldn't have lied to me about those paintings. There's an explanation here. A solid explanation. If I can't trust those two I can't trust anyone. They helped me. John Finnerty and the rest, they told the police everything I said about Dexter. Well, I said worse things about Dexter to the Lundgrens. And they didn't breathe a word."

"Then why won't they talk to the police about the paintings?"

"We've got to see those files, Timmy."

"Listen, we can ask." My attorney is soothing. "And we can keep digging on this question of the money and the paintings and the Lundgrens. Just because the prosecutor thinks he's settled the question, it doesn't mean we have to think that."

"I want to see Larry's files. I want to know who he did business with."

"Kevin, I'll make a motion that we be allowed access—"

"I'm not going to jail on account of some bullshit—"

"I don't like the drift here, Kevin."

"—bullshit legalism."

"If you're talking some scheme to get at those documents. Forget it. That's a one-way ticket to jail with nothing I can do to help."

Turning away, I look down the courthouse corridor.

It happened very fast. I should be happy. I'm sitting in the Lundgren's real estate office waiting to sell Indian Peak to an investor dug up by Simpson the banker. My money troubles will soon be eased considerably. And yet I'm not happy.

"Tell me again," I ask, "when are you going to the police?"

"I'll make an appointment tomorrow." Pat sets out coffee and cakes. "It's outrageous. Now we know what it's like to be falsely accused. Really, I don't care what Larry's papers say. The icon is a reproduction. It costs us a few hundred dollars, not a hundred thousand. All you have to do is look at it."

"For God sakes, Pat, tell that to the police!"

"I wanted to. But Jack insisted we have a lawyer, as a precaution. Because, well, suppose Larry *used* us in some scheme, like, maybe to cheat the IRS. You better than anyone should know the terrible things that can happen to perfectly innocent people."

"Let the police see the painting. Let them see it isn't worth anything."

"We plan—"

"If they're ever going to find out where Dexter's money came from you've got to tell the truth!"

"We intend to. We will." She's looking me square in the eye, balancing a saucer and cup—with not a tremor.

I feel guilty doubting her. The Lundgrens have done so

much for me. And yet, my mind races back to the medieval painting over the fireplace, Jesus, looking mournfully to heaven.

Pat disappears into the outer office behind a wall of dark suits. They're mostly lawyers so you can bet they know my story. Maybe they've even seen me on TV, in handcuffs.

I catch them now staring through the glass wall of this office. A bug in a bottle, I want to stand up and shout, "I'm innocent."

Haines, the buyer, bends, listening to Simpson. *Bourque ran amuck at the bank. Thank God he'll be locked away soon.* Haines looks my way. And, in turn, so does everyone else in the room. God, I feel hot and dizzy. And yet I've got to go through with this.

Haines has agreed to buy Indian Peak. The deal will bring enough money to save Susan's house. With Pat and Jack to thank for putting it together—and for convincing Kikki to sign.

"I was through that house you boys built."

I look up at Haines, an old Yankee carpenter turned contractor. He's stiffly uncomfortable in a suit and tie. "Good job," he says.

"Thank you."

"Must have cost."

"Well, my labor was cheap."

"Don't see how you make a profit."

"If I was making a profit I wouldn't be here," I declare.

"True enough." He turns, but comes back to ask, "What do you do now?"

"I don't know. It's tough to get work. In my position."

Hire the accused. Well, believe it or not, I'm thinking maybe Haines feels sorry for me, maybe he's going to offer a job, which I could use. But instead he walks back to the lawyers and bankers.

As Pat returns with coffee, Haines intercepts her at the door.

"What are we waiting for, girlie?"

"For my husband to come back with Mrs. Dexter's signature."

Everything had been done in such a hurry that Kikki sent back the purchase and sale agreement without a signature. Jack volunteered to run over and get it, right beneath mine. No problem.

"Well," Pat tells me brightly, "you'll be in the chips now."

"I'll be out of the poorhouse."

"We should celebrate. We'll go over to my house. Open champagne."

Jack Lundgren comes sweeping through waving the purchase and sale. The lawyers converge on him. They mutter, heads shake.

Suddenly, Pat is whispering. "She won't sign."

"What? I thought—"

"I talked to her less than an hour ago. She said she'd sign. Never gave a hint she wouldn't. But when Jack went over, she flatly refused."

"What's her problem?" I groan. "Is it the contract?"

"She wouldn't even look at the contract."

"Then what? It's a damned good price."

"I don't think she cares. She said she won't sign. Ever. She told Jack, 'if you don't like it you can sue me.' "

Jack is at the door, frustrated and depressed. The lawyers are picking up their coats. Haines seems disgusted, Simpson in shock.

"How am I going to sue her? I don't have any money."

The Lundgrens exchange glances.

"But she knows that," I nod. "She's just trying to screw me. Isn't she?"

Jack clears his throat.

"She let this whole farce go along. Never intending to sign."

Jack shrugs. "It looks that way."

"And not a damn thing I can do. I can't sell a goddamn divot without her."

No reason to celebrate now. Driving to the Lundgrens, Pat tries to calm me. I want to bang on Kikki's door and have it out. "You know she's got a boyfriend?" I ask. "The cops are trying to cover that up—but I found out. And somebody ought to ask Mrs. Dexter—where was loverboy when Larry was killed? Somebody ought to ask her that."

Pat brakes for a red light.

"Did you know about her boyfriend?" I turn to Jack in the back seat.

"We never heard that," Jack replies.

"Doesn't sound like Kikki," Pat insists.

"I should ask her. I should demand to know that guy's name."

"Somebody should do that," Pat agrees. "But not you."

"Better stay away from her," Jack warns.

"Oh, sure. Great advice." I'm so angry . . . Christ! You think they'd have made sure the damn thing was signed before dragging me over there!

Pat is going on about how the deal can still be made. Talk, talk, talk. She never stops selling. "I'm still on good terms with Kikki. I can drum some sense into her. I mean, she only hurts herself acting like this."

"That's what I told her," Jack says.

"There's no reason to get depressed."

Do I look depressed?

"Every deal, there's a glitch. Never goes smooth. Does it, Jack?"

"No. Almost never."

At Pat and Jack's, the middle-aged sitter gives me a squint-eyed glance.

"What are you looking at?" I demand.

"Uh, nothing."

"Take the kids to the playroom." Pat steps between us.

I sit in the kitchen, feeling cooler, my head on the table. The bad news is that I have no money. Virtually all my mail begins, "Last Notice. . . ." The good news is that the collection agencies will never find me in state prison.

"Let's have lunch." Pat opens the cupboard. "And then we'll figure a way to get this property sold. There's always a way. . . ." She goes on and on.

Jack pours me a beer. Why are these people so nice? So many friends have long since jumped ship. Pat slides a turkey sandwich under my nose.

I had my suspicions about these two even before Terri mentioned their names. Looking beyond the kitchen, I stare at the icon over the fireplace.

"Those assholes in suits. Standing around *talking about me!*"

Pat says, "No one said anything—"

"Don't tell me! I'm not stupid. I could see the way they looked. The way everybody looks at me. Jesus. My head is splitting."

"Can I get you an aspirin?" Pat asks.

"You should have had her sign before you dragged me into that circus."

"You're right," Jack says softly. "I guess we were hoping that if I took the papers over, she'd just sign like she promised."

"Fucking circus. And I was the clown."

"No."

"Haines wants to know what I'm going to do next. I'm going to fucking jail for the rest of my life!" I slam the table, spilling beer.

Pat shuts the door. She doesn't want the children to hear.

"We want to help." Jack seems truly sympathetic. Is it all an act?

I take a breath. "Pat? Maybe I shouldn't bring this up. But I heard you and Larry had something going a few years ago."

"Me and . . . ?" She looks to her husband in astonishment.

Jack actually stifles a chuckle. "Where did you hear that?"

"I . . ." I sense I'm not even close. "I heard it."

"I can guess where," Pat says.

"Okay, forget that. Let's get down to the real, real nub of the thing. Let's get down to that."

"What?"

"The painting you say is worthless and the prosecutor says costs a hundred thousand dollars."

"Well, he's just wrong."

"Really? Well, why didn't you just tell him that?"

"That's my fault," Jack says, "I was being overcautious. I wanted legal—"

"You need a lawyer to answer a simple question? Did you pay Larry Dexter a hundred thousand dollars for three antique paintings?"

"No," Jack replies.

"Then explain how come he had receipts from you!"

"Lies!" Pat roars. "Those receipts are lies. Do we look like the kind of people who'd pay a hundred thousand dollars for pictures?"

"I wanted the lawyer." Jack is apologetic. "We wanted to know the ramifications of the questions. How they'd affect us, how they'd affect you—"

"Oh, come on."

"Cool down, Kevin," Jack says. "You're among friends."

"Let's be sure," I say.

"Let's be sure?" Pat asks.

"All I'm saying is let's have someone look at your paintings."

"There's only the one," Jack insists.

"Fine. Okay. Let's get an expert to appraise it. Appraise the value."

"If that's what it takes," Jack says.

"No," Pat interrupts.

"If that's what it takes to put Kevin's mind at ease."

"You mean if that's what it takes to prove we didn't kill Larry for a hundred thousand dollar painting. Isn't that the bottom line, Kevin?"

"I'm not accusing anyone—"

"Hear what Kevin says, Jack? He says we're pretending friendship." The words almost choke her. "Hoping they'll send him to jail for what we did."

Suddenly Pat turns on her heels and makes for the living room. She returns clasping the painting to her bosom. But while the face of Christ shows piety and love, Pat's lips are a thin line of rage.

Yet, I don't expect what happens next. Taking the painting in both hands, she slaps it—WHAP!—into the Formica table top, smashing the wood and its holy image into a hundred pieces. Splinters fly up and hit me.

"Pat!" Jack cries. "For God sakes!"

I gasp. And now I see what should have been obvious to a carpenter, the unmistakable traces of machine tools. The wood might be old, but it was recut and painted recently. On close examination an amateur could spot it.

Reflexively, I stoop, trying to pick up the pieces. But the wood is very dry, its remnants mostly too small to recover. "No, oh no . . ."

"If you want to sweep that up for the police," Pat spits, "be my guest."

"Pat," Jack tries to soothe her.

"Don't." She jerks her arm up, avoiding his touch. "And if you're still not convinced, put me on a lie detector and—"

"Pat!" Jack shouts and she hurries tearfully from the room.

Call it superstition, but a stab like ice runs through me. What Pat has done is a sacrilege bound to spill bad luck all over *me*. I stand slowly. "I better go."

"I'll drive you home," Jack offers.

"No. No, I . . . I feel like walking."

"Everyone . . . everyone's upset."

Outside, I realize I've probably lost my best friends. Now, when I need friends more than ever.

*　　*　　*

All night I see that ancient block of wood exploding on the table top, obliterating the face of Christ. I toy with the idea that Pat and Jack were scammed by Dexter, that he'd sold the reproductions as genuine antiques. Discovering the deception made the Lundgrens mad enough to kill.

But it's a scenario that won't work. Only a fool would invest a hundred thousand dollars in such an obvious fake.

Another possibility is that a facsimile has been substituted for the real painting. I suppose I should consider this. In fact, it's too convoluted. Pat spoke like someone taking an oath. She promised that Dexter sold her a painting costing only a few hundred dollars. I believe her.

The police claim to have found antique paintings in Dexter's closet. Okay, who appraised them? Some guy in black boots to his knees—the state police art expert. Ha. No doubt, they jumped to the same mistaken conclusion that I just did.

· *11* ·

I sleep all day. There doesn't seem much point to getting up. Whether Kikki Dexter's lover, the Lundgren's painting, or John Finnerty's terrorist cousins, I ask all the questions and all I get back are more questions.

By afternoon, I rouse enough to remember that I'd promised to collect Molly from dance class. Well, at first, I think I won't go. I'll tell Susan I'm not up to it. I'm having a rough time. I want to stay in the room and . . . what? Do what? Vegetate until the police come to collect *me*?

Suddenly, I realize that it's vital, in my few days left, that I be with the kids, talk to them and hold them. I leap into the truck, check my watch, and worry that I won't reach the school on time, that Molly will be gone, brought home by some concerned instructor or neighbor.

Dance class is held in the grammar school. Every afternoon children in Norham are ferried all over town to such programs. Soon Molly will have to withdraw from after-school activities. The money's just not there.

My daughter, sweeping across the stage, is a revelation, as if a spotlight has picked her out among the others. I stand in the shadows and I want to cry for her talent and beauty. I've put her on the brink of an upheaval. I try with all my wit and strength, but I don't think I can protect you from it, Molly.

The tempo picks up. Some of the kids watch their feet, measuring each step. A teacher shouts encouragement. But my girl is on her own, scarcely touching the floor, eyes half-closed as she absorbs the music.

"You dance great," I tell her in the car.

She smiles. At stop signs and traffic lights I stare at her. Finally, I ask, "Did I ever—Molly? Did I ever tell you how much you mean to me?"

"Dad."

"No, really. You're . . . up on the stage, you're like a dream. I feel so proud."

She looks away. "You're weird, dad."

"Am I?" I laugh.

At the house, Susan is ferrying groceries from the car. I notice at once that her face seems to have aged years in the span of weeks.

She looks up. "Thank God you remembered Molly."

"Where's Michael?"

"With the Walshes. Cathy took him and Liam to a movie."

"Oh." This is a disappointment. To see Michael I'll have to wait. Of course, that also means being stared at by Cathy Walsh.

I bring in the bundles. Susan sits at the table, examining the register tape for overcharges. Once, as I come in, she rises to hold the door.

Her movements remind me of Molly. Of course, Susan was a great dancer in high school. In admiring Molly, I see a reflection of her mother.

At the table, I rave about my daughter's dancing—a safe subject. Susan glows. "So," I say, "don't forget. I'll be taking them to the mall. Friday night. My birthday. And you'll have extra time on your hands."

"I could use it."

"Yeah. You look like you could use some rest."

"It never stops." She clutches the tape. "I'm full time at the library. The money's bad, but the hours are flexible. Most days I'm home before the kids."

"Most days? What, what happens when you're not home?"

"Cecilia agreed to watch them."

"That's good."

"I offered to pay her. But she won't take any money. I know she's got her hands full with her own kids."

"That's good she takes them," I say.

Susan goes flush and her eyes fill with tears. "I just want to rest, sleep. I'm always tired. There isn't a moment to just have fun. I'm always shouting. . . . I make them so unhappy." She puts the back of her hand to her eyes.

I rush over, stroke her hair. Oh, Susan, it can't be that bad. "This is a rough time. But after a while it will be easier."

"I hope so," she sobs.

"You've got to keep up your spirits. Forget me. Get out and meet new people."

"What?" She looks up.

"You've got to face the fact that, you know, I'm probably not going to be around anymore. So you've got to—"

"Meet new people. I heard you." Something hard has come into her voice and the tears stop. "When do I do this? Kevin? When do I meet these new people?"

"I . . . I guess whenever you can."

"Meet men. That's what you're saying. I should meet some men."

"Susan, we've got to be realistic."

"Don't you listen? I barely have time to go the bathroom."

"I know, just now—"

"I'm not you, Kevin. *You* have time to meet women.

You're not up all hours with crying kids. You don't have to clean the house, make the supper, put out the garbage. . . . I can't do it, God, I can't do it all. It's too much!"

"I just . . . I only—"

"You went off to your little whore and left me to do my job and your job too."

"I help as much as I can."

"Unless you're here every hour, every night, you can't help enough."

"Listen. It wasn't my idea to leave."

"You weren't satisfied with me! You made it clear. I loved you with all my heart, all my heart. My life revolved around you."

"That's not how it seemed to me."

"I gave and gave and you pushed me away."

"I pushed *you* away?" I protest.

"How do you think that made me feel?"

"Susan, you never showed that you really loved me—"

"That's a lie."

"If you cared you would have tried to please me. I didn't ask so much."

"Just the impossible." She stands, almost smiling at this chance to set the record straight. "Your complaint wasn't what I did or didn't do. Your complaint was with me. What I am. The person I am. I'm sorry. I wish I could be different for you. But I can only be myself." She begins to cry.

"I, I can't help being the person I am, Susan. I didn't plan to be unhappy. I just was. And I couldn't see the advantage of pretending."

"So you went off."

"You threw me out. You keep forgetting."

"And you went to her. And what has it got you? Her boyfriend murdered. You get blamed. You used to be smart. But now you act so stupid I can't believe it. Like, you can't see what's perfectly obvious to everybody."

"What? What's perfectly obvious?"

Suddenly Susan is inches away, digging her nails into me.

"Don't you see? She's going to get rid of you. Like she got rid of Larry."

"You don't know."

"Jesus! Jesus Christ has she put you to sleep or something? Open your eyes, Kevin, and see."

"She has an alibi . . . She's—"

"She's killing you. *Killing you!*"

For a long time I had the illusion that Susan and me had just, as they say, drifted apart—like a lazy day on the lake. The truth is we've been wrenched in two, violently. Our family will never know another day without a certain sadness over this terrible thing.

I should have done it differently. I know, I know. But if I'm ever to make it right again I must save myself. And to do that, I must know if Susan is correct about Terri Pratt. For hours I drive around, working it out in my head.

Admittedly, Terri could not have killed Larry herself. At the time of the murder she was reading to some old lady in the nursing home. So, it's damned suspicious that she repeatedly fails to produce a photo of ex-husband Eddie.

Of course, Terri's been helpful to me. She set up the meeting with John Finnerty and raised my suspicions about the Lundgrens and Susan. But was that really helpful? Or was she purposely sending me up one blind alley after another, wasting what time I have left?

Finally, I've never known a woman as exciting as Terri. And it stands to reason you've got to pay for fun like that.

I arrive home late. Climbing out of the pickup, I reach for the mail—mostly dunning notices, I'll bet. The letters are half in and half out of my box.

I step to one side as a car comes up behind me. Headlights make the rusty box bright. Over my shoulder, I see only glare. The car bears down. "God!" I dive into the brush. A crack, the sound of breaking glass, and the thing is gone, roaring to the state highway.

I climb out cautiously to find my mailbox pointed in an altogether different direction.

A group of officers take my statement while examining the bent mailbox and broken glass. "Shouldn't you get impressions of the tires?" I ask.

"From gravel?"

"You could try," I insist.

"Aren't you the guy with the motion detector?"

Of course, they run around with flashlights examining *my* truck. "Am I not getting through to you guys? This isn't a traffic accident. Someone is trying to kill me."

"We're investigating, Mr. Bourque. I don't know what more you want."

I turn away, disgusted. Someone wants me dead because I'm close to something. If I don't find it fast I might not survive much longer.

Radiators hissing, the nursing home lounge is oppressively hot, but Mrs. Carney remains alert, listening carefully to my question.

"Yes," she says, "I remember the murder. It was terrible. And so close. And I remember earlier in the day, Mrs. Pratt reading to me. Between six and seven. That sounds about right. Then we found out that she knew the man. Oh, my Lord, all next day she was very upset. Very upset."

"Do you remember what she read?" I ask.

"Well, now, let me see. *Reader's Digest.* That was it. I haven't the eyes to read myself anymore. Even when they have books with big type isn't it always the modern ones. I'm too old for four-letter words an inch high."

I nod. Terri's alibi has held. Working alone, with most all of her charges asleep, the possibility existed that she could have slipped out of the nursing home to meet Larry Dexter at Indian Peak—fifteen minutes away—killed him, and slipped back. It would have been difficult, but having pulled it off, she would have established a convincing alibi.

Mrs. Carney has neatly disposed of that theory—along with Susan's dark suspicions. Terri was probably reading "My Most Unforgettable Character" at the precise time the gold-colored nails were fired into Larry Dexter.

As I thank Mrs. Carney, she asks, "Will you come again? I do wait so long for a visit."

"Well," I answer softly, "I might come by again to say hello. Why not?"

"I go month after month without a phone call or a letter. You could send a card. You used to send a card."

"Excuse me?"

"I told everyone you called at Christmas. Even though you hadn't."

I'm slowly standing.

"It's hard. My friends see *their* children every week. I get so lonely."

I feel as though I've been hit by a truck.

"Did I tell you?" Mrs. Carney smiles suddenly. "I'm taking a walk today. Through the garden."

I'm driving past Terri's house for the second time today and where the hell is she? It's her day off so I suppose I shouldn't worry that she's out.

On the other hand, since early morning I've been all over town, past the Finnertys' house, the Lundgrens', and even, by chance, Susan's. None of their cars showed evidence of having run into my mailbox.

I don't know what that proves. A headlight is easily repaired. And surely these attempts on my life are the work of a stranger, the blank face gazing down from Long Bridge.

Still, a look at Terri's car—and her ex-husband—would ease doubts. Because let's fact it, her alibi for Larry's murder is shot to hell. (You wonder about an investigation that takes the word of a senile woman.)

I remember Terri, eyes aglow, describing the power of her sexuality. What greater kick than luring two men to death and prison? Sometimes I see her lay the nail gun on Larry's forehead. As he screams, she pulls the trigger.

But I made love to this woman. If she is a killer wouldn't I have seen it in her eyes, heard it in her voice? Wouldn't I have stayed away from her?

I should go down the driveway and check Kikki Dexter's cars.

I'm across the street, idling, trying to decide. The Dexters' Tudor home is below the road on a three-acre lot with an unobstructed view of the North River. Yet the blinds are drawn, as if Kikki can no longer bear the sun.

The Mercedes and BMW are parked nose to the garage door. I could run down, unseen, and get a good look at the headlights and bumpers.

I'll tell you what I'd like to do. I'd like to do more than check her cars. Better if she explained this character from the Chinese restaurant. Does your boyfriend have an alibi? Did the two of you want Larry out of the way?

Now, if she's got a reasonable explanation, I'll listen. And then, maybe, in that spirit, she'll listen to my side. Which I'm certain she's never heard before. So, finally we'll sit together and figure out who really killed Larry.

"Getaway, getaway from my house!"

"What?" I look up.

"You bastard. Son of a bitch." She's across the street, at the top of the driveway, no coat, wearing jeans and a blouse. Her face is drawn and once-tight clothes hang like bags.

I climb out of the truck. "Look, I didn't come to cause trouble, Kikki."

"Get away from me, get away from my children!" Her voice is hoarse with anger and emotion. She heaves a handful of gravel. I cover up. Tiny stones rain on my truck.

It isn't starting out as I'd hoped.

"I just want to talk, Kikki. Please."

"The police are coming," she announces.

"Kikki, please . . ."

"You're going back to jail where you belong."

"Just, just give me a chance."

"Go to hell, bastard. GO TO HELL!"

I've made a mistake even being here. I back away. She hisses, "You're going to prison as soon as the police get here."

And I can't resist, I come back to say, "Just remember. When they get me. The real killer gets, goes off scot free. Or is that what you're hoping?"

"I hope someone does to you what you did to my husband."

This is pointless. Two of the older children are running up the driveway. "Ma, ma, don't go near him!"

Kikki won't leave the property, but leans over the road, still shouting. "Good you came. You'll be back behind bars tonight."

"Yeah?" I call over my shoulder, "How about your boyfriend? He's not a secret anymore, Kikki. Better have some answers—"

The oldest boy, about thirteen, comes sailing past his mother, right for me. Christ, a butcher knife! I sidestep and manage to push him. His red face and white teeth flash past. He staggers, falls, the knife snapping to pieces as it jams into the pavement.

Kikki screams, "Leave him alone!"

Which I'd gladly do, but the kid is quickly afoot, coming at me with the jagged remains of the knife. Again, I knock him to one side. He careens across the street, tumbling into the brown lawn. Kikki charges next.

"No momma don't!" a girl cries out. More Dexter children are racing up the driveway. And behind me, the neighbors begin to appear.

"I only want to talk!"

Kikki Dexter pounds me with her fists. I cover up, try to retreat. Got to watch for the kid with the knife.

"Leave my mother alone!"

This whole family is nuts.

Gently, I push. Kikki goes more easily than I expect, back, back, arms swinging, finally tripping and tumbling hard on the tarmac.

At this juncture, the police arrive in three cruisers.

We are separated by five officers. Kikki howls. Larry's murder has unhinged this woman—or was she insane before? I mean, look how she acts.

Another policeman is interviewing the neighbors.

Officer Matt O'Keefe has just returned from herding one of the kids back to the house. He says, "You shouldn't have come, Mr. Bourque."

"I had a good reason."

"He hit me," Kikki screams. "Why isn't he in prison? In the name of God, put him in jail!"

"We're handling it, Mrs. Dexter."

O'Keefe says, "This could be construed as harassment, Mr. Bourque."

"No way. I was just looking. Someone tried to kill me last night. It seems like people can try to kill me and no one gives a damn. I'm minding my business on a public street and I'm attacked by a madwoman."

"Lying bastard. Don't listen to him."

An officer tries to shout louder than Kikki. "Will you please come inside, Mrs. Dexter? I'll take your statement."

"I just wanted to see if her car had a broken headlight. Whoever tried to kill me broke their headlight on my mailbox."

"He was trespassing!" Kikki shouts. "Criminal trespass."

O'Keefe asks, "Did you go on Mrs. Dexter's property to look at the headlights? Did you walk down the driveway?"

"No, I did not. But somebody should. The woman is crazy."

"He hit me!" She holds up a skinned elbow. "I'm bleeding!"

"Mrs. Dexter says you hit her," O'Keefe says.

"I pushed, pushed her off me. In self-defense. You guys saw it. Just as you pulled up. Now that's twice she's attacked me."

Three officers create a wall, nudging Kikki and the children back down the driveway. But just when she seems subdued she sweeps around them like a running back, coming at me, shouting so I can't understand a word. Her eyes spill out hate. I've never seen such a look.

"Why is he on the streets?" she demands as police scramble to box her in. "Why is he here in front of my house? He murdered my husband. God. Haven't I suffered enough? Can't we be left alone in our pain?"

"Yes, Mrs. Dexter."

"Where is justice? Where is justice in this country?"

"Please, Mrs. Dexter."

"Put handcuffs on him," she points. "That bastard."

Even as she heaps abuse on me, I can't help seeing this from Kikki's point of view. If she didn't kill Larry, if she thinks I did it, well, maybe her anger is understandable. She's had a lot of tragedy in her life. But on the other hand, all this rage creates an excuse not to answer questions.

I urge O'Keefe, "Tell them to check the cars while they're down there."

"I was just down there," he says, "I didn't see any broken headlights."

"Oh."

Kikki and her children are gone. And I realize that I'm surrounded by police. It's Indian Peak all over again.

"What's . . . why don't you guys give me some room?"

It's a cold day, but I feel hot and sick. I remember vividly the smell of the Norham lockup. "I didn't do anything wrong, I was just sitting on the street."

O'Keefe nods, scribbles something in his notebook.

"This is crazy. You can't arrest me for sitting on a public street."

"I explained, Mr. Bourque, some might consider that harassment."

"Somebody tried to kill me. Was that harassment?"

"Are you accusing someone in particular?"

"I don't know who did it."

"Well, neither do we."

"For Christ sakes, that kid came at me with a knife. And she, she was pounding my face."

"Want to file a complaint?"

I take a breath. "No. No, I don't. But why arrest me?" My voice breaks. "Dear God. If I go to jail. Matt, I'll never get out. Free I have a chance. Maybe I can prove I'm innocent. But in jail, no one's going to help me."

Officer O'Keefe walks away, consulting his notes. Still trying to catch my breath, I feel dizzy. "Do I frisk him?" an officer asks.

"Wait," O'Keefe replies.

Jesus, help me.

The cops huddle. Handcuffs dangle off thick black leather belts.

Hands in my pockets, I'm afraid and angry. I won't let them lock me up. God. I'll fight you guys. *I didn't do anything!*

"Listen Kevin," Matt says, "call your lawyer as soon as you get home."

Home! I try not to smile with relief.

"I'm sure Mrs. Dexter is going to file some kind of complaint." He looks down on the big house. "I understand she has a lot of influence."

"Yeah."

"We're not holding you now because one of the neighbors backed up your story. We're not holding you. But I'm afraid that might not be the end of it."

"Okay. Okay, Matt. I appreciate this. God bless you. I mean it."

"Kevin. Don't come near here again."

"No."

"I'm sticking my neck out for you. Again."

"I appreciate it. You won't be sorry."

"Keep your nose clean. Or it's going to be your ass. And my ass too."

"You can count on me." I'm backing away toward my pickup. And freedom. Climbing in, I hear Kikki scream.

"What have you done?" Tim Regan's voice pulls me from an unsound sleep. "It couldn't be what I heard you did. Because I know you're not stupid."

Gripping the phone, I describe what happened at the Dexter house.

"Oh, no," he says. And, "Oh, shit." Until he groans, "Oh, Kevin . . ."

"I . . . I probably made a mistake."

"Probably?" He becomes subdued, doesn't chew me out, as if things are too far along for that. "They're trying to get your bail revoked."

I swallow. I'm wide awake.

"They may have already done it."

I gaze at my room, the morning sun in yellow streaks across the floor. What a pleasant place this suddenly seems to be.

"It's possible you'll be rearrested this morning."

"This is all a misunderstanding, Tim. I never meant to—"

"You shouldn't have gone near Mrs. Dexter! Period." After a silence, he asks, "Have you seen the morning paper?"

"I . . . no, I just woke up. What does it say?"

"It's not good. I guess the Foleys have friends in the media too."

Outside a thin layer of frost covers everything. I'm careful not to slip on the stairs. I drive to a nearby store for a newspaper. On an inside section, a prominently placed column is headlined . . . AND THE NIGHTMARE GOES ON.

Catherine Dexter expected courts to bend over backwards on behalf of her husband's "alleged" murderer, Kevin Bourque.

After all, it isn't called the victim justice system.

She wasn't surprised when the accused made bail, despite overwhelming evidence against him. She wasn't surprised when highly paid lawyers began pushing the court date back and back so that justice was a faraway island in a sea of paper. She wasn't surprised when the suspect demanded the right to profit financially from the murder.

"What is this bullshit?" I hear myself say. Highly paid lawyers? And I'm not demanding profits, I'm fighting to stay out of the poorhouse. I mean, get real here.

She was more than surprised, however, to find the alleged killer on the front lawn taunting her and her children.

Jesus Christ.

"What kind of country do we live in," Mrs. Dexter asked, "that I have to be afraid to look out my own window?"

Norham police arrived to see Bourque push Mrs. Dexter to the ground. Claiming self-defense, the muscular home builder was allowed to leave, presumably without a pat on the back from his friends in blue.

In one of the most savage crimes in Plymouth County history, Larry Dexter, Kevin Bourque's business partner, was found riddled with three-inch nails from a pneumatic hammer. The case against Bourque is so strong the boys at Cedar Junction are already planning his furlough.

Recently, the accused objected bitterly when

Mrs. Dexter blocked the sale of their jointly owned real estate, a move that would have gained Bourque additional thousands.

Unbelievable how distortion and omission can paint black for white. And what now? Do I write a letter of complaint to the editor? I bunch the paper into a ball. "Mother of God!" The whole world is against me. But, after a time, I can't resist flattening the paper to read the rest.

Judge Andrea Sussman, who allowed bail over the prosecutor's objections, refused comment yesterday. But a spokesman insisted that the bail was "very, very" high. In fact, it took fifty thousand dollars to unlock the revolving door that is the state correctional system. The developer raised it in three hours.

Meanwhile a terrified widow and her five children are powerless against slick lawyers who treat the law the way TV evangelists treat lonely widows. The innocents remain prisoners in their own home, while Larry Dexter's accused killer owns the streets of Norham.

Oh, please. Don't let it bother you. Let them think and say what they want. I'm in the right and it gives me strength.

Only when you've battered your head against the wall for so long with nothing to show for it. . . . God, you want to say the hell with it and give them what they want, what they're going to get eventually anyway, which is me.

I head home to wait for them. At least my arrest will end the awful uncertainty. But turning off the state highway, I see a police car rolling past the battered mailbox and into my driveway. I stop, swallowing hard.

Quit? Consider the implications. A long life in prison. If I'm lucky. I throw my car into reverse.

I don't dare call anyone. Tim Regan will insist I turn myself in. So I drive. Somehow, I feel safer in this tiny space, the heat blowing, radio blasting. Then again, maybe, maybe I should call Susan. Talk to Molly and Michael while I'm still free to do it.

Listen kids. I said I wasn't going to jail. Only sometimes things work out different than we expect. Just believe me, I never did anything wrong.

They'll ask, when you coming home, Dad? Are you taking us out on your birthday? It's a few days off. Will I be in jail then? Happy birthday, Kevin.

Depressed, exhausted, I drive around for hours before parking on a wooded back road and falling asleep in my truck.

Larry Dexter's law office is in Patriot's Square Office Park. He had a long-term lease, so his name is still on the sign. I hope they haven't yet moved his things out.

It's well after midnight, cold and black, quarter moon clouded over. The cluster of two-story buildings is white with blue shutters, meant to suggest colonial homes. In Norham even the office park has class.

I gently set my ladder against the back of the building. The freezing aluminum stings as I climb. The doors and windows downstairs are locked. People aren't so careful on the second floor.

Up here, I overlook the industrial area, now deserted. Anyway, nobody's going to see me, unless the police come roaring around the corner.

The hall window won't life. Shit. I climb higher, wind whistling through the ladder. Shivering, I peer at the lock. It's secured . . . but . . . wait. My breath creates fog on the glass. Wiping it clear, I see the lock is turned only part way, catching on the edge.

I stick my fingertips beneath the molding and give the window frame a jiggle. Damn. Still won't budge. Christ. I'm not going to fool with it much longer. I don't want to break the glass—that might attract attention—but I will if . . . if . . . I'm pulling at the thing again. Terrific! It finally opens.

I stop. Listen. No alarm. Unless there's a silent alarm.

Climbing inside, I hardly want to breathe for fear someone will hear. Yet the place is certainly empty. The hall carpet feels so thick, like walking on air. I unzip my coat, loosen my collar, but I'm already soaked with sweat.

Work to do. I turn on my flashlight, close the window, and move quickly downstairs, unlocking the back door. I carefully, quietly return the ladder to my truck behind a dumpster on the far side of the lot.

Inside, I slip past the office of Dr. Richard Dunn, D.D.S., and find proud gold letters announcing Lawrence W. Dexter, Attorney at Law. Larry took his professional status seriously. Even his golf clubs were engraved *L. W. D. Atty.*

I'm no thief. But I know doors. I set a crowbar level with the lock and work it in carefully, using a strip of pine to reduce marks. God, this causes tremendous noise. But then, there's no one to hear at two in the morning.

The door and casement strain, the wood makes cracking sounds. I can't help noticing the poor quality of the lumber and workmanship. The frame bends easily—for a minute I think it's going to split—and the door pops open.

Again, I wait for the alarm. Nothing. I close the door behind me, though it will not shut completely. (I'll fix that when I leave.)

First thing, I get a nasty turn. Every drawer of the secretary's desk is open and empty. Christ, no. The whole office has been cleaned out!

I hurry, stumbling to Larry's office. I swing the flashlight around. Thank God. This room is full of books and filing cabinets. It is as it was when Larry was alive, as if he'd worked here today.

I stand over the desk, hands shaking. Once I get at this stuff I'll have the truth and no one will care which laws I broke to get it. I pry open the top drawer with my crowbar and rummage through the papers by flashlight.

Words flip past. Memos on divorce and accident cases. Notes about Indian Peak. A Christmas card on blue construction paper from one of the children. Hurry up. Can't, can't get more than a vague sense of each document. What am I looking for?

European Import Consultants. The name or a reference to it. Perhaps a note on "business in Europe" or "paintings." Anything relating to immigration, or Ireland or Austria. A trace of money.

Nothing useful in the top drawer. Wish I had more light. But one window overlooks the main street. I'm nervous enough about the flashlight.

Plenty of time. Workers won't start arriving for over three hours.

I inspect each drawer, even tap for hidden compartments. That's Larry's speed, false bottoms and the like. Yet I find no such thing.

Stacks of paper fall sheet by sheet beneath my flashlight. Nothing interesting. Nothing to catch my eye.

It's in a file cabinet, I decide. Something incriminating wouldn't be in the desk. Got to be filed away.

I face two such cabinets, four drawers each. One is unlocked. I leave that for later. Question is, how to open the locked file cabinet?

I jam the crowbar into the top drawer. The lock, on the upper right-hand corner, is stubborn. I must catch my breath . . . okay, try again. Pull! Sweat runs down my face. I glance out the window, half expecting the racket will attract the police.

The drawer begins to warp and as it does I hear a pitiable screech, as if someone is inside crying out. I see the files, tightly packed. But bent is not the same as open. I can't get at them.

To hell with subtlety. Using the crowbar like a hammer, I smash the protruding lock from the side. A few good whacks sends it flying, while something falls within the cabinet. The drawers are opened to me at last.

And then! Jesus, Jesus, Jesus. The room is light, light everywhere, light pointed at me! I dive for the floor. God. Not now. Let me inside that cabinet first. Please.

A car pulls past the window and into the rear parking lot. Somebody must've heard something and called the police. And now I've been seen. The lights were right on me.

"Shit!"

I crawl beneath the desk and hope they go away.

But, God, obviously, the police are not going away.

I wonder if they'll panic and shoot me. The flashlight looks a bit like a weapon so I turn it off and gently push it away.

For a while I hear nothing. Then, slamming car doors and voices that are loud and not exactly sober. Can't be cops. A key clatters, struggling to find a keyhole.

Someone is coming in here. God knows why at this hour. Of all the damned bad luck.

Two voices, man and a woman. Coming down the hallway. If they haven't seen me already, then they're bound to notice the door to Dexter's office is not quite shut.

"Which office is yours?" the woman asks. I can't hear the man's reply, but she says, "I'm just in for a filling," and bursts out in drunken laughter.

"Shhhh," he says.

"Who's going to hear us?" she asks.

They don't reach Larry's door, but turn into the dentist's office.

"Where is it?" she asks.

"Right here," exclaims the man.

"I know where that is honey. Where's the bed?"

The walls are thin. I hurt, wondering if Dexter ever brought Terri here.

"There's no bed?" she asks indignantly.

"I told you. We push these couches together."

"No couch. Forget it!"

"It's not a couch. It's two couches."

"I don't care."

"I've got a very comfortable chair."

"You said you had a bed."

"Let me show you the chair. It has more positions than—"

"Hey, forget it. I'm not doing it in a dentist chair."

I don't dare move while the two are in there. If they stay all night, I'll be trapped.

Meanwhile, Dexter's file cabinets are standing before me, waiting to give up the name of his killer. Goddammit! Let me at them! But just pulling the drawer open is bound to make the godawfulest squeak.

"If you didn't have a bed why couldn't we get a room?"

"I didn't think we needed a room, darling." His voice goes low again.

"You put your pants back on because if you want to fuck me you better come up with a bed."

"Pearl."

"Don't Pearl me."

"Well, the rug in the reception room is deep pile—"

"I'm not doing it on the floor! What do you think I am?"

"Pearl honey, I don't have the cash for a room. If I had the cash I'd take you to the Ritz. I don't have it. I just don't."

"You have credit cards."

"Come on. My wife pays the credit card bills."

"I'm nobody's cheap date."

"Of course you're not—"

"What was that?" she asks.

Blue light crashes off the walls and ceiling of Dexter's office. I'm entranced. The police. First one cruiser, then another, then another. Why are they here? For crying out loud, is this an open house?

Shoes on the pavement. A flashlight. An officer walks the perimeter of the building. Christ, they only have to check the opposite end of the parking lot to spot my pickup. And they'll have me.

Someone knocks loudly.

"Police are at the front door," Dr. Dunn explains.

"We didn't do anything. We don't even have a bed."

"Shut up one minute please. Let me think. We. We must have tripped . . . tripped the silent alarm. I forgot all about it."

The police knock again.

Dr. Dunn instructs, "Stay here and be quiet. I'll get rid of them."

To think, I'd been cursing my luck. Surely, *I* had set off the silent alarm. If the horny dentist hadn't happened along I'd be headed for jail right now. Instead, the blue lights are soon extinguished. The police drive away.

"What are you doing?" Dr. Dunn asks, wounded.

"Putting on my coat."

"Pearl."

"You . . . you know, you brought me here under palse fretenses . . . I mean . . . you know what I mean."

"Don't be like that." He pleads all the way down the hall. "If I was a prince I'd take you to a palace. But I'm just a dentist."

After a few minutes, car doors are slammed shut and the frustrated couple roars away. I take a breath, try to calm myself.

Don't waste a minute. I pull open the cabinet drawer. The files are alphabetical. I go immediately to "E" but find no European Import Consultants. Next I try "F" for Finnerty, then "S" for his cousin, Sullivan. No luck. So. Start at the top and work down.

I don't have time to take out each file, nor to read any completely. I skim them, the flashlight pointed into the drawer.

I find correspondences between Larry and his clients, Larry and other attorneys, the courts and Larry. None deal with immigration. Mostly, they concern divorce and accident cases.

I can't help reading some sad, too-common stories of how these dozens and dozens of families came apart. It's funny because I never imagined so much of the misery being collected in one place like this.

A woman's letter reports, "I'm at the end of my rope. The landlord is removing us on Thursday if I don't pay him. I call and beg. I tell Ron it's for the children. He says he'll send the money, but it never comes. . . ."

A memo is direct. "Mr. S—— called. In tears. Children again refused to accompany him on weekend visit. Mrs. S—— laughed. . . ."

A court order disposes of the custody of Derek, three, and Kim, five, in pages of legalisms, but someone has included pictures of innocent, smiling angels.

I discover other pictures, telephoto shots, a middle-aged couple having sex in the woods somewhere. I suppose somebody's got to be a lawyer, but I'll feel better about being a carpenter after this.

Then, forgetting I would find it, the "Ps." Terri Pratt. God. I go cold.

I lay the thick folder on the desk. At the last, I don't want to touch it, never mind open it—as if I know already what's inside. Two U.S. passports protrude from the bottom. Jesus.

I pick up the passports first. Issued four years ago in the names of Louraine and Kelly Pratt, Terri's youngest, they are stamped for Austria.

I take a breath. God.

Inside the folder, amidst the brief record of the Pratt divorce, is a four-year-old copy of a letter from Mrs. Theresa T. Pratt to the State Department requesting passports for her minor children. Attached are photocopies of birth certificates for Kelly and Louraine.

Another lie. The worst yet. It's as if Susan is grabbing me again. Open your eyes. Face the facts.

Terri scoffed at the suggestion that she'd accompanied Dexter on his travels. *How could I go to Europe? What would*

I do with my kids? Well, I guess I know now. And I know why the air fare was so expensive.

From one passport drops Dexter's canceled check for three hundred dollars. Terri's signature covers the back. Why did Terri's lawyer pay her?

For a long time, I stare at the check and the passports. I wish she was here now. Can you explain these things, Terri? And she'll have to tell why the trip was made and how it led to Larry's death. She'll have to tell the truth at last.

Good news, but I don't feel particularly happy.

· 12 ·

I've bought the morning paper. Happily, my name isn't in it. I begin to wonder if the police *are* after me. I haven't been all that difficult to find.

Sunrise and I drive home to my cottage. I did a good job of disguising the forced entry at Larry's office. It might be days before the break-in is discovered. Of course, the office is a mess—I tore that place apart.

Under my seat is Terri's folder. Excepting the passport material and the check, there's no useful information in it. Yet, I treat the thing the way a miser treats his gold. At every red light, I take it out, look at it, and get hotter and hotter.

At last, I've got her figured out. Because even if she could prove her innocence in Dexter's murder, Terri knows of the European trip and Larry's secret business. And while I need every scrap of information to survive, she tells me nothing of it! God, I'd like to get my hands on her.

Bent with exhaustion, I carry the ladder to its resting place under my deck. Trouble is the police won't make much of the checks and passports. Dexter and his mistress went to Europe and came back with something—I'm guessing it's antique paintings—which brought him lots of money. So what. They've already conceded that Dexter made thousands selling art works.

I've got to confront Terri, make her talk. Somehow.

I slide the ladder under the deck and pause to look out on the pond. It's all so tranquil. But if the police want me, this is the first place they'll come. So, I'd best get moving, find a place to sleep. God, I need to sleep.

Would Susan let me sleep at home?

Susan and home. My real home. The mere thought is warming. She only wants what's best for me. And to think I'd actually suspected Susan. Terri put that idea in my head. Just as she pointed a finger at the Lundgrens.

I hurry inside. A quick call. Then, I'm out of here.

As it rings I whisper, "Susan, Susan, Susan . . ." Suppose she doesn't want to hear from me, much less hide me.

"Hello?"

God, she sounds tired. Poor Susan. Then, I remember. It's very early.

"Susan?"

"Kevin? Kevin is that you?"

"Susan, honey. I had to call." I feel like crying. I'm so damned weary. "Uh, how are you?"

"I'm okay."

"Good. Good. You sound tired. I know you work hard. And it's—everything you do is for the kids. And I had to call to say I appreciate that."

"Well . . . thanks." She seems confused.

"Sometimes. When I think of things. I don't know why we're apart. I . . . I guess there are reasons. But sometimes I just don't know what they are. You know?"

"Kevin. What . . . what's the matter?"

"Uh, are the police looking for me? Do you know?"

"Not that I know of."

"I was afraid they might be."

"Is something wrong?"

"I was wondering, Susan. I was wondering if I could ask a favor."

"What? . . . Well, of course."

"Just. I don't know. I'm so tired and I need a place to sleep."

"You mean here? You want to sleep here?"

"If it's too much trouble—"

"Do you mean now?"

"Uh, I'm afraid to stay at the cottage, you know. I'm afraid. Because somebody tried to run me down. And the police. If the police come after me. I just, I just don't want to be found. I'll understand if you say no."

"Of course you can stay here," she says.

"That's great of you. Great."

"I could come and get you. It might be better if I do. You don't want them to see your truck here."

"No. That's okay. I'll park it in the garage. And I'll be right over."

"What . . . Has something happened? You sound . . . different."

"Well, I'm tired. But yeah. Something happened. I've found something. It's good. Maybe it won't prove I'm innocent. But I think, I hope it will help. And, and I haven't told anybody. Not even my lawyer. I didn't even tell him yet. Because I wanted to tell you first."

"What did you find?"

"Some, some passports and stuff. I don't know. Looks like, maybe you were right about Terri Pratt. I don't like to think so. But. She wasn't straight with me. I caught her in lies, just very serious lies."

"I see."

"Was I kidding myself with her? Susan?"

"Uh, I know at times you're too trusting. People take advantage."

"Yeah. What a mistake listening to her. She tried to poison my mind against everyone. My friends. Like . . ." I won't tell Susan she was on the list. ". . . Like the Lundgrens. They'll probably never talk to me again. Tell them, tell them I'm sorry. If you see them . . ."

"I still don't understand. What did you find?"

"Like I said. Passports. For Terri Pratt's kids. Which shows she herself went to Europe with Larry four years ago. After telling me she didn't know anything about it. You know? How could you not know about a trip if you went on it?"

She doesn't answer for a moment, as if she can't understand the significance. Then, she says, "I'm glad it looks better. Thank God."

"Yeah."

"And you can come over."

"Thanks."

"I'm glad to help, Kevin."

"I want to tell you something."

"I've been waiting for you to ask me to do something. I'm willing to help. I'll do anything I can to help."

"I want to tell you, Susan. I want to say I still love you. You know?" She can't see me cry.

"I . . . I didn't know that. No."

"I do. I couldn't stop if I wanted to."

"I'll always love you," she says.

I hang up, tears streaming. I sit on the bed to compose myself. For a moment, because I'm so tired, I kick off my shoes and lie back, closing my eyes. When I open them it's dark and the black barrel of a handgun points directly at my forehead.

"Get up."

"What?"

"Get the fuck up."

I know how much trouble I'm in right off. I was thinking police. But hearing that voice, I feel I've been tossed back in the ice water. It's the man from the bridge.

I come to a sitting position. Having slept in my coat, I'm damp with sweat.

"Get up."

I get up with a sick, despairing sense of death in my gut. I must have seen people pointing guns a million times on TV.

Yet I never fully appreciated how persuasive they are. Every second, I'm waiting for the thing to go off and make a hole in me.

No, it can't happen. I remember fighting my way to shore after he threw me off the bridge. That was like surviving a plane crash or something. And you don't survive a plane crash just to be shot weeks later. No way.

So I'm standing. A voice in my head says, *Do whatever he tells you.*

"What do you want?" I try to sound calm. But he's behind me and I can't see what he's doing. A shiver runs up my back. As I begin to turn he gives a hard push. I stumble toward the door.

Still more frightening, this guy can't keep still, he bounces about, his voice breaks. He means to kill me. But not until he works up the nerve.

My eyes well up remembering that I just told Susan I loved her. All the bitterness of our divorce seems to have fallen away. And perhaps this is the reason I was saved at the bridge.

"Outside."

"Why?"

"Move."

"Where we going?"

"Jesus," he shouts, "just move!"

"Right, right."

"Don't piss me off!"

He's not sure of himself. No wonder he botched the job twice before. And maybe, if I keep my wits, I can escape or even talk him out of it.

"I gotta, gotta get my shoes if we're going out."

"You won't need them."

"What . . . what are you going to do?" I turn, but he gives another shove forward. "Listen." I struggle to keep my balance. "You don't want to do this."

"Put your shoes on."

I do it. Good, good. I need shoes. I'm going to be out

there a while. Maybe we'll walk or something. I breathe easier. Or is he just saying that because he heard the terror in my voice? Pacified, I'm easier to deal with.

He's not going to shoot me. He's not. He's not. I'm so scared that I don't know how I manage to put one foot in front of the other. But I do.

I go down the front steps, wishing I could wake up.

Keep your eyes open. He's bound to make a mistake.

It's night. I guess I slept a long time. I turn again hoping to see his face.

"Eyes front."

Eyes front. In the driveway is an old Ford compact, beat up, shattered headlight. I memorize the plate. 328 HBP. I imagine, sometime in the future, reporting it to the police. In the future. An optimistic phrase.

I flinch seeing the trunk open.

I'm not getting in there. Not the trunk. I see a million news photos of shoeless gangsters found dead in trunks. "You don't want to do this."

He nudges me toward it.

"This is unfair. My God, I haven't done anything!" I want to cry. "This is . . . this is stupid."

He doesn't answer.

"I mean, I'm going to jail. Isn't that enough for you?"

We've reached the car. I begin to speak very fast.

"Who are you doing this for? Is it Big John? John Finnerty? Well, then who? Is it Kikki Dexter? Or Bill Foley? I've a right to know who sent—"

"Shut the fuck up, asshole!"

"It's Terri. Isn't it? I know it's Terri. And you're making a mistake to trust her. Take it from me. Look. She's always going to have it over you. She's . . . " Pushed hard, I very nearly tumble into the trunk.

"Get in," he says.

"Uh, wait." Inside, it's layered with junk, chains, rags, and an old gas can. I smell oil. I don't want to get in there.

"Jesus, Jesus, help me." I close my eyes. I feel dizzy. "Holy Mother . . ."

I can't see it, but I know the pistol is near the back of my skull.

"Get in. I won't say it a third time."

"Okay, okay." I'm careful not to move suddenly. It's painful climbing into the tiny, cluttered space. I still haven't seen this guy. When he was before me all I saw was the gun. He has no trace of an Irish accent.

I lie down and he slams the lid shut. It's black.

The car begins to rumble like a tank. No muffler. Jesus. My ears ache and everything vibrates. Shouldn't have gotten in. Christ. Now, he can do anything he wants to me.

I get my first whiff of exhaust.

Sure. No need to look me in the eye. Just pump carbon monoxide into the trunk. I spin, panicked. "Let me out!" I gasp. Give me air. I smash my elbows and knees. Something sharp cuts the back of my head. I'm bleeding.

Air. I can't breathe. "God, help me."

The car bounces over the dirt driveway. I slam into the roof of the trunk. "Aww!" The damn thing roars so I don't have the satisfaction of hearing myself cry out.

A crack of faint light appears near the wheel well. I push my nose to it. A hint of fresh air. I can breathe. Thank God.

But I remain helpless. And while we're quickly on pavement, the car has virtually no springs. Every pothole jerks me into something hard. I have no room to turn. Or to straighten my knees. My muscles cramp.

Why did I climb in here? I should have run. Or stood up to this thug.

Trying to drive me down the other night, he couldn't manage the job and ran away. He's afraid. Remember that and take advantage of it.

Who am I kidding? I'm the one who's afraid. Why should he be afraid—he's got the gun.

Over the roar comes country western music, songs of cheated lovers and broken hearts. Surely, the man who listens to these has a sense of fairness. I can appeal to that.

After what seems hours of driving, perhaps aimlessly, we are back on dirt. My own driveway again? No, it's a long road. I am tossed brutally. My hip aches where I lie on the damned chains. The stench of oil and exhaust sickens me.

After such a ride, how can I react to defend myself once I get out—if I get out. The car stops and silence follows. I strain to hear, but I'm half deaf now. There is the distinctive pop of a can, beer or tonic.

I figure he's building his courage. To do what? Choices come to me in vivid, horrifying detail. Open the trunk and fire. Shoot through the trunk. Set the car ablaze. Run it into a lake. Or simply leave me to freeze or starve, as I was once left to drown.

God help me, I should have refused to get in. He would have had to kill me face to face. And I don't think he's able to do it.

I'm praying to be out—almost despairing—when the trunk pops open. I shiver at a welcome blast of cold. I look up to stars and trees. We've stopped in a lonely place, very dark, not even a street light visible.

"Out," the kidnapper says from somewhere.

I emerge with difficulty. "Oh . . . ah, jeez . . ." It's a moment before I can stand upright. "God." I hurt everywhere.

"Get the chains."

"What?"

"Take out the chains."

"The chains?"

"Just do it." He comes up to me. In the dark, I get a vague glimpse of his face. He's of medium height, but strong—I still hurt where he pushed me into the trunk. He's wearing old clothes. Also, he's oddly familiar. I mean, I can't put my finger on it, but it's like I know him from somewhere.

I fish out the first chain, covered in rust.

"Wrap it around."

"Wrap it around what?" I ask.

"Around you."

"How . . . how am I supposed to do this?"

"Over the shoulder." He comes close in the dark. I smell beer breath. "Like a bandolier."

"A bandolier?"

"Like this, asshole." He points. Then withdraws.

I find three lengths of chain, one short, but as thick as an anchor chain, and he has me carry these over both shoulders, crisscrossing my stomach.

I'm encouraged. He wouldn't chain me if he meant to kill me. More likely, I'll be held somewhere.

But why? And who is this guy?

"Let's go." He points to the woods.

I can barely see the trail and he wants me to lead. "I . . ."

"Come on!"

"These things are heavy."

"Want to stay alive? Then do what I say as soon as I say it! Clear?"

Why so worked up? After all, he's got the gun.

Thinking escape, I clank along like Marley's ghost, branches slapping at my face. The damn chains keep slipping off my shoulders, catching on roots and branches. Add to that I can't see more than a few feet in front of me.

I try to take steady, measured breaths. The darkness makes me sick at heart. Can't forget when I asked for my shoes. *You won't need them.*

Climbing steadily. The only light is the moon and stars. We are in the country. I turn every so often, hoping to see his face. What does he plan for me?

He's going to find a spot far from the world and shoot you in the back. It's obvious. Oh, God. I fight it, but tears streak my face. It's just so unfair. I didn't kill anyone.

At one point, I stop. "I don't . . . I don't know which way it is." I've lost the trail and I sense that he can't find it either. Eventually he gives me a rough shove, so I climb forward.

I fall more than once, landing painfully on rocks or on the frozen earth. "Ah . . . aw, God."

"Get up."

Then, softly, as I get to my feet I say, "Jesus . . . Jesus, help." I've never been religious, but I feel God beside me now, a forgiving friend.

God, if I had time—even in prison—I could make amends for all the wrongs I've done. Particularly to Susan. And Molly and Michael.

I'm not going to die. I won't accept the possibility. Find an out. Keep alert. God will show the way.

I could run into the dark. But the chains. It would take time to rid myself of the chains. I'd be dead before they hit the ground.

Fact is, the guy could have shot me in bed. Instead we take a drive, then sit a while. Now we're hiking through the damn woods.

If this man killed Larry, if he plans to kill me, it's because he's been goaded into it. He screams and shouts to psych himself up because he really hasn't the stomach for murder, is doing everything to delay it. Which maybe means he can be turned.

I try a friendly tone. "I don't think I'd recognize this place with the, with the lights on. . . . Are we going somewheres in particular?"

He makes like he hasn't heard me, so I raise my voice, "What . . . what is this all about anyway?"

No answer.

"Why are you doing this?" my voice wavers. "What have I done to you?"

"Keep moving."

But I turn. "I have two kids. Little, young kids. For their sake—"

"Shut the fuck up!" The gun swings. I catch a glancing blow on the temple.

"Jesus, God." I back away more frightened than hurt. Jesus, Jesus, that thing could go off. The way he handles it. It could go off by accident.

He says, "After what you did to them babies, I don't want to hear any shit from you about kids."

"Babies?" My head spins trying to figure what he means,

what he knows, what he thinks he knows. Is this Terri's ex-husband and has she told some ugly lie about me and her girls? Or do those passports somehow put Terri's children in jeopardy? Perhaps he means some other babies, maybe the Dexter kids?

"Who are you?" I plead.

"Move!"

The topography has changed dramatically. We move over a moonlit waste of boulders, dirt, and granite slabs until finally I stop at the edge of a vast hole, like a black sea with no far shore. It frightens me, as if I might be sucked into it.

Yet, a stiff breeze comes from its depths, carrying with it a bizarre phenomenon—snow, flying up at us, returning to the sky. I back away.

He walks past, careful that the weapon still points at me. Reaching the edge, he leans to look into the void. His hair blows wild with the snow. His face seems full, unshaven. He kicks a rock over. For a long time I hear nothing. Then, faintly, a splash.

Turning to me, the kidnapper is partly obscured by shadows. The weapon I see clearly. The clouds gone, light plays off its ugly snout.

"You can put that down," I say hopefully. He doesn't answer, doesn't even seem to watch me. Yet as I lean left, the barrel follows.

"Can I get rid of this stuff?" I shift the weight of the chains.

"No."

By now, they are digging into my shoulders, sapping my strength.

Reaching into his coat, he flashes two steel padlocks. He throws these on the ground before me. "Wrap them chains tight. Then lock them secure."

"What?" I stare at the locks. Because I know why we are here. The chains are for weight. So the body will sink to the bottom of the quarry. The body. Me.

"Lis—listen, we should talk."

"Do it."

"If it's Terri's folder you want. You can have it back."

He brandishes the gun.

Okay, okay. Stop shaking and think.

He can't do it. Not face to face.

"I . . . I mean . . . this doesn't make sense." I shuffle slowly backward, along the lip of the great black hole. And he follows. Step for careful step.

Soccer-style, he kicks the two locks. One bounces off my leg. "Pick em up."

The gun is pointed at my gut. Another step backwards. The wind is stronger, the snow thicker. Where's the edge? I should look where I'm going but I can't take my eyes off the gun.

I gaze into his eyes. Plead with them. Two specks of light in the black. Unmoved, he doesn't blink. Maybe I should just do as he says.

No. Then, I'll be helpless again. He's had time to kill me. He can't. And all that's left is to call his bluff.

"I . . ." The gun comes closer. Pointed directly at my chest. It won't fire. "Don't. This is murder."

The thing is inches from my heart.

"You don't want that on your conscience."

His finger finds the trigger.

"You don't want to do this—" And I know him. He's the temporary help, the wild one roaring up the street in Kikki's Mercedes, nearly running over Larry's foot as he delivered a brown package. "You—you worked for Larry!"

He fires.

I don't hear it. Sparks leap from the barrel and land all over my chest.

I fall back on the rocks, a hole in my chest, the exploded heart shutting me down like a machine, eyes, ears, the sense of touch. And death is not a release, but a cup of pain and regret for a life full of mistakes.

Death does not live up to expectations. I'm surprised to be watching the gunman, staring down at me for some time before shoving the gun in his coat and turning to kick about in the grass and rocks. Of course, he's looking for the padlocks.

I've read about this. An out-of-body experience. At any moment, I'll begin floating skyward. I will see myself, lying still, a huge hole where my heart had been. Anyway, I guess I'm grateful to be done with it all at last.

Except, after an interval, I'm still earthbound and I don't see white lights or dead relatives and my back is hurting like hell.

This is some surprise. Because I saw the gun fire. I think I saw the bullet even. It was aimed directly at my heart from less than a foot away. I felt the impact. So, I've got to be dead. Only it seems I'm not.

Slowly, carefully, I feel about and find, despite soreness, that my coat, my chest, my heart are all intact. Figure this one out. I remember my prayer. *Jesus help.* And I wonder if He somehow intervened, interrupting the fatal course of the bullet.

I'm alive by the grace of a God. Only why save *me?*

I'm alive, but not out of the woods in any sense. The gunman approaches, padlock in hand. Gentle thoughts of miracles and Jesus are fast receding. I find a large, jagged stone is in my hand.

The gunman squats. He's pulling at the chains which fell away as I fell, which are at my arms and legs. He means to lock them tight and push me into the void. I remember the bridge, the water seeping in.

I come up swinging.

He turns, eyes wide, as if facing a ghost.

The rock catches him on the head. "Agh!" Rising for an instant, he wobbles and falls on all fours alongside the excavation.

I scramble, rock in hand. He fumbles for the gun in his pocket. Son of a bitch. I hit the bastard again, solidly, on the back of the head.

He grunts and collapses over a sheet of granite that rims the quarry. The pistol clatters, resting on the edge.

He's still moving, reaching for the gun. But I'm hunched over him, following. I strike out again. "How do you like it?" Dragging the chains behind me. "How does it feel, *asshole*?"

He cries as I cried in the water, "Help."

"No one's—"

He's trying to get away, crawling toward the gun.

"No one's listening." Swinging desperately, I won't let him up. But he wriggles away!

And suddenly I find myself on my knees alone with the wind and the swirling snow. It's a moment before I wonder if he's slipped off the rim, gone into the black, gone without a cry. He might splash as he hits the water, but I don't hear the sound. Perhaps I'm too stunned.

It's a trick. I lean cautiously over the edge and see nothing. "What . . .?" And, when I understand finally, certainly that he's fallen, I give an involuntary laugh. "Ha."

I come unsteadily to my feet. God, I'm sweating, shaking with terror. Got to collect myself. Do . . . something. The chains.

I whip them out, soaring toward the moon. Minutes seem to pass. I was meant to go with them. Then, faintly, the splash.

"It was you or me," I say, leaning over. "You or me."

To be safe I kick over any number of loose rocks in case there's blood or something on them. Then, accidentally, I find the gun. Christ, another bit of luck. I'd assumed it had gone over the side with the owner.

I set to heave it as well. But, something stops me. Maybe I feel safe with the thing in my hand. I push it into my coat pocket.

I never intended the guy to fall. The responsibility is all on him. Dexter's temporary helper. What was his name? He was part of Larry's scam. And who else was involved, people I've never met, never heard of? Suddenly, I'm more confused than ever and the truth seems very far away.

Got to . . . got to get out of here. That's the priority. I see headlines. BOURQUE IN SECOND MURDER. I run, sometimes stumbling, downhill.

Nobody can connect me to this. Someone will spot the body in the water. But maybe not until summer. By then— no, wait. They'll find the car and go looking for him. Shit.

I should inspect the car. The registration will give a name to the man who three times tried to kill me.

It's almost impossible to follow the trail. Frequently, it goes off in several directions. Deep in the forest, I run smack into a tree, "Shit!" bruising my forehead. Shake it off. But it aches like a punishment.

Had to keep hitting him. So long as he was going for the gun. He was dangerous and I had to defend myself. It's not like I pushed him. He fell. He was moving for the gun and fell.

Or was he simply trying to get away because I kept hitting him?

I was fighting for my life. God saved me when the gun went off, but thereafter I was expected to save myself. That guy pulled the trigger, he intended to dump my corpse into the quarry. He winds up in there himself. And I can't make myself feel bad about that.

I plow through a grove of small evergreens, like Christmas trees. I go like mad, downhill. Branches whip my face. Then I find myself on macadam, gasping for breath, falling to my knees.

Well, I've missed the car and the dirt road as well. Should I go back? A steep, wooded hill looms. The chances of finding a car in there are not good. Did I leave anything in the trunk, evidence connecting me to what has happened tonight?

I stand. God. Head won't clear. Can't concentrate. What could I have left behind? Still got my wallet. There's nothing else I can think of.

If I'm connected to the body it's over. No one will believe that he shot me pointblank in the heart but, somehow, the bullet "evaporated." Must have been . . . some kind of misfire.

What do I say if police come round tomorrow asking questions? For the first time, I must deal with the hard work of lying. "I've been sleeping all night, officer. Why?"

I walk the middle of the road, wondering what to do next. And it roars out of the night, lights catching a face contorted in horror. I leap for the shoulder. It rocks, bangs, and shakes the trees. But I am far into the woods when the eighteen-wheeler actually passes.

Oh Christ. My nerves are gone to hell. Help. I've got to get help.

· *13* ·

Tim Regan yawns as we drive the empty interstate. His pajama collar crawls out of the top of his coat.

After a long, frightening walk in the dark, I'd finally stumbled onto the interstate and a pay phone at the Hopewell exit.

"I appreciate your coming, Tim. I . . . I didn't know who else to call."

"Just don't make this a regular routine or something."

"Does it come under lawyer-client privilege? This, this, picking me up tonight? The fact that you've done it?"

"Interesting question." He looks over. "What went on out here?"

I stare at the headlights reaching out into the black. It feels strange driving so low to the ground. I don't belong in a jazzy sports car. My coat is torn and stinks of oil. My face is bruised and scratched. And the gun in my pocket tugs my coat to one side. I suppose I should get rid of it.

So far, I've ducked all Tim's questions and he doesn't like it. Fact is, I don't know how much I can safely tell him.

For one thing, he'll want to go back and make certain the guy is dead or something. But he's dead for sure.

I study my hands, remembering how I tried to smash his skull, how he slipped away and, apparently, over the edge. Had to do it. Except for a miracle I'd be in a quarry instead of him. I touch my chest, which is still tender—though the coat, incredibly, is not even soiled.

The engine hums. Am I finally out of danger? I take a deep breath. "The police aren't looking for me?"

"Not yet. They moved to revoke bail, but all those headlines got the judge's back up. The lady doesn't like to be pressured. So she took it under advisement."

"What's that mean?"

Tim says, "Let's hope nothing."

"They're not after me for anything else? The police?" I'm thinking of the break-in at Dexter's office.

"Like what?"

"Like . . . well, I don't know . . ."

Tim shakes his head. "Going to tell me what you're doing out here?"

"Like I said, uh . . . I was with this guy, he claimed he knew Dexter."

"What guy?"

"I don't know his name."

Tim shakes his head. "Why'd you come half way across the state?"

"I, uh . . ." I'm casting about for answers. "This is where he wanted to go."

"Where is he now?"

"Ah, he was just a crank. So, I left. And I was hitching home but I wasn't getting rides so I got cold and scared and I called you."

Tim has a pained expression. "The guy picked you up at your house?"

"At my house, yeah. I think he was a crank or something." I look out the window. "A crank."

After a few moments, Tim says, "You know, if you're

so anxious to go to prison, Kevin, you can manage without me."

"What?"

"Lying to your attorney is just about the surest way there."

"I know how it sounds. But it's true. The guy, I think he saw me on TV and wanted to meet me or something." Christ, it's a lame story and Tim makes me go over it three or four times. It's just as well because I'd better get it right for the police.

After a long silence, Tim says, "Susan called me last night. Worried. Said you were due at her house. But you never showed up."

"Yeah," I nod. "I should have called her. I couldn't make it. I fell asleep. Then, later on. This, uh, guy showed up, like I said."

"You better call as soon as we get to a phone. She's worried sick."

"I will."

"Susan, she's very loyal."

I nod.

"I always admired your wife. One of those women. You can see right off she's got class."

"Yeah. Better, better than I deserve." I stare at the road. "Susan." She still cares. "Take me there, Timmy. Take me to Susan."

Susan's sheets are freshly laundered, the room clean, bright, with white curtains. It's a dizzy turn from last night's dark horror. On the closet shelf are my sweaters and slacks, neatly folded as if awaiting my return. My old gym bag is here—I stash the gun in it, under a couple of towels.

I sleep most of the day. Awakening, I vomit in the bathroom.

Clean up. I'll feel better if I can wash. But, undressing, I'm stunned by a peculiar red curl raised on my chest. I stare into the mirror.

It corresponds to a link from a chain. With a flash of gunfire, neither of us remembered that I was crisscrossed by steel. The chain, not Jesus, caught the bullet. And if I'd so much as shrugged I'd be dead.

Light headed, I sit down. This is a message. To stay alive and free I cannot rely on miracles. I must examine each unanswered question. And pick apart everything I know. Possibly, the solution stares me right in the face.

Why, when I am certain to be sent to prison for life, was someone trying to kill me? To keep me from the truth, of course. Clearly, I remain on the verge of something explosive—or someone thinks so.

Suddenly, I hear Dexter's ironic mutterings, *"This is what passes for temporary help. . . ."* The wild man in the quarry lacked the attitude of an ordinary employee when he accepted the boss's package weeks ago. Nor would Larry allow a stranger to drive Kikki's Mercedes.

Given Terri's sordid habits, it's not impossible that her husband Eddie and her lover Larry were acquainted. And couldn't they have gone from sharing the same woman to sharing the same crime?

Terri will think I'm a ghost when she sees me. I'll demand Eddie's picture. Then, I'll wave it in her face. This man tried to kill me last night. And I'll let her guess the result.

At last, I'll show the passports and the check. I got it figured, Terri. You, Eddie, and Larry Dexter worked some art scam. I don't know the details except it made lots of money. And that's how Larry got killed, a fight over money. You two killed him.

Then, when I got too close to the truth, you sent Eddie to kill me too.

Hearing that scenario, she'll just assume I have the proof and she'll confess. So I'll be free, finally.

Can't wait. I dial Terri's number. No answer. I call the nursing home, but she's not working. Perhaps, realizing Eddie is dead, she's run off.

Except . . . except, well, I might have details confused or the whole thing ass-backwards. After all, a few days ago I was so confident of Terri that I took her to bed. I must be careful to consider everything.

The kidnapper could have been Kikki Dexter's lover or one of John Finnerty's cousins. Am I too hasty in condemning Terri? Is it possible there's an innocent explanation for the passports? I can't imagine one, but . . .

The would-be killer talked of "them babies." Well, what does that mean? How does it tie into Larry Dexter's art scam? (Assuming there was one.) Could the paintings be peripheral to the murder?

Suppose the hedonistic Eddie Pratt faced a perversion even he couldn't stomach. What if Larry Dexter was molesting his children?! I sit upright.

For one thing, he'd be inclined to act on his own—couldn't bring Larry to the cops without revealing his involvement in . . . I don't know what, peddling smuggled paintings, sex orgies, whatever.

Dexter lies at the foot of the stairs, terror frozen on his face. And at last I know that I *could* do that. Lay a hand on my children, I could do worse.

I hear voices. Slowly, I descend the stairs. It's late afternoon.

Susan is hosting the Lundgrens. Outside, our four kids play loudly. The window is open—it has become mild, giving a sudden hint of spring.

It seems Pat has forgotten our argument, gesturing for me to sit beside her. "My God, look at his face. Jack, look at his face."

Jack leans on the stove, sipping coffee. "Hope you got the number of the truck that hit you, Kev."

"Actually," I sit, "I was out walking and—in the dark—and I ran into a tree. Believe it or not. I never saw it." A half lie. Will I be able to keep my stories straight? Yet, it's essential Susan not know the truth about last night. No longer my wife, she could be forced to give evidence against me.

"I keep telling him he should have it looked at," Susan says.

"You should," Pat agrees. "That could get infected."

For a moment, no one speaks. It's like they all know I'm lying. I make it worse—can't help it—by looking down and away.

"I called Pat and Jack yesterday," my wife explains. "For help. When we couldn't find you."

"We were all very worried," Pat says.

"Well, I'm okay. Really."

"Kevin called yesterday," Susan's voice tightens. "About someone trying to . . . run him down." Her eyes fill.

"He's safe now, Susan," Pat moves to her. "He's safe and sound." But she looks almost as distressed as my wife.

As soon as they start asking questions, I excuse myself for the living room. I call Terri again, heart pounding as the phone rings. I've got to *see* you. Right away. Come on, answer! I wait several minutes before giving up.

Then, on impulse, I call information for the number of Edward Pratt in Revere—but it's unlisted. Maybe no one would answer anyway.

Back in the kitchen, I apologize to Jack and Pat. "The way I acted the other day. Well. You guys deserve better than accusations from me."

"Forget it," Jack says. "I want you to know we've talked to the police. To explain about the painting. Right, dear?"

"I shouldn't have blown up like that," Pat says. "Just when you need understanding and help. I wasn't, I wasn't being a good friend."

"My fault, I'm sorry." In fact, I still don't quite trust them—I don't trust anyone except Susan.

"Shouldn't you sleep?" My wife reaches toward me. "You look tired." She's been like this since I got here, thoughtful, caring, as if there aren't all these hurtful things between us.

"I'm okay. I've got to take the kids out." I tell Pat, "It's my birthday."

"Happy birthday," she says.

My wife looks alarmed. "You're not going out."

"I promised we'd all go to the mall. So, I'm going." I smile. "But it's nice to have you worry about me again."

"I never stopped worrying about you."

Pat says, "Susan told us about Terri Pratt, about the passports you found. What do you think they mean? What'll you do with them?"

Goddamn! I go from affection to rage in a beat. "Who told you to go blab that around?"

Susan twitches. "It was just, just Jack and Pat. I thought—"

"Who else did you tell?"

"No one."

"Jesus!" I'm trying to disguise my concern. "Yeah, well. We trust Jack and Pat. But. You can't go around shooting off your mouth—"

"I won't. I didn't."

"We won't tell," Jack pledges.

"I know you won't." I nod, though I'm not really sure of anything. Once that information gets out the cops will ask, *Where'd he get the passports?* When the break at Dexter's office is detected they'll have the answer.

"Please, Susan. Don't talk about my case *with anyone.*"

And she finally says uneasily, "Well, at least Jack and Pat had some good ideas. Tell—Pat? Tell Kevin your idea."

"Only this," Pat responds. "With everything you've told us. About Larry and Europe. You haven't found anything illegal he did over there?"

"I can't prove he did anything illegal, no."

"Well, maybe the murder had nothing to do with Europe. Maybe it was just her."

"Her?"

"Terri. She was losing him. And she couldn't accept it. So . . ."

"You're saying Terri killed him?"

Pat shrugs. "It's only a guess, of course."

I ask, "What about all the money Larry made? All that money and if it didn't come from you guys it came from somewhere. Where?"

For a moment, they look uncomfortable.

"He might have made the money legitimately," Jack says. "Legal work. Say, he made a hundred thousand. But he pays—what did they tell us? Twenty thousand. Supposedly. For paintings. Only the paintings cost a few hundred. And the receipts are as phony as Larry. So, at the end. He deducts the twenty thousand as a business expense. But it's really in his pocket."

"Cheating the IRS." Pat smiles. "Sounds like our Larry."

"It's illegal," Jack adds. "But it's no cause to kill anyone. Love is the better motive."

"But . . ." I'm trying to work through this one. "Terri killed Larry . . . only the way he was killed . . ." I look up, thinking of the hours of lovemaking, the sweet things we'd said to each other. "Could a woman do that?"

"Yes." Susan replies so emphatically that we all stare. "Well . . ." She clears her throat. "Women can be savage. It's a known fact. Like, like the mother protecting her cubs . . . I . . . I've heard."

And I'm still staring as Molly, Michael, and the twins, Tony and Jessica, rush in, arguing loudly about something, pleading to us for justice.

Once the Lundgrens are gone I borrow Susan's car to drive past Terri's house. It's apparently empty. I stop next at the nursing home, searching for her car. Where is she?

Suppose I never see her again. Can I prove my innocence without her?

"What'd you say, Susan?" I'm preoccupied, having just hung up the phone. Still no answer at Terri's. Frustration is giving way to desperation.

"Do you still insist on taking the kids out?"

I stand, pace. "Didn't I promise? It's my birthday." Keep to schedule. Don't do anything that might look suspicious later.

Later. When the body comes bobbing to the surface of the quarry.

I force a smile. Molly stares back dreamily. The kids are thrilled to have me home. "Want to go out, pal?" I ask Michael. Do they see how frightened I am? Does it show that I've killed someone?

At the mall we go from the toy store to the candy store to the ice cream parlor. We don't buy much (I haven't got any money) but they enjoy looking.

People are everywhere, and stretching down the concourse—cars, the racer that won Indianapolis, sedans from a local dealer. We settle on a bench apart from the crowd. Michael stares at the autos. "Dad?"

"Yeah."

"Why are polar bears white?"

"Uh . . ." I see swirling snow, and I am alone in the dark. Surely, he fell.

"Dad?"

"What is it, pal?"

"Can you go away so far that nobody sees you?"

"I . . . I don't know. I guess you could."

Molly is in good spirits. "Are you and mom back together?"

"What? Back together? I don't know. We'll see."

She turns to her brother. "That means yes."

"No, no," I warn. "It means what it says."

"You are," she insists. "You and mommy are back together."

I argue, but I wonder if she sees something we adults have missed. And yes, how nice if things could be put back where they were before our separation. But it's a forlorn hope with a life sentence over my head.

"Hi, Kevin."

Terri Pratt is smiling, carrying a shopping bag. Stunned, I can't speak.

"How are you?" she coos. "How are you, Mikey? Molly?"

"None of your business." Molly curls her lip and stares at the floor.

"Where the hell have you been?" I leap up.

"What?"

I push her away from the children. "I've got to talk to you."

"You're . . . please Kevin."

I look down. I've got her wrist in a tight pinch.

"I want to see that picture of your ex-husband."

"What?"

"Somehow you never remember to have it, do you?" Her eyes grow cloudy with doubt.

"I want that picture. Understand?" My teeth clench.

"I haven't got one on me." She acts shocked.

"You got one at home, don't you?"

"Well, yeah."

"Let's get it!"

"Okay."

"Now! I'll go with you!"

"Okay . . . Please, let go of me."

"Didn't expect to see me here, did you?" I ask. "You didn't expect to see me again, ever."

"What?"

"I want to hear about the passports, Terri. And the checks. And why your divorce lawyer writes out checks to you."

She just shakes her head, as if she hasn't a wide-eyed clue what I'm talking about. I want to put her fucking face right through a window.

"You won't be able to deny it when I hold the things in my hand. When I hold them under your goddamn nose."

"I . . . don't know anything about this, Kevin. Please. What have I done?" Tears. Goddamn tears come to her eyes.

It's a performance. Damn me! Somehow, I wish I could believe her. I cared for her once. And that's what she's counted on from the beginning.

"Let's go," I say.

"What? Where?"

"To get the picture."

"But I've got to meet my mother and the girls in front of—"

"Do you think I'm going to let you out of my sight?"

"I just mean we should take our kids home. And I'll get the picture and meet you at your place."

"Oh, no." Except, for some reason, I turn to see Michael on the bench and Molly is . . . Molly is . . . Oh, shit. This is all I need.

I rush to the bench. "Where's your sister?"

Michael is surprised to discover she is not beside him.

Oh, God. Oh, God. I turn again and Terri has vanished as well.

On my toes, I peer down the crowded mall. I can't see either one. And I know that this is no coincidence. God help me!

Pulling Michael behind, I rush into the nearby bookstore. I walk past the aisles. No Molly. Even racing to the back we can't find her.

I ask the cashier, urgently, "Did you see a little girl? Seven years old. With dark hair? Pretty little girl? By herself?"

"When was this?" asks the young man, very goddamn casual.

"Just, just now. In the last few minutes?"

"No—"

I'm gone before the next word is out of his mouth. Standing on a bench, I scan the mall in both directions. So many people and cars, a little girl is easily missed. "Molly," I shout. "Molly, Molly, Molly!"

"Who are you looking for?" a woman asks.

"Little girl." I show her height with my hand. "Dark hair. Red coat."

"I'll keep an eye out," she promises.

Yanking my frightened son by the hand, I rush past the candy store, hobby shop, and toy store, giving each a quick, careful look. I don't see her.

At the information booth, a mild, gray-haired woman takes Molly's name and physical description. Then, she calls security.

I lean over. "You've got to seal the exits?"

"We don't have the manpower to do that, I couldn't—"

"I've got reason to believe my daughter has been kidnapped."

It's a comfort of sorts that she becomes almost as panicked as I am. She gasps into the phone, "Yes, the man seems very serious. He says . . . yes, that his daughter was kidnapped." She looks up. "Did you see who took her?"

"No I didn't. Look, I'm going down the main entrance. Do what you can."

"No, wait. Just a minute. Mr. Bourque!"

I run, Michael in my arms. I must *do* something. My eyes sweep every store, every aisle. Sometimes I climb a bench and scan the crowd. And yet I can't see around corners. Or behind that fat woman. Or inside the gleaming cars on display.

At the main entrance, I race outside into the cold. Across the vast, crowded parking lot, red clouds of exhaust mark where cars are exiting to the street nearly a mile away. Molly might be in one. I imagine that she is terrified, calling for me. And I am not there.

Whoever tried to kill me, has taken Molly. Nor was it coincidence that she was snatched as I was distracted by Terri Pratt. No doubt, they want to swap Molly for Terri's folder.

Well, they can have anything. Just give back my daughter.

Michael cries, "Dad, let me down." I hold on, weaving my way back to the information booth. Soon, I'm met by Mr. Baldwin, mall security. "You the fella with the missing daughter?"

"You found her?" I reach out in gratitude.

"No. No, I'm sorry. We haven't found her. No."

I turn around and around. "Where could she be?"

He puts a hand on my shoulder. "We've called the police. We need to know what makes you so sure she was kidnapped?"

"She was! This is wasting time. You've got to guard the exits."

"Think about this, Mr. Bourque. Mr. Bourque? Please. Now. I hate to say it, but if your daughter was kidnapped. She's gone. She was out of here within a minute of being missed. It's just logic. If someone snatches a child, he isn't going to hang around waiting to be caught."

"Oh, Christ. Oh God." I'm still turning, sick to my stomach.

"Is it possible she wandered off on her own?"

"Yes. No. She wouldn't. She's never done anything like that. Christ. It's my fault. I should have stayed away." I squeeze Michael hard against me.

Mr. Baldwin telephones Susan. I carry little Michael all over the mall, searching frantically, flashing a wallet photo of Molly to sales people and cashiers. I'm assured that they've been alerted to watch for "the little girl." I'm not soothed. She's gone. That's the horrible truth.

Susan is pacing Baldwin's office. I can't speak as she pulls Michael from me. Whining softly, his fist is at his eyes.

"These situations," a policeman says. "In our experience they're almost always runaways."

"This is not a runaway! Get it through your head, she's been snatched up, God."

"What makes you so certain, Mr. Bourque?"

"Do you know who I am? Do you know I'm a suspect in a murder? That there've been attempts on my life?"

He's got no idea what I'm talking about.

"How?" Susan's eyes are worn and red. "How?"

"I . . . I just turned away a few minutes."

"You didn't see who took her?"

I sit down, run a hand through my soaking hair. "Terri, Terri Pratt came over to me. And next thing I knew Molly was gone." I turn to the policeman. "Terri Pratt, find her.'" I give the address.

"You mean," Susan stands, "you mean you were talking to *her* when our daughter was—?" She stops herself, a look of contempt and barely suppressed rage on her face. I have to look away.

"Are you accusing this Pratt woman of taking the child?" the officer asks.

"With an accomplice. Yes!" Too late, I see Susan was right about Terri.

"Is it possible," Baldwin asks, "that Molly just decided to walk home?"

"We live miles from here! Come on."

"She wouldn't." Susan is still staring at me.

"I know with my kids," Baldwin continues, "every day they do something they've never done before, something I don't expect."

"Maybe." I stand. Yes, it could be. She just wandered off. And soon she'll return to us. "But I don't know. Why would she run off like that? There's no reason."

"Oh, God," Susan is stroking Michael's hair while trying not to cry.

I find it difficult to look at her. "I'm going to search," I say in a low voice. "Take Michael home. Take a cab. I'm going to find her."

First, I circle the huge parking lot. But I'm wasting time. She is gone. The streets around the mall are largely deserted. Once, I see a small figure. I slow. But it's a boy, who regards me with suspicion.

I'm facing facts finally. All my problems trace back to the same person. Of course, I just gave Terri's name to the police. But you can't rely on them to do anything. *These situations are almost always runaways. . . .*

I step on the gas and head for Terri's house.

* * *

Terri's mother smiles, "Terri just left."

"Just left? Left for where?"

"She didn't say."

"She was at the mall tonight. She said you were with her."

"That's true." The old woman's smile fades fast. "She was."

I push the door open and barge in. "Where is she?" I look about.

"I told you, she's not here!"

I go from room to room, even checking the basement. "I told you she's not here," Terri's frightened mother repeats several times.

Apparently, she isn't, but I find her girls sleeping in one large room. One groans softly as I stand at the door. Three beds. Three children. I walk over to each. Where's my Molly?

Terri's car is waiting outside my cottage. A light burns inside. The lies are finished. She will demand the passports and canceled check in exchange for Molly. I'll give anything to see my little girl safe.

I check under the front seat of the pickup. For a moment, panic, the folder isn't here. But wait. I reach further back and find it. Hurriedly, I check the contents. Thank God. Here are the important things, the passports, passport application, and the check.

I take one passport and the canceled check. Leave the rest here for security. Then, I continue to the cottage.

"How did you get in here?"

Terri is at the table, coat on. "The door was open. It, it was like this."

Books are toppled, the rug is like a teepee in the middle of the floor, sugar and flour are heaped on the counter. I don't even have to ask why. Terri—or someone connected to her—has been searching for the folder.

"What happened?" she asks.

I don't answer. Let her talk.

"I've . . . I've got the snaps." She lays them on the table, three photos of her husband. I sweep them up, examining one after another.

Eddie is an inoffensive-looking guy, not the sex maniac she described. I see him cutting his grass as Terri looks on, squinting into the sun, and clowning at the beach with his kids.

I place the pictures under the light. I killed this man last night. His body floats in the quarry. I stare at his face. "Is this the best you got?"

"I don't have many pictures of him. Sorry."

I'm not seeing the guy, okay? These are grainy, blurry, and they don't quite tell what he looked like. Except . . . God . . . I have to admit. He does not resemble the kidnapper. Of course, I saw him in glimpses, by moonlight, scared half to death.

The photos don't settle it. I return them to the table and glare at Terri. It seems years ago that she sat there playfully stripping off clothes. The woman worked hard to keep our affair alive, even paying my bail. Why?

"Where is Molly?"

"She's not home?"

I slap down the canceled check atop Eddie's smiling face. "Tell me why your lawyer pays money to you."

"I think . . ." Brow furrowed, she studies the check, then brightens. "This was a long time ago. We went somewhere. And he, he forgot his checkbook. So I paid. And then," she points to the check, "he paid me back."

"Explain that." I slap down Kelly's passport.

She lifts it gingerly, turns it over. Her eyes narrow, "I . . . I don't know . . ."

"It's a passport."

"I can see—"

I tear it from her hands, open it. "Look at the dates. The

dates, Terri! This child went to Europe. See? Austria. Four years ago. Same time, same place Larry Dexter went in Europe."

"No." She's shaking her head. "Kelly never went to Europe. That . . . I mean, she didn't. She was just a baby."

"Don't lie to me." I'm over her. "Don't lie to me now. I want the truth."

"I'm, I'm telling you—"

"She went to Europe." I wave the passport in her face. "And you went with her. And Louraine. And probably Robin too."

"No. I don't know what, what's going on but I never saw this—"

"I don't have Robin's passport. Or yours. But I've got a Xerox of the kids' passport application with your signature on it."

"I didn't." She shakes her head, hard. "I've never been out of the country even. In my life."

"You went to Bermuda with me. That's out of the country."

"Bermuda—"

"You went to Europe with your lover. With Larry Dexter. You said you didn't. But you lied, Terri. Because you applied for passports for your kids over a month before. And you all went."

"No."

She's going to deny everything. Goddamn. She's going to sit here and deny, deny, deny with the evidence staring her in the face. Well, fuck it. She's not getting away with it.

"This is your husband?" I lift the snapshot.

"Yes."

"The guy I saw last night."

She gives not a glimmer of acknowledgment.

"Is he the guy I saw last night?" I demand.

"I don't know who you saw last night."

"Don't you?" I'm standing so close she's got to lean back in her chair to look up at me. And she does. She doesn't dare look away.

"Did your husband ever do jobs for Larry Dexter?"

"No."

"I think he did. I also think he helped you kill Larry. And last night you sent him after me. You probably told him lies first. I can guess what you said, Terri. How you convinced him to kill me. To do the job right finally."

She's shaking her head emphatically. "This is insane, I wouldn't—"

"He's dead, Terri. Or. At least. I left him for dead. Did he come back? Did he maybe show up at your door this morning? And did you send him out to snatch my baby?"

She gives a little shudder.

"Did you?"

"I think . . . you're very upset, Kevin. And . . . maybe, maybe you should talk to someone."

"I'm talking to you."

"I mean, someone professional. You know, I mean—"

"Let's get to the point, Terri. At long last, let's get to the fucking point."

She nods, but goddamn she won't say anything.

"I know you snatched Molly."

"Just, why don't you just, just tell me what's happened to Molly."

"Give my daughter back and you can have anything you want."

"I don't . . . I don't . . ."

"Oh, stop this bullshit charade!" I take the chair, lift it off the floor, then slam it violently down. She slaps her hands to the seat to save herself from toppling. "I want my daughter."

"I don't—"

"I'll give you the folder, the passports, everything."

I've got her scared. Okay. But self-control is slipping away and God knows where all this ends.

"All these weeks, I gave you the benefit of the doubt. I've played by the rules, Terri. But you take my daughter and I'm not playing anymore."

"I haven't—"

"*Stop* when I got the passport application with your handwriting all over the fucking thing."

She doesn't speak, holding back.

I take the lapels of her coat, pick her out of the chair, and slam her into the bookcase. She begins to cry.

"Don't you know if my children can disappear so can yours?"

"Oh God, no."

"You filled out the passport applications."

She's biting her lip.

I crash her into the bookcase again. Hard. Books, photos, and knickknacks fall to the floor. "Didn't you!"

"Yes."

"And you went to Europe with Dexter."

"No—"

I slam her again. She gives an involuntary cry. "I didn't. I swear. I filled out the application for the kids. Larry wanted me to do it."

"Why? Why'd he want passports for your kids?"

"I don't know." She's blubbering."

"Did he take the girls to Europe?"

"No."

"What were the passports for?"

"I don't know. I swear."

"What was Dexter doing in Europe?"

"I don't know, I don't know," she's crying, sobbing. Her head drops.

"Look at me." I take her roughly by the chin, jerk her face up. "Look at me! Tell me. Tell me why he wanted passports."

"He never told me."

"What *did* he tell you?" And when she won't answer I slap her.

She gasps. The outline of my hand is on her face.

"What did he tell you?"

"He told me . . . he told me it was better I not know."

"Why didn't you say anything about this before?"

She's still trying to catch her breath. I raise my hand.

"I didn't . . . I was wrong . . . I was afraid. I should have told. I'm sorry I didn't . . . I was afraid I'd get implicated. In a federal crime. Larry paid me. The check. He paid me for the passport stuff. And he made me promise not to tell. He said I'd go to jail if I told. I'd go to jail and lose my children."

"You'd go to jail?" This is unbelievable! "*I'm* going to jail for the rest of my life *because you didn't tell.*"

"No. It was years ago. And you said yourself. Something four years ago. It couldn't be connected to the murder."

"I never said that, Terri. You said that."

"I . . . I helped all I could. I pointed you in the right direction in case there was a connection. I told you about Larry getting indicted for illegal immigrants. I told you that. Didn't I? And I would have told everything if that's what it took to save you."

"You stayed close to me. Until you knew everything about me. So you could frame me for Dexter's murder."

"No."

"And you're still keeping tabs. To make sure I don't find out that you killed him. You killed him because of Europe. Or because he wouldn't marry you. Whatever the reason. But you did it!"

"I wouldn't ever involve you in such a thing. I love you."

"When will you tell the truth?" I give her hair a yank, jerking her head back.

She screams and then cries, "I do love you, I do. . . . Oh, God, believe me, Kevin. All I want is to be with you—"

"Where is my daughter?"

"I don't, I don't know—Awww! I'm telling the truth—"

I pull at the front of her coat, swinging her around, throwing her into the table. The table topples loudly and the light crashes into pieces. In the dark, Terri staggers, landing on her back, on the bed. "Please," she cries.

I'm straddling her. "Where's Molly?"

"I don't know."

"Why did you kill Dexter? Was it money? You like money. You're not exactly honest, are you?"

"I wouldn't hurt him."

"No," I cry, "you wouldn't hurt anyone."

"No, Kevin."

All this hell and she's the cause. I'm swept by rage, I feel it on my face like fire.

"Please," she groans, "please don't kill me."

My hands are on her throat.

"Where is my daughter?"

She tries to speak, can only shake her head. Her color changes, her mouth opens, tongue protrudes. She coughs.

"When will you tell the truth?"

Gagging, panicked, her legs buck. I tighten my grip. She digs her nails into my arms, while rocking violently. But I don't let go. Tears and sweat splash the pillow. Blood speckles the sheets. A stink of urine fills the room.

"Where is Molly?!"

She gasps, in a tiny voice, "Kill me." And I'm frightened by her eyes, without urgency. She no longer struggles. But I can't stop. I've taken it for so long that it's good to give it back at last.

And all this time, the phone rings.

The phone seems to have been ringing a very long time. "Hello?"

"Kevin?" It's Susan. "Kevin, is that you?"

"Yes." And then. "Yes, it's me."

I guess it doesn't sound like me, because only after a pause she begins, excitedly, "She's home, she's back."

"What?"

"She's here with me. Thank God, thank God." Susan laughs.

I sink slowly into the stuffed chair beside the telephone table. "Oh."

"She walked home. Walked! I don't know whether to hug her or paddle her."

"She just . . . she just walked home?"

"You said you couldn't think of a reason why she would just walk away. Well, I thought of one. It was that friend of yours. Lady friend. Molly was jealous, upset because you went off to talk to her. Can you believe it?"

"Uhh," I stroke my forehead. "Then . . . then Molly's all right."

"I gave her hell. But. Oh, God, she's safe, she's safe."

"Thank . . . God."

"I know you'll want to talk to her. If you want. I'll wake her."

"No, that's all right. Let her . . . let her sleep."

I hang up and stare ahead. Somehow, the refrigerator is open. A shaft of light crosses the floor. What a mess. At some point I'll have to repair the damage. Where to begin?

Terri is wheezing. I don't know what to do or say. As she stumbles from bed, gathering up her coat, she nearly falls. I'm staring straight ahead, like I said. Except for Terri it's quiet.

Molly is safe. I ought to rejoice.

Terri passes a few feet away. I can smell that she's soaked herself.

Maybe I should help her. I should try to . . . try to . . . what?

I was wrong to suspect Terri in Molly's disappearance. But in my rage, I got another bit of truth from her. I'll strip away lie after lie and get the whole story eventually.

Terri applied for passports she says she never used. Well, more likely she did use them, was at Dexter's side in Europe. Moreover, I still believe that she and an accomplice killed Larry over the money, expecting that I would be blamed. Finally, last night, she sent her confederate to kill me.

No wonder she won't confess all that, even at the point of death. If she did I just might kill her anyway.

I hear her fumble at the door. She drops her bag. She squats, picking up the contents in the dark. When she sobs I almost feel sorry for her.

But as she closes the door, I know the pretense of love is over. She couldn't have ever cared for me and hidden these things. And I realize at last that I never really loved her. I just loved the act she put on.

Compared to the Norham Police, who treated me with some consideration, the state cops make me feel like Al Capone or something. They wake me, banging on the door. As if my house isn't messy enough, they make it worse, clomping about in muddy boots.

In the back of the cruiser, I'm separated from a detective and a trooper by a thick metal screen. I move from side to side, seeking room to stretch. God, it's hot. I'm sweating, carsick.

"Pretty messy place you live in," the detective says as we drive.

"Yeah, it's the maid's day off."

He looks over the gashes Terri left on my arms. "Hot date, huh?"

I pull down my sleeves. "I told you I'm not answering questions. Okay. Why don't you let me call my lawyer?"

"As soon as we get to the barracks."

"This is a waste of time. He's not going to let me talk to you."

The detective turns away and we drive a long time before he turns back and says, "It's not about the Dexter murder."

"What?"

"The questioning. It's not about that. The Dexter murder. This is something else. Something different."

"What? What is it?"

"Why should I talk to you," he asks, "if you won't talk to me?"

What now? At least he didn't say anything about arrest or revoking bail. Has Terri charged me with attempted murder or something? Or did they discover the break at Dexter's office? Then, there's the guy in the quarry. Assuming he was ever in the quarry.

Here's the joke. These guys expect answers from me. I've been poking my nose into everything and I'm more confused than when I started. What happened in Europe? Who paid

Dexter thousands of dollars and why? Who are my friends and who are my enemies?

Last night I was certain of Terri's part in a plot to put me away for Dexter's murder. Today, I remember her eyes at the end, a look—more chilling than fear—of indifference. It's something I wish I hadn't seen.

·14·

They lead me to an interview room. "You should have let me call my lawyer. He could have met us. Instead of this bullshit waiting around."

I'm loud so they won't see I'm scared. I smell disinfectant from the cells. Suppose they lock me up. Maybe I'll never know another free day.

Left alone, I face a strange dark mirror. Surely a two-way mirror. What do they expect to see? Head on the table, I close my eyes. I'm finished fighting. Better to run. Open the door a crack and I'm gone. Long gone.

Yeah. My head comes up. I look at the mirror and see a small town, a thousand miles away. I arrive with a new name. I do odd jobs. Maybe work on a farm. Keep to myself. Get a place in the woods. The climate is warm. People friendly. So, I live out my life in peace.

Far from home, I leave a lot behind. But if I stay I go to prison forever.

It's not an easy choice, nor fail-safe. Disappearing among two hundred and fifty million people isn't as easy as it sounds. You see the recaptured fugitives on the evening news all the time, sorry-looking bastards. But that doesn't mean *I* couldn't avoid their mistakes and stay free.

Cut off all contact with home—tell no one where I've gone. I have no wife, no children, no family whatsoever. Send no letters that can be traced back to me. Make no phone calls. Arrange no meetings, no visits.

Become a *new* person. Abandon carpentry and manage a restaurant or something. Take up new hobbies. I won't be at the gym playing basketball.

Cut my hair. Grow a beard. Gain weight—that shouldn't be difficult. Maintain the changes. And maybe someday I'll feel safe.

Better if I can alter my fingerprints. Because there's always the possibility—no matter how careful you are—that you get stopped for something. And they print you. And they've got you.

But how do you change your fingerprints? Acid? I'm looking grimly at my fingertips when Tim Regan walks in with Toomey, the assistant D.A.

Tim asks, "What have you told them?"

"Nothing."

"Good." He turns. "We have nothing to say, Mr. Toomey."

"I'm sure your client could clear this up rather easily."

"Clear what up?" I ask.

"Do you know Bill Foley?"

Tim isn't objecting, so I say, "I met him once. Larry's father-in-law."

"William Foley Junior."

"Junior? You mean the son? No," I shake my head.

Toomey explains. "This is Kathleen Dexter's brother I'm talking about."

"Never met him." I remember Foley Senior mentioning him. "He's . . . he's retarded or something?"

"Where were you, night before last? Between nine PM and four AM?"

"Why?" My lawyer is waving for me to keep quiet.

Toomey glares at me. "Were you with someone who can vouch for you?"

"Don't answer!" Tim says sharply. "What's going on, Mr. Toomey? What's this all about?"

After a moment Toomey takes his eyes from me. "Foley Junior was fished out of the Hopewell quarries this morning. Head crushed. Ever been to Hopewell, Mr. Bourque?"

"Why . . . why should I—"

"Shut up!" Tim wheels on me, his face crimson. "Don't open your goddamn mouth unless you have *my* permission. Understand?"

I nod.

"I want to speak to my client alone."

"Fine."

"Outside. Where we can't be overheard."

"You won't be overheard here," Toomey insists.

"Let's go," Tim gestures to me.

"Just prove you weren't there," the assistant district attorney says, "and we can eliminate you as a suspect."

"Don't say a word," Tim instructs. "Don't, don't speak. Nothing!"

Tim leads me on a quick march, out into the cold, through the parking lot, and down the road.

Foley. Kikki Dexter's brother. In the quarry, just before he shot me, I thought I remembered his face from when he nearly ran over Larry's toes with Kikki's Mercedes. In fact, I barely glimpsed him then. But I saw his photo all over his father's office. I realize that he actually resembled Kikki.

No wonder the police refused to investigate the possibility that Kikki had a lover. They knew all along that the fight in the Chinese restaurant involved Kikki, her husband, and her brother. The Foleys had covered it up to shield nutso Billy.

This guy I never met before in my life tried three times

to kill me. Where do I fit into this? Did he also kill Dexter? Was he acting at Kikki's direction? What was the motive? I keep thinking new information will make everything fall into place. Instead it gets more confusing.

My God, am I up against the entire Foley family with their serpentine political connections? But what did I ever do to them? Am I merely a convenient fall guy for Larry's murder?

With her volcanic temper, it's possible that Kikki killed Larry in a fit of jealousy. Afterwards, she called in her protectors. Daddy, daddy. You and Billy have got to get me out of this.

Damn! Why don't the cops investigate her?

I'm uneasy after putting a name to that fellow in the quarry. Still, I keep in mind that it was supposed to be me floating down there. And that's the part I can't figure. Because if they'd wanted me convicted for Larry's murder . . . Christ, I was well on my way. So, why kill me?

Tim is walking fast toward a white-steepled church. I'm not surprised that he's angry. "I just want to say—Tim?"

He turns and glares.

"Look, I'm sorry. I should have told you about Foley. I didn't—"

He walks. I must hurry to catch him.

"Honest to God, I would have told you what happened. But I thought it would be safer for you if I didn't."

Glancing about, making certain we're not observed, he takes my elbow and growls, "I told you from the start. Don't lie to me."

"I'm sorry. I shouldn't—"

"You can't pull this shit on me." He looks away, muttering, "My own goddamn fault. I knew you were lying and let it pass."

"Timmy, it was an accident. He just went over. I didn't push him. And besides no one saw me. They can't put me at the scene."

Tim stops. "I can put you at the scene."

"Come on."

"What do you think of that? I saw you at the scene. And if you suppose there's some ethical obligation to cover for you—"

"Please, Tim."

"There's no reason not to tell them how you called me from Hopewell—"

"You know what that would do to me?"

"I'm not worrying about you, *cousin*. It's one thing to lie. It's another to involve me in your shit!"

"Timmy, I swear to God, this was an accident."

"Everybody warned me. Don't represent your fucking relatives, they'll screw you every time."

"Please, Tim. Give me a chance."

"You haven't got a chance. You never had a chance." He looks me in the face. "This case was a loser from the get-go."

It's a splash of cold water. Never had a chance. Never. Everybody else can see it. I am as good as convicted. "Tim . . ."

He turns his back.

I make a last effort. "Timmy, please listen." I march around to confront him. "I didn't kill him. He fell. It was an accident."

When he waves me off again I know I must get away.

Tim Regan heads back to the state police barracks. Maybe he'll really inform on me, maybe there's some legal thing that compels him to do it. But even if he keeps quiet, I expect the state police to come after me for the murder of William Foley, Junior. I start to run in the opposite direction.

At the nearby general store, I call the last person I can count on. "Susan?"

"Kevin, I just called you—"

"Listen, I need help. I need money. Lots of it. Maybe several thousand."

"Several thousand?" She almost laughs.

"And I've got to have it by tonight."

"But . . . what for?"

"Just, I need it." I'll tell no one—not even Susan—my plan. Just go. Leave only a tangle of loose ends for the police and the Foleys to follow. That's assuming I get out of the state.

"Where do I get that kind of money?" Susan is asking. "The bank's not going to hand over thousands of dollars this afternoon. No questions asked."

"Please deposit ten cents for an additional three minutes. . . ."

I fumble for a dime, muttering about the phone company.

"What is this all about?" Susan speaks over the recording. "Has something happened?"

I drop the dime. But, dammit! the recording continues. *". . . if you do not deposit ten cents your call will be terminated . . ."*

"Goddamn fucking phone company," I complain. "Try the Lundgrens. They might have that kind of cash. Tell them you'll pay them from the sale of the cottage. Tell them we need the money . . . to pay a source. Okay? It's to pay off a guy. A source of information. For my investigation."

"Is that really true?"

"One thing more. I need some things. You know my old gym bag up on the top shelf in your closet? Bring that. Don't put anything in it. And don't take anything out. Understand? Just bring it. Okay?"

"Are you running away, Kevin?" There's a catch in her voice. I lean my head against the side of the phone. I'm alone, at the rear of the store. Up the aisle, the cashier is bent over her newspaper.

"I won't be at the cottage. Bring the money to the Indian Peak house. Tonight. And make sure, above all, make sure you're not followed. Susan?"

"You're running away, Kevin . . . Aren't you?"

"No."

"Tell me. Tell me where you're going. I'll go too. We'll all go. I want us together like it was. If we have to live in a car, that's all right with me."

Jesus, make her stop. "No." I swallow. "No, I'm not running away. I just need money. Okay?"

"You tell me what to get and I'll get it. You tell me where to go and I'll be there."

A state police car passes outside. Okay, okay. Don't get excited. It doesn't mean they're looking for you yet. The barracks is around the corner, cars coming and going all the time. Still, I better get away from here.

"Kevin, tell me what's happening so I'll know what to do."

I can feel Susan loves me. I wish I was near enough to touch her, comfort her. Why did we separate? I can't remember the reason.

I see my mistake now. It's too late and I see my mistake.

"Susie . . ." I can't explain all I'm feeling, the words won't come loose. I finally blurt out, "Just, you know, just have the money for me. Tonight if you can. At Indian Peak. And everything's going to be okay."

"*Please deposit ten cents for an additional three minutes . . .*"

"Shut up!" I slam the box. "Where's my fucking three minutes?" The cashier looks up. I stiffen, trying to control myself. "Goddamn phone company."

"Do you have the change?" Susan asks.

"No. No, I'm out."

"I'll call you back. Give me the number."

"There's no number. It's gone. Scratched off or something."

"Call me back. Get some change and call me back."

"*. . . your call will be terminated in fifteen seconds . . .*"

"I can't. I've really got to go. See you tonight. Just. Make sure you're not followed."

"By who?"

"By anyone."

"But who would want to follow me?"

"Don't come if you think you're being followed."

"Tell me you love me."

The line goes dead, and when I say it, "I do, I love you. I love you," she cannot hear me.

At the cash register, I buy candy bars, sweet cakes, and an apple. I haven't eaten all day. The woman slides over my change. A man comes in to browse at the newsstand. He fails to even look my way.

I feel intense hostility from both, as if they know who I am and why I no longer belong, will never again belong to their settled, peaceful town.

Out the door, I have a lump in my throat, remembering how unsure and alone Susan sounded. With nothing I can do for her, nothing. The air is cold.

I hustle across the street, watching for police. I leap a rotting rail fence, plunging into a meadow waist high with brown grass. I don't slow until reaching the woods. I can't stop shivering.

At every point I expect them to come plowing across the field in their cruisers, leaping out, guns drawn. I don't really believe I'm going to escape, but I will try.

I keep to wooded back roads. Once I scramble into the forest as a police car appears. Soft earth gives and I slide down an embankment into a wet tangle of thorns. Scraped and cold, frightened and humiliated, I sit, heart pumping. Did they see me? Are they even looking?

I cease to breathe until the cruiser whishes past.

Perhaps I should stay here until dark. I wolf down the apple. I eat the cakes with the tips of my wet and dirty fingers. This is the future, cold, lonely, and miserable. Christ. Don't start feeling sorry for yourself.

Four miles down the road is Indian Peak. It might as well be four hundred. I imagine roadblocks, swarms of squad cars. What's more, the police are probably smart enough to be there waiting for me.

An elderly man in a new Buick picks me up. "Some problem?"

I wince. Does he know? In fact, he thinks I've had car trouble. I look too respectable for a hitchhiker. A few days on the road should change that.

The colonial house with its grand columns is dark, echoing, forbidding. I remember the place swarming with carpenters, all of them having some connection to John Finnerty. Is that what Terri's passports were for, to slip more Finnertys into the country? But where does Billy Foley fit in?

I'm still missing something.

I turn on the electric blower in the bathroom, the only heat. Perched on the toilet lid, I stare at the wall. Hours drag by. The little room grows warm and I sleep beneath the gold fixtures in the spacious whirlpool, my coat for a pillow. When I wake every muscle seems to ache.

I sit up in alarm. "God." I hope Susan hasn't missed me in here. Surely, she would have heard the fan, come to inspect.

Just, isn't it taking her a long time to arrive? No, no. Don't worry about time. Wouldn't want to be on the road until dark anyway.

I watch through the bathroom window while rehearsing our farewell. Unavoidably, at the last, I must lie. And convincingly. Because she mustn't know that I'm running away. I don't want her to be implicated in my escape.

Will Susan understand why I've gone? I would have stayed if I had the smallest chance of remaining free. I would have stayed with you.

Sometimes Terri comes to mind and I get a sick, sick feeling. It's possible that she told the truth, finally. She'd given Larry the passports, not knowing why. After protecting herself, she meant to help me by revealing Dexter's work in bringing in immigrants.

Sometimes I still see the dead look in her eyes. And I'm trying very hard not to see it, to forget all that entirely.

I try to understand the few things Foley Junior said at the quarry. Something about "them babies." Was he protecting his sister, the mother of so many babies, from a murder charge?

Or did Foley act, thinking I'd killed his brother-in-law and left the "babies," his nieces and nephews, fatherless. In fact, Kikki—or Foley Senior—might have encouraged him to strike at me for that very reason. In other words, it's possible that he had nothing to do with Larry Dexter's killing.

I open a candy and eat. Then I kneel, emptying my wallet on the toilet seat lid—credit cards, money, old receipts, union card, photos. I take out anything that identifies me. Here and now Kevin Bourque ceases to exist.

I drop all traces of my old life into the toilet tank. I pocket the cash, about forty dollars. I'll ditch the wallet. Why haven't I got an ID? Well officer, I lost my wallet. The thousands from Susan will go into my coat lining.

Finally, only family photos remain, spread on the seat. Got to be tough now. It's dangerous hanging onto these shadows of the past. They might betray me, weaken my determination not to contact my family.

Take a long, last look at Susan, Molly, and Michael. I swallow a lump of chocolate that has no taste and stare up at the heater with its whirring fan. Never see or hear from them again. Except for tonight. Because possibly Susan will have to bring the children—it'll be too late to find a sitter.

The thought cheers me. Yet, I must find a way to say good-by and not let them know that it is good-by. Got to prepare. I must be calm and comforting as I tell of my love. Using the perfect words because this meeting will be the last they'll ever see of me.

The thought pulls me up short. I mean, really, what do I say? It must reassure yet resonate for them and be remembered down through the years.

I try to invent such a message. I think long and hard and can't get much past the first words. This is too tough. I look away from the photos.

Maybe I should yield a little on this idea of no contact. I could write, driving hundreds of miles to post the letter. But if they can't write back, how do I know the letters are even received? How do I know if everyone at home is okay?

Poor little Michael will call out on his sick bed and no amount of soothing words will explain why I'm not there.

Christ, I feel the walls closing in.

Stick to the plan. They won't understand now. But as adults they'll say, "I'm glad he's free. I hope he's had a good life."

Still, what should I say to them tonight? I gaze at those smiling faces on paper. "Jesus . . ." I must look away.

Mind your mom. Remember I love you more than anything. You'll be in my thoughts always. And . . . what? What else? We'll hug and kiss. And maybe, years from now, at a low point, they'll feel my arms around them.

What if Susan finds a sitter, after all? Oh, God. I pace the tiny room. If they don't come. It means the last time I saw Michael I was in a frenzy, dragging him about the mall. While Molly was in a jealous rage.

I've got to write. Now. I can say more and say it frankly in a letter. I search for paper and pencil. I scan the floor, go from room to room. Damn! Not a scrap in sight.

In a second floor walk-in closet, which we used as an office, virtually everything has been taken by the police, only the telephone remains on the floor. Downstairs, the kitchen cabinets and drawers are empty.

I need paper and lots of it. I've got to write page after page. I must explain this difficult decision to vanish forever.

Try and understand. I didn't want to leave, but I would have gone to prison. For something I didn't do. Got to stress my innocence.

It's all so complicated. How can I make them see the truth?

Christ, I can't say anything without paper. I circle the basement, then troop upstairs, revisiting every room. Finally, I find a stubby carpenter's pencil on the dining room floor. So, I carry that, poised to write but with nothing to put it to. I grow so wild I kick, exploding a section of drywall.

Suddenly, I spot the building permit on a window sill. I

could write on the reverse! Grinning, I get comfortable and ready on the gleaming hardwood floor. But once pencil touches paper I can't find a single word to say.

This isn't the way. Go look at the snapshots, at their faces. I want to imagine I'm speaking to them. I hurry to the bathroom.

Kneeling, I position the permit on the toilet seat lid. Then, I touch the photos. Michael, smiling carelessly. Molly with no front tooth. Susan, young, happy.

How do I say good-by so it doesn't hurt?

I'd do anything for you all. I'd give my life.

So why don't you stay, daddy?

Because—I—

How do you cut off your family? Wouldn't prison be better? At least I could see them, write letters, get letters and photos in return.

I stare at the pictures. Seconds pass. Then minutes. Always those kids in front of me. My father had been there to offer help and advice until long after I was grown. Poor Molly and Michael, on their own already.

I stand. Dizziness hits me like a wave. And very suddenly, I know who killed Larry Dexter, and why.

Upstairs in the closet, I dial information for the number of Professor Gary Healy, formerly of the U.S. Department of State.

· 15 ·

Hours later, I'm still on the floor, the phone on its cradle beside me, listening to footsteps on the brick walk.

The door opens and someone enters the foyer, a light step, like a woman. Susan. Cautiously, I don't stir. After a few careful paces in the dark, she says softly, urgently, "Kevin?"

The woman is not Susan. For a moment, I'm sure this is a police trap. I'll be shot down as soon as I show my face, never telling what I've learned.

"Kevin, where are you?"

I recognize Pat Lundgren, of all people.

She gasps as I emerge on the stairs above her. "God, you scared me."

"Where's Susan?"

"She couldn't come. I'm sorry I'm so late."

I move down to peek out the window. Pat's wagon sits alone on the street. The plywood house next door, Larry's death house, is a massive black shadow. "Why didn't Susan come?"

"Police were over to see her twice today. She was afraid, if she came, she'd lead them right to you." Pat fishes through her purse. The gym bag, a dead weight on a nylon cord, is hanging off her arm. "She got the money."

I snatch the bag, stuffed with shorts and jerseys, among other things.

Pat hands me an envelope so thick it must consist entirely of small bills. Laying down the bag, I thumb through it, astonished, because after the tens and fives at the top, it is mostly thousand dollars bills. "Holy Christ. How much is here?"

"Twenty-five thousand," Pat says softly.

"Twenty-five!"

"Susan thinks you'll need it."

"But how . . . how's she going to pay it back?"

"Don't worry about that," Pat declares.

"I never meant her to put herself in the hole. A few thousand I said."

"Don't worry. Really. Jack and me. We want you to know. Whatever happens, Susan and the kids will be all right. Anything they need, we'll be there. We give you our word, Kevin."

I'm deeply affected, staring at Pat. "Well," I say haltingly, "thank you." I stuff the envelope into the gym bag.

"I brought Jack's driver's license," Pat says.

"Driver's license?"

"I've got a plate too. In my car. Jack says to put it on your truck. If you're stopped. No one's looking for Jack Lundgren."

"I appreciate that . . . only, why do I need Jack's license and tags?"

She gives a shrug, "We all know you're going, Kevin. That's, that's what the money's for. Isn't it?" When I don't answer, she adds, "I've got some brochures. Jack's uncle lives in Costa Rica. If you can get there. Twenty-five thousand will go a long way. And it's possible we can send more."

"I'm not going anywhere, Pat."

"But Susan—"

"I can see how Susan got that idea. But. I could never leave."

She shakes her head very slowly. "Don't you know, Kevin? Kikki Dexter's brother. He's been killed. And they're looking for you. There's been another huge uproar about why you got bail in the first place. You're on every radio station. Television. It's bad, Kevin."

"I didn't kill Foley."

"I'm sure you didn't, but they're going to arrest you for it anyway."

"Do they say that?"

"They're looking for you. They're going to arrest you. That's what they say."

For a long time neither one of us speaks. We're standing in what will be the family room. I can't see her too well. It's quite dark on the end of this street with no lights. She's plainly nervous.

"I don't understand," she says. "Did Kikki's brother kill Larry?"

"What makes you think so?"

"Well. Why else was he killed too? It couldn't be a co-incidence. I'm just speculating. But. What if he was mixed up in killing Larry Dexter? Him and—I know it's terrible to say. But him and his sister. Him and Kikki. They killed Larry together. Then, I don't know. They had a fight. And she—"

"Killed her own brother?"

Pat shrugs, her lips come tight as if she's already said too much.

"Foley didn't kill Dexter," I reply. "And Kikki didn't kill anybody."

She takes a deep breath. I guess we're both scared at this point.

I lower my voice and explain, "This Foley was crazy. And he made a big mistake. He believed the newspapers. He believed it when they said Kevin Bourque, me, that I killed Larry. All the Foleys believed that. And they're a tight, loyal bunch. So, I guess, they wanted revenge. And maybe junior had this half rational moment and he thought killing me would win him some respect from his father. Don't we all want to please the old man? So, he tried to kill me. Three times as a matter of fact. He wasn't good at it. But, still, it's only a miracle he didn't succeed."

"But who . . . who killed *him*?"

"I'm sure it was an accident."

"I see." Her voice is very soft.

"I didn't kill him, Pat."

She nods.

"And I didn't kill Dexter. You know that."

She's not moving or speaking, like she's nailed to the floor.

I take a breath, "See, Pat. I always thought, behind this whole thing, was money. Money Larry made in Europe. Money from nowhere. No explanation. Except Larry's records. That say he was paid a hundred thousand from you. For paintings. We know that was bogus."

"It was."

"So where'd he get an eighty-thousand-dollar return after a few days in Europe? That's the question. For a while, I thought it might have to do with John Finnerty and his relatives from Ireland. But, you know, too much argued against that. For one thing, I didn't find a shred of evidence connecting John to Dexter outside of work. For another, these Irish don't have money and we both know Larry didn't do things for people unless he saw a big payoff down the road. Finally, I can't figure why anybody would need help to enter the U.S. It's too easy to get a tourist visa or to just walk across the border. Dexter might have helped them after they were here, but there was no reason for him to go to Vienna. Not for John Finnerty's family."

"So . . . what—What was it?"

"You know, just, just today, while I was sitting here waiting for you, I got this idea. And I made a call. To this state department guy my lawyer knows. I asked him again about imports from Eastern Europe. Like, maybe there's some commodity he overlooked. Something to make a quick buck on. Because, like I said, I had this idea what it might be."

"It's not the painting."

"No."

"It was worthless."

"Well," I smile, "it had a purpose. Remember, I worked with Larry so I know how he operated. How, if he made a play that wasn't legal, like bribery, he'd have a cover worked out for in case he got caught. Like he'd convince the guy he was getting a valuable antique painting but if anyone blew the whistle the thing would turn out to be worthless and Larry would shrug his shoulders and ask how you could seriously call it a bribe."

"Larry could sell," Pat says, as if it were a professional evaluation.

"He used paintings as a cover for this scam too. If anyone, customs, or anyone, questioned him about the money. He planned to tell them he'd earned it by importing antique art. Like the icon. See, he could confess to smuggling. Because the stuff was fake. He'd look like a fool who, technically, wasn't guilty of much more than overpricing some flea market paintings. Which, the buyer wasn't going to complain. Because the buyer knew what Larry was really bringing in."

"Drugs?"

"No."

"Diamonds? What? What would fit in a picture frame?"

"Larry didn't hide it in a picture frame. It came home on his arm."

"I don't know—"

"Don't you? Pat? I think you do."

God it's quiet. Just a sound like the house settling. And she's backing away, slowly, in tiny steps.

"You've been nice to me, Pat. So eager to see me get away. Disappear."

"We . . . I didn't want you to go to jail."

"No. Nobody likes to see an innocent man sent to prison."

How different this moment is from what I'd imagined and hoped for. I can't work up much rage or hate. I feel cheated in a way.

"Someone messed up my place, looking for something." I shrug. "I thought it had to be an accomplice of the guy who tried to kill me. But then I find out it was Foley tried to kill me. And his accomplice. Well, no halfway intelligent person would rob a piggy bank with him for a partner. Not even Kikki. So Foley didn't have an accomplice. But then. Who made the mess?"

She gives a blank stare.

"Were you looking for the passports, Pat? Susan told you about them and you knew what that meant. Everything was about to unravel. You had to get them back. But, you weren't thorough. Very uncharacteristic. You tore my house apart and never looked in the truck."

"I didn't—"

In the shadows, I can see her mouth, tight, twitching. Don't get the impression I feel safe, even holding the gym bag.

"Larry might have told Kikki where he was going that morning. Who called. But you didn't care because you weren't planning to kill him. You only wanted to talk sense into him. Only he wouldn't listen. And there was some kind of scuffle. And Larry got pushed down the stairs. Which is where you saw a chance to solve your problem forever. You'd watched me operate the nail gun. I'd left it loaded and ready. You only had to pick it up. Turn on the compressor. Wait a minute or so. Then fire. And keep on firing till you emptied it. You, Pat. That was your work. Wasn't it?"

She's grim, not saying anything. Cautiously, I withdraw from the bag. At last, it's turning my way.

"Come on out, Jack. Don't be shy." Foley's gun glistens black, like it did in the Hopewell quarry. Except, it looked bigger from the other end.

Jack Lundgren shuffles in from the living room. I heard him from the start. Though he doesn't look particularly fierce, a not very tall, overweight, middle-aged man, I take care. I hope he's not armed because I haven't a clue how to use this thing I'm holding.

"Let's go," I gesture with the gun, "to your car."

We walk the long gravel driveway to the street and the Lundgrens' green Chevy wagon. I can't see their faces, but I know too well how they feel with the future suddenly a very grim prospect.

"Pat drives. Jack in back. I want to see you both at all times."

Pat stares at the gun and I say, "Can't take your eyes off it, can you? That's how I've been living. Every minute, like there's a gun to my head."

"We're not your enemies, Kevin."

"You can prove that at the police station."

"We're going to the police?"

I've got the idea, half-formed, that putting my accusation on record makes it more difficult for them to disappear. And maybe, who knows, they'll just see their situation as hopeless and confess. As easy as that.

Anyway, a confession might be my only hope. The police and assistant district attorney have pretty much decided that Kevin Bourque killed Larry Dexter. They won't easily admit a mistake. Pile the evidence as high as the courthouse and they'll just turn away, saying, "We know you did it, Bourque."

Foley will remain a nagging loose end. And yet, who can prove his plunge into the quarry was not an accident? As far as that goes, I've decided that Tim Regan, my lawyer, my own cousin for God sakes, will swallow hard and invoke lawyer-client privilege on the matter.

The thing is I haven't done anything wrong and I keep hoping against hope that they'll get it right finally.

I climb in, showing the gun. I don't expect trouble. Pat and Jack know I'm desperate and therefore dangerous.

"Start the car."

Turning the key, Pat's some distance from me in this big American car.

"You've really got the wrong idea, Kevin," Jack says.

"Do I?"

"I don't know what you think we've done."

"I know what you've done. Okay?" I lean towards Pat. "Let's go." We drive up the darkened, lifeless scar of a street that was to make my fortune.

"Really. You can't believe we did anything to Larry," Jack persists.

We're on Grove Street, making for Norham Center.

Jack says, "A lot of people had grudges against Larry. Reasons, reasons to kill him. Why blame us?"

"Because you and your wife had the best reason of all. In fact, I might have done the same thing in your place. I realized that today."

We drive for several miles in silence. And when I speak it's half to myself, rehearsing what I plan to tell the police.

"I was talking with this state department guy. About Eastern Europe. And exports. Got a whole education on exports." I watch Jack in back, bundled in his big coat, hands in his pockets, collar up to his chin, eyes down.

"You know what countries export, Jack? They export what they got plenty of. Surpluses. And you know what's the surplus in Eastern Europe? People. I don't know how it is now with all the changes, but go back four years and life there used to be pretty depressing and the only fun. Well, it was the old-fashioned kind."

All the time I look from one to the other, one to the other. I don't take chances with this pair because I know how much they stand to lose.

"People had their fun. But then there were shortages of things like condoms and pills. Had to wait in line for them like everything else. Except, sometimes, you know, you can't wait. So you ended up in another line. At the abortion clinic. And if weren't quick you got past time. What I mean is, they had kids born. Nobody wanted them. And the state had to care for them."

The gun in my lap points in Pat's direction, my finger near the trigger. She concentrates on the road, keeping just below the speed limit.

"Anyway, some of these governments, they used to see the babies as excess population. So what happened, they sold them. To couples from the West. It wasn't called selling, of course. Adoption. With a fee. People in the West have money. So the state unloaded its burden and got hard currency in return. Everybody gained. New parents got kids. White kids. Blue eyes, blond hair. And no moms coming around later saying they changed their minds. Also, less chance that the kids would someday go off looking for their 'real' parents. And if you got a smart lawyer to act as middleman there weren't a lot of problems about health, background, age. So, if the father was old, a little overweight, not in the best health. This was probably their only chance to adopt. Of course, it cost. But I imagine, the way some see it, what you got for your money was priceless."

Pat sighs deeply.

"Larry was the ideal middleman. He'd brought people into the country before. He had his father's contacts in the East. And no scruples. He flew over, arranged to buy—I should say adopt. Adopt a baby, twins in fact. Getting them in the country, they were the Pratt babies of Norham, complete with passports, traveling with uncle Larry. Maybe the passports had to be doctored, but usually they don't even look at a baby's passport. So, it worked like a charm. You and Jack were happy. Some of us might have wondered how after so many miscarriages you could bring twins to term. But then you were careful to disappear months beforehand. Supposedly in the hospital. So there was no questions, only smiles. And it would have been a happy ending all around, except for stupid-ass Larry. Who couldn't leave well enough alone."

She slows for a stop sign.

"Time came Larry needed money. Money to keep Indian Peak going. He kept telling me he had this source he could tap. Which, what it was, he was leaning on you guys. And I know just how his mind worked, the stupid son of bitch. 'If they don't lend it I'll mention all I've done for them. All the laws we broke getting those kids. And I'll mention what would happen if the state came round to look at the adoption papers. And Pat and Jack won't like that. But they'll come across with the money. Then, eventually, they'll get it back. And everybody will be happy.' Except for one problem. The problem that Larry never knew who he was dealing with."

"He'd *borrowed* money twice before," she says, waiting at the stop sign, though there isn't a car in sight. "He said it cost to keep things secret. But he was just greedy. There wasn't going to be any end to it."

"He was bluffing, Pat. He couldn't have caused trouble without exposing himself. Getting disbarred. And if he had gone to the authorities, I doubt they'd ever touch your kids."

"We couldn't take that chance!" Jack declares forcefully.

"Of course they would," Pat says. "They'd take our children and never give it a thought. That's the law. And the law's not on our side, Kevin. Maybe it was once. But no more. Now it's for people who kill their babies in the womb. The law's for them. Because the law serves selfishness. Not people, a family like us. Who . . . we'd do anything for our children."

She turns to me. "That's why I killed him. To save my babies. Larry Dexter held their lives in his hands. And he proved he couldn't be trusted. If ever anyone sent those angels back . . . They don't know anything about where they came from. Those people didn't want them. I'm their mother. And I wouldn't let him or anyone harm them." She looks straight ahead. "No one will ever take them from me."

"It was for the children," Jack comments from the back. "Understand, Kevin, we never had anything against you. Isn't that right, dear."

"We were horrified when you were arrested," Pat replies earnestly. "I thought, once he was found, they'd think he was killed by some dissatisfied client. He had enough of them. I never dreamed they'd blame you. I pray that they'll drop the charges against you. And I tried to help you. We both did."

Well, it might be true. All the same, I'm not throwing the gun out the window. In fact, I'm a little chagrined to hear that I was not a victim of some evil plot, that I was merely the bumbling innocent bystander in the wrong place at the wrong time. "Let's move," I nod to the police station down the street.

She squeezes the steering wheel. "In the argument. He fell. Larry. That part was an accident. Except that gun was there. You say I watched you use it. I only remember picking it up and knowing how to turn it on."

"Pat is very mechanical," Jack says softly, admiringly.

"Jack," she gives a little smile, "couldn't do it. It isn't in him, that sort of . . . So I had to. Which didn't bother me because, you see, Larry Dexter brought it on himself."

I say, "The courts will take all your reasons into consideration, Pat. And if you come forward on my behalf, that'll be to your credit—"

Into the intersection, she turns left, away from the police station.

"Pat!"

She flattens the gas pedal. We jerk forward, engine screaming like an aircraft on takeoff.

Pat cries out, the pitch of her voice rising as our speed increases.

"Turn around." I wave the gun. "You're going the wrong way."

Trees and houses whip by. Horns blare. Oncoming cars pull prudently to the shoulder. We pass a truck which looks to be standing still.

"Stop!" I shout.

Eyes on the road, at least she's stopped yelling. I reach to switch off the ignition, but it will not turn. A hard twist and the key breaks in my hand.

"Make her stop!" I tell Jack.

The gun is useless. I mean, she *is* driving the goddamn car! I can't shoot her without killing us all. So I lean close and shout into her ear.

"Stop!"

She acts like I'm not there.

"She's crazy!" I drop the shift into neutral. She slaps it back to drive, her hand remaining on it. And when I try to force it into reverse, to stop this car but good, something like lead hits me on the back. The wind knocked out, I gasp. Then, I'm hit again.

Sinking to the floor, I raise my arm up to protect myself. From a Jack Lundgren I've never seen before. He leans into the front seat, pounding at me with an ugly black tire iron, his cheeks flushed and bulging.

I'm stunned, but not panicked. He swings like an old lady.

"No . . . don't, Jack. Shit!" He catches my elbow, the pain so sharp and lasting that it makes me mad. I want to hit him back, the bastard. "Stop!"

The iron slams harmlessly into the dash.

"The gun!" Pat shouts. "Get the gun!"

The tire iron is large and Jack can't get a full swing. *Whack,* it slashes the ceiling. *Whomp,* stuffing from the seat flies. *Crack,* the dome light shatters.

But I have no place to run. "Cut . . . cut it out, Jack." Each time I try to get off the floor I must dodge one of his attacks.

The big wagon vibrates, then swerves. Cars honk angrily. Tree limbs overhanging the road appear and disappear in a blur. I mean, Christ, it feels like we've left the fucking ground.

I reach for the iron. It dances away. Teeth bared, Jack stabs at me. It angles off my palm. Turn my head! I'm hit, a glancing blow, behind the ear.

I'm bleeding. "Goddamn! Fucking bastard." I'm afraid. And angry. My God, I can't get up. They'll kill me. Like they killed Larry and for the same reason.

"Get him," Pat shrieks.

He's maneuvering for a better swing, watching for an opening. One skull-cracking hit to finish me.

I raise my hand without a conscious thought. The gun is in it.

Jack's face opens in sudden fear. As if he'd forgotten the gun, or never believed I'd use it. The barrel floats a few inches from his eyes.

"No!" Pat lunges for it.

I squeeze the trigger.

The car swerves crazily.

Open-mouthed, Jack looks old, hair gray and thin, upper molars mostly missing. A metallic click and I wait for him to vanish in a mist of blood.

We smash into something solid. Bits of wood fly over the windshield. I feel a draft. The door behind me has opened of its own accord. The car shudders violently as I slam into the underside of the dash. It didn't go off. I moan. Goddamn, the gun didn't go off!

I'm sitting on someone's lawn. My head swims and when I touch gingerly at the back, I feel a gash. I suppose I got bounced out the door.

I should be thankful—nothing broken—and I should get up.

The big wagon, some yards away, shudders to life. It tilts toward the road, the rear perched on a hillock. In its wake are the remnants of a white picket fence.

On a side street of ranches and capes, I smell the ocean. Dogs bark, lights go on. People appear at doorways. "Call the cops," someone says.

The station wagon rocks back onto the road.

"Where's he going?" a man calls out.

Dazed, I rise and move for the road, thinking that I must stop them.

The car travels half a block and makes a quick, wide U-turn. I step over the remains of the fence, then stumble off the sandy shoulder to the road. At precisely the wrong time.

The car, left headlight destroyed, is bearing down on me, the passenger door open and waving like a flag.

Too late, I wonder what became of the gun. The car picks up speed! I think to run left or right, but I'm too tired and confused to do either.

I close my eyes and brace for the impact. When I open them, the station wagon is gone, the road silent.

·16·

I'm sure the Lundgrens are headed home to gather the twins and begin a journey they'd meant for me. To prove my innocence I must stop them.

I guess they've been prepared for this since the murder. They produced my twenty-five thousand dollars pretty quick. And I'll bet they've got an even bigger pile of cash for themselves, plus passports and air tickets.

Costa Rica is a likely destination.

As I work to clear my head, neighbors filter onto the street, long coats over their pajamas. "What happened?" they murmur.

"Did you see them?" someone questions me.

"Were you hit?" a woman asks. "Here. This man was hit by the car."

"No," I say.

"Son of a bitch." A man kicks the wrecked fence. "Son of a bitch."

"Anyone get the license plate?"

"What did you see?" someone asks.

"Nothing," I reply. "I, uh, heard it coming and jumped out of the way."

"What were you doing out there?"

"What's your name, pal? Do you live near here?"

I find a dozen or more people gathered round.

"I've really got to get going." I back away.

"The police should be here any minute."

"I didn't see anything." I turn, loping up the street.

"You should wait for an ambulance. You're hurt."

"Hey! You gotta make a report!" They call after me, but they're confused and they don't give chase, thank God.

On the main road, traffic is sparse, yet I manage to stop a delivery van. The driver agrees to take me as far as Main Street, a few miles from Pat and Jack's.

He keeps glancing at me. Well, I'm dirty and beat up. "Listen," I ask, "no chance you'd take a little detour up Main Street?"

"What?"

"I could pay you. . . ." I reach for the forty dollars in my pocket.

"*I'm on a schedule.* I shouldn't pick up riders at all."

He gives me another careful look. I cover the torn knee of my pants.

They're getting away! I could offer him a thousand, but the gym bag and its envelope stuffed with bills is in the station wagon.

I assume the gun is also in the car. Which isn't a problem. Pat and Jack probably don't realize they've got it. Besides they're not killers at heart. They could have escaped clean away if they'd run me down back there.

Christ, don't kiss their feet because they drew the line after whacking you with a tire iron, heaving you from a moving car, and sending you to prison. See how they act when they discover I'm still dogging them. It was because she felt cornered that Pat turned on Dexter and killed him.

I hike up Main Street. It's cold, my muscles aching, skin chafing. I hear the traffic coming from a long way off. "Come on, come on," my thumb is out, "stop. Please stop!"

I don't see the cars really, just headlights in the dark, speeding past, leaving only a taunting gust of freezing wind.

I run a bit. Nearly half an hour has passed since Pat and Jack sped away. Let's see. Fifteen, no, ten. Ten minutes to get home. (Pat's not afraid to speed, obviously.) Dismiss the sitter. Grab the cash, tickets. Suitcases and clothes. Pull the kids out of bed, pile them in the car. And drive away.

They might be gone already. God.

Goddamn! Run faster! But suppose I catch them. Then what? Without the gun, how do I hold them?

Well, I'll say, "You guys misjudge your situation. People are going to sympathize with you. The public will not allow the state to take your kids away. With a good lawyer, I doubt they'll ever convict you of anything. Except, you can't run away. You must clean the slate, tell the truth."

I dive behind a hedge as a police car approaches. Don't get picked up. I picture myself pleading with the cops. *My God, I didn't murder Larry Dexter. The Lundgrens did. They did it and they're getting away!* Then I'm tossed in the back of the cruiser. Tell it to the judge, ace.

If they get away, the police will pick between a suspect in custody, me, or people vanished from the earth. They can announce, "We nailed the killer," or "Gee, sorry, they slipped through our fingers."

A young man in a beaten old VW picks me up outside the town center. "Pretty cold night for walking."

I nod, catching my breath.

He shuts off the radio. "You from Norham?"

"Huh, what?"

"Are you from Norham?"

"Yeah—I mean, no. I used to be."

He'll drop me a block from the Lundgren house. Finally, I must form a plan. I don't have the gun and maybe Jack does. I still feel the click as I pulled the trigger. I meant to blow his face away and no doubt he's been thinking on that.

But then, it's very possible they've gotten clean away already.

Suddenly, I'm certain of this. They knew I'd give chase

and they made allowances. Perhaps if I'd been a real threat they *would* have killed me.

I'll bet they didn't even go back to the house. Realizing that I was close to the truth, they were packed and ready to run. They probably sent the kids ahead yesterday.

I put my face in my hands. What do I do now?

"You with me?"

"What?" I look over at the driver.

"I asked if you had trouble." He nods at my torn pants.

"Umm. I get off up at the mailbox here."

He pulls over and I leap out—"Hey!"—before he's quite stopped. I expect I'm on a fool's errand.

I climb a chain link fence and pick my way carefully through trees and fallen branches. Emerging from the woods, I come to the pool covered in a giant black tarp, like some toxic waste dump.

I remember pool-side cookouts, Pat among the guests, "Can I get you anything? Having fun?" With her obsessive sense of order, parties ran like clockwork. Perhaps that's why, when things went wrong, she ran amuck.

Neither light nor movement is visible through the sliding glass doors and giant windows. I mount the porch quietly. But, God, obviously they've gone. Neither car is in the drive-way.

With an ear on the cold, glass door, I hear something. Is it merely the furnace? I try the knob. It won't turn. Damn.

No one's in there. The place feels empty. Still, I must be certain. I'll run round to the front and peer into the windows.

Tired and discouraged, I cross the wide driveway. A frigid wind cuts through my clothes. After all my efforts, I'm still outside, shivering.

I hear a *thump* and stop. The automatic garage door lifts slowly, as if it is the curtain and I the audience. Onstage, Pat and Jack Lundgren talk in low voices alongside their little blue Subaru.

"Hurry," Pat says.

Pale, sweaty, Jack disappears through the door into the house. Pat leans into the car. "Sleep now, angel. Good girl." She buckles in the twins. From behind, I see white blond hair as one dozes against the other. She strokes their faces.

Pat goes next to the door and calls urgently, "Let's go." After a moment, she also disappears.

When the Lundgrens return, Jack carries a brown package tied with string. I dangle the keys to the Subaru. "Who wants to call the police?"

It's a moment before Pat recovers. She reaches into her coat. The gun? God, no. "I've got another set of keys." She holds them out.

"It . . . it doesn't matter, Pat. I'm not letting you go."

They don't move.

"You should give yourselves up. It'll go better for you."

One of the kids whines sleepily. Damn! I can't take the sound of crying babies, not now. Pat looks stricken, staring into the car. With me between her and the children.

Jack comes forward. "Let us go."

"Oh, sure."

"No, really. Let us go. Let us get away."

"Let you get away and I take the blame? I don't think so."

"Look, Kevin. As soon as we're gone, you'll be exonerated."

"Or accused of four more murders."

"If we disappear," he gestures, "we've left tracks. Withdrawn money. Liquidated assets. It'll look like we were planning to run away and we did."

The child cries more loudly, perhaps sensing something amiss.

"Please," Pat asks.

"It's all here." Jack unties the brown package, revealing a shoe box. "All the documents. Papers on the kids. Notes. Even tapes."

"We taped his calls," Pat adds. "When Larry started threatening us. We were going to get him arrested. Maybe we should have. Only, we were scared they'd take the kids away. It's happened. Babies taken from their moms."

"I can't let you go," I say, though I wonder exactly how to stop them.

Jack offers me the box. While I don't know what's on the tapes, I see forms with foreign writing.

He pleads, "You don't need us, Kevin. Others are implicated. Terri Pratt. She must have had an idea what the passports were for. Put all this in front of her. She'll admit her part. Confess."

The child still cries and my face is hot, uncomfortable.

"Please." Pat brings her hands together prayerfully. "Forgive us the pain we caused, Kevin. Remember, what you said. In our place, you would have done the same. To protect your family."

"I don't want to hear that!" I see my hands around Terri's throat.

The little girl cries, "Momma, momma . . ."

"We tried to help," Jack reminds me. "Gave you money. We would have done anything to get you off."

"Except to step up and take the blame yourself."

"If you'd been convicted we would have—"

"Bullshit."

"If it had been only ourselves to consider we would have come forward."

"Easy to say."

Jack lowers his voice, "Kevin, if we go to jail . . . our children will be left alone in the world. We have no close family. Only each other."

"That's your lookout."

"I can't bear to think of them left with strangers." Pat is crying.

"For their sake we ask you to give us a chance," Jack says.

"A chance?" I snicker. "Don't you think I thought about running away, Jack? You can't do it. You get found. Especially dragging kids along."

"I can't leave them alone and afraid." Pat's eyes burn. "Maybe you won't let us go. But I will never be separated from my babies. Never."

I take a step back. I understand what she's threatening and I don't doubt that she would do it.

After a pause, Jack says softly, "We didn't cause all this."

"Neither did I!"

"I know, I know. See, Kevin. We're innocent victims. Just like you."

"Not just like me! Don't give me that bullshit because you've no idea the hell I've been through—Christ. Why doesn't that damned kid *SHUT UP!*" If I wasn't so weary I might be able to think. I want to put my fist through a wall. Of all things, I don't intend to feel sorry for them.

"I'm going to my baby," Pat says. "Let me pass. She needs me. And then she'll be quiet. She needs her mother."

I take a step backward and she is past me.

·17·

Susan never complains, though it's a big job, settling in a new house, in a new town—and thanks to Larry Dexter's insurance policy it's one of the richest towns in the state. Already, it looks like home, the living room immaculate, white curtains billowing in a warm summer breeze.

She glows. "Oh God, I love this house."

"I'm glad it makes you happy."

She reaches out and I stretch for our fingers to meet.

When Michael and Molly pass they look on us with obvious delight. And I feel a sense of things put right, my family made whole again.

"Where do you think they went?" Susan asks suddenly.

"Who?"

"The Lundgrens. Where do you think they went?"

"I told you before. I have no idea. They could be anywhere."

"They'll be caught," she says confidently. "You just watch." Susan will never forgive Pat and Jack. She's puzzled that I don't share her anger.

Other bystanders wound up worse than me in this affair.

The cause of William Foley, Jr.'s, death is still undetermined. His father, incidentally, suffered a stroke a few weeks ago and isn't expected to recover. I hear Kikki Dexter went gray overnight and looks twenty years older. If she knew of her brother's efforts to kill me—well, it would be difficult to admit that.

And Terri. She's had her name in the papers a lot and once she was on TV, hurrying from the courthouse, looking scared and tired. She claims she never understood why Larry wanted the passports, but God knows if the grand jury will believe her. I feel for Terri, but I guess a girl like her lands on her feet.

See, I still think about her—sometimes I see her nude at the window. She turns to me, skin so smooth. And the rising sun seems to set her hair afire. I wanted her as much as I've ever wanted anything. And that's the main point I've learned in all this, the difference between what you want and what you need.

I've tried to meet with Terri, but she wouldn't answer the door when I called and she hangs up whenever I phone. Maybe someday she'll let me tell her I'm sorry and wish her the best. And I'll also say that there's no need for her to brood on what might have been. I've returned to my wife and kids. I would have done this in any case. I belong here.

"You look far away," Susan says.

"What?"

"You look a thousand miles away."

"I'm just tired."

"You know, I wish there was a way I could make you forget everything that's happened. And you could be happy."

"Happy?" I smile. "I'm as happy as I can be."